With An Eye to the Future

Sir Osbert Lancaster's two autobiographical memoirs are re-printed here for the first time in one volume, with a new intro-duction by Richard Boston. Famous as the creator of Maudie Littlehampton in the *Daily Express* and the author of the de-lightful *A Cartoon History of Architecture*, Lancaster has writ-ten a brilliant and sparkling autobiography that reflects his unique genius with both brush and pen.

'Mr Lancaster's style is a perfect vehicle for these witty and ironic memoirs' *Guardian*

'The wittiest and wickedest of pocket cartoonists, Osbert Lancaster touches the summit of satire' *Yorkshire Post*

'This most informative and most entertaining of writers is here embalming the corpse of an upper-middle-class society so that future generations may study it with awe and love' *Tatler*

'Enchanting ... the picture of a vanished age, of Edwardian England ... so deft, so evocative that the whole dead era seems to be infused with life' *Daily Telegraph*

Richard Boston was the founder and editor of the magazines *Vole* and *Quarto*. He now works at the *Guardian* newspaper, and is the author of *An Anatomy of Laughter*, *Beer and Skittles* and *Baldness Be My Friend*. He is currently working on a bi-ography of Osbert Lancaster.

D1344624

With An Eye to the Future

Osbert Lancaster

Introduction by Richard Boston
Illustrations by the author

Century
London Melbourne Auckland Johannesburg

© Osbert Lancaster 1953 (*All Done From Memory*),
1967 (*With An Eye to the Future*)
First published by John Murray

© This edition Osbert Lancaster 1986
© Introduction Richard Boston 1986
All rights reserved

This edition first published in 1986 by Century, an imprint of
Century Hutchinson Ltd,
Brookmount House, 62–65 Chandos Place, London, WC2N 4NW

Century Hutchinson Publishing Group (Australia) Pty Ltd
PO Box 496, 16–22 Church Street, Hawthorn, Melbourne, Victoria 3122

Century Hutchinson Group (NZ) Ltd
PO Box 40–086, 32–34 View Road, Glenfield, Auckland 10

Century Hutchinson Group (SA) Pty Ltd
PO Box 337, Berglvei 2012, South Africa

ISBN 0 7126 9467 6

Printed in Great Britain by
Richard Clay (The Chaucer Press) Ltd,
Bungay, Suffolk

Introduction

Though fourteen years separated the original publication of *All Done From Memory* from that of *With an Eye to the Future*, the two books are so intimately connected that even after repeated reading of them I still sometimes have difficulty in remembering in which of the two a particular description, character or incident occurs. Now that they are united here in one volume it is clearer than ever that they comprise a single work, and one with a structure of considerable intricacy.

The late Sir John Betjeman described his old friend's autobiography as 'profound and moving' but also as 'curvilinear', and the narrative does indeed loop backwards and forwards on itself like one of those Celtic designs which form an endless knot. Both books start geographically in the part of London where the author was born, though not at the time of his birth but more than thirty years later in the very different London of the Second World War – not the London of organ-grinders, muffin-men and crossing-sweepers but a city of barrage balloons, blackouts and air raids. Then, with a regard for chronological order that can at best be called relaxed, the author tracks his course through the period *entre deux guerres*, to the First World War, to the years before *that* war, and ends up where he started in Kensington and the Blitz. The narrative pattern is like one of those Anglo-Saxon decorations that show an animal biting its own tail. Curvilinear indeed.

All Done from Memory first appeared in 1953, in a limited edition of forty-five copies, and did not receive its trade publication for another ten years. This gap was out of respect for the feelings of the author's mother, who was still alive at the time when the book was written. Such is Sir Osbert's explanation, which of course one accepts, but I do find it a little odd since the portrayal of Mrs Lancaster comes across as an affectionate

v

one, albeit the product of a pen which cannot fail to be comic. If anyone is a victim in these books it is the author himself: the drawing of some of the self-portraits is pitiless.

Sir Osbert is a dandy, like his much-admired Carthusian predecessor Sir Max Beerbohm, with whom he shares much in common (even the moustache). The dandy's usual attitude is one of quizzical amusement. Rarely does the author display anything like anger. When this does happen, the provocation usually turns out to be a bully. One was the prep school sergeant in charge not only of drill, boxing and gym but also the punishment squad. For this 'fat and greasy sadist' the author feels an undying hatred. Another is a fat, arrogant *Sturmbannfuehrer*, witnessed in a Hanover beer-hall with his attendant storm-troopers, wearing shiny leather gloves and 'with wet red lips and a great deal of face-powder'.

These are exceptions. In his writing, as in his drawing, Sir Osbert is rarely ruffled. For the most part the people he describes, even if caricatured, are shown in a warm light. And what a rich cast they are, from the great-bearded patriarchal Victorian grandfather Sir William Lancaster, and the countless aunts and female cousins which populated the author's childhood, to the eccentric dons of his Oxford years and such wonderfully dotty characters as his parents-in-law: Sir Austin Harris, who was under the impression that when Blériot made his historic cross-Channel flight it was in Sir Austin's company, and Lady Harris, who made crazy amateur films, travelled with her own bidet and had a huge macaw which would shout 'Fuck off, you silly bitch' at inappropriate moments.

In these books Sir Osbert is not a social historian, and does not purport to be. Readers in search of information about working conditions in the Lancashire textile industry, or the living standards of farm-labourers in Essex, will seek in vain. What the author does is to write from his own experience, which is that of a well-off metropolitan. In thus depicting that corner of the world which he knew at first hand, he produced in *All Done From Memory* one of the most vivid of all accounts of that *Wind in the Willows* Edwardian England that perished in the First World War, following it in *With an Eye to the Future* with an equally sharp, informative and entertaining picture of Oxford and London society in the 1920s and 1930s. In recent years many descriptions of the Oxford of the Twenties have appeared, in the autobiographies, biographies, memoirs, letters and diaries associated with the names of such people as Evelyn Waugh, Cyril Connolly, John Betjeman and C. Day-Lewis. *With an Eye to the Future* is not only one of the first of these; it is still the funniest.

This book traces the life and times of the author only up to his mid-thirties. At that time most of his major achievements in a variety of fields lay ahead of him. There were still books of verse and prose to write; pictures to paint and countless covers and illustrations for books; lectures and speeches to make; cartoons to produce day after day; a distinguished career as a Diplomat in a difficult and dangerous situation in Greece at the end of the Second War; designing some of the most attractive stage sets and costumes for plays, operas and ballets that have graced the English stage . . . All these, and much else, lay in the future, and one would not expect mention of them in a book which does not even bring us up to the end of the war.

But even by that time there were solid achievements, and ones that this book either passes over or about which it is silent. He had written four books. *Our Sovereigns* is a short, witty series of sketches of the kings and queens of England, produced for the Coronation in 1936. In the same year *Progress at Pelvis Bay* appeared; it is still the deadliest and funniest satire on town-planning ever penned. These books were followed in the years immediately before the War by *Pillar to Post* and *Homes Sweet Homes*, which (taken together) are still unsurpassed as an introduction to European architecture. Furthermore, since the beginning of 1939 he had been producing his daily pocket cartoons for the *Daily Express*.

Nowadays pocket cartoons are a standard feature of journalism, and very good many of them are. One has to remind oneself that (at least as far as Britain is concerned) the pocket cartoon is the invention of Osbert Lancaster. Its success was immediate and enormous. There wasn't always a lot to laugh about in a Britain under the very real threat of Nazi invasion. Osbert Lancaster's contribution to maintaining national morale is not to be under-estimated. His daily one-liners were avidly devoured at the breakfast-table, on the buses and trains, and re-told and retailed in the pubs and offices, in the shopping queues and air-raid shelters. His celebrity was enormous. He was a national institution.

The fact that we would know none of this from his autobiography is not simply a matter of the author's reticence or modesty. In some ways this autobiography tells us curiously little about the author, but then it does not set out to be a work of boasting or of breast-baring confession. Indeed, the introductory chapter states specifically that the author's intention is 'not primarily autobiographical' but is rather 'by using thematic material from a few commonplace incidents of childhood, an attempt to raise not a monument but a small memorial plaque to a vanished world'.

That sentence, whether intentionally or not, reverberates with echoes of Wordsworth. It reminds one of 'Intimations of Immortality from recollections of childhood', and the 'fallings off, vanishings' of that great poem. The high comedy of Osbert Lancaster's autobiography is accompanied by deeper, darker notes, and they come from this Wordsworth-like attitude to the act of recollection. There is a clear distinction between autobiographies and memoirs which record events, and those which remember them. The title of *All Done From Memory* states to which category it belongs, the point being emphasised by the epigraph taken from Delacroix's *Journals*. The passage is full of the kind of nuances that are lost in translation, and Osbert Lancaster was wise to leave it in French. However, to paraphrase crudely, what Delacroix says, is that experiences, especially early experiences, however intense at the time, are even more so when remembered afterwards.

Likewise with Proust (a writer greatly admired by Sir Osbert), in his search for time past it was not the *madeleine* that was the intense experience, but the memory of it. Wordsworth famously said in the Preface to the *Lyrical Ballads* that the origin of poetry is 'emotion recollected in tranquility'. What is probably his best-known poem is not so much about the daffodils as about the experience of loneliness and the recollection of the flowers. He wanders 'lonely as a cloud', and though 'jocund in their company' the time when his heart fills with pleasure is when they flash upon the inward eye which is the bliss of solitude.

This connection between the inward eye and the outward

eye, between solitude and memory, is also to be found in Osbert Lancaster's autobiography. Throughout his life he has been the most sociable of men, immensely clubbable, never known to have turned down an invitation for any social occasion. But, like Proust, he was an only child, and he is no stranger to solitude, or melancholy. Comparisons with Proust and with Wordsworth may seem strong meat; but readers of this joint autobiography will soon find that they are not inappropriate.

The following account of Osbert Lancaster's first childhood encounter with Venice shows not only the precision of his visual observation and the powerful effect that architecture (his great passion) holds over him. It also describes a moment of Wordsworthian exaltation, and it is again one in which the writer emphasises that he was alone at the time:

> Waking very early next morning I went out into the brilliant sunshine on a solitary exploration before breakfast, and after negotiating several narrow alleys found myself in a long arcade hung with canvas awnings through which the sun filtered in a golden glow and one of which after a moment's hesitation I firmly pulled aside. For what was then revealed—the whole Piazza backed by the west front of Saint Mark's, all the golden balls and crosses gleaming and shimmering in the rays of a sun that was only just above the Doge's Palace—I could not have been less prepared. Slowly, in a state of exalted trance, I crossed the great Square, at that hour empty of all but pigeons, and then, having arrived opposite the glittering façade, I glanced right and saw for the first time that most staggering of all views, S. Giorgio Maggiore floating above a dancing sea framed between the twin columns of the Piazzetta.

Not the least of Osbert Lancaster's achievements is that he can write such descriptions without their going over the top and becoming mere purple passages.

Those in whom the act of memory arouses such powerful sensations usually associate them with some idea that they are living in a period after the Fall, and that what they are recalling is a pre-lapsarian Paradise. The Fall may be anything from a social transformation (such as the Industrial

Revolution) to the personal experience of the loss of child-hood innocence. And not only is the past another country; it is a better one. Wordsworth again:

> But yet I know, where'er I go,
> That there hath passed away a glory from the world.

Osbert Lancaster describes not one but two vanished worlds. Born in 1908 (the year in which *Wind in the Willows* was published) he came to consciousness in the world which perished (as did his own father) in the battlefields of the First World War, just as the world of his adolescence and early adulthood was shattered by the events following the invasion of Poland in 1939, news of which the author heard on the wireless of the public bar of the Holland Arms in Kensington. *With an Eye to the Future* is as much a 'memorial plaque to a vanished world' as is *All Done From Memory*.

But enough of this gloomy talk of memorials. The blue notes are there all right in Sir Osbert's autobiography, but they accompany a work in which the predominant theme in the writing and in the drawing is one of delight. You have a treat ahead of you, and I will delay you no longer.

Richard Boston
1986

Contents

Je crois que le plus grand attrait des choses
est dans le souvenir qu'elles réveillent dans le
cœur ou dans l'esprit, mais surtout dans le
cœur ... Le regret du temps écoulé, le
charme des jeunes années, la fraîcheur des
premières impressions agissent plus sur moi
que le spectacle même.

Delacroix's Journal

1. *"Keep the home fires burning"*

THE PUBLIC BAR of the Holland Arms was full to bursting. Some of those present were doubtless regulars but the majority, of which I was one, had clearly just dropped in for the one o'clock news. With the six pips, conversation became desultory and faded away altogether as the announcer, in tones rather less dispassionate than those to which during the next five years we were to become accustomed, began to summarize his disastrous bulletin. The Polish frontier crossed at four separate points . . . massive air-raids on the capital, whole quarters in flames . . . three German panzer columns advancing on Cracow . . . Polish Second Army surrounded . . . more raids on Warsaw, refugees streaming south. Audience reaction was strangely unemotional but tinged, or so it seemed to me, with that embarrassment induced in all right-thinking men by any mention of God outside of church. Some of the regulars shook their heads slowly from side to side; one old man cuffed his fidgeting dog with sudden, unnecessary vehemence; but the only spoken comment came from a respectable-looking middle-aged woman in a white coat, perhaps the manageress of the near-by dairy, who kept repeating in a flat, dull voice, wholly devoid of emotion, "The buggers! O, the dirty buggers!". And, indeed, it was not until I had returned to the Post a few minutes later that I myself received the full impact of that moment of truth, now rendered more powerful by a sudden realisation of the wild incongruity of my surroundings.

It would be hard to imagine any setting less in accord with contemporary events, or indeed so manifestly unsuited to be an Air Raid Warden's Post, than Leighton House. The fountain in the pool in the Arab Hall tinkled irrelevantly, emphasizing rather than breaking the silence; the squares of sunlight on the marble floor were cross-hatched by the patterns of the carved wooden grilles which covered every window; in the fretted squinches, supporting the dome, gold-leaf gleamed in the bluish transmuted light reflected from the peacock tiles. Highly inappropriate as such a décor must always have been, even when, on far distant Varnishing Days, it had framed a gaggle of Victorian Academicians and artistic duchesses, it was doubly so now. Even a large canvas by G. F. Watts representing, according to the legend beneath, 'Chaos Disrupting the Arts of Peace', which might possibly be thought to have possessed a certain topicality, seemed in the contemporary predicament only to offer a wholly inadequate generalization, conceived in a period of unbroken tranquility and totally lacking any hint of prophetic menace. In fact the only visible evidence that Queen Victoria was not still on the throne, and Lord Leighton presiding over her Academy, was provided by the presence of a telephone, a first-aid box and the colleague whom I had come to relieve.

Outside in the Melbury Road, which at that date was still largely unchanged from its original conception, Norman Shaw's revived-Queen-Anne façades glowed warmly in the September sunshine, the crockets and pinnacles of the Burgess house were bravely upstanding against a cloudless sky, and in a few moments' time the aged Lord Wrenbury would be taking the last pair of

Dundrearies in London for their afternoon airing. It was hard to think, but at the time we did think it, that in a matter of days, or hours even, all this solid enclave of late-Victorian culture might well be reduced to a heap of smoking rubble, only to be distinguished from whole quarters of Warsaw by the colour of the brick and, perhaps, a handful of broken terra-cotta enrichments on which Walter Crane's familiar sun-flower was still faintly discernible.

On the departure of my colleague I fell to reflecting on how far removed were my present emotions from those displayed by my parents' generation on that other sun-drenched day on Littlehampton beach almost exactly a quarter of a century ago. Then, while apprehension had doubtless touched the more thoughtful, the brass-band and light cavalry approach to war was still general and to all but a minority the actual onset of disaster had, despite a few ancestral voices, come as a surprise; whereas for their children, who had lived so long with the prospect, the actual outbreak of hostilities, despite a far clearer idea of what it was likely to entail, was accompanied by a feeling almost of relief. For some the tension had started as long ago as 'thirty-three', for others from the time of the Spanish Civil War, for the majority since Munich, but in my own case, thanks to my mother's eschatological enthusiasms, dread had long pre-dated any of these events.

*   *   *   *   *

The first German war was not yet over when my mother decided that that conflict was not, as she had previously supposed, Armageddon but merely a trial run, and that the vials of wrath were still to be outpoured. She had come to this cheerful conclusion largely as a result of her own remarkable gift of precognition but she had been much encouraged to discover, after prolonged research, that her views were fully supported by such unquestioned authorities as the Prophet Ezekiel, the Great Pyramid and St. John on Patmos. This intelligence plunged her only child, a pious but perhaps over-imaginative lad, into a state of gloom bordering on panic not noticeably relieved by her cheerful assertion that all these heralded disasters were but a prelude to the Second Coming when all the redeemed—among whom, as fully paid-up members of the Lost Ten Tribes, we had a very good chance of being numbered—would be caught up out of their gross, terrestrial bodies and transferred to the Astral Plane, there to grow in wisdom and holiness throughout eternity. For although only just nine years old I had a strong feeling that my gross terrestrial body offered possibilities of enjoyment as yet un-exploited and I took a rather dim, in both senses of the word, view of the Astral Plane. My childish sentiments, in fact, are best summed up by some lines written many years later in a different context.

'For Thy coming, Lord we pray,
But let it be some other day.
On Thy return our hopes are set;
Thy Will be done, but not just yet.'

To what exactly my mother's life-long pursuit of Hidden Wisdom, for which she always seemed to me to be tempera-mentally quite unsuited, owed its origin I have never been able to decide. Was it, perhaps, a form of escapism encouraged by the conditions of her early life? On the death of her mother her father, who shortly married again, had returned to China leaving her in the care of her grandmother, a formidable old lady who had found salvation at the feet of that pillar of the Low Church, Prebendary Webb-Peploe, then Vicar of St. Paul's, Onslow Square, and who ran her household on strictly Evangelical lines which my mother may well have felt unduly restricting. More-over, searching the scriptures for hints of things to come, preferably unpleasant, has always been a favourite pastime of extreme Protestantism and this may well have come to play a compensa-tory rôle in an otherwise not very colourful childhood.

Or did this strange preoccupation with The Beyond develop later, when my mother was in her 'teens, as an unconscious sublimation of rather different longings which in her day and class were quite impossible of fulfilment and of the nature of which she was quite certainly ignorant? She did once tell me that she had first become aware of her psychic powers, of which I must disloyally confess I never witnessed any very convincing manifestation, while at finishing school in Brussels where she had been much in demand for seances and table-turnings usually held, she coyly added, presumably by way of social justification, in the Japanese Legation. There can, however, be small doubt that her enthusiasm was much strengthened, and received its peculiar colouring, in the studio of G. F. Watts, then passing through his final, apocalyptic phase, whose last surviving pupil she lived to become, and was further reinforced by a close study of the Pre-Raphaelites.

In her appearance there was not, at any stage of my mother's life, any marked suggestion of otherworldliness. Very short, robust, with great width of jaw and very beautiful pale blue eyes never, in my experience, illuminated by anything approaching a mystic gleam, she habitually radiated a cheerful determination to get her own way that had led the better disposed among her relations to describe her as 'very capable', others as 'bossy'. Sensibly, rather than smartly, dressed the only discernible hint of the greenery-yallery which her presence afforded was occasioned by a deplorable weakness, which she never quite overcame, for artistic jewellery laboriously handwrought in what was hoped was a Celtic style by a distressed gentlewoman in Glastonbury.

After marriage my mother's psychic and artistic gifts remained for a time unparaded. Nor was this surprising as my father, a cheerful, irreverent man whose spiritual requirements were undoubtedly fully met by Freemasonry and his duties as church-warden and whose preferred artist was Phil May, can never have provided an ideal audience for revelation. Moreover, his leisure hours were fully taken up with getting sufficient outdoor exercise, an advantage of which all Lancasters were determined not to deprive themselves or others, and to exploit which in the fullest possible measure we temporarily abandoned Kensington.

The chief, and in my mother's eyes only, merit of our new

5

residence in Sheen was the opportunity it afforded my father for riding in Richmond Park before breakfast; an opportunity of which he had, alas, but a short time to avail himself. The house, just off Sheen Lane, was a largish, pebble-dashed and white-balconied number with a spacious garden that was yet not sufficiently so to compensate for the inconvenience of the internal arrangements. The only room of which I retain today any very clear recollection was the drawing-room which my mother, greatly daring, had decorated in a Chinese style inspired by several visits to a highly popular oriental drama called *Mr. Wu* in which her favourite actor, Mr. Matheson Lang, was currently appearing.

East Sheen was, at that date, going through an uncomfortable period of transition. Surrounded on all sides, save on that adjoining Richmond Park, by the stifling red-brick and fancy tile-work of Edwardian suburbia, the centre of the village still displayed faint traces of the rural, Rowlandsonian past. The Bull Inn had not yet been rebuilt in Brewer's neo-Georgian and not only retained its courtyard and dignified brown-brick façade, but once a week, when with much hornblowing my uncle's four-in-hand drove up for the first change of horses on the weekly run from The Berkeley to Hampton Court, fulfilled its original function. Opposite, at the bottom of Sheen Lane, there still stood an enormous chestnut in the shade of which a few old gaffers were accustomed, perhaps a trifle self-consciously, to sit on summer evenings, while Sheen Lane itself was flanked for much of its length by eighteenth-century stables and high demesne walls above which loomed the tops of gigantic cedars.

But all these vestiges of a dignified past were quite powerless to reconcile me to the odious present. Richmond Park I hated, contrasting its wide open spaces, dotted with blasted oaks and inhabited only by deer, unfavourably with the jolly social whirl of the Broad Walk with its dignified elms. It induced in me a feeling of loneliness and depression and in all the long, grey afternoons, during which I was mercilessly dragged through its far too extensive rides, the only incident I can recall with pleasure was an encounter with two ladies of, to me, fabulous elegance and

6

distinction driving in an open victoria under violet-tinted para-
sols. With rare presence of mind Nanny called me smartly to
attention, for I was wearing my sailor suit, and bade me give a
proper naval salute to which Queen Alexandra and the Dowager
Empress of Russia gravely responded with a gracious inclination
of the head.

In retrospect our period at Sheen remains inescapably identified with the gloom and misery of the First War, and whereas
Kensington and the Bayswater Road are forever bathed in the
perpetual sunlight of the days before 1914, over Sheen and its
surroundings the clouds are low and grey and the wind blows
coldly with a hint of sleet. Of the war itself I recall little enough—
a captive balloon breaking away from its moorings in Richmond
Park; a purple-lettered poster, seen from my pram, in the Upper
Richmond Road announcing the death of Kitchener; leaning from
an upstairs window to watch a daylight air-raid, hundreds of
little balls of dirty cotton-wool drifting and expanding against the

London sky with, way above them, barely detectable, a cloud of scattering mosquitoes. What, however, has not faded is the memory of the overall and increasing depression which, even for a child, coloured life on the home-front during that earlier conflict and which was so mercifully absent during the last. The endless casualty lists, the appalling prevalence of mourning which turned London into the magnified likeness of one of those French provincial towns which seem to be inhabited exclusively by widows, and, later, the constant hunger which neither the too frequent appearance on the nursery table of a horrible ersatz concoction known as honey-sugar, nor generous helpings of lentil-soup, seemed ever wholly to satisfy—all combined, in a way in which queues, bombings and blackout never did, to induce a permanent lowness of spirit. Perhaps the only real advantage (for a personal safety in war-time is not invariably an advantage for the civilian population) which the First War had over the Second was the absence of sirens. For the brave tooting bugles blown by boy scouts on bicycles, so far from turning the stomach over, promoted a feeling of pleasurable, if faintly comic, bravado.

On my mother the war had, at first, a distinctly bracing effect. Contemplation was abandoned for action and that side of her character which her appearance so strongly reflected found, for perhaps the only time in her life, full scope for development. For despite her transcendentalism my mother was always a New Woman at heart; in her younger days when she had moved in the intellectual circle centring round the Cobden Sanderson house on Chiswick Mall, she had been staunchly pro-Boer, a keen, although not militant, supporter of Women's Suffrage, and she always remained a dedicated Shavian. Forewarned from Beyond of the imminence of war she had, in the years immediately preceding the outbreak, taken a series of courses in First Aid and become an enthusiastic recruit to the newly formed Red Cross, so that she now found herself well equipped by experience, and still more by temperament, to raise and train a local detachment. In this great work of education, I, too, played my part, spending many a long evening on the platform in schools and church halls being bandaged and unbandaged in demonstration of the correct procedure to be adopted to meet every variety of wound and fracture. Incidentally, it was in the same cause that I made my first appearance on any stage, when, dressed in rags and representing Gallant Little Belgium, I was clasped to the protective bosom of a local Britannia in a patriotic *tableau vivant* that produced, so I have always been given to understand, a very powerful effect.

My reaction to my father's death in 1916 was one of shattering disappointment rather than overwhelming grief. He had been away for seemingly so long that, although he had always remained a cherished and deeply missed figure, his image was fast becoming legendary. It was all the more bitter, therefore, that the dreaded slip of paper should have arrived on the very day he was due back on leave and that instead of his jovial presence in the nursery restoring and revitalising my love and appreciation I should have been confronted with weeping relatives in the drawing-room. Of the following weeks I retain only a confused memory of memorial services and black-edged writing paper, of crêpe arm-bands being sewn on my jackets and overcoat, and of desperate and futile efforts to obey the constantly repeated injunction to be a comfort to my mother. She for her part, once the first shock was over, concentrated more fiercely than ever on her Red Cross activities so that I now found myself increasingly in the exclusive company of Nanny and the domestic staff which, although deeply appreciated, was not, perhaps, that best calculated to fit me for the rigours of school-life in which I was shortly to be enmeshed.

Occasionally, however, I was privileged to accompany my mother to the headquarters of the Red Cross, to which she had recently been transferred, in a large and gloomy mansion on the corner of Eaton Square. The tedium of these visits, during which I was enjoined to sit quietly with a good book while my mother got on with her work, was considerable and would have been insupportable had I not made, quite early on, an interesting discovery. Owing to some technical deficiency the overflow from the lavatory alongside my mother's office, which was on the top floor, cascaded straight into the street below, immediately opposite the front door. And by skilful manipulation of the plug this flood could be controlled and timed to coincide with the arrival of visitors. The best, and last, catch of a distinguished bag was Lady Northcliffe, an imposing figure in magnificent sables, who provoked investigation by commenting in some bewilderment on the sudden downpour from a cloudless sky which had drenched her on alighting from her car, an unnatural phenomenon which marked the end of my visits to Eaton Square.

With the coming of peace my mother's first action was to shake the dust of Sheen off her feet and move straight back to Bayswater. St. Petersburg Place, where she purchased a recently erected terrace house in the neo-Georgian style, was, and indeed still is, a short street off the Bayswater Road better endowed ecclesiastically than any other street of its length in London. At one end towers the West End Synagogue, twin-turreted in vaguely oriental red brick, at the other stands the Greek Orthodox Cathedral, conventionally if unconvincingly Byzantine, and in the middle St. Matthew's (C. of E.) raises to Heaven a lofty and uncompromisingly Evangelical spire; while just around the corner in the Queen's Road is, or was, the Ethical Church, the only place of worship in London adorned with a stained glass window of George Bernard Shaw.

However, none of these fanes save, occasionally on wet days, St. Matthew's, which was normally too bleakly Low even for one brought up in the shadow of St. Paul's, Onslow Square, received my mother's patronage. On Sunday mornings she resumed attendance at St. John's, Notting Hill, from which, alas, much of the pre-war glory had departed (not a frock-coat in sight and only Sir Aston Webb still sporting a top-hat), but in the afternoons made pilgrimage to far less orthodox shrines propagating an extraordinary variety of esoteric doctrines.

The years immediately following the First War witnessed the emergence in London of a whole host of thaumaturges and mystagogues both lay and clerical, and of the latter there can have been few at whose feet my mother did not at one time or another sit. As I grew older my unenthusiastic presence beside her was more frequently insisted on, but of all these innumerable Magi I retain clear recollections of only one or two. There was the Reverend Fearon who had at one time been curate to Arch-deacon Wilberforce, a prelate for whom my mother always retained a peculiar reverence, and who presided over the destinies of the Church Mystical Union in a particularly depressing brick church in Norfolk Square wearing a scarlet cassock and a short, blond bob. In his sermons, which were long and largely incomprehensible, the word 'anthropomorphic' used exclusively in a pejorative sense, was of frequent occurrence, and the ritual was marked by long, long pauses of total silence during which we were exhorted to empty our minds of all extraneous thoughts and concentrate on Perfect Oneness. Try as I would, despite clouds of encouraging incense, the successful accomplishment of this feat always eluded me and, long before I came within spitting distance of Perfect Oneness, extraneous thoughts came crowding back, most of them lubricious.

After my mother finally broke with the Church Mystical Union, for reasons which I have long since forgotten, there followed a period spiritually dominated by a portly faith-healer who was also, I think, a lay-preacher whose services, to which mercifully I was only infrequently taken, consisted, as far as I can remember, almost entirely of silent prayer. Of his successor, however, the Bishop of Basil Street, my memories are vivid. This ecclesiastical ham whose charlatanism was, even for a schoolboy, palpable, claimed to have been consecrated by the Old Catholic

Archbishop of Utrecht and wore the conventional purple-piped soutane and skull cap of a Roman bishop. His cathedral, known, if I remember rightly, as The Sanctuary, a Jacobean-style hall tucked away behind Harrods, was furnished, along with more familiar *bondieuseries*, with statues of Buddha, Zoroaster and

Pythagoras, and boasted in addition a lavishly gilded bishop's throne in Wardour-Street Gothic which had once belonged, so the Bishop claimed, to Sarah Bernhardt. The congregation, numerous and well-heeled, was largely feminine but included one or two prominent merchant bankers whose credulity, so naïvely exalted was my childish estimate of Lombard Street

shrewdness, never ceased to astonish me; the services were litur-
gically elaborate but despite the Bishop's wide experience and
carefree borrowings there always clung to them a faint suggestion
of improvisation inducing an embarrassment which at length
out-weighed the fascinated curiosity which first acquaintance had
aroused. On the whole, therefore, it was a great relief when my
mother finally abandoned The Sanctuary and joined a Lodge of
female Freemasons from attendance at whose rites my sex debarred me.

That my mother escaped the besotted absorption, and inevitable
exploitation, to which so many of the richer female members of
such congregations fall victim, was due to an unusual combination of qualities. All her life she retained a robust sense of
humour and a curious ability to achieve, suddenly and without
warning, an almost cynical detachment when the spectacle of
others' credulity would provoke her to hoots of happy laughter.
Moreover she was safeguarded financially both by a recurrent,
although fortunately erroneous, conviction that she was as poor
as a church mouse and also by a strong feeling that there was
safety in numbers. Never at any moment did any one creed
command her exclusive allegiance, and to the variety of movements and organisations with which she maintained contact the
periodical literature that accumulated in the Chinese drawing-
room (her first exercise in oriental decoration had been repeated
on a more lavish scale in St. Petersburg Place) bore abundant
testimony.

There was the *Occult Review*, displaying on its orange cover a
wide selection of cabalistic signs and symbols, of which the
contents were usually improbable but only occasionally fascinating; tall stories of reincarnation alternated with articles on
ectoplasm and long accounts of Tibetan wonder-workers. Altogether classier and better produced, rather in the style of the
Burlington Magazine, was the *Rosy Cross*, the official organ of the
Rosicrucians. This was largely devoted to the exposition of the
teachings of Rudolf Steiner but published from time to time
fascinating photographs of the extraordinary buildings, in a style

midway between Erich Mendelsohn and Arthur Rackham, which were being erected at the cult's headquarters in Weimar. And once, curiously enough, there appeared an article by Arthur Symons on Toulouse-Lautrec, not one would have thought the most other-worldly of artists, which first fired my enthusiasm for that painter's work. To the *Theosophists' Monthly*, packed with hot tips from the Krishnamurti stable and fighting leaders from Mrs Besant, my mother's devotion was short-lived, her subscription being promptly cancelled after hearing a thing or two about the private life of Dr. Leadbeater.

But of all the innumerable periodicals from which she from time to time derived comfort and instruction that to which my mother remained the most abidingly loyal, maintaining her readership up to the day of her death, was the *National Message and Banner*, the official publication of the British Israelites. In outward appearance there was little, save the crossed flags of Britain and the United States reproduced in colour on the cover, to distinguish it from the average parish magazine; but the contents, although often fraught with menace, reducing me in my younger days to a pitiful state of terror and apprehension, were irresistible. There were learned articles demonstrating that the circumference of the inner circle at Stonehenge if measured in cubits was exactly equal to the height of the pillars in King Solomon's temple multiplied by twelve (a number of portentous significance); there were closely reasoned arguments, which even as a child I judged slightly specious, showing that the popularity and antiquity of 'Danny Boy' provided powerful support for the theory that the Irish were, in fact, of the tribe of Dan. Nor were current affairs neglected, always being approached from a strictly Conservative angle and usually interpreted in the light of that certain knowledge which a close study of the Great Pyramid alone afforded. Indeed it was these editorial comments which most frequently sent me shivering to bed and coloured my dreams when I got there. For no matter how cheerful the news nor how quiet the international situation, the wrath to come, here on earth, was inescapable and getting very close now. The fact that the English-speaking peoples, provided that they did not go whoring after strange gods such as the League of Nations and never adopted the decimal system, would, thanks to the promises given to their forefather Abraham, emerge triumphant in the end, did little to reassure me; the length and nature of the tribulations which would have first to be undergone suggested too low a rating for my personal chances of survival. That the plan and dimensions of the Great Pyramid, or rather their interpretation, provided on occasion less than completely accurate information on the shape of things to come was small comfort. If some particular date to be marked by irreparable disaster passed without incident this was invariably attributed to some marginal error in the measurement of the Passage to the Tomb-chamber and the load of woe transferred a few years ahead. Only when they were retrospective could I regard such re-adjustments with equanimity, as when the year 1923, which had long been forecast as the beginning of the end, having drawn to its close unmarked by any very spectacular calamity, it was discovered that the sinister crack at that particular point in the Passage was a clear reference to our resumption of the Gold Standard. A lamentable decision, doubtless, and one with far-reaching consequences, but which left me as a schoolboy comparatively unmoved.

One strange feature of this astonishing publication which puzzled me at the time, but which subsequent experience has led me to regard as generally indicative, was the high proportion of naval officers, both active and retired, among the contributors. Why is it, I wonder, that no cause, from Homœopathy to Fascism, is so dotty that it cannot attract loyal support from at least one Rear Admiral (Retd.) or Captain, R.N.?

My mother's studies were not, however, confined exclusively to periodical literature; our bookcases groaned beneath the weight of innumerable volumes with such titles as *Behind the Beyond* or *The Yogi Way*. Fortunately for me, a child much given to browsing, this esoteric flood never completely overwhelmed the shelves reserved for Thackeray and Kipling, nor those which reflected my father's taste on which both Saki and W. W. Jacobs were well represented. But as time went on books tended increasingly to stray from appointed sections and I shall never forget my surprise and delight when one day I discovered, tucked away between *In Tune with the Infinite* and the poems of Rabindranath Tagore, *More Gals' Gossip* by Arthur Binstead of *The Pink 'Un*, discreetly jacketed in plain brown paper.

How carefully, in fact, my mother studied all the massive tomes which she acquired in ever-increasing numbers I was never wholly certain. On more than one occasion, having departed to bed with the *Bhagavad Gita* or *The Cloud of Unknowing* prominently displayed beneath her arm, I subsequently discovered her, when I went to say good-night, deep in the latest work of Miss Ethel M. Dell. Always on such occasions her response, uttered in a very reproachful tone, to any expression of surprise was the same, "You know quite well, dear, that the bent bow must be unstrung."

Fortunately for me my mother never found any difficulty in pursuing her less specialised interests, among which the theatre ranked high. This was in a way curious as in the evangelical surroundings of her childhood the playhouse was anathema. But fortunately her grandmother had, before her own salvation, been a devoted playgoer with a marked preference for opera and ballet (I still possess an ivory model of Vestris' leg which the old lady used as a seal) and seldom tired of recalling for the benefit of her grand-daughter the exact nature of the temptations to which the fortunate child would never be exposed. But if she had long outgrown these early prohibitions, my mother always retained a slightly puritanical attitude towards playgoing that was reinforced rather than diminished by her Shavian loyalties. Thus musical comedies and revues were regarded with marked disfavour as being certainly trivial and probably immoral. Exception was made in favour of *Chu Chin Chow* on account of its oriental setting, and, curiously enough, the music-hall which, although she herself never displayed much enthusiasm for red-nosed comedians, she held to be justified, in so far as I was concerned, by my father's preference for that form of entertainment. And it is entirely thanks to her unselfish attitude that I can now recall such figures as Alfred Lester, George Robey and Harry Tate in their heyday, a privilege for which I remain eternally grateful.

Mysticism, luckily for me, did not make much impact on the theatre of the 'twenties but whenever it did my mother was right out there on the touch-line and it is on record that she attended no less than twenty-two performances of *The Immortal Hour*. On one occasion in Paris, having been informed by an American spiritualist painter of her acquaintance that a Hindu dancer, whose performance was fraught with mystic significance, was currently appearing at the Casino de Paris, I was taken to a revue called *Paris en fleurs* in which, rather to her surprise but not, I think, altogether to her regret, the other performers included Maurice Chevalier and the Dolly Sisters, and which was from time to time enlivened by dance-routines that were not remotely tinged with mysticism.

While opera, apart from *The Immortal Hour*, had little or no appeal for my mother, although out of respect for my father, an ardent Wagnerian, she always referred to *The Ring* in a very reverential way, she had inherited to the full her grandmother's passion for the ballet and it was to this that I owed the first great aesthetic experience of my childhood.

The ease and completeness with which so many people seem able to recall over a lapse of many years every roulade and entrechat of some historic production arouses in me a doubtless unjustified scepticism. Certainly any such feat of total recall is quite beyond my powers; and of the 1919 Diaghilev production of *The Sleeping Beauty* almost all that I can now remember is Lopokova as the Lilac Fairy, the dazzling beauty of the Bakst sets and the intensity of my own response. Nothing I had ever seen had in any way prepared me for the magnificence that was disclosed on the rise of the curtain of The Alhambra, and for weeks afterwards my drawing books were packed with hopeful but pathetic attempts to recapture something of the glory of that matinée, and there and then I formed an ambition that was not destined to be fulfilled for more than thirty years.

17

While nothing else in my theatrical experience as a child ever achieved so great an impact, several notable performances still remain vivid: Mr. Henry Ainley as Mark Antony; Mr. Miles Malleson as Lancelot Gobbo in a production at The Court Theatre in which the great Jewish actor Moritz Moskowitz won universal praise for his interpretation of Shylock, a performance of which I remember not one single line nor gesture; a quite unknown young actor called Coward in *The Knight of the Burning Pestle*; Miss Dorothy Green as Lady Macbeth in the dear old half-timbered theatre at Stratford and, needless to say, Mr. Matheson Lang playing Matheson Lang in a whole series of cloak-and-dagger dramatisations of novels by Rafael Sabatini, an author for whose work I had the keenest admiration. Occasionally these memories are not wholly of enjoyment; of *St. Joan* what I now most clearly recall is my resentment of the *faux-naif*, breathless tone of voice, suggesting a particularly maddening girl-guide at a rather difficult stage in her development, which Dame Sybil saw fit to maintain throughout, that almost outweighed my excited appreciation of the play itself and of the outstanding beauty of the costumes designed by Charles Ricketts.

While my mother's determination to keep abreast of all that was worthiest in modern culture remained constant she could never bring herself, anyhow when I was young, to include the cinema as coming under that heading. It was, in her view, invariably an undesirably sensational form of entertainment that always took place in the most unhygienic surroundings, and the grave risk of 'catching things' reduced my visits to a minimum. Almost the only exception was made in favour of the Polytechnic in Regent Street, whether because the connection with Quintin Hogg was considered to have a sterilising effect, or because the film of Scott's expedition to the Antarctic had first been shown there, I never knew. Personally, I always felt this ban to be monstrously unfair, the more particularly as it did not apply to my little cousins who never missed an episode of *The Perils of Pauline*, and I can still recapture the pangs of frustrated longing aroused by the sight of the powerfully conceived posters for *The*

Birth of a Nation. In later life, however, my mother's attitude was somewhat relaxed and, accompanied by her devoted maid, she was accustomed to make regular weekly excursions to her local. But she always remained a trifle ashamed of these dissipations and her reaction when taxed was the same as that aroused by any adverse comment on her devotion to the works of Ethel M. Dell.

One reason, I fancy, why my mother never wholly surmounted her guilt feelings about the cinema lay in the fact that it was so frequently preoccupied with sex, a subject which she found not so much distasteful as virtually incomprehensible. With her, as with so many well-educated women of that generation, emancipation was conditioned by background and, while she never wavered in her conviction that men and women were equally entitled to the same freedom, she never for one moment doubted, in so far as pre- or extra-marital experience was concerned, that this was best achieved by restricting the male rather than by any extension of indulgence to the female. Nothing infuriated her more than to hear any light-hearted reference to the sowing of wild oats. Deeply as she had loved my father, physical passion, I am convinced, in her case played but a small part in their relationship: a view in which I was confirmed many years later when on the eve of my own wedding she took the bride aside for a little good advice. "Now, dear, I want you to promise me that you won't let Osbert be tiresome. I know what those Lancasters are like when given half a chance and I was always very firm with his dear father."

Towards less orthodox manifestations of the sexual urge she displayed an engaging tolerance founded on total ignorance. Among her numerous artistic acquaintances there were several djibbah-clad couples whose mutual affection would, to a more sophisticated eye, have seemed long since to have passed the normal bounds of feminine friendship but in whose relationship my mother saw nothing remotely equivocal. And once, when staying with friends in France where a distinguished writer was a fellow-guest, she wrote me, "There is a Monsieur Gide staying here at present. I must say I find him very courteous but they tell me he is a little like Oscar Wilde—you know what I mean, dear." I did but remained doubtful whether the knowledge was shared.

To the art of painting my mother's attitude was enthusiastic but confused. Well-trained, first in Brussels, then in Watts' studio and subsequently, round the turn of the century, at St. Ives, her practice (for immediately on our return to London she rented a studio) remained strictly orthodox; but the fact that she continued, year after year, to exhibit well-painted but conventional flower-pieces at the Royal Academy in no way inhibited her appreciation of those more experimental works for which she had first conceived an enthusiasm at the historic Grosvenor Galleries exhibition in 1912. Unfortunately her admiration did not go so far as to lead her to purchase any examples; on the very few occasions when she brought out her cheque-book it was almost always for the acquisition of some opalescent water-colour in which ill-defined forms loomed through violet clouds, painted, it was claimed, under the direct control of a spirit-guide. This was in a way curious as the nearest she herself got to mysticism in her own work was the occasional introduction of a wooden statuette of Buddha into a solidly conceived still-life. Nevertheless, if she neglected many a golden opportunity (either from recurrent fears of imminent financial disaster or from a well-justified apprehension of the alarming reaction which the patronage of contemporary art would undoubtedly provoke in her in-laws), her approach always remained, to my infinite advantage, professional and catholic, and from a very early age I was not only encouraged in my own efforts but was her regular companion at private views at the Leicester Galleries and the winter exhibitions at Burlington House. Indeed, it was to this determination that I should enjoy as wide and as early an acquaintance as possible with the work of the Masters both in painting and architecture that finally led her to overcome her reluctance to venture on the post-war continent without adult male protection.

*   *   *   *   *

My first visit abroad, every detail of which remains strangely vivid, took place in 1920 or '21 and was purged, in my mother's eyes, from any suggestion of frivolous pleasure-seeking by its primary objective, a visit to my father's grave. Only when this was duly accomplished did she feel herself justified in spending two nights in Paris and embarking on a short motor-trip round the châteaux of the Loire. For me the whole outing was euphoric; for years I had nourished an intense passion, much stimulated by constant study of that colourful series of Messrs. Black's *Peeps at Many Lands* to cross the Channel, and abroad had taken on an extraordinary magic as a place where everything was quite, quite different and far, far more highly coloured. That in the event I was not disappointed was due not only to my childish determination that I should not be, but also to the period. In those distant days before even the limited post-war reconstruction of the 'twenties had got under way, abroad *was* vastly different from the homeland. Now when it is possible for none but the expert to detect any visible difference between his point of departure and that of arrival, and only the language of the advertisements, adorning the inevitable curtain-walled office blocks and the all

too familiar façades of identical coffee-bars patronised by the same indistinguishable jean-clad customers, affords the smallest clue as to whether one is in Teheran or Clermont-Ferrand or Coventry, it is, as never before, far, far better to travel hopefully than to arrive. But then, from the very moment the Channel packet slid alongside the quay at Boulogne, dominated by a vast poster of that repellent Savon Cadum baby which was subsequently said to have exercised so powerful an influence on Picasso's middle-period, everything was utterly and fascinatingly unfamiliar.

The bloused porters who rushed on board in a cloud of garlic and ferocious high spirits, the waxed-moustached gendarmes, the formidable alpaca-bosomed ladies rummaging in the *douane*, had none of them any counterparts in my experience, and shared with the shutter-hung façades and the awaiting rolling stock (Compagnie Internationale des Wagons-lits et Grands Express Européens, Paris–Basle–Milan–Venise–Belgrade–Bucarest–Athènes–Istanbul) towering above the non-existent platform, a quality of defiant and intoxicating exoticism. To this visual strangeness was added that, rather subtler and more abiding, invoked by the smell, which in later years I should be able to break down into a mixture of caporals, garlic, pastis, coffee and cheap Belgian coal without, alas, ever quite recapturing the original, first-encountered pungency. Moreover, one gained a distinct impression that one had travelled not only in space but also in time, for in the immediate post-war period in France the average age of the male population must have been sixty-plus, and many of the greybeards sitting outside the cafés might well, so far as the sartorial evidence went, have served as models for Steinlen and Caran d'Ache or even have stepped from the pages of *Les Malheurs de Sophie*. Of these the one I most vividly recall as being, indeed, the first Frenchman I had ever consciously seen at close quarters, was the gentleman of whom my mother enquired the whereabouts of the local train to Arras, fork-bearded and grey-cotton gloved, wearing a very narrow-brimmed boater and a flowing Lavallière.

That the subsequent journey across the tedious miles of Picardy

and Artois did not in fact prove an anti-climax was entirely due to the fact that everything—the plush upholstery of the carriage surmounted by lace doylies embroidered with the magic legend 'Chemins-de-fer du Nord', the occasional small château with pepper-pot turrets, the fleeting sight of a priest in soutane and shovel-hat bicycling down a long avenue of poplars—provided abundant evidence that I was, at long last, and indisputably, abroad.

Arras, when we arrived in the late afternoon, wore an equally foreign but rather more sombre aspect. In the roof of the railway station no pane of glass survived intact, the magnificent Grande Place was shattered and forlorn, and the nave of the neo-classic cathedral, which we immediately visited, for my mother was the most conscientious of sight-seers and the light was beginning to go, was blocked by tons of fallen masonry. The next day was bleak and windy and the drive across the mournful plains, still pitted with shell-holes and of which the monotony was only occasionally relieved by a clump of shattered trees rendered, somehow, even more forlorn by the new growth pushing up round the roots, or a roofless farm, taxed even my capacity for enjoyment. Nor was much cheer added by the conversation of our driver, one of those pathetic, big-boned Englishwomen, of whom at that date there were many who, having found emancipation in the newly formed women's services, were now faced with the problem of re-adjustment to civilian life. As an alternative to the usual chicken-farm she had set up as a chauffeur taking tourists round the battle-fields, an enterprise which, so she repeatedly informed us in a voice like a cracked gin-bottle, was not proving an unqualified success.

Confronted with the war cemeteries it was difficult, even then, to experience any but piously induced sentiments. The scale was far too large for personal feelings; in the long perspectives of identical headstones, stretching away across the uplands like some vast dolls' housing estate, the individual message was successfully blanketed by the general testimony to man's ruthlessness and folly. Mercifully, for like all children I dreaded emotion when displayed by grown-ups, my mother was wholly free from the lachrymose necrophilia of the Victorians; not for her the pious outings to Kensal Green so regularly indulged in by the other members of her family, or the hushed references to 'the dear grave'. Indeed I am convinced that her journey had been undertaken far more from a sense of duty than to satisfy any deeply felt emotional need, for she had always held strongly to the opinion that the moment the spirit had departed, the body had no further connection with the person one had known and loved, and possessed 'no more significance, dear, than a broken gas-mantle'. With such convictions her attitude towards death's trappings had always been decidedly robust, and funerals invariably afforded her material for hilarious, if occasionally macabre, reminiscence. One of her favourite anecdotes, which she never tired of recounting, concerned a large family mourning one of its younger members with whom she had gone to condole when as a young woman she was district-visiting in the slums of Wandsworth. All were gathered round a substantial meat-tea of which she was immediately asked to partake, and when the last cup had been drained came the inevitable enquiry, to which she knew the answer had by tradition to be affirmative, as to whether she would care to see the dear departed. Immediately the cloth was whisked away and the coffin-lid raised, revealing the inanimate form of little Willy, off which for the last half-hour they had all been tucking into muffins and pickled pork.

When, finally, after much consulting of maps we located my father's resting-place it evoked, in that neatly laid-out valley of bones, hardly more emotion than an entry in the telephone directory. After laying some flowers and standing for a moment in silence we returned to the waiting car and its lugubrious driver.

The train journey to Paris the same afternoon was slow, uncomfortable and overcrowded, but rendered memorable by my first sight of a genuine, old-fashioned, *bien pensant*, French general, now, alas, an extinct species. Seated in the corner of, until our clearly resented intrusion, an empty first-class carriage his was a formidable presence. Against a dark skin, tanned doubtless by the Saharan sun, a small imperial and neatly curled moustache shone with a silvery radiance; across an horizon-blue chest stretched a

rainbow patchwork of decorations; the boots and gloves were of the finest leather; and alongside on the seat lay a scarlet, gold-encircled kepi. I had at the time a strong, and perfectly correct, feeling that I should not look upon his like again.

Paris, which today is probably, anyhow in the centre, the least changed of European capitals, nevertheless seems in retrospect to have possessed, when it first presented itself to my delighted gaze, a certain additional quality of colour and Frenchness that has weakened with the years. There were then none of those all too familiar posters advertising English language musicals or Biblical epics bringing a resented whiff of Broadway or Piccadilly Circus to the Champs-Elysées; Pernod rather than Scotch was the aperitif most in demand on café-terraces; the taxis might have been those which rushed General Gallieni's reinforcements to the Marne; and, what struck me more forcibly than anything else on that first magical evening, many of the cyclists pedalling homewards along the *quais* carried, slung to the handle-bars, a Japanese paper lantern.

The phenomenal success of our tour of the châteaux, upon which, having inspected the Louvre and Notre Dame, we embarked on the following day was a tribute to my mother's inspired choice of itinerary for my first foreign outing. Like all well-conditioned children I was at the age of twelve a devotee of the picturesque and a keen mediaevalist (how bitterly I resented the L.C.C.'s recent refusal to allow Messrs. Liberty's to erect the half-timbered façade of their new premises right on Regent Street) and if my preference was given to such uncompromisingly feudal piles as Loches and Chinon, the fantastic silhouettes and romantic siting of such castles as Amboise and Azay-le-Rideau, recalling as they did 'La Belle au bois dormant' with all the overtones of Dulac and Bakst, completely reconciled me to Renaissance details which elsewhere I should have so bitterly resented. Of my first visit to Chartres, curiously enough, I recall little except the awe induced by the extraordinary depth of blue in the glass and my deep disapproval of the neo-classic group in white marble above the high altar, while the Trianon, which today I rank high on the list of the world's indisputable masterpieces, had for me at that age no message at all.

*   *   *   *   *

In the years that followed, the range of our travels was annually extended. To my mother's eternal credit she was not one of those grown-ups who invariably turned down all hints and requests with the maddening response, "Wait a little longer, dear. You'll appreciate it all so much more when you're a little older"; an observation quite unjustified by the minute particle of truth embodied in it. On revisiting the pilgrimage centres of my childhood I have always, naturally, found much that on first acquaintance I had entirely overlooked or which, if noted, had evoked no response, but the intensity of my first reactions has never been surpassed and only occasionally equalled. In particular I recall an experience in Venice which ranks with the rise of the curtain at the Alhambra matinée as one of the two great moments of revelation of my childhood.

We had only arrived late the previous evening and what I had seen from the gondola on the way to the small hotel tucked away behind the Piazza had inspired a certain gloom. Not only was the Renaissance far too much in evidence for my taste but many of the façades were adorned with round-headed windows that re-awoke a strange irrational terror which certain streets in the Notting Hill area, similarly fenestrated, had induced in my pram-borne days but which the conscious mind had long since forgotten. Waking very early next morning I went out into the brilliant sunshine on a solitary exploration before breakfast, and after negotiating several narrow alleys found myself in a long arcade hung with canvas awnings through which the sun filtered in a golden glow and one of which after a moment's hesitation I firmly pulled aside. For what was then revealed—the whole Piazza backed by the west front of Saint Mark's, all the golden balls and crosses gleaming and shimmering in the rays of a sun that was only just above the Doge's Palace—I could not have been less prepared. Slowly, in a state of exalted trance, I crossed the great Square, at that hour empty of all but the pigeons, and then, having arrived opposite the glittering façade, I glanced right and saw for the first time that most staggering of all views, S. Giorgio Maggiore floating above a dancing sea framed between the twin columns of the Piazzetta.

For the rest I found Venice oppressive and slightly alarming; it is not, I think, a city for children who unconsciously react to that aspect of it so subtly presented by Thomas Mann while remaining quite unmoved by the beauties extolled by Ruskin. Burano in particular, which I have never revisited, remains forever endowed with a terrifying noonday menace that haunted, although in a less concentrated form, the whole lagoon and which I was to re-experience many years later on first seeing the early canvases of Chirico. Florence, on the other hand, generated no such terrors and was exactly tailored to my childish requirements. The Ponte Vecchio, the Bargello, Giotto's campanile, even the appalling west front of the Duomo ("Entirely nineteenth century but still no good," as Sir Maurice Bowra once remarked of Cologne) all filled me with uncritical delight, and the only building to which I could in no way respond was the Pitti. My mother, too, was, I think, happier in Florence for the appreciation of which her Pre-Raphaelite past had, in a rather specialised way, fully prepared her. Moreover she for once found herself among friends, slightly older contemporaries for the most part, ladies in wide straw hats swathed in batik scarves whom we constantly encountered in Donney's, or on the Ponte Vecchio acquiring vast quantities of leather-work and Della Robbia reproductions.

Such contacts were normally of rare occurrence, for among my mother's many gifts, that for friendship was not very highly developed. Partly, perhaps, because of a lonely childhood passed mainly in the company of her elders, partly thanks to a lifelong inability to suffer fools gladly, and admittedly in some measure due to an unshakeable conviction that she knew far better than those concerned what made for their true happiness, my mother's circle was always small and steadily contracted as the years went by and her attitude to life became increasingly managerial. Latterly the simplest social occasion involved, for her, weeks of detailed planning, and for her guests the strictest compliance with the most elaborate instructions; and while no last minute changes or postponements would be tolerated if proposed by others— prompted, as they so clearly were, by a shocking thoughtlessness or even downright selfishness—she always reserved to herself the right which, as she grew older she exercised more and more frequently, of wholesale re-adjustment or total cancellation. Furthermore, as all these preliminary discussions were rendered the more burdensome by the fact that my mother came of a generation which, while it had finally mastered the business of getting on to the telephone, had never acquired the far more difficult art of getting off, it was hardly surprising that at length her acquaintance was almost exclusively confined to elderly relatives and a few others of the same age-group whose circumstances were sufficiently reduced to render them amenable to discipline. For her immediate family, and in particular for her grandchildren, the genuine pleasure her company afforded—for she remained exceptionally high-spirited to the end—was, in her later years, increasingly overshadowed by the appalling negotiations necessary to enjoy it.

The Second War, of the coming of which she had naturally received advance information from the Other Side, my mother took in her stride. Refusing absolutely to retire to her seaside villa at Rustington which she was convinced, whether by strategic arguments or psychic warnings I never knew, would certainly be singled out for prolonged bombardment, she remained throughout in the top flat of a large Victorian block in Kensington. The only concessions she made to war-time conditions were to move a wicker garden chair down to the shelter where during the noisier part of the Blitz she spent her nights, and to resume work on a large drawn-thread tablecloth which had occupied her leisure hours during the previous conflict and which she was alleged to have started during the dark days preceding the relief of Mafeking but which was always relinquished in time of peace. She admitted, however, to suffering from boredom, and not even the more than usually complicated preparations, which were now for everyone the necessary preliminaries to any social activity, compensated her for the difficulties, and finally the impossibility, of maintaining regular attendance at British Israelite gatherings during the blackout.

During the ten years which elapsed between the end of the war and her death the tempo of my mother's life slowly slackened. The same flower-piece remained unfinished on the easel for months on end; the organisation which even a tea-party involved now seemed to her so overwhelming as almost invariably to lead to a last-minute cancellation; and she seldom, I fancy, managed to read more than two pages of even the *National Message* without falling asleep. Fortunately, however, her conviction of the immense busyness of her life and the number and importance of her engagements, which fully justified in her mind the autocratic attitude she was occasionally forced to adopt, never left her. She was fortunate, too, in that however many friends she might finally drive to distraction, she always inspired in her retainers, most of whom had been in her employ since before the First War, a loyalty and an affection which never wavered no matter how frequent or maddening her changes of plan.

In the last years of her life her spiritual adventurings were gradually abandoned and she came finally to rest in the bosom of the High Church. Nevertheless her acceptance of ritualism was never whole-hearted, the early discipline of St. Paul's, Onslow Square, allied to her strong sense of the ridiculous proved too strong for that, and her genuflexions and 'Hail Marys' were always made, as it were, in inverted commas.

For her end, which came after a few hours' illness in her eightieth year, she was, I like to think, at long last after so many years of frenzied searching which had never modified a fundamental child-like piety, fully prepared.

2. *"Lord, dismiss us with Thy blessing"*

EVEN IN normal times Worthing can never have been a very glamorous resort. Situated on the most depressing and featureless stretch of a dismal coast where an endless expanse of cold grey shingle, relieved only by breakwaters, faces a cold grey horizon relieved by nothing, it had long since lost, if indeed it had ever possessed, the homely charm of Littlehampton and had never acquired the architectural distinction of Brighton. In the last winter of the First War such features as may at the height of a peace-time summer have enlivened its promenade only served to emphasize the general desolation. In the fretwork shelters on the front a few old ladies crouched shivering; occasionally a bathchair fought its laborious way past in the teeth of a biting east wind; on the neglected pier a handful of wounded soldiers in their bright blue suits and red ties stared glumly at the working model of a suffragette being forcibly fed or failed to derive any manifest pleasure from what the butler saw. The municipal flower-beds supported nothing but weeds, in the bandstand was stacked a vast pile of tattered and salt-encrusted deck-chairs, and the passing traffic was confined to an occasional South-down bus, rendered dangerously unsteady by the sagging gas-bag covering most of the top-deck. Indeed the only sign of animation in all that dreary marine landscape was provided by the ragged column of St. Ronan's boys out for their Sunday afternoon walk.

In front marched the master in charge, tweed-capped and furiously pipe-smoking with alongside him, hopping and skipping to keep up with his purposeful strides, two or three of the more sycophantic of his little charges sustaining an ingratiating stream of futile conversation. Every now and then a halt would be called, the laggards, among whom Lancaster was invariably to be found, rounded up and the show-offs, who had broken ranks to display their skill at ducks and drakes, hauled up from the water's edge. And once we were all brought to a standstill by our cicerone suddenly striking a dramatic pose with uplifted arm and calling for complete silence. When at length the last chatter had died down he removed the pipe from his mouth and announced in consciously impressive tones,—"Listen, boys, the GUNS!"—and from far away to the south-east we heard, or anyhow pretended that we heard, above the noise of the surf, the low, distant rumble of the great artillery barrage launching the last German offensive.

On the whole, Sundays at St. Ronan's, despite the gloom induced by the walk, were a relief. Not only were there no classes save Scripture, at which I shone, but, far more important, no games, at which I did not. Moreover there was cake for tea, a fact which in 1918 was of the greatest possible significance, and afterwards the Headmaster would read to us. His choice of works was praiseworthy and his diction excellent so that one crept finally to bed still in a state of pleasurable terror evoked by his hair-raising presentation of the ghost-stories of M. R. James or of Arthur Benson. Had it not been for evening chapel the day would have been almost enjoyable but this invariably generated a melancholy which not even the strong possibility that the Rev. Urch would start foaming at the mouth during the Psalms could do more than alleviate. "Now the day is over, Night is drawing nigh,"—the depressing and expected harmonies reinforced the doleful message that tomorrow was also a day and that our brief weekly respite was at an end.

The fact that I was, anyhow during my first few terms, thoroughly and constantly miserable reflects no great discredit either on the masters or on my fellow fiends. As an only child brought up exclusively by women and almost completely bereft of any playmates of my own age I could hardly have been worse adjusted to school life. I had never before been subject to teasing, let alone bullying, and only after long and bitter experience was I able to evolve a technique for dealing with it. Moreover, the day-dreams of shining on the playing-field which, with Heaven knows what justification, I had entertained in the nursery were all brought crashing in rapid succession. When after a very brief period it became obvious to me, and even more quickly to others, that Lancaster was unlikely ever to win any laurels on the soccer field I comforted myself with the baseless conviction that rugger would prove to be my game. Came the Easter term and my ineptitude in this far more disagreeable and dangerous sport was very soon exposed and all my hopes were set on cricket. But the leaves were not yet fully out when it became apparent to all that my lack of skill at the wicket was only surpassed by my hopeless-ness on the bowling crease, while a total inability to throw the ball more than a few yards seriously reduced my usefulness to the side even at long-stop. Only at swimming did I manage to hold my own, and even once won a very small cup, but this was not a very highly regarded sport, as success afforded no proof of team-spirit.

At any school at this period failure at, and still more lack of enthusiasm for, games would have been a grave disadvantage but at St. Ronan's the social results were comparable to those arising from some crippling and ludicrous physical disability. Our head-master, the great Stanley Harris, was probably one of the finest all-round athletes this country has ever produced, and while soccer was his preferred sport—Captain of Westminster, of Pembroke, of Cambridge, of Corinthians, of England—wardrobes full of club and county ties and long rows of tasselled caps hanging in glass cases in his study testified to a hardly less spectacular prowess at cricket and rugger. In the circumstances it says much for him that he took the interest in my school career that he did and if I never quite attained to membership of the small inner ring of preferred favourites, likely blues, most of them destined for his brother's house at Lancing, we were in my final year on the best and pleasantest of terms, and I was even made a prefect.

While athletic distinction remained the highest of all goals, the pursuit of knowledge was certainly not neglected, and the teaching, given the difficulties of the times, was excellent. Indeed I doubt very much whether my subsequent studies at Charterhouse and Oxford in fact added anything of importance to the conventional learning I acquired at St. Ronan's. This was the more surprising as the majority of our teachers were amateurs, either too old or too frail for active service, some of whom were conspicuously eccentric. Apart from poor old Mr. Hoffman, who suffered from a tendency to epilepsy and the conviction general among his pupils that he was undoubtedly a German spy, the most memorable of these was certainly Miss Eakin, the only woman on the staff. Tall, with a high, Roman nose delicately pink in colour, she always remained conscious of the fact, in which she took enormous pride, that her presence among us, by releasing a man for the armed forces, made a direct contribution to the defeat of Kaiser Bill, and of all the staff she it was who took the keenest interest in the news from the Front and saw to it that we shared it. At the beginning of each term we were encouraged to provide ourselves with maps on which the progress of the Allies was to be indicated by little flags, an activity for which it soon proved difficult to sustain much enthusiasm as the Front remained stationary for months on end or else advanced so small a distance as to be completely indetectable on all but those of the largest scale. Had it not been for General Allenby's spectacular successes against the Turks, which of course necessitated the acquisition of a whole new and more glamorous set of maps, it is doubtful if even the awe, not to say terror, which this formidable woman inspired would have been sufficient to prevent the wholesale abandonment of our strategic studies long before final victory was in sight.

The methods by which Miss Eakin maintained her sway were thoroughly underhand but just as effective as the strong-arm treatment occasionally handed out by some of her colleagues. We were always on our honour to do well and any failure in *dictée* or unseen carried with it a terrible stigma of broken faith and trust betrayed. With what fearful apprehension we awaited her first appearance in class each morning! If she marched briskly in, wreathed in smiles and scattering slightly out-of-date slang—"Ripping morning, boys!"—or whistling "Pack up your troubles in your old kit bag", and wearing her deer's-foot brooch set with cairngorms, we knew that all was well and relaxation spread around, but if that thin mouth was set tight as a mantrap, the tip of the nose more than usually flushed, and the shirt-waist unadorned, we braced ourselves for the wrath to come. This always developed along the same lines; tapping the pile of exercise books on the desk before her with an irritated pencil she would survey the class in quiet bitterness for what seemed an eternity and finally break silence with an indulgent reference to her current favourite.

"Now, little Burnett here may not be very clever but at least he TRIES! I don't mind anything so long as a boy is really TRYING! But Wethered who has been in the class far longer doesn't even TRY!! . . ." As the list of delinquents grew longer personal alarm increased an hundred-fold, for bitter experience had taught us that the full exposure of the real monster of sloth and ingratitude was always reserved till last when she had worked herself up into a highly emotional state. "Now we come to Lancaster sitting there looking so smug . . . HE doesn't TRY! O no, he's far too pleased with himself . . ." On and on went the catalogue of iniquities, its speed only occasionally reduced, as the nose grew steadily redder, by desperate swallowings and sniffings until finally the strength of her feelings overcame her completely and the lace-edged handkerchief was withdrawn from the belt and one was left feeling relegated to the moral level of Nurse

35

Cavell's murderers, and convinced that too casual an attitude towards *l'imperatif affirmatif* had not only broken Miss Eakin's heart but had also, quite possibly, in some mysterious way imperilled the lives of the gallant boys in Flanders. Nevertheless, bitter as were the tears I shed, and many the nights rendered miserable by anxiety as to tomorrow's reception of the evening's prep, I must confess that it is to Miss Eakin alone that I owe my unfailing ability to cope with *genou, hibou, joujou, pou.*

Very different but no less successful was the technique of instruction employed by Mr. Jevons under whom we acquired the rudiments of Latin and made our first acquaintance with English verse. To this wholly admirable man had been given in abundant measure the power of communicating enthusiasm, and if on occasion he failed quite to infect us with his own passionate interest in the correct use of 'ut' he had other methods of enforcing attention. One had only to let one's gaze stray to the window for a very few seconds, or to take the stealthiest glance at the copy of *Chums* concealed beneath the desk, to experience a sudden agonising pain in the ear occasioned by a piece of chalk thrown with a force and accuracy I have never seen equalled. But it was only in Latin class that I found myself very often in the target area, for in English literature he never needed to fall back on this peculiar skill to maintain my interest. Tennyson was, I think, his favourite poet and I can still thrill to the memory of his rendering of the 'Ode on the Death of the Duke of Wellington' accompanied by great thwacks on the desk to emphasise the metre, for he was rightly determined that we should fully appreciate the importance of technique and not be encouraged to think that poetry was just a matter of expressing poetic sentiments. Nor, on the other hand, were we left in any doubt that poetry was sense as well as sound and woe betide the boy who, although word-perfect, recited in a monotonous, uncomprehending sing-song.

"Row us out from Desenzano, to your Sirmione row,
So they rowed and there we landed, O venusta Sirmio."

"Now, Lancaster, what does 'venusta' mean? Barty-King, who

was the tenderest of Roman poets nineteen hundred years ago? Wigram, please translate 'Frater ave atque vale'." In my case Mr. Jevons' reward came many years later when, finding myself at San Virgilio gazing out over 'the Garda lake below' in the company of Harold and Vita Nicolson, I was able to go through the whole of the first verse while Harold was still scratching his head—the one and only occasion in my life when I have managed to achieve both the appropriate quotation and the appreciative audience at exactly the right moment.

To the second master, Mr. Vinter, whose unenviable task it was to teach me mathematics, no such posthumous triumph was ever granted. I possessed no aptitude whatsoever for figures and as quite certainly neither science nor accountancy, if I had any say in the matter, would prove to be my destined career, I failed to see why I should make any effort to overcome a natural distaste. Today, when I am quite incapable of the smallest calculation involving more than two figures, I still feel that this attitude was logical and justified; to spend long hours explaining quadratic equations to such as me would seem as pointless an activity as teaching tonic-sol-fa to the tone-deaf. However, it says much for Mr. Vinter's patience and determination that I finally achieved the necessary proficiency to pass the Common Entrance. Safely over that hurdle, and once past the School Certificate, I never again paid the smallest attention to any maths master, and today all I can remember of so much painfully acquired knowledge is that the square on the hypotenuse of a right-angled triangle is equal to the sum of the squares on the other two sides—a fascinating theory, doubtless, but one for which I have never discovered any practical application and which when quoted, no matter how aptly, seldom scores a big conversational hit.

For only one member of the St. Ronan's establishment did I ever feel a real undying hatred—the school sergeant. How on earth this fat and greasy sadist came to be tolerated for as long as a week I have never been able to understand. He it was who not only drilled us in the quadrangle and superintended boxing and gym, but also took charge of the punishment squad. Any

37

master wearying of the setting of lines or unable to maintain order by the usual methods could hand his victim over to the sergeant for half-an-hour's disciplining in the free period between the end of morning school and lunch. This took the form of being made to stand with arms outstretched grasping a pair of very heavy iron dumb-bells for anything up to ten minutes while sergeant marched up and down twirling his little waxed moustaches and catching one a sharp crack on the back of the knee with his drill-stick at the first sign of wavering. When one was finally released one was, as like as not, subjected to a sinister demonstration of bonhomie which involved being clasped tight to his bemedalled breast while, in an overpowering cloud of whisky-laden breath, he rubbed his close-shaven but still abrasive chin up and down

one's cheek, behaviour which seems to me in retrospect to have required rather closer investigation than, so far as I know, it ever in fact got. Revenge was long in coming but none the less sweet. Some ten or fifteen years later on answering the telephone one winter's evening I heard again that once dreaded voice. "Is that Mr. Lancaster, sir? It's your old sergeant 'ere—you remember old sarge at St. Ronan's, sir! 'Ow are you keeping, sir? I'm still fit and well but just at the moment, sir, I'm in a bit of temporary embarrassment and I was wondering, sir, whether for old times sake . . ." I am sorry to say that it was with keen if unworthy pleasure that I pleaded total ignorance, and no cock crowed.

Of my fellow-pupils I recall little of interest; they were, I fancy, no better and no worse than any other selection of upper-middle-class boys of that age-group, which is to say that they were, collectively, hell-on-earth. St. Ronan's at that date was not a particularly smart school and we could boast only one peer, and Irish at that, and a single baronet, the latter a tiresome lad in a

Norfolk suit, much favoured by Miss Eakin, who was everlastingly according one the inestimable privilege of inspecting his family-tree complete with hand-coloured quarterings, and while many of my contemporaries have doubtless subsequently acquired great distinction in their own spheres few of us have hit the headlines. Hugh Molson and Roger Fulford had both gone on to Lancing the term before I arrived and the only budding statesman I once saw plain was Patrick Gordon-Walker, a year or two my senior, a keen, persevering, but not, I think, outstanding footballer whom I chiefly remember enthusiastically charging up and down the touch-line like a conscientious chimpanzee.

But neither boys nor staff could really compete in interest with the overwhelming personality of the Headmaster. Stanley Harris was an extraordinary figure in more ways than one. Strikingly good-looking and excessively high-minded he commanded the unwavering and totally uncritical adoration of all; no member of his staff would for one moment have dreamt of questioning any of his decisions and for a boy any attempt at ragging would have seemed like the sin against the Holy Ghost. A friendly hug or a manly pat on the back from him remained the highest possible accolade, and his lightest reproach cast one into the depths of depression and self-loathing. Even with parents his magnetism never failed and many a widowed mother was encouraged, by the sight of 'S.S.H.' in spotless flannels advancing to the wicket during the fathers' match, to dream dreams which, I now realise, were in the highest degree unlikely ever to be fulfilled. By and large he relied on this personal relationship to maintain the right spirit of sportsmanship and high endeavour but he never shrank from corporal punishment if the circumstances required it. This he administered with all the skill and enthusiasm which he brought to every form of physical exercise, employing what was generally held to be (and I think probably was) a sjambok inherited from his father, an ex-Colonial Governor. It affords some measure of the admiration which he inspired that, on the first occasion when I was beaten, my initial reaction was an immediate conviction that so good and kind a man could not possibly be aware of the acute pain he was inflicting; but when I turned round to explain I discovered that this was in fact a false assumption, for acting on which I promptly received an extra stroke. Nevertheless, my idol was only temporarily set rocking on his pedestal and long before the welts had turned from purple to blue I was back in the mood when I would not have been remotely surprised had I noticed, the next time he read the lesson in Chapel, a glowing halo encircling that noble head.

But with all his sterling virtues Stanley Harris was neither an intellectual nor a man of the world. Although he took the scholarship class in French I never recall seeing on his shelves any work of literature save *Tartarin de Tarascon* and the *Lettres de Mon Moulin*, nor can I ever remember hearing him quote any poet except, very occasionally, La Fontaine. His remoteness from life, of which I was naturally not at the time fully aware, was most effectively demonstrated when he was called upon to deal with what are so curiously known as its Facts. As soon as it became apparent that one had reached the age of puberty there came, one Sunday evening, a summons to his study for a little chat. Perched on the club fender beneath the white painted overmantel loaded with silver cups and photographs of celebrated Blues one listened appalled as, with infectious embarrassment, the poor man proceeded to beat endlessly around what in the circumstances could fairly be described as the bush. At long last, the rather prominent Adam's apple bobbing nervously up and down above the I Zingari tie, he finally achieved an almost comprehensible reference to the tricky subject of self-abuse. He was, needless to say, against it, not only on moral but also on hygienic grounds. Fortunately it was a temptation that could quite easily be overcome by steadfast prayer, the sacrament of Confirmation, and in my case, increased keenness on the rugger-field. If it were not overcome, however, the results were inevitable and truly awful. First I would start dropping catches in the out-field and finally my spine would turn to jelly. As I had never yet succeeded in holding a catch in any part of the field I judged my prospects to be gloomy indeed. Unfortunately he had quite failed in the course of his explanation to mention the natural phenomenon of involuntary ejaculation with the result that for months to come after every wet dream, and they were not infrequent as I was a lusty little lad, I spent most of the next day running my fingers up and down my vertebrae nervously testing for incipient softening.

The sequel to this painful interview came in one's last term when, having been excused prep, one spent the evening marching round and round the cricket-pitch enjoying a man-to-man talk intended to equip one for dealing with the difficulties and temptations of life at a public school. He started by stressing that at Charterhouse I would undoubtedly find myself in the company of boys who had not enjoyed advantages equivalent to those St. Ronan's afforded and whose standards of behaviour might well be lamentably different. He relied on me never to forget that I was an old St. Ronan's boy and to keep myself uncontaminated by evil communications and firmly to eschew swearing, surreptitious smoking, clandestine visits to public-houses and all such unworthy diversions. There followed then an awkward pause during which I noticed that the Adam's apple had gone into the old embarrassment routine; finally he hazarded a guess that it was just possible that some totally degraded youth might make to me certain disgusting suggestions which he wanted me to promise him I would unhesitatingly reject. This I readily did but as no further explanation was forthcoming I remained in a state of total bewilderment as to the possible nature of the perils to which acquiescence would expose me. After this his brow cleared and he went on to discuss less specialised aspects of public-school life, and I assumed that the worst was now over. However, I was wrong, for very soon the movements of the Adam's apple and a certain far-away look in the keen blue eyes indicated that we were once more approaching dangerous ground. After a brief reference to the painful subject of our earlier talk he said that he supposed that I had often wondered how babies came. In fact there were few subjects about which I had so rarely speculated but, ever anxious to oblige, I readily agreed. It was, he said, all very simple and really rather beautiful, but his manner did not suggest that he himself found it so. Then, inevitably, he fell back on botany and explained at some length how the bee, visiting some male flower, involuntarily acquired some pollen which in the course of its rounds was deposited on the stamen of a female flower which in due course, as a result of this impregnation, produced seed and finally more flowers. "Well," he concluded, "you see it's exactly the same with men and women," adding, rather regretfully it seemed to me, "except, of course, there is no bee."

Retrospectively to exaggerate the horrors of public-school life is a fairly widespread failing. It is of course a form of self-congratulation—how tough and long-suffering must one have been successfully to have withstood such hardships—and is usually accompanied by the complacent assumption that things are now, of course, quite different, and that such trivial inconveniences with which a new boy may today be faced are as nothing compared to the barbarities one had to suffer oneself. Thus on the eve of my departure for Charterhouse my uncles were at pains to assure me that there was nothing to worry about, that the beatings and bullyings of their youth were things of the past, now as obsolete, they understood, as the thumbscrew and the rack, and that school was a totally different place from what it had been thirty years ago. In the case of Charterhouse they were, I think, wrong; not only were conditions almost exactly the same in the early 'twenties as they had been in the 'nineties but a great deal of thought and effort had been expended in order to achieve this result.

In my father's time the formidable Dr. Haig-Brown, one of the 'great' Victorian headmasters, was still reigning but on his retirement a year or so later had been succeeded by Dr. Rendall, whose sole qualification for the task would seem to have been that he was the brother of the headmaster of Winchester, and under whose direction the school rapidly sank into the deplorable state so vividly described by Mr. Robert Graves.

On his departure he was succeeded by Frank Fletcher, formerly headmaster of Marlborough who, by such draconian measures as the sacking of the whole of the Sixth Form, soon restored the high moral tone and the conditions of life that had prevailed under Dr. Haig-Brown and, moreover, maintained them, so that when I first went there, Charterhouse was a fossilised but fully function-ing survival of the Victorian age. The clothes we wore, the idiotic slang we were compelled to converse in, the sanitary ar-rangements were all exactly the same as they had been in my uncles' day. Several houses still had earth-closets and the doctor who attended to my ailments, and incidentally owed the job to the fact that he was a nephew of Haig-Brown, was the self-same medico whose ministrations had landed my father with rheumatic fever.

When, in the early 'seventies, the school had been moved out of London great pains had clearly been taken to select the most wind-swept spur of the Surrey Downs on which to erect an extensive concentration camp in Early English Gothic. Aes-thetically the result could hardly be considered an unqualified success although, very occasionally, when seen from the Godalm-ing–Guildford road, silhouetted against a sunset sky, this extra-ordinary cluster of spires and pinnacles momentarily achieved the romantic aspect of a rural version of St. Pancras Station; functionally it was a disaster despite the fact that when the winter

43

winds howled through the cloisters and arcades those, and they were many, who placed great faith in the health-giving benefits of total exposure could claim that in one respect at least fitness for purpose had been fully achieved. The bleak plateau on which the school stood was divided by a steep gully down which ran the road to Godalming; on one side were the school buildings, class-rooms, library, chapel and the three block-houses; on the other the sanatorium and the outhouses. Of the latter some had been built for their purpose and resembled isolated extensions of Wormwood Scrubs; others were late Victorian mansions to which at various periods arbitrary additions had rather carelessly been made. Of these my own house, Pageites, was one and the inconvenience of the internal arrangements was fully equal to, if it did not surpass, that prevailing elsewhere. However, we were in one respect fortunate as a separate 'Long Room' for work and leisure had been added a term or two before I arrived; formerly one had eaten, worked and played in the same hideously over-crowded common-room, a system which was still functioning in the majority of houses. Studies were limited to half-a-dozen and reserved for monitors and members of the Sixth.

The first thing that struck me when, on a grim autumn after-noon, I was introduced, along with two other snivelling new boys, to my new surroundings was the smell—an appalling mixture of stale frying-fat, cocoa, damp and feet—and my reaction was all the stronger for the fact that St. Ronan's had been scrupulously clean and the atmosphere overwhelmingly antiseptic. Apart from our housemaster, a courteous, good-looking old classical scholar who, I think, never at any one time knew the names of more than a very small proportion of the boys in his house and had the greatest difficulty in recognising those and with whom my con-tacts during the next few years were to be minimal, the only other persons we had encountered were the matron, always known as the Hag, and the porter. Until a very few years before, the Hags had all been Mrs. Gamp-like figures of humble origin but recently some houses had taken on distressed gentlewomen whose medical knowledge was probably even slighter than that of the Mrs. Gamps and whose activities were severely limited by an overwhelming preoccupation with social status. The Pageites Hag was in the latter class and our little chat had been largely concerned with establishing her position and family connections. The porter, on the other hand, was a tough old soldier of uncertain temper but fundamentally kind-hearted who had regaled me with his reminiscences of my father and uncles. Now, utterly abandoned, we three newcomers sat in the Long Room apprehensively awaiting the arrival of the school bus.

We had not long to wait; very soon a roar and a pounding of feet announced the presence of our elders and betters who, after swarming around finding lockers, reading notices, and greeting each other, came over in groups to inspect us. Judging by their reactions mirth was the most charitable of the emotions our appearance inspired. To add to the indescribable inadequacy of our persons we were, it seemed, sitting in a part of the room reserved exclusively for those in the Upper School, and we were told, not once but many times, that on this one occasion, having regard to our natural ignorance, our insubordination would be overlooked but that if ever we were found there again we could expect the worst.

It is curious but undeniable that most boys, contrary to popular belief, in fact like regimentation and regulations although it is not, in my view, a fondness which merits encouragement. If it were not so why should they spend so much time and ingenuity evolving and enforcing so many drivellingly pointless rules and taboos in addition to those necessarily promulgated by higher authority? At Charterhouse these were legion, governing every aspect of daily life. First-year boys had to have all three buttons of their jackets permanently fastened and to wear plain black socks, in our second year we could undo the top button and were allowed coloured socks; one section of pavement was reserved exclusively for those who had their house-colours while only school bloods could walk in the road itself; ordinary speech was rendered almost impossible by the fact that so many things, places and activities had to be referred to by special traditionally hallowed names that were, in most cases, as misleadingly inexpressive as they were philologically uninteresting. For the acquisition of all this specialized knowledge we were allowed a fortnight's grace during which we were excused fagging and were free from the danger of physical assault and each given a 'father', a boy of a term's standing, to instruct us. At the end of this period we sat for a detailed examination and woe betide the lad who had failed to grasp that 'tosh' was a bath or could not identify the house colours of Weekites. The only reward which success brought with it was an end to suspense and an immediate introduction to hell.

For me the most depressing feature of life during my first term at Charterhouse was the isolation; for company and conversation one was virtually restricted to one's 'father' and one's fellow new boys, not in my case a very stimulating band. To speak unaddressed to any boy even a couple of terms one's senior was asking for trouble while no communication with anyone in another house, even if a relative or a family friend, was tolerated for a moment. To ask the way or the time was, at best, to be greeted by a stony silence and a shocked stare, at worst, to provoke a major ticking-off for gross impertinence. So permanently inhibiting did this tradition prove that even today I find it almost impossible to overcome my reluctance to address a word to anyone, from a fellow-passenger to a shop-walker, to whom I have not been formally introduced. With fagging, on the other hand, I soon found it fairly easy to cope. So incompetent was I at shoecleaning, running baths, making toast, so hopelessly inaccurate were my versions of the messages with which I had been charged, that the impression was soon general among the monitors that I was not quite right in the head and it was not long before the command "Send any fag but Lancaster!" became an established formula.

That Stanley Harris had been right when he surmised that I might find myself in the company of boys accustomed to slightly different standards from those upheld at St. Ronan's was soon apparent, even to me. Words the exact meaning of which escaped me, but of which the implications did not, were in common usage

46

and I shall never forget the blush of shame which mantled my cheek when one of my little companions in a fives court said "Balls!" and I suddenly realised that this was not a technical term connected with the game, which was new to me, but one with physiological overtones. Nor were the personal habits of some of my schoolmates such as would have been tolerated for a moment at St. Ronan's where scatology was unknown; when during prayers on my very first evening the boy next to me broke wind and I realised that this mishap was far from being involuntary I did not know where to look so great was the shock and embarrassment. However, it was not long before I overcame my prudishness and I was soon taking as much pride as anyone else in the enviable reputation enjoyed throughout the school by one of our number possessed of the rare accomplishment of being able to fart the opening bars of 'Abide with me' in perfect tune. To the other temptations of which my old headmaster had spoken I was fortunately not exposed. No one pressed me to visit public-houses or encouraged me to smoke and so high was the moral tone, or so resistible my charms, that I still remained for long unaware of the exact nature of the suggestions against which I had to be on my guard. (Indeed the only time when they have ever been made to me was many years later by a Mexican diplomat in an hotel in Prague, an occasion on which I found no difficulty whatever in behaving like a perfect St. Ronan's boy.) Throughout my school career my sexual experiences were limited to the occasional intrusion into my trouser pocket of a friendly but alien hand and now and then participation in a group wolf-whistle as the reigning beauty made his provocative way to the choir stalls in chapel.

Discipline, in so far as compliance with tradition and the maintenance of respect for one's seniors was concerned, was rigidly enforced and the threat of the rod was ever-present. Personally I have no rooted objection to corporal punishment provided that it is administered immediately and with the minimum of fuss (Bernard Shaw never spoke more sense than when he said "Never strike a child except in anger"), but at Charterhouse the process was endlessly prolonged and hedged about

47

with various rituals all nicely calculated to achieve the maximum anxiety. Having committed some offence for which one knew that the penalty was a 'Cocking-up' one was only charged with it after sufficient time had elapsed to encourage the optimistic belief that it had remained undetected. Then one was gravely informed by the head of the house that, much to their regret 'Hall' had decided after prolonged reflection that there were no extenuating circumstances and chastisement was unavoidable, but, unfortunately, he was rather busy just at the moment and the ceremony could not therefore take place until the following Monday. When, after a grim weekend, the inevitable fag-call came one was sent off at a brisk trot to the school-sergeant to acquire half-a-dozen green 'whipping rods' which were at once tested for strength and suppleness. If one was unlucky, or the head of the house was in a tetchy mood, all were rejected and one was sent back for a further supply. Finally after one's clothing had been endlessly re-adjusted and no pads or protective devices discovered, one was stretched tight across a table and the cane was solemnly chalked. This ingenious refinement, subsequently banned but too late for me to benefit, by leaving a clear white line across the bottom enabled a skilful operator, and the heads of Pageites seemed invariably to be also captains of racquets, to get all the six strokes in exactly the same place. When all was over one dashed from the room, through a crowd of boys who had been pressing their ears to the door, desperately trying to restrain the tears until one had reached the comparative privacy of the lavatories. Usually, however, by the afternoon one had sufficiently recovered to visit the swimming-baths and gratify one's exhibitionist tendencies by displaying one's harlequin bum to all beholders.

One of the principal differences between life at St. Ronan's and at Charterhouse arose from the status of the masters; at the former their personalities and influence had been all-pervading while at the latter they were, with the exception of the Headmaster, an almost negligible quantity. My housemaster I saw only at prayers and at meals when his justified nervousness in the presence of his little charges imposed on him almost total silence.

Of the teaching staff I can now recall only such eccentrics as Colonel Smart in whose class one spent most of one's time singing 'Ich weiss nicht was soll es bedeuten' with the gallant colonel giving a very spirited performance on the rostrum, and old Mr. Pilsberry, a high-collared, pince-nezed hangover from my father's day, who suffered from a curious inability, needless to say fully exploited by all, to hold his water if he heard the sound of whistling. Owing to the number and regularity of the services in chapel a rather clearer picture remains of those who were in charge of our spiritual welfare. There was the Rev. Bryant, grey-moustached and white bow-tied, who was so uncompromisingly Low that for him even a black stole smacked of Popery; there was the Rev. Allen, a jolly, kindly man, an elder brother of the well-known vinophil, Warner Allen, inclined to be High, known for reasons that were even then obscure as 'Jazzing Jesus', an ex-naval chaplain and for a time my form-master, whom it was pitifully easy to lead on by disingenuous questions and casual hints from 'Arma virumque cano' to his personal reminiscences of the Battle of Jutland; there was the Rev. Selby-Lowndes who was alleged to have served in the Foreign Legion and was thought to have taken Holy Orders with the sole object of acquiring a rich living in his family's gift of which the actual incumbent was proving to be unco-operatively long-lived; and last, but not least, there was the Rev. Jameson, the perfect example of that pathetic phenomenon—the professional old boy who, after the briefest possible period at the University, had straightway returned to Charterhouse where, despite his invincible cheeriness and passionate self-identification with every aspect of school life, he was regarded, particularly by those in his house, as dangerously *faux-bonhomme*.

In their presentation of the Gospel message these worthies all differed widely. The Rev. Bryant preached Redemption through Grace in tones so monotonous that the whole congregation immediately gave themselves up to playing noughts and crosses or the compilation of ideal cricket teams or even less innocent pursuits; the Rev. Allen adopted a breezy, nautical style which occasionally landed him in metaphysical difficulties which he did not always succeed in resolving; of the exact theological position of the Rev. Selby-Lowndes it was not easy to gain any very clear impression as on the extremely rare occasions when he mounted the pulpit he was almost totally inaudible; while the Rev. Jameson by his wide use of similes drawn from school life and his constant employment of Carthusian slang induced a general embarrassment that found its inevitable outlet in waves of contagious giggling. In fact the only sermons we ever heard that had any intellectual content at all, and grim was their message, came from the Headmaster, who was also a lay-preacher.

Far more striking in character and appearance than any of the masters on the active list was the founder of my house, the great Thomas Ethelbert Page, who lived in retirement close by and was frequently to be seen wandering round the school radiating weary melancholy. Immensely tall with long hair falling over his coat-collar and a growth of stubble on his massive chin, which never reached a point where it could quite qualify as a beard, he was the one personage con-nected with the school whose reputation ex-tended beyond its boundaries. Reputedly a grandson of George IV he was undoubtedly one of the great classical scholars of his day whose edition of the Aeneid I believe still holds the field. Many, many years previously he had purchased a large roll of light grey Donegal tweed, which had become legend-ary even in my father's time, from which all his trousers had subsequently been cut. Although a permanent and much appre-ciated feature of the Carthusian landscape he was by no means immobile and was likely to turn up in the most improbable spots; on one occasion I found myself op-posite him in the restaurant car on the Blue

Train, on another I encountered him strolling down Bond Street with Mrs. Asquith on his arm.

Less picturesque but more immediately formidable was the personality of the Headmaster whose appearance suggested a cross between Genghis Khan and the late Lord Beaverbrook but whose manner was unmistakably that of Jowett's Balliol. Himself a scholar of note, he found it difficult, I think, to take any very keen interest in the intellectual progress of those who were not in the classical Sixth, but this indifference did not extend to their moral and spiritual welfare about which he kept himself constantly, if not always accurately, informed. Personally I found little or no favour in his eyes, and he once decreed the formation of a special football game for those whose notorious incompetence (or evasive skill) had secured them rejection from all the established teams solely on the grounds that he was sick and tired of seeing Lancaster wandering around doing nothing.

Intolerably irksome as Charterhouse seemed to me at the time and lamentable as the education provided seems to me today, in one respect at least I count myself lucky to have been there, for by great good fortune there existed a long tradition of excellence in the graphic arts, which went back to Thackeray and Leech, in which considerable pride was taken and which was—and I am happy to say, I believe, still is—stoutly maintained. The studio was well equipped and the library was particularly rich in examples of the work of the great illustrators, among whom Max Beerbohm and Lovat Fraser naturally took pride of place, and if one was judged to be serious no discouragement was offered to spending what little free time one had there. In the studio teaching was in the hands of a kindly, enthusiastic water-colourist affectionately known as 'Purple Johnson', whose appearance— thick tweeds, Rex Harrison hat, small sideboards, spotted bow tie—was typical of the artist of the old school, today as extinct as the masher and the knut, and whose works frequently appeared on the walls of the R.W.S. and the Academy. Under his régime drawing and painting (water-colours and lino-cuts only; oils he held, not unreasonably, to be too messy safely to be entrusted to adolescents) were not regarded as useful forms of occupational therapy but primarily as crafts of which the technique had first to be properly acquired before they could with advantage be employed as media for self-expression. Once, however, one had achieved a certain degree of proficiency, and provided that one did not altogether neglect to turn out a certain number of academic pencil studies, one was left quite free to choose one's subject matter and I spent many a happy hour composing large historical or oriental scenes in a style which I flattered myself nicely combined the more striking characteristics of Lovat Fraser, Boutet de Monvel and Bakst. In the autumn the purely representational was abandoned for the decorative and everyone was busy painting and varnishing vast quantities of little wooden boxes and book-ends with which to delight long-suffering relatives at Christmas time.

Every half-holiday in the summer term we all went sketching, a straggling group of school-capped cyclists whizzing through the deep Surrey lanes heedless of the booming warnings of Purple Johnson—"Have a care, boy, have a care!"—majestically upright sailing along at an even, dignified pace, like a great galleon surrounded by darting pinnaces. Eventually at some old lych-gate or ruined mill a halt would be called and we each, not invariably without some display of precocious artistic temperament, selected our preferred view-point, set up our camp-stools and took out our Watman sketching pads. First we drew the scene lightly in pencil and then covered the whole with a wash of yellow ochre to the smooth, unbroken flatness of which P.J. attached enormous importance. Only when this had been seen and passed were we allowed to carry on; if it was patchy or streaked, back we were sent to square one with the injunction "Always remember, boy, to take a nice FULL brush!" Pedantic as this insistence always seemed to me at the time I owe to it a simple accomplishment which has proved unfailingly useful, and I remain eternally grateful.

Having finally achieved the required degree of smoothness we were allowed to go ahead, always remembering to use a great

deal of purple in the shadows. (Upon reflection I think it must have been his fondness of this particular technique that had originally gained P.J. his nickname.) Finally, after careful inspection and considered criticism, we put our pads and paints back in our saddle-bags, those who had abandoned art for nature and gone off chasing butterflies were rounded up and rebuked, and we all set off to free-wheel back through a still rustic landscape, doomed all too soon to become a commuters' paradise, with the low sun sparkling through the elms, gilding the clouds of midge hanging above the hedgerows and turning the thatch on the old-world cottages from burnt umber to raw sienna beneath a crimson lake sky noisy with rooks.

The enlightened Carthusian attitude to the visual arts extended also, although more reservedly, to music. That this played the rôle that it did in our lives was no doubt in part due to the fact that Vaughan Williams was an old boy, which was held satisfactorily to counteract any suggestion of frivolity, but far more to the skill and enthusiasm of Dr. Thatcher, subsequently Director of Music at the B.B.C. This excellent man, in addition to supervising the Music School, playing the organ in chapel and coaching the choir, not only each term arranged concerts by the Guildford Symphony Orchestra at which distinguished soloists regularly appeared, of whom Alfred Cortot has left the most vivid memory, but also, more important by far, gave before every concert a series of lectures which although not compulsory were always packed, when he discussed and analysed with the aid of gramophone records the music we were going to hear. He also organised and conducted the school orchestra, an enthusiastic if not outstanding body of players, in which I was numbered among the flutes. Never, perhaps, a virtuoso, I nevertheless came out very strongly in the Polovtsian dances from *Prince Igor* and if my performance never quite achieved the effortless melodic flow of my fellow flautist, Harry Oppenheimer, I personally attributed this to the fact that he had a far more expensive instrument.

Towards the end of my third year the breeze of change which had blown up with the 'twenties was just beginning, very gently, to eddy round the Victorian windbreaks of Charterhouse. Old taboos were not so strictly enforced, the prestige of the athletic element began slightly to diminish, few any longer made the smallest pretence of taking the O.T.C. seriously. That this was not a purely subjective impression, the result of now finding myself in the Upper School and free of fagging and other disabilities, was proved by the emergence of a figure who perfectly embodied the *Zeitgeist* whom I encountered for the first time one dull afternoon in the school bookshop where I was idly thumbing through the works of Henry Seton Merriman and he was making enquiries about *Those Barren Leaves* which, as he pointed out rather tartly, he had had on order for at least a week.

In any society Ronnie Cartland would have been outstanding; at Charterhouse he had the impact of a supernatural phenomenon. A year or so my senior, and before this encounter known to me only by sight and reputation, he possessed a charm, against which even the Headmaster was not proof, that enabled him, not once but many times, to get away with the Carthusian equivalent of murder. Outrageously snobbish, he openly deplored his parents' error of judgement in sending him to so distressingly middle-class a place of learning with the traditions and customs of which he not only made no effort to comply but which he loudly derided, and he frequently announced his intention of adopting an old Etonian tie as soon as a decent interval had elapsed after his departure. Compared to him even the most dashing of our contemporaries seemed like Dornford Yates heroes trying desperately to keep up with Clovis Sangrail or Comus Bassington, and the aura of sophistication with which he was encompassed, and which he knowingly sustained by casual references to Mrs. Wilfred Ashley or the Ritz Bar, was much strengthened by visits from his sister Barbara the sight of whom, becloched and incredibly short-skirted, displaying a generous quantity of pink silk thigh as she alighted from a low-slung scarlet Lancia, was among my earliest erotic experiences. His energy and enterprise were alike prodigious; regarding both *The Carthusian* and *The Greyfriar* as hopelessly bourgeois and pedestrian publications he started a new magazine called, if I remember rightly, *Green Chartreuse*, to which he himself contributed short *contes* in the manner of Michael Arlen as well as a gossip column rather in the style which at Oxford was brought to perfection in *The Cherwell* and distantly foreshadowed *Private Eye*, and which regularly ran the paper into trouble with the authorities. But even at that age it was politics that aroused his keenest and most deeply felt enthusiasms, and found forceful and prolonged expression in the Debating Society which he dominated and inspired, and it was at its meetings that one became dimly aware of the deep sense of purpose concealed behind the scintillating *persona*, distinguishing him in the final analysis from the typical Saki hero on whom he might have been thought to have modelled himself. That the Headmaster, not the most indulgent of men, allowed him so much licence was, I think, in a large measure due to the fact that he at least was not blind to latent qualities that were to carry his protegé, at a very early age, to an outstanding position on the Tory back-benches, which he did not hesitate to imperil by his outspoken opposition to the Party leadership at the time of Munich, and were to find their tragic but perfect fulfilment in 1940.

55

At about the same time a further crack in the barriers which cut us off from the outside world, which Ronnie lost no time in enlarging, was caused by a rather dashing young master who started a literary discussion group which met in his rooms on Sunday afternoons where such authors as Galsworthy, H. G. Wells and, at Ronnie's insistence, Aldous Huxley, came up for study and analysis. Even I, who at that time was going through my nineties' phase, abandoned *The Yellow Book* for Lytton Strachey; and very soon the name of Noel Coward was on everyone's lips; *The Green Hat* achieved almost as wide a clandestine circulation as *La Vie Parisienne*, and a hitherto rather despised member of the Tennant clan gained a sudden kudos by claiming actually to have met the Sitwells. Parallel efforts made by an infant Dadaist called Edouard Roditi to spread the gospel in the studio, however, met with no success thanks to the discouraging attitude of Purple Johnson who continued to regard the Ecole de Paris and all its works with profound distaste.

The outward and visible sign of this sudden blossoming arose from an accompanying preoccupation with matters sartorial. During term-time the sumptuary laws sadly limited the scope for experiment and there was little the more determined dandies could do but stealthily to increase the width of their trousers and to substitute black pullovers for waistcoats, but on arriving and taking off at the beginning and end of term, or at the annual Exeat, members of the Upper School enjoyed the privilege of flaunting their holiday clothes, known as 'sportings', of which the fullest possible advantage was now taken with, in some cases, surprising results. The golfing set, who were rather common and very rich, favoured plus-fours of extravagant bagginess in striking checks which the more advanced wore with dark stockings and black-and-white co-respondent shoes in emulation of the Prince of Wales; less aggressively sporting types favoured flapping flannel trousers in the palest obtainable shade of grey or even, in the case of extremists, lavender or *bois-de-rose*; Ronnie Cartland, needless to say, eschewed all such flamboyance and relied on perfect cut,

a pearl-grey homburg and a clove carnation to achieve an effect that owed not a little to Mr. Jack Buchanan.

It was during my final Exeat—a three-day break in the middle of the summer term—that I experienced the full effects of my recent conversion to contemporary fiction. London, which previously I had accepted as the familiar humdrum background of my home-life and which I had never considered as in any way qualifying as romantic in the sense that I as a matter of course applied the term to Paris or Venice, was suddenly transfigured. In a large measure this was due to the influence of Michael Arlen, a once much overrated but now, I suspect, unduly despised author who, thanks to a transforming imagination and an alien eye, managed in the best of his short stories to invest the contemporary setting with a Disraelian glamour. But even without this literary stimulus I could hardly have failed to respond to the beauty of the London scene. It was June at its rare and brilliant best; in Berkeley Square, still innocent of car showrooms, with its skyline unbroken by slabs of neo-Georgian concrete, the leaves of the plane trees, just stirring in the almost non-existent breeze, alternately threw back and transmuted the rays of a blazing sun; outside Gunters there waited a long line of glittering limousines and a single dowager-occupied carriage and pair; bobbed and short-skirted girls carrying mysterious, but unquestionably expensive, parcels shot up and down the steps in Lansdowne passage. But thanks to my reading and the enthusiasm of my companion, an even more devoted Arlen fan than I was, a further dimension had been added. The sight of an Hispano-Suiza outside an eighteenth-century doorway in Hill Street was invested with an extraordinary significance; the robust ladies in shawls and black straw hats proffering violets on street-corners were transformed into figures of high romance; the sound of a distant barrel organ playing 'The Sheik of Araby' outclassed the music of the spheres.

In the evening we were taken to *No, No, Nanette* where the audience was studded with our school-mates of whom we made a careful count of those who were not, as we were, in dinner-jackets and cast envious eyes at the few, all members of the fast set in Hodgesonites and ostentatiously smoking, who were in tails and were undoubtedly going on to the Berkeley or the Embassy, which we were not. For my mother, although no foe to the bright lights, was strongly of the opinion that dinner at a modest restaurant followed by the theatre provided quite sufficient dissipation for the young and certainly did not see herself accompanying us to a supper-resort or night-club, establishments of which she had formed a rather over-coloured picture and which she had no intention, very reasonably, of allowing us to visit on our own. However, she did on one occasion make an exception in favour of

Princes', a then popular cabaret functioning beneath the R.W.S. galleries in Piccadilly, which she had once visited before the war when it was a fashionable roller-skating rink, and to which I was taken by the parents of a school friend and where I was privileged to hear Jack Smith, the Whispering Baritone, sing 'When the red, red robin comes, bob, bob, bobbin' along'. A daring visit to the old Café Royal in the company of an Etonian friend from St. Ronan's, where we consumed a ritual crême-de-menthe, took place without her knowledge and was anyhow more in the nature of a pious pilgrimage than of an evening of pleasure.

This sudden awakening to the attractions both literary and social of the adult world induced, not unnaturally, a mood of restlessness and dissatisfaction which coloured my remaining time at Charterhouse. In due course I achieved a study, which I shared with Robert Eddison whose thoughts were already turning from the mission field to the stage; became a monitor, a position in which I have an uneasy feeling I provided a convincing demonstration of the truth of Lord Acton's dictum about power; and was even for a time on good terms with the Headmaster who summoned me to join the exclusive circle of those invited to take part in the Shakespeare readings regularly held in his house. But once safely over the hurdle of the School Certificate, which secured my entrance to the University, and with no encouragement for thinking I was ever likely to achieve a scholarship, I finally persuaded my mother that I would for the intervening period be more profitably occupied at an Art School and was allowed to take an early but not precipitate departure. Whether or not because he regarded this as an act of base ingratitude or because of some undisclosed misdemeanour, the Headmaster took the opportunity provided by my leaving report to record his conviction that I was, he feared, 'irretrievably gauche' and had proved 'a sad disappointment'.

3. *"The Varsity Drag"*

AMONG THE many differences distinguishing the world
we live in today from that in which I grew up, the principal, it seems to me, is that formerly one had room to
move: and not only to move but also to see and appreciate both
architecture and people. Today, in cities such as Oxford, the
façades of the buildings are wrecked by the fact that the basement
storeys are permanently masked by phalanxes of parked cars,
and the eminent and picturesque figures who were once accustomed to take their *personas* for an airing down The Broad or
The High would now, did any such still survive, be cut off
from their appreciative public by a scurrying throng of suburban
shoppers and housewives from Cowley. Quite otherwise was the
situation forty years ago; then, if those celebrated thoroughfares
were not quite so unencumbered as they appear in the early
lithographs, wherein The Broad is shown as quite empty save for
a flock of sheep in the middle distance and a couple of dons in the
foreground, they approximated far more closely to this ideal than
they did to the urban Gehenna of today. Motor-cars there were,

mostly little snub-nosed Morrises with an occasional Bentley, its bonnet secured by a strap, belonging to some rich American in The House, but they rolled swiftly by and were accommodated in garages, not left lying around ruining the architecture. On market days the sheep were still there and the Dons, undistracted by the lure of television and the Third Programme, remained prominently in the foreground, grave and distinguished figures for the most part, some, like the President of St. John's, so venerable as to have been untouched by reform, and able to claim Verdant Green among their youthful contemporaries.

Of all the senior members of the University Dr. Homes Dudden was undoubtedly, and appropriately, the most striking in appearance. Always outstandingly good-looking he had acquired in the years which had elapsed since I had last seen him gracing the pulpit of St. John's, Notting Hill, an added *gravitas*; the thick curly hair was now silvery-grey and the profile that of one of the more reputable Flavians. Although the longed-for bishopric had eluded him there had been impressive compensations—a canonry at Gloucester, the Mastership of Pembroke, and the Vice-Chancellorship of Oxford, all rôles in which he conducted himself with the utmost distinction and to which he brought an unrivalled panache. A powerful and moving preacher, he was also a man of the world and at least one rather *naif* undergraduate was startled to recognise in the relaxed, fur-coated figure lying full length in a first-class carriage on the last train back from London, smoking a large cigar and reading the final edition of the *Evening Standard*, the divine who in the University pulpit the previous Sunday had so feelingly described the trials and afflictions to which all flesh is subject in this vale of tears. However, although a Doctor of Divinity and a theologian of impeccable orthodoxy, it remains possible that he was not as unquestioningly reconciled to his lot as his appearance and performance suggested, for many years later a friend reported that on one occasion, when he had been dining at High Table in Pembroke, the Master had turned to him and remarked, *à propos des bottes*, "As an ordained clergyman of the Church of England I am constrained to believe in a future life, but I don't mind admitting, my dear fellow, that personally I should much prefer extinction."

If no one could quite rival the impressiveness of the Vice-Chancellor's passage through the streets there were many other passers-by who attracted almost as great notice and, maybe, roused an even livelier interest. There was Dr. Phelps, the Provost of Oriel, the last clergyman habitually to wear a black straw boater, who was regularly visible tearing down The High bent almost double, hands clasped tight beneath the tails of his short cutaway, not infrequently talking to himself. As befitted an old Carthusian he was a staunch believer in *mens sana in corpore sano*, and greatly prided himself on the cold bath with which he started the day both winter and summer; that his enjoyment of this ritual may have been less spontaneous than he maintained is suggested by the experience of a visitor to the Provost's Lodgings who, on passing the bathroom door, was startled to hear his host exclaim in agonised tones, "Come now, Phelps, be a man!" Unfortunately this pre-occupation with self-discipline and toughness (it is not, perhaps, irrelevant that at Charterhouse he was a near-contemporary of Baden-Powell) may finally have in some measure clouded his judgement and encouraged unwise enthusiasms, for on the last occasion that we met, in a railway carriage shortly before Munich, he passed the  journey loudly regretting the political prejudice which had, in his opinion, coloured the University's decision not to send a delegation to the Third Reich on the occasion of the millenary celebrations at Heidelberg.

Others there were whose appearance, if less frequent and spectacular, occasioned, thanks to their almost legendary fame, an even greater excitement. The celebrated Dr. Spooner was still occasionally to be seen popping into New College where the

Warden, H. A. L. Fisher, seldom tired of recalling at length his experiences in Mr. Lloyd George's Cabinet, and in Addisons Walk one was likely from time to time to come upon President Warren courteously chatting, with a beautifully blended mixture of deference and authority, to the lordly offspring of some ducal house. In addition to the Dons proper there were also several local characters who, although but vaguely connected with the University, yet made their own contribution to the Oxford scene. There was Father Hack, the seventeen-stone incumbent of St. Mary Magdalen, the only man who was ever aware of what he described as "that nasty pull-up at the top of Beaumont Street", who was usually to be seen on Saturday evenings in The George discussing High Anglican politics with the tenth Duke of Argyll over a bottle of champagne. There was the venerable and dearly loved Dr. Counsell, with his broad-brimmed hat and Inverness cape, who lived in what were generally held to be the Duke of Dorset's old lodgings opposite the Roman Emperors, all too soon to be swept away to make room for the monstrous new Bodleian, whose medical knowledge might not quite have kept pace with the advance of science but who was universally acknowledged to have a magic touch with clap.

Among the undergraduates, Harold Acton having recently gone down and Bunny Roger not yet having come up, there were few, hard though they tried, who could rival such figures in visual appeal. Nevertheless the student body as a whole formed an admirable chorus-line against which the principals could make their exits and their entrances. On the one hand were the hearties, grey flannel-trousered or elaborately plus-foured, draped in extravagantly long striped scarves indicative of athletic prowess; on the other the aesthetes, in high-necked pullovers or shantung ties in pastel shades from Messrs. Halls in The High, whose hair in those days passed for long and some of whom cultivated side-burns. Apart and consciously aloof were the Bullingdon and their hangers-on, always in well-cut tweeds and old Etonian ties, or jodhpurs, yellow polo-sweaters and hacking jackets slit to the shoulder-blades. These enjoyed one great advantage over the other two, far larger, groups for they could, and frequently in those traffic-free streets did, display themselves on horseback.

My own college, Lincoln, was small, picturesque and not particularly distinguished athletically or scholastically, and its chief claims to fame rested on the reputation of the late Mark Pattison and the possession of the best seventeenth-century glass in Oxford. Its connection with Charterhouse was close, a little too close for my comfort, for not only were the Rector, the Dean and several of the Fellows old Carthusians but the J.C.R. and most of the undergraduate societies were dominated by my former school-mates. Welcoming as was at first the impression thus created, the reality became before long restrictive. In the interval that had passed since my departure from Godalming I had attended art-school in London and survived the General Strike, for my services during which I had received an illuminated and signed testimonial from H.R.H. Princess Marie Louise in whose canteen I had been induced to work after having, fortunately perhaps, failed to obtain employment as a bus driver. Naturally after such formative experiences in the great world I was dis-inclined to reconcile myself to what seemed all too likely to amount to an extension of my school-days; moreover with few of my fellow Carthusians, except Stanhope Furber and Max Harari, had I ever been on close terms, so that a gradual disassociation from college life presented few problems and aroused little com-ment. However, before withdrawal I committed one ghastly error. The incurable optimism which had at St. Ronan's sustained my belief that there must be one sport at which Lancaster was destined to shine was not, even yet, finally quenched by bitter experience and when the President of the Boat Club came round on a recruiting drive I proved a sucker. After a very few days on the river it became abundantly clear to me why rowing had in more rational societies been confined to the criminal classes and prisoners of war, and not all the efforts of Sefton Delmer—then a willowy, curly-haired heart-throb, the toast of St. Hilda's—to whom my instruction in the rudiments of what it would be ridicu-lous to call either an art or a science had been entrusted, could arouse, let alone maintain, my enthusiasm, so that after a grim two weeks I cast in my lot with the aesthetes, laid down my oar and joined the O.U.D.S.

In 1926 the University Dramatic Society was at the height of its fame. Thanks to a series of spectacularly successful productions culminating in Max Reinhardt's *A Midsummer Night's Dream* in Magdalen deer-park the summer before, the club's finances were in excellent shape and its well-equipped premises in George Street a major centre of social life. The first production in which I was privileged to have a rôle was *King Lear,* for which the services of perhaps the greatest producer of his day, Theodor Komisarjevsky, had been obtained; that my part was as prominent as it was, was due to an extraordinary and distressing incident rather than to any immediate perceptible suitability. It so happened that *The Cherwell,* the less reputable but by far the livelier of the two undergraduate magazines, was at that time edited by John Betjeman who published a cod photograph, with a ribald caption, of the O.U.D.S. rehearsing. The club, which in those days took itself very seriously, was furious and both Denys Buckley, the president, and Harman Grisewood, who was playing Lear, insisted on the poet's immediate expulsion. Unluckily this resolute but rather hastily considered move involved a major reshuffle of the cast less than a fortnight before the first night, for Betjeman was playing the Fool, a major rôle which had now to be taken over by John Fernald, who relinquished the part of the Duke of Cornwall to Peter Fleming, until then only the Duke of Cornwall's servant, to enact whom I was now promoted from the anonymous ranks of Goneril's drunken knights.

Keen Shakespeareans will readily recall that the Duke of Cornwall's servant, although not a very large part, has one highly important and spectacular scene of which, I flatter myself, I made the most. The honest fellow, appalled by his master's treatment of the unfortunate Gloucester, bids him stay his hand, is promptly set upon by the incensed Duke and, after a prolonged sword-fight, slain. Thanks to the Mappin Terraces with which Komisarjevsky had filled the entire stage—a device which in

those days, at least in England, was looked on as revolutionary—
the sword-fight, for which we had received special training from
the University sabre champion, became one of the highlights of
the production and each night I confidently awaited the horrified
intake of breath with which my dying fall from the topmost ledge
was regularly greeted. That I survived a week of this, relatively
intact, was due to luck, careful timing and the maintenance of
strict precautions in the matter of body-armour; others were not
so fortunate, or so careful, and Peter Fleming, ever impetuous,
on one occasion, when he had scorned to put on his helmet, received
a nasty crack on the head from my four-foot blade (steel, not
papier-mâché) and on another, having forgotten his mail gauntlet,
received a wound which lent dramatic emphasis to his exit-line,
"I bleed apace!" Nor was he the only victim, for one night as I
swung Excalibur over my left shoulder a loud groan signalled
that I had dealt an effective back-hander to one of those old men
whom Shakespeare so frequently leaves hanging about the stage,
invariably in one of the pools of darkness without a superfluity
of which no continental producer can possibly make do. The
very next evening my trusty weapon finally failed, snapping off
smartly at the hilt, flying across the stage, tearing through a flat
and, after narrowly missing Miss Martita Hunt who was playing
Goneril, buried itself in the prompt-side wall.

While no other production in which I was involved ever quite
achieved the success of *King Lear,* casualties were even higher in
Romain Rolland's *Fourteenth of July* directed by the same producer
the following year, during the run of which the ambulance was
almost permanently at the stage door. This was largely due to
the thoroughness with which the women of Paris, recruited from
the frustrated daughters of North Oxford, rendered almost
hysterical by the glamour of the footlights and their first gin-and-
limes, armed with broom-sticks, flails and rolling pins, stormed
the Bastille. In the rôle of Marat I was in a particularly exposed
position as Monsieur Rolland had apparently convinced himself
that I could stem the onrush and prevent a general massacre by
hoisting a repellent child on to my shoulder and saying, "Listen

to our little sparrow!'', an invitation which the women of Paris understandably disregarded. That the child in question survived the holocaust to score a notable success as *Alice in Wonderland* in London the following Christmas I held to be entirely due to my presence of mind and total forgetfulness of self.

After the last night of the run it was customary for a large party to be held, allowed by the Proctors to continue till dawn, in Dr. Counsell's house in The Broad. It was attended not only by the whole cast but also by former members of the Society, some of whom were already firmly established in the London theatre. The principal entertainment was provided by musical members past and present repeating the numbers which they had composed for O.U.D.S. smokers, many of which—such as 'How now brown cow'—had, after some slight modification of the lyrics at the request of the Lord Chamberlain, reappeared in West End revues. On the first occasion on which I was present we had to wait a long time for this ritual treat as Komisarjevsky, whose temperament was exaggeratedly Slav, despite his local triumph and the long and favourable notices in the London press and his successful seduction of the leading lady, was suddenly overwhelmed with gloom and retired to a corner where he monopolised the piano for hours on end playing a melancholy and interminable Russian folk-song with one finger. For me the evening was also rendered unforgettable by my first cigar which combined with an all-night session, sustained on alternate draughts of whisky and mulled claret, to produce my earliest and most horrible hangover.

The unique atmosphere of these parties was in no small measure due to the presence of the actresses; this was the result not so much of their professional glamour as simply of their sex, for in those days in Oxford women played a very small part in our lives. There were, it is true, the women's colleges but their inhabitants were for the most part unknown and unregarded and their entertainment, which took the form of morning coffee at the Super, was left by right-thinking men to the scruffier members of the dimmer colleges. Exceptions, however, there were, and each year one single student enjoyed, thanks to her personality or looks or both, a success denied to all her sisters. In my first year it was Miss Margaret Lane; in my second a girl from Somerville who played Miranda in *The Tempest*—the first occasion on which the O.U.D.S. had used the services of a non-professional for a female rôle—with whom many were in love, and to whom not a few were engaged; in my last it was Miss Elizabeth Harman, now Lady Longford, who even achieved the unique distinction of being admitted into the charmed circle surrounding the Dean of Wadham. And for some reason or other, possibly the guilelessness of the nuns, the girls of Cherwell Edge seemed always to enjoy a circulation never attained by the members of other women's colleges. Female visitors from London were normally rare although, in the days of Hamish Erskine who with one or two other old Etonians maintained close links with the Bright Young People, weekends in the summer were from time to time enlivened by the appearance among us of such contemporary celebrities as Miss Elizabeth Ponsonby and Miss Brenda Dean-Paul and, on one memorable occasion, Miss Tallulah Bankhead.

Despite the absence of women, social life was nevertheless intense. As always University society was divided into various sets and cliques most of which to a certain extent overlapped although the great divide between hearties and aesthetes was seldom completely bridged. The latter, after the collapse of the Hypocrites, tended to find their centre in the O.U.D.S., while the former gravitated round Vincents and the Grid. Vincents I never set foot in and my single appearance at the Grid was unfortunate. I was lunching with Christopher Hobhouse, who was also entertaining Ernest Thesiger (who happened at that moment to be appearing at the local theatre) when the Captain of Boats, a strikingly handsome youth, passed our table; whereupon Ernest remarked in his beautifully modulated but carrying voice, "My dears, what wouldn't I give to have been that boy's mother!", an observation which reduced the whole room to silence and prevented our host from entering the club for the rest of the term. The smart set from Magdalen and The House tended chiefly to frequent the Bullingdon, a club dedicated in the first instance to steeple-chasing and confined largely to old Etonians. Not unnaturally I was never a member but from time to time was privileged to attend its dinners as a guest when I never failed to admire Peter Fleming's unshaken ability to keep his head when all about him were looking for theirs under the table.

In addition to these wide groupings there were innumerable small circles usually centring round some hospitable don. In Balliol the celebrated Sligger Urquhart, on whose shoulders we were encouraged to believe that the mantle of Jowett had fallen, albeit he was only the Dean, now confined his entertaining both in his rooms and at his famous châlet in Switzerland to those members of his own college whose abilities were likely in his view to carry them far in the service of the State; while in The House Dr. Dundas extended his inexhaustible sympathy and excited interest to all those he considered to be in urgent need of sexual advice. But by far the most influential of all the dons who took an interest in undergraduates that went beyond the purely pedagogic (a comparatively small proportion), was undoubtedly the

Dean of Wadham, and among the more illustrious of my contemporaries who had cause to be, and were, grateful to him for the unquenchable and astringent enthusiasm with which he proffered both sympathy and encouragement during their formative years were John Betjeman, the late Hugh Gaitskell and the present Warden of All Souls. His hospitality, which was expansive, was never confined to members of his own college or even to undergraduates, for on Saturday evenings senior members of the University like Roy Harrod and David Cecil and distinguished old boys such as Cyril Connolly, Evelyn Waugh and from time to time Bob Boothby were conspicuously present. A formidable and uninhibited conversationalist himself he possessed, to a degree which I have never encountered in anyone else, the power to stimulate the brilliant response even among those whose reactions were not normally lightning-quick; with the Dean everything seemed speeded-up, funnier and more easily explicable in personal terms. Abstract ideas, a passion for the endless discussion of which was elsewhere the first infirmity of alpha-minds were, in his company, always firmly treated as extensions of personality. Himself an expert in the art of going too far, our most daring flights were never  censured for being too outrageous; only if they were quite clearly prompted by a desire to shock rather than to illuminate were they pointedly ignored. The noise was invariably colossal, for our host was never one who hesitated for a moment to exploit his great reserves of lung-power to gain a conversational advantage, so that his opponents were forced either to turn up the volume, or, like David Cecil and Isaiah Berlin, redouble the speed. Drink flowed and only if we were clearly in danger of passing out were we encouraged to cool off in the garden. But one inviolable rule there was—No Breakages. Infringement entailed the immediate departure of the culprit. Neither apologies nor protests were of any avail and I shall never forget the admiration with which on one occasion I watched our host's handling of Igor Vinogradov, an amiable, enormous but clumsy historian who appeared reluctant to withdraw after having, with one expansive gesture, demolished a whole tray of glasses; before you could say "Pindar" the Dean, whose resources I had hitherto mistakenly judged to be largely intellectual, had manhandled the over-excited moujik down two flights of stairs and out into the quad.

Very different, albeit many of the guests were common to both, were the Sunday morning receptions of Colonel Kolkhorst. This highly ridiculous but dearly loved figure, whose very existence was denied by the Dean of Wadham who held that he was nothing but an intellectual concept thought up by Betjeman, was a Reader to the University in Spanish and Portuguese, dedicated to the maintenance of the values and traditions of the 'nineties. His rooms in Beaumont Street, now demolished to make way for the Taylorian extension, were, in the sense in which the term is employed by house-agents, undoubtedly 'rooms of character'. His landlady, of whom he was mortally afraid, kept a succession of dogs which she had never succeeded in house-training and had for years failed to trace a persistent leak of gas, so that the smell which greeted one in the small hall was so fierce as to deter all but devoted admirers; aloft on the first floor, which was occupied exclusively by the Colonel, this was enriched rather than eliminated by the joss-sticks which he always optimistically lit before the arrival of guests. In the sitting-room where he received one could just discern through the Celtic twilight, induced by clouds of incense and very grubby Nottingham lace curtains, an extraordinary collection of objects of dubious virtue to all of which he attached enormous aesthetic or financial value. There were suits of Japanese armour in which whole families of mice had made their homes; there were innumerable occasional tables crowded with oriental figurines of a quality which suggested that they

had originally come out of crackers but which were nevertheless carefully protected by glass domes; the walls were adorned with fly-blown kakemonos and pseudo-Beardsleys; Oxford book-cases groaned beneath the weight of *The Yellow Book*, Wildeiana and an unrivalled collection of novels of school-life; while on the mantelpiece, flanked by black Nell Gwynn candles and a pair of outstandingly hideous Satsuma vases, a photograph of Walter Pater, always referred to as the Master, was prominent; and from the ceiling, regularly enriched with a décor of postage stamps tossed there on coins by the more daring of his disciples, there depended a magnificent brass gasolier with pink glass shades in *le Modernstyle*.

Originally known as 'Gug', the Colonel had subsequently, for reasons that were purely perverse as no one could possibly have displayed a less martial air, been generally accorded a mythical commission in the Portuguese medical corps—an honour against which he had at first protested but to which with the passage of time he had become so attached that he now much resented its omission in correspondence. His conversational style was elaborate in the extreme; well-prepared epigrams were carefully introduced at what he judged, after much forethought and contrivance, to be the exactly right moment, their advent signalled by a wave of the spy-glass which on public occasions he always wore on a black moiré ribbon, and were invariably followed by explosive giggles. As a foil to his brilliance he was usually accompanied by a very dim member of the Exeter Senior Common Room called Toby Struth who prided himself on his conventionality and always displayed a down-to-earth, no-nonsense attitude, appropriate to one who had for a brief space in the last war held His Majesty's commission, which admirably qualified him to be the accepted but unconscious butt of his patron's circle.

First discovered some years previously by 'Cracky' Clonmore, the Colonel owed the exalted position which, when I went up, he enjoyed as a public figure largely to the enthusiasm of John Betjeman and Denis Kincaid who had been so successful in their promotion that in the course of time attendance at his salon had become *de rigueur* for all the smarter aesthetes. Every Sunday morning of term, punctually at half-past twelve, a distinguished band climbed those malodorous stairs and were formally received by the Colonel standing alongside a table on which were a tray of glasses and two socially significant decanters, one of sherry and one of marsala. If one's relationship with the host was unclouded one was handed a glass from the former but, if in some mysterious way one had blotted one's copy-book, one had to make do with the latter. It was not always easy to discover the precise grounds on which any particular guest had been relegated to the marsala class but the most usual causes of offence were a slight tardiness of response to one of the Colonel's bons-mots, or too appreciative a reference to Maurice Bowra of whom he was excessively jealous, or even some disloyal witticism, rumours of which had reached Beaumont Street.

Looking back it is difficult to reconcile the childish character of the ritual jokes with which, usually under Betjeman's direction, the proceedings were regularly enlivened with that sophistication on which we all so prided ourselves. At a given signal those present would sway from side to side, chanting in unison "The Colonel's drunk! The Colonel's drunk! The room's going round!", or some wag standing with his back to the fireplace would laboriously inscribe four-letter words beneath the mantel shelf where it was hoped, usually justifiably, they would escape the Colonel's notice but not that of the female students to whom, seated on a low sofa before the fire, on Monday mornings he gave his first tutorial of the week. From time to time a postage stamp would be sent winging up to the ceiling and if there was a full house all present might break into what had come to be regarded as the school song, to the tune of John Peel.

      "D'ye ken Kolkhorst in his art-full parlour
         Handing out the drinks at his Sunday morning gala?
      Some get sherry and some marsala
      With his arts and his crafts in the corner.

"O and Toby's there in his dirty woollen scarf
    With his acolytes and overcoat and sycophantic
        laugh.
    He only gets marsala and he's puzzled by the chaff
    Of the High Church nancies in the corner."

Such outbreaks would be treated by the Colonel with ill-simulated rage and perhaps some vague attempt, doomed to frustration (for at these moments he quite lacked the Dean's alertness and presence of mind) to expel the principal culprit, usually either Betjeman or Pryce-Jones. If, however, the behaviour of the company had not been too outrageous and there had been sherry all round, the Colonel might be prevailed upon, after a show of reluctance that would have done credit to a Victorian debutante, to move into the back room and there delight us with 'Questa o quella' sung in a very juicy tenor to his own accompaniment on the harmonium.

It is not easy at this distance in time to decide exactly what it was which so endeared this figure of fun to so many of the brightest of my contemporaries. It was certainly not scholarship for, despite frequent impressive references to Lope de Vega, few were convinced that his knowledge of Spanish was more than nominal, while his comparative fluency in Portuguese was due rather to a childhood spent in Lisbon, where his father owned the municipal tramways, than to any extensive research. Intellectually there were few of his fellow dons with whom he could compete on equal terms and to the quality of his aesthetic sensibility his apartment bore lamentable witness. And, although exceedingly generous, his hospitality was not lavish, for until the death of his father, when he moved into what he hoped was a Jacobean manor-house near Kidlington, which he filled with what he insisted was Portuguese Chippendale, he was far from rich. The explanation, I think, lay in his possession of certain qualities of which perhaps we were not at the time consciously aware but to which we instinctively responded—great kindness of heart (a commonplace virtue, maybe, but not one of which senior common rooms can invariably boast a surplus), a genuine fondness for the company of youth which was totally devoid of any hint of patronage and a touching tenacity of purpose which sustained him in his chosen rôle—already outmoded when he had first adopted it—long after he had ceased for a moment to take himself seriously.

The enthusiasm which the Colonel's personality aroused among undergraduates did not, however, extend to his fellow dons, only two of whom, apart from the inevitable Struth, were ever known to appear in Beaumont Street—my Anglo-Saxon tutor, John Bryson, whose friendship dated from their undergraduate days, and that great and good man, the Professor of Byzantine Archaeology and Modern Greek, the late R. M. Dawkins.

No eccentric professor of fiction could possibly hold a candle to the reality of Professor Dawkins whose behaviour and appearance placed him, even in an Oxford far richer in striking personalities than it is today, in a class by himself. Ginger-moustached, myopic, stooping, clad in one of a succession of very thick black suits which he ordered by postcard from the general store of a small village in Northern Ireland, he always betrayed his whereabouts by a cackling laugh of great carrying power. (Once when passing alongside the high wall of Exeter, startled by this extraordinary sound, I looked up and saw the Professor happily perched in the higher branches of a large chestnut tree hooting like a demented macaw.) His claims to scholarship, unlike those of the poor Colonel, were indisputable and his edition of the *Erotokritos*, that great mediaeval Cretan epic, is admitted by the Greeks themselves to be far the best available.* Of his powers as a lecturer it was difficult to judge as he had managed over the years successfully to discourage anyone from reading modern Greek. When, very occasionally, some misguided female student, despite every obstacle he could devise, inscribed herself for the course, his first, and last, lecture of the academic year was always of such shattering indecency that the unfortunate young woman immediately decided to take up Icelandic. His philhellenism was,

* Or rather would be were it still available, for the Delegates of the University Press saw fit to pulp down the whole edition during the war-time paper shortage without a word to the editor.

however, far from being confined to literature and linguistics; he knew every corner of the country, displayed a passionate interest in its political complexities and had formed an admirable collection both of ikons and Lear watercolours, the latter then far less widely known and appreciated than they are today. In the First War disguised, it is hard to believe very convincingly, as a Lieutenant-Commander, R.N., he had, along with Professor Myres, conducted cloak-and-dagger operations in the Aegean and intrigues in Athens, and his account of life in the Greek capital at that time, and of the under-cover activites of the Allies, was not only wildly funny in itself but provided a useful corrective to the published memories of Sir Compton Mackenzie. Fortunately for us the Professor was no recluse and was much in demand as a luncheon and dinner guest not only for the sake of his engaging personality but also for his reminiscences of such figures as Ronald Firbank and Baron Corvo with both of whom he had at various times been on close terms. Unfortunately it was seldom easy, and always demanded much patience, to appreciate these at their full worth owing to his tendency to be overcome by hopeless mirth provoked by the absurdity of the situations and characters he was recalling which rendered the end of his stories virtually incomprehensible. Occasionally, much to the astonishment of those present who were meeting him for the first time, he would slide, completely overwhelmed, under the table, hooting madly; there he would remain for a couple of courses to re-emerge with the savoury, articulate but with tears of laughter still trickling down his cheeks. In the last years of his life his mobility, formerly excessive, was much impaired by a broken hip imperfectly mended, which he found infuriating. But his end was blissful; one fine June day, having lent down to smell a rose in Wadham College garden, he suddenly drew himself upright, cast aside his crutches and with his face irradiated by a seraphic smile fell back dead at the feet of Maurice Bowra.

Of all the undergraduate regulars at the Colonel's Sundays the most memorable was, perhaps, the late Denis Kincaid. Although only a year or so my senior his appearance was that of a well-fed forty; heavy-jowled, his chaps always faintly quivering with suppressed laughter, with a complexion which suggested he had been weaned on dry sherry and whipped-cream walnuts, for us he was always encompassed by an air of unattainable maturity. Never one to stand for a moment when he could sit, at every party he was invariably to be found solidly ensconced in a corner whence he had no occasion to move to dominate the whole assembly, wheezing and, as the evening wore on, lightly beaded with sweat, surrounded by open-mouthed admirers, like some self-indulgent Buddha who had decided that his mission could best be accomplished from a favourite table at the Closerie des Lilas. As a raconteur I have never, in all the years that have passed, heard his equal. Although his imitations were outstanding, mimicry played but a subordinate rôle in his art which achieved its most notable effects by a sustained fantasy and perfect timing. Taking some relatively ordinary incident or encounter he would develop it and embroider on it in a way which beautifully served to illuminate and enlarge the characters of those involved to a point where they assumed mythological status and, as life notoriously copies art, those figures on whom he chiefly delighted to expound began after a time to conform in their behaviour ever more closely to the rôles to which he had assigned them. Thus some dim but pompous light of the Union would, after Denis had got to work on him, develop a capacity for spouting painstaking nonsense far greater than that with which he had naturally been endowed, and such a character as the Colonel himself achieved fame and found fulfilment by enthusiastically overacting his own, Kincaid-created, legend.

On going down Denis followed a long line of forebears into the I.C.S. and was lost to Europe, but from time to time there appeared a novel of Indian life, sensitive, compassionate and, according to those in a position to know, displaying a remarkable insight into alien attitudes and traditions but, curiously enough, deliberately unrelieved by wit. And then came the first volume of what would surely have proved to be his masterpiece *A History of English Social Life in India* in which knowledge, sympathy and humour were triumphantly blended. Alas, shortly after its appearance and before he was fairly started on the sequel, he was drowned while bathing near Bombay, the first and not the least remarkable of my contemporaries to take his departure.

Although as time went on extramural activities tended increasingly to weaken the links with my college, it was in Lincoln, nevertheless, that I found two of my greatest friends, Stanhope Furber and Graham Shephard, with whom in my last years I shared rooms, first above Adamsons, later in Beaumont Street. The latter, the son of the well-known illustrator, E. H. Shephard, was one of a remarkable generation of Marlburians that included John Betjeman, Louis MacNeice, Philip Harding, and Bernard Spencer. Graham's great friend was Louis MacNeice whose regular visits to his rooms generated in Lincoln, a college where aesthetes were almost unknown, a constantly renewed and not wholly appreciative excitement. And, indeed, it had to be admitted that Louis' appearance was at that time of his life uncompromisingly and defiantly poetic; the curly black hair, the carelessly draped scarf above the brown velvet jacket, the walking stick, all combined with an habitual air of bored and slightly arrogant detachment to arouse intense astonishment without immediately inspiring sympathy. Although he was never one of the party-going poets he made no effort to maintain the hermit-like seclusion of Wystan Auden, tucked away in a do-it-yourself Thebaid somewhere in The House to which few were privileged to make pilgrimage, but his public appearances grew far fewer after he had been lassooed and incorporated into her 'little band' by Mrs. Beazeley, the Madame Verdurin of Boars Hill, whose social position had recently been much strengthened by Lady Ottoline Morrell's abandonment of Garsington.

Of the numerous poets then active in Oxford none achieved quite the visual impact of Louis MacNeice although most conformed in their appearance to some accepted poetic ideal. Thus Stephen Spender who came up in my second year was type-cast for the young Apollo golden-haired, a rôle to which he brought all the touching grace of a performing bear; Norman Cameron, tough and shaggy, approximated more closely to the Robert Graves conception; Bernard Spencer, while retaining the side-whiskers and walking stick popularised by his schoolmate, was distinguished by a certain additional intensity that foreshadowed the new poetic look of the 'thirties, first introduced into Oxford by Arthur Calder-Marshall; while Betjeman, idiosyncratic as ever, made a sustained and successful effort to present a convincing impersonation of a rather down-at-heel Tractarian hymn-writer recently unfrocked.

In those halcyon, pre-slump years none of these youthful bards was as yet politically engaged; only when International Nickel had dropped to twelve-and-a-half, and most sensible parents had started their economy drive with their children's allowances, did Marxism add an extra string to their lyres. Tom Driberg, alone, justified politically by Faith but spiritually redeemed through Works, was already way out on the Left Wing but his poetry, of which he gave a memorable recital to the accompaniment of typewriters and flushing lavatories in the Music Rooms, owed, as I recall, rather more to Dada than to the Communist Manifesto. Political awareness, and that of a highly traditional kind, was in fact confined almost exclusively to the Union, an institution visited by the majority of undergraduates solely for the sake of its lavatories, which were exceptionally commodious, but wherein a small but determined band laboriously prepared themselves for those high offices to which, unfortunately, rather too many of them subsequently attained. Indeed the only occasion I can recall on which any political excitement was generated outside its walls was once during an election when I noticed a large crowd, blocking The High opposite the Conservative Committee Rooms, being passionately exhorted from the first floor window by Quintin Hogg. At first I thought they were held spellbound by the power of his oratory and it was not until I noticed wisps of smoke snaking up the façade that I realised that they were in fact rooted to the spot by an understandable curiosity as to how soon the speaker would be consumed by the fire which, unbeknownst to him, had broken out in the piano-showroom on the ground floor.

At the end of my first year I made another unfortunate choice similar to that which had landed me in the college boat club, but this time irremediable; having passed my History Previous without much difficulty I forthwith enrolled myself in the Honours School of Eng. Lit. What inspired this disastrous decision I cannot now for the life of me imagine, and it was some time before I appreciated the full horror of my situation. Of the manifest inadequacy of this branch of learning, as pursued at Oxford, Mr. Stephen Potter made a full exposure many years ago to which there is little I can add save to testify that my own experience completely supports his findings.

Firmly discouraged from exercising what little critical faculty one might possess one was forced to accord as much attention to an affected bore such as Spenser as to Chaucer and spend far more time mugging up all those tedious horror-comics which had, one must assume, some sort of message for the Elizabethan *lumpenproletariat* but absolutely none for me, than one did reading Shakespeare. Personal judgements were not called for; what was required was the largest possible collection of *idées reçues*. In addition there was Anglo-Saxon, for the inclusion of which in the syllabus every sort of specious explanation is constantly being brought forward, all designed to conceal the fact that those responsible for its retention have a vested interest in maintaining the sale of grammars and critical editions of which, in most cases, they themselves are the authors. However, my misguided enthusiasm for literature was unexpectedly rewarded by the personality

of my tutor with whom, had I not been his pupil, I should have been unlikely to come into contact.

The exact age of Canon A. J. Carlyle was even then a matter for excited speculation; he was known to be the last of the Christian Socialists and the only surviving friend of F. D. Maurice, and in his worldlier moments could be induced to reminisce about the beauty of Paris in pre-Haussmann days. He had at one time or another lectured in seven different schools and the five volumes of his *History of Medieval Political Theory in the West* remained a standard work. At one time he had been the chaplain of University College, a position from which he had been most unfairly removed as a result of a trivial display of absentmindedness; having on one occasion, so it was alleged, mounted the pulpit and announced his text, "Suffer little children to come unto Me and forbid them not for such is the Kingdom of Heaven", he had proceeded to give a perceptive, but in the circumstances unexpected, lecture on the later novels of Zola. Nevertheless, if occasionally hazy, he was a man of great practical saintliness and although his roots were so deep in the past, his charitable activities were closely geared to the times; his was the first soup kitchen to open in starving Vienna after the Armistice and in the promotion of such international activities as those undertaken by the Society of Friends he was indefatigable. As a tutor, however, he was not perhaps the ideal. Sitting at ease in a low armchair in his study in Holywell, Morris wall-papered and adorned with many a faded sepia photograph of Paestum and the Acropolis and many a wide-mounted etching of Norman church and Florentine cloister, he would dismiss in a very few words the replies for which the examiners, to whom he always referred as 'those silly empty-headed donkeys', were hoping and then proceed to discuss what in fact Dryden or Donne was trying to say, whether it was worth saying and if they had in fact succeeded in making themselves clear, always ending with a warning that any mention of such conclusions in one's papers would undoubtedly cost one a good degree. With modern literature he kept as closely in touch as the maintenance of a self-imposed time-lag would allow; he made it a rule never to read a book until it had been out ten years, holding that by then it would have become generally clear whether or not one was in danger of wasting one's time. When I first became his pupil he was starting on Proust and pointed out to me an interesting similarity between the handling of love in *A La Recherche du Temps Perdu* and in *Troilus and Criseyde*, a comparison which immediately fired me, modish little snob that I was, with a fresh enthusiasm for Chaucer.

Very different, although not, alas, any more practically effective, was my Anglo-Saxon tutor, John Bryson. Only a few years older than I was, he very soon, I fancy, came to realise that to arouse let alone maintain, my interest in the doings of the insufferable Beowulf or Sir Gawain and the Green Knight was a task well beyond his powers, and it was seldom long before we had abandoned Grendel and his mother in their gloomy mere and gone on to discuss the latest performance of *Les Biches* or the social complications arising from Graham Eyres-Monsell's party the previous Saturday.

Far removed from the studied indifference with which I welcomed the masterpieces of the Anglo-Saxon's limited imagination was my response to contemporary culture. For the 'twenties, too often regarded as a period of sustained frivolity, were in fact a time of great creative vitality. The fertilizing stream of aestheticism, driven underground in the mid-'nineties by the Wilde scandal, had flowed powerfully on, throwing up occasional gushers such as Firbank and Norman Douglas, to re-emerge in full flood after the First War, temporarily overwhelming such idols of the intervening years as Kipling, Wells and Bennett, to mingle its waters with those from fresher springs rising in Paris and Berlin. Even the Diaghilev Ballet, perhaps the greatest single formative influence of the period, had its roots in *Mir Issteva* and *art nouveau*, and Bloomsbury itself was linked by its francophilism with the world of Arthur Symons. Naturally at Oxford it was the aesthetic rather than, as at Cambridge, the intellectual, aspect of the period which aroused the greatest enthusiasm. On every wall Van Gogh's sunflowers bloomed in reproduction alongside the coloured horses of Franz Marc, and in more sophisticated apartments the odalisques of Matisse had finally overwhelmed Holbein's Medici-framed studies of Tudor courtiers and were now enjoying an uneasy relationship with the costume designs of Bakst. The orange cushions on the black settee glowed with a daring radiance in the light transmuted by the pleated parchment lampshades and the mauve tulips elegantly drooped in the converted glass accumulator jar. On low, lacquered tables *Life and Letters* and *The Enemy* were prominently displayed and on the portable gramophone in the corner, still laboriously hand-wound, 'L'Aprés-midi d'un Faune' alternated with 'Johnny spielt auf'; while in the looking-glass over the fireplace alongside the Commem Ball tickets was stuck a printed reminder that *The Cabinet of Dr. Caligari* was now showing at the local flea-pit in Walton Street and on the mantelpiece itself a pair of streamlined jade elephants wilted under the strain of supporting a tight-packed row of recent novels.

It was a great time for fiction 'and on looking back now, when I hardly open a new novel from year's end to year's end, I am astounded at our consumption. It seemed that then no week went past without a new Huxley or Lawrence or Virginia Woolf and one eagerly absorbed an unrationed quantity of lesser men's imaginings; Richard Aldington, Stefan Zweig, Carl Van Vechten all had for us a message which might today, I fancy, be a little difficult fully to explain. Moreover, alongside contemporary works, those of such writers of the recent past as Saki and Ronald Firbank were for the first time becoming readily available in collected editions. It was not perhaps surprising, therefore, that so many of my contemporaries were heavy with novels; Graham Shephard was engaged on a long family chronicle which appeared shortly after he went down; in Trinity Marcus Cheke, in the three weeks during which he was gated for throwing a bicycle at John Edward Bowle, completed and had published an elegant Directoire fantasy entitled *Papillon*; and in Lincoln, of all colleges, a rather dim undergraduate startled all who knew him by producing a now-forgotten best-seller called *Rats of Norway*.

Apart from fiction the key-works, to which we most eagerly responded, were *The Waste Land, Southern Baroque Art, Si Le Grain Ne Meurt, Goodbye To All That* and the writings of Wyndham Lewis, particularly *Time And The Western Man*. In my first years at least, Germany had not yet supplanted France as the day-spring from which we all derived our inspiration and in my own case vacational visits to the world of Roquebrune reinforced this francophil slant. At the end of my last visit there I was given a list of works to acquire at the local bookshop without a knowledge of which the daughter of the house could hardly pass me, despite three weeks intensive reading, as being adequately equipped intellectually; for its period flavour it is perhaps worth citing in full: *La Chartreuse de Parme, Eupalinos, La Trahison des Clercs, Nourritures Terrestres, Dominique*, which I never succeeded in finishing, *Les Maries de la Tour Eiffel* and two volumes of Paul Morand's short stories for light reading on the train.

Culturally lively as were the 'twenties they were also in Oxford a period of conspicuous consumption, the last perhaps that undergraduates were ever to know. A comparatively high proportion of youth was still lavishly gilded and credit was unlimited. Lunch parties normally continued until four or five o'clock in the afternoon and every weekend after dining beneath the swaying punkahs at The George or, if cars were available, tucking into the rather folksy fare and Chateau Neuf du Pape at The Spread-eagle at Thame (why, incidentally, do undergraduates of every generation always make a beeline for Chateau Neuf du Pape?) we all made our way to a gay social gathering in somebody's rooms frequently rendered the more exciting by the possibility that it might be broken up by the hearties headed by Edward Stanley. These latter, usually rowing men, despite their fierce training and superb physique, were by no means invariably on these occasions left in possession of the field, and I recall one heroic evening when they fell like ninepins before a barrage of champagne bottles flung by Robert Byron from a strategic position at the head of the stairs with a force and precision that radically changed the pattern of Oxford rowing for the rest of term.

The most spectacular parties were usually those in celebration of the host's twenty-first birthday and several which took place in my time made social history. Particularly memorable was that given by Harry d'Avigdor Goldsmid who had hired a river steamer for the evening complete with a brass-band and loaded to the plimsoll line with champagne. The experience of many on that occasion conclusively proved that, contrary to the generally accepted view, sudden immersion does not immediately produce a sobering effect, but may well indeed temporarily increase inebriation. (I myself was instrumental in saving several of the brightest and best who were just about to go down, singing merrily, for the third time.) The fact that all the guests made a point of wearing boaters and arriving in hansom-cabs marked it as one of the first Oxford functions to be influenced by that wave of neo-Victorianism, started originally by Harold Scott and Elsa Lanchester, which was shortly to produce *Bitter Sweet*, the Players Theatre and the temporary renaissance of the old-time music-hall and was to remain a powerful force throughout the 'thirties until it finally petered out after the war in a depressing waste of B.B.C. drolls in false whiskers singing 'A Bicycle made for Two'. While it lasted, however, its manifestations were by no means confined to the revue-stage and fancy-dress parties but were also detectable in more serious fields; the novels of Trollope and Disraeli now enjoyed a fresh vogue, Kenneth Clark's *Gothic Revival* and Evelyn Waugh's *Rossetti* both appeared in 1928, Betjeman's *Mount Zion* a year or two later, and from this period dates the beginning of that revival of Victorian typography which was later so markedly, and for the better, to change the look of title-pages and fascia boards.

The weekend gaiety at Oxford attracted, not unnaturally, a stream of visitors from London, particularly during the summer term. Some were well-remembered characters recently gone down who for a brief spell had torn themselves away from the clubs and deb-dances of the metropolis, others were talent-scouts from publishing houses and ministries discreetly disguised, and some there were, like two identical Hungarian barons both equipped with those rimless monocles which appear to be kept rigidly in position by some surgical operation, whose lavish use of face-powder suggested reasons for their presence not at that time readily admissible. Among the more notable of these repre-sentatives of the wider sphere who came regularly among us was undoubtedly that extraordinary figure, Harry Melville. Almost the last of the professional diners-out, whose social programme was said in his heyday always to have been fully booked from early May until after Goodwood, his legendary powers as a raconteur had recently been made the subject of a short story by Osbert Sitwell, *The Machine Breaks Down*. Exquisitely neat and fine-drawn he looked at this time, save for the white hair, much as he did in the portrait by Jacques Emile Blanche, high-collar, cloth-topped boots and all, painted many years before, which used, in the days when it was still permissible to admire Edwardian portraiture, to grace the walls of The Tate but which has long since followed the Wertheimers down to the cellars. His stories, which were frequently hair-raising (my wife recalled that as a young girl she was always sent straight up to the nursery the moment Harry was announced in her mother's drawing-room) gained enormously in effect by being invariably delivered in a tone of voice not far removed from the clerical. "I'm telling this to *you*, my dear friend, because *you* have just the *sort* of intelligence fully to *grasp* the *implications!*" (Harry's use of emphasis was like Queen Victoria's underlinings, arbitrarily selective) was the unchanging preface, and the final climax was always marked by a delicate dabbing of the corner of the eye with a neatly folded pocket-handkerchief. For us he had an interest that verged on the archaeological; an attested friend of Oscar Wilde, one who had encountered Proust when both were sitting to Blanche, he seemed to embody all the fabled sophistication of a period of which we were disposed to take the rosiest view.

For some years to come Harry continued to lend tone to the Bachelors Club and regularly to attend all the more dashing parties and finally died, as it were, in harness. Having contracted pneumonia he entered the immensely chic but slightly wayward nursing-home run by Almina, Lady Carnarvon, where he made such good progress that his bed was one day moved out on to the roof so that he might enjoy the spring sunshine. Unfortunately he was forgotten and passed a night which was marked by several heavy showers in this exposed situation; when in the morning his absence from his room had been finally noticed he was dis-covered in a high fever courteously addressing a neighbouring chimney-stack, "I'm telling this to *you*, my dear friend . . .", and died during the course of the day. According to Dolly Wilde the cause of death should properly have been certified as 'pernicious Alminia'.

As time went on, it was not only social delights and theatrical interests which made such heavy inroads on time that would more properly have been spent on the Anglo-Saxon Chronicle and *Paradise Lost*. After working for a year on *The Isis* under John Fernald I moved over to *The Cherwell*, a rather livelier sheet which could number among its recent editors Evelyn Waugh (who had done the lino-cut on the cover), Robert Byron, Christopher Sykes, John Betjeman and Tom Driberg, where I shared the direction with the present editor of *The Daily Telegraph*, Maurice Green. No one, so far as I know, ever got paid and what cash we could lay our hands on came from flogging review copies. The business manager, and I think part-owner, who handled all the advertising was a Grimes-like character called Evill, loud-checked and ginger moustached, who conducted most of his business from the public bar of The Mitre where, after exactly the right number of Scotch-and-sodas, it was occasionally possible to extract from him small sums for running expenses. The tone of the paper, which was surprisingly well printed and laid-out, in many ways foreshadowed that of *Private Eye* some forty years later, although naturally with the proctors always waiting to pounce it was considerably more inhibited. (Even some of the victims were the same for I well recall threats of legal action from Quintin Hogg which were not finally carried into effect thanks to the restraining influence of the Senior Censor of the House, Roy Harrod.) Of the many difficult interviews we had with authority, which usually we were able to bring to a comparatively satisfactory conclusion by pleading total unawareness of the scabrous or libellous implications which some readers alleged that they had detected in a, to us, wholly innocent comment, the most disastrous was with Stanley Casson—a proctor of exceptional toughness whose experience editing a regimental magazine during the First War had, he claimed, given him the advantage of knowing exactly what he was talking about—who fined us ten pounds apiece for publishing an indecent joke about Godfrey Winn.

Halfway through my third year it became clear, even to me, sanguine and inventive as I was, that my researches into our literary heritage had as yet been on insufficiently extensive a scale to enable me to sit for my finals with any degree of confidence. It was accordingly decided that I should stay up for a fourth year during which all my non-scholastic interests would be abandoned, my social life cut to a minimum, and my whole attention directed to the operation of Grimms Law and the appreciation of *Piers Plowman*. In furtherance of this radical policy I handed over *The Cherwell* to Angus Malcolm, made my farewell appearance on the stage of the O.U.D.S., and the better to avoid the temptations offered by society moved out to lodgings off the Iffley Road. All would doubtless have been well, and the new régime firmly established, had I not suddenly been confronted with a wholly new, and admittedly much worthier, cause of distraction.

In that year the Ruskin School of Drawing, which had been moribund for as long as anyone could remember, was re-established on a new basis by Albert Rutherston, and inevitably the pull of the life-class proved in the end irresistible. Originally my intention was to confine myself strictly to one morning a week simply in order to keep my hand in, but very shortly the old familiar smell of turps and the presence of those long-bobbed, charcoal-smeared girls in ostentatiously dirty overalls proved too strong a lure, and hours during which I should have been listening to interesting lectures on *The Prelude* were increasingly frequently spent astride my 'donkey'.

But not, I think, ill-spent, for Albert Rutherston had gathered round him a remarkable team which included Gilbert Spencer, Eric Ravilious and Barnett Freedman. Of these it is the last whom I now most clearly remember. Cursed with wretched health, born and brought up in the East End in conditions of the greatest hardship, Barnett had had to overcome formidable obstacles to establish himself, and for him, even after he had attained fame and was universally acknowledged as being the foremost lithographer of the day, Creative Artist always remained synonymous with Exploited Victim. Extremely voluble, no conversation of his could long continue without one's attention being forcibly drawn to the iniquities of publishers, advertisers and other such patrons of the arts who were all, according to him, actuated by the single-minded determination to do down at all costs the poor artist to whom in every case their prosperity was self-evidently due. In another man this arrogant assumption of indispensability and never dormant sense of grievance would in the end have proved intolerable but such was the charm of this rotund little Jew, forever indignantly booming adenoidally away in a strong Cockney accent, that he was, as far as I know, entirely without enemies, and even those whose motives were the most constantly and outrageously impugned never withdrew their patronage. As a teaching draughtsman he was first-rate and if now, viewed in its entirety, his enormous output— book-jackets, advertisements, illustrations, posters—seems to suffer a little from a certain lack of stylistic variety it is only necessary to take a look at what went before to appreciate his impact. With the single exception of McKnight Kauffer no man in this country did more to re-store the standards of commercial art, and no young artist should forget that it is in no small measure due to Barnett's ceaseless promotion and propaganda that he gets the price he does today for a book-jacket or a brochure.

But as time wore on, despite the enthusiasm generated by the Ruskin, my absorption in art became increasingly guilt-laden and in the summer term panic set in. My command of Middle English was minimal, of Anglo-Saxon even less; I had not finished *Paradise Lost* nor started *Paradise Regained*; Grimms Law remained as incomprehensible as the Second Law of Thermodynamics without an understanding of which we have Lord Snow's authority for saying that no man can count himself educated. Only in Chaucer and the Metaphysicals could I claim to be reasonably well-grounded and they, as well I knew, were not going to be enough. Of the ordeal itself, of the questions asked and my imaginative but seldom wholly relevant answers I have mercifully no recollection, and the only incident which relieved the monotony of those interminable hours in the Examination Schools that I can now remember was the lordly action of an eccentric racing man at the next desk who, after scribbling away busily for ten minutes, summoned one of the invigilators, gowned and awe-inspiring figures who could only be addressed in case of the gravest physical necessity, and handed him a telegraph form with his bets for the two-thirty at Newbury. The Viva, however, left me scarred for life and the moment when a particularly aggressive female don thrust at me a piece of Anglo-Saxon unseen, of which the only intelligible words were 'Jesus Christ' which I promptly and brightly translated, leaving her with the unfortunate impression, as they were followed by unbroken silence, that I had employed them expletively, still occasionally haunts my dreams. After this shattering interview my hopes were not high and it was with relieved surprise that some weeks later I learnt from *The Times* that I had been awarded an honest Fourth.

Although my additional year had not only served its announced purpose of just enabling me to get a degree but also afforded an unexpected bonus in the shape of the Ruskin, it had not, perhaps, proved to have been an unrelievedly enjoyable extension. Many of my closest friends had gone down, some like Peter Fleming and Maurice Green covered with glory, others like John Betjeman and Alan Pryce-Jones involuntarily. (In the former's case a failure to gain a pass-degree in Welsh had been partially compensated for by the knowledge that in order to gratify this strange ambition Magdalen had been put to all the trouble and expense of importing a don from Aberystwyth twice a week, first-class.) And moreover, in a hitherto azure sky a cloud, considerably bigger than a man's hand that had been waxing over Wall Street since the previous autumn, was now moving rapidly westward and the air was growing chill.

In the years immediately following my departure, during which I frequently returned, Oxford underwent some profound and to me depressing changes. Aesthetics were out and politics were in, and sensibility was replaced by social awareness. Figures such as Crossman, 'broad of Church and broad of mind, broad before and broad behind', who as undergraduates had been widely regarded as jokes, as young dons now loomed large with prophetic menace. In Blackwells the rainbow hues of the Duckworth collected Firbank were soon overwhelmed by the yellow flood of the Left Book Club, and the recorded strains of 'Happy days are here again' floating across the summer quad were drowned by the melancholy cadences of 'Hyfrydwl' chanted live by Welsh miners trekking southward down The High. Martinis and champagne had given way to sherry and beer; serious-minded, aggressive pipes had ousted the gold-tipped Balkan Sobranie of yesteryear; Sulka shirts and Charvet ties were now outmoded by thick dark flannel and hairy tweed. And along the corridors of the Union and in the more influential J.C.R.s Party members proselytized with a discreet zeal that had formerly been the monopoly of Campion Hall, and everywhere the poets hymned the dictatorship of a proletariat of whom they only knew by hearsay.

Already, even before the outbreak of the Spanish Civil War, all over Oxford the lights, if they were not yet actually going out, were starting ominously to flicker.

4. "Wien, Wien, nur du allein"

AS THE innumerable brass bands thundered out the Rákóczy
March the excitement of the crowds sweating and laughing
in the hot sun steadily increased. The music grew louder
and round the corner of the Old Palace came a couple of mounted
police in their menacing Tartar helmets; then more bands,
cavalry, infantry, the fire-brigade and finally the swaying canopy
above the sacred relics borne by the Cardinal Prince Archbishop,
glorious in crimson and ermine and encaged by the elaborately
damascened halberds of the Noble Guards in their white cloaks
and plumed helmets, at the first sight of which all the red-booted
peasant women fell to their knees and started frenziedly to cross
themselves. Immediately behind the crowd of bishops, mon-
signori and censer-swinging acolytes marched the Regent,
Admiral Horthy, together with members of the government
among whom the tail-coated representatives of the bourgeoisie
were, I noted, in a marked minority. Close on their heels followed
all the rank and nobility of Hungary, some traditionally booted
and be-furred with velvet dolmans slung across silk-embroidered

tunics, others wearing the full-dress uniforms of the old K.u.K. Armee, but all ablaze with the forgotten orders of a vanished chivalry. As they passed, one was conscious of a slight smell of formaldehyde. The tail-end of the procession was *plus folklorique*; groups of peasants, long-skirted herdsmen from the plains with bunches of flowers bobbing in their jauntily cocked black hats and head-scarved or bewreathed maidens from the remote Carpathians, testified by their joyful presence that all was still well in this last outpost of feudalism.

With a keen interest in military uniforms and a strong tendency to romanticise the *Franzjosefzeit*, to which the recent release of Erich von Stroheim's 'Wedding March' had powerfully contributed, I was in a state bordering on euphoria. With what excitement and satisfaction did I identify the cap-badges of the Deutschmeister Regiment and the Radetzky Hussars! How wholeheartedly I responded to those martial and long familiar airs! What pleasure I derived from the recognition of the insignia of the Golden Fleece! But of all the groups in that exotic turn-out it was the crowd of Boyars and Magnates, moustachioed and monocled, the heron's plumes sparkling like fountains in their fur caps, striding arrogantly behind the Regent on whom my interest most keenly focused. Needless to say the thought never crossed my mind that they were in fact hardly more picturesque, and scarcely less ridiculous, than the beefy, tartan-wrapped lairds from whose appearance at Oban and Braemar I had in my time derived so much quiet fun; and so overwhelmingly romantic was the whole Hungarian set-up that not for one moment did I, nor for that matter the majority of my countrymen, pause to reflect that no single social group in Europe had caused so much trouble in so comparatively short a history.

Saint Stephen's Day in Budapest came as the glorious climax of a prolonged tour undertaken during my first Long Vacation. Having been presented with fifty pounds worth of traveller's cheques by my mother I had set off with Graham Shephard for a week on the Loire, ending with a few days in Paris during which we had haunted the Dôme and the Rotonde, then at the height

of their fame, where we fancied we had identified Ernest Hemingway and were certain we had recognised Nina Hamnett. I had
then joined up with John Fernald and a friend and gone on to
Munich, which was at that time rapidly becoming a home from
home for Oxford undergraduates, whence, after ten days or so,
we had proceeded by river-steamer from Linz to Budapest,
spending a couple of nights in Vienna. And now after a week in
the Hungarian capital, so fortunate was I in my generation when
the pound was worth a pound, when fourth-class still existed on
most European railways and one could eat as much as one could
hold at a farmer's ordinary in the Sendlingertor Strasse for a
mark a-head including beer, I had just sufficient left from my
fifty pounds to stand myself a second-class sleeper all the way to
Calais, arriving home with exactly sixpence in hand.

During all this extensive wandering only one sight had in any
way suggested that the prevailing tranquillity and cheerfulness
of the European scene might possibly prove illusory—that of the
freshly blackened ruins of the Justizpalast in Vienna. Only a week
or so before our arrival a quite unexpected and seemingly purpose-
less riot had broken out on the Ringstrasse developing into a
savage uprising in which many policemen had been massacred,
public buildings set on fire and which it had soon become obvious

was far too well organised to have been
wholly spontaneous. This deplorable outbreak of mob violence, of which lurid
photographs were still being sold on the
streets, coming at a time when the stock-
markets were booming and the Credit
Anstalt solvent, when faith in the League
of Nations was still high and it was generally assumed that every day and in
every way everything was getting better
and better and better, had left public
opinion profoundly shocked. Finally, in
default of any rational explanation, it was
optimistically decided that it was an

isolated phenomenon to which no sequel would be attached and one best forgotten as quickly as possible: nevertheless the post-cards and the gaunt ruins on the Ring remained productive of a certain unease which even the sight of Frau Sacher, encased in black satin and pearls, with her French bulldog on her lap, still reassuringly installed outside her hotel puffing away at a long black cigar, could only partially dispel.

In the long summers which followed most of my vacations were spent either in Germany or Austria. Sharing to the full the contemporary passion for Baroque, first aroused by the Sitwells, I trekked from Ottobeuren to Melk, from Pommersfelden to Wurzburg and few were the masterpieces of Lukas von Hilde-brandt and the Asam brothers with which I was unacquainted. Whether they would today, when I am tolerably familiar with a far greater range of architecture, have quite so powerful a message I cannot say as I have never revisited them, but I rather doubt it. Even then my enthusiasm, although boundless, was not exclusive; the memory of the dazzling sunbursts and whirling stucco, overwhelming as was their immediate effect, did not on my return home blind me to the sterner beauty of the less ecstatic manifestations of religious devotion evolved by Butterfield and Street to which John Betjeman had first introduced me. But the appeal of southern Germany was by no means wholly architec-tural; there was also music and I became during these years, when it was in its heyday, a regular visitor to the Salzburg Festival.

Honesty compels me to admit, however, that the beauty of the setting and the glamour of the occasion exercised a perhaps more powerful attraction than the operas themselves, for in the matter of musical appreciation I was decidedly a late developer. Hotly as I would then have denied it I experienced at that stage of my career long stretches of something very like boredom even when listening to what was the most famous of all casts in *Der Rosen-kavalier*—a production of which I can now recall little save the beauty of the second act set by Ernst Stern and Richard Meyer's performance as Baron Ochs.

Of the social delights I was more immediately appreciative;

every morning the Café Bazar was crowded with friends from London and Oxford as well as with such celebrities as Emil Jannings and the glamorous house-guests from Leopoldskron, while on the near-by Wolfgangsee half the *höhe gesellschaft* of Vienna, to a number of whom Angus Malcolm, who on two occasions was my companion, had introductions, were established in their summer villas. An industrious student of the *Almanach de Gotha*, I at first experienced a romantic satisfaction at finding myself in this illustrious company but even my starry-eyed snobbism was not ultimately proof against disillusionment. Of all these Maxis and Putzis, apathetically pursuing the seduction of such English debs as came their way after a winter spent propping up Sachers bar bemoaning their vanished grandeur and lost estates (albeit several of them by adopting Czech or Hungarian nationality had managed to keep a firm grip on properties which compared quite favourably in extent with an English county), few, I was pained to discover, displayed the I.Q. of a mentally underprivileged member of the Bullingdon or, save when they were exercising their professional charm, had nearly such good manners.

On looking back it sometimes occurs to me to wonder how far the widespread reluctance of the English upper classes to face German realities in the following years was due to these annual get-togethers, and whether the enthusiasm for baroque abbeys and Mozart operas, for *schulplattler* and 'Kongress Tanzt' in which we all shared, coupled for some with an agreeable schloss-life with hosts several of whom hunted in the shires and all of whom had excellent shooting, did not make a powerful contribution to the process of softening-up. At all events there can, I think, be small doubt that such contacts were largely responsible for one of the most widespread and dangerous illusions then current—namely, that the Bavarians and Austrians were kindly, sensitive peoples, the predestined and unwilling dupes of the brutal and callous Prussians to whom all the more disagreeable phenomena of German history were exclusively attributable. Certainly this point of view was tirelessly maintained by the *hochwohlgeborene* on the Wolfgangsee who never spoke of the Reichsdeutsch save with the most profound distaste which, however, when the crunch came, most of them experienced small difficulty in overcoming. One young count in particular I recall, who owned the smartest villa on the lake and appeared regularly at deb-dances in London where his demonstrative anglophilism afforded much pleasure to simple minds. Many years later I heard that he had spent the latter part of the war as an honorary attaché at a German Embassy where the popularity of his smart little dinner-parties with the local nobility did not finally survive the realisation that an increasing number of the guests tended mysteriously to vanish on the way home, never to be heard of again.

Not all my vacations, however, were spent church-crawling round Mittel Europa; in the spring I returned to Roquebrune where the Bussys and the Van den Eeckhoudts continued to maintain their close relations with Bloomsbury. The village had not at that time been developed and remained, perched on its hill-top, quite detached from Monte Carlo and Mentone both of which cities of the plain it surveyed with a certain lofty consciousness of intellectual superiority. A small number of villas there were but their owners, with the spectacular exception of an Italian princess whom the Van dens always spoke of as being 'd'une indécence folle', by no means conformed to the established Riviera norm. In one lived old Gabriel Hanotaux the historian, a member of the Academy and for a short space during the Dreyfus case a particularly disastrous Minister of War; next door there resided Admiral Lacaze with whom Paul Valéry used frequently to stay. The latter, although his appearance did not immediately suggest the poetic rôle, was capable on occasion of publicly accepting it. Once at a tea-party of the Bussys, on being confronted with a chameleon which his hosts were currently cherishing, after a prolonged scrutiny, he raised his hand for silence and announced in oracular tones:

"Vert parmi les vergers,
Rose parmi les fraises,

Dans les apartements,
Il grimpe sur les chaises."

The proximity of Monte Carlo, although tacitly ignored by the
majority of the Roquebrune élite, had for me certain advantages.
I could from time to time, on the pretext of cashing a cheque or
sending a telegram, walk down for a nourishing lunch at the
Hotel de Paris as a justified change from the cuisine at the villa
which, owing to the chronically delicate condition of Monsieur
Van den's 'foie', tended to be austere, and afterwards to wander
around what still remained, in those days before Mr. Onassis
and the speculators had got at it, the perfect architectural expression of the nineteenth century's idea of pleasure. The formal and
elaborate gardens, palm-dotted, here achieved not only the
intended effect of disciplined gaiety, after which those at Torquay
and Eastbourne so pathetically strove, but also a perfect relationship with the adjacent architecture; the sculpture-laden and
purposefully busy façade of Garnier's masterpiece, as successfully
over-emphatic on its own terms as those of the Bavarian abbeys
I was accustomed to survey with such unquestioning reverence,
beautifully re-echoed the complexity of the canna-packed geo-
metry of the hoovered turf. The elaborately ornamental lamp-
posts, the windows of the patisseries with their dragée-filled glass
bottles and abundance of gold copper-plate, the canopied
victorias drawn up outside the Casino, all spoke, as did the
occasional bursts of rifle-fire from the *tir-aux-pigeons* on the terrace
below, of an age when leisure was taken seriously and there was
plenty of it to take; an age of which, among the short-skirted
matrons and lustrous gigolos outside the Café de Paris, a few
living survivors were still identifiable by their clothes and deport-
ment, some, like old Berry Wall with his grey bowler and horrid
little dogs, familiar to me from the albums of Sem.
There was, however, one intrusion from the strictly contemporary world to which even I, period-besotted as I was, gave an
ungrudging welcome—the large poster at the entrance to the
Opera announcing the forthcoming season of Diaghilev's Russian

Ballet. Thanks to the admirable local bus service, regular attendance was easy and night after night I cultivated that passion of which the seeds had been sown many years before at the Alhambra matinée. Many times afterwards I saw the company performing in a variety of different theatres but never in one which so admirably complemented their art as did Garnier's ridiculous, mirrored auditorium; both the ballets themselves and the piano-duets of Auric and Poulenc, which in those days enlivened the scene-changes, seemed to gain in effect from the comparative intimacy of the setting. Moreover the repertoire frequently included ballets which were subsequently dropped, or were seldom given in London, such as *Barabau*, *Pulcinella* in the Picasso décor, and the Berners-Sitwell *Triumph of Neptune*. But of all the works to which these surroundings lent an additional glitter, it is *Les Biches*, that here seemed a brilliant contemporary extension of the world immediately outside, of which the memory remains the most vivid. Nor was the foyer, with, in the intervals, an international audience drifting to and fro between the bar and the Rooms, without its excitements for it was here that I once, and once only, saw Diaghilev plain, monocle, white mèche and all, hurrying through the respectful throng with an anxious cortège of aides-de-camp and hangers-on close on his heels, like some Napoleonic marshal striding through the glittering ante-rooms of a requisitioned Schönbrunn.

Educative in the widest sense as were these continental excursions they did not by themselves, any more than did a fourth-class degree in Eng. Lit., serve to resolve the vexed question of my immediate future, and there came a day when I was sent off to see the head of the family, my uncle Jack, for a serious talk. For the Lancasters, work, to which they attached a moral value far exceeding that imposed by economic necessity, was something carried out during regular, preferably long, hours in an office; art, which they were prepared grudgingly to tolerate as a hobby, did not therefore qualify, and in their experience those who made it their profession not only forewent all the moral benefits which real work afforded but almost invariably failed to achieve any

solid financial advantage. "It's all very well," said my uncle, "drawing funny pictures but it don't get you anywhere". "Why," he continued, "I remember there was an awfully clever chap in my form at Charterhouse who did wonderful caricatures of all the masters. We all thought he had a great future but I've never heard of him since. Can't remember his name but he was a half-brother to that actor fellow Tree." (Curiously enough, well as I came to know him, I never found quite the right moment to repeat this anecdote to Max.) Finally it was decided that I should as a compromise read for the Bar, a course on which my mother had set her heart, for while it was very doubtful whether the law really rated as work in the sense that business and the Civil Service did, and certainly the record of the only barrister in the family, my uncle Harry, encouraged doubts, it was a respectable profession which fortunately involved arduous study. Why my mother, who had no legal connections of any kind save her brother-in-law whom she did not much like, was so keen on my being called to the Bar I was at a loss to understand. Only on going through her papers after her death did I come upon the explanation; an elaborate horoscope which she had had scrupulously cast at the time of my birth foretold for me a glittering career in the law for which I had a quite exceptional aptitude and practically none for anything else. So on my return from the Salzkammergut that autumn I acquired a number of incomprehensible volumes on Torts, departed each morning to a crammers in Chancery Lane and began to eat a series of unappetising dinners in the Middle Temple. In due course I sat for my exams of which, at the time God intervened to put an end to this dreary farce (for I had if anything even less natural sympathy with felonies, conveyances and Lord Birkenhead's Act of 1926 than with Beowulf and Grendel) I had failed Roman Law once, Common Law twice and after having taken one look at the paper on Real Property had gone straight out to see the Marx brothers.

A few days after this last evasion I was seized while in my bath with a violent fit of coughing at the end of which I was appalled to find the towel covered in blood. Apart from the usual childish complaints I had never had a day's illness in my life and, although not markedly hypochondriacal, was totally unequipped to rationalise so alarming a situation; despite an almost unlimited capacity for self-dramatisation it was some time before I could see myself in the rôle of either Violetta or Mimi and my immediate reaction was panic. There followed then a long succession of specialists and consultations and X-rays which proved largely inconclusive, for no one could make their minds up as to whether certain dark areas in the lung were 'patches' or old pleurisy scars, radiography being then an even less exact science than it is today: but despite the fact that I felt perfectly well, except when I was identifying with Chopin, and had no more haemorrhages, it was decided that as I appeared to have lost some weight I should go for a spell to a sanatorium in Switzerland.

*   *   *   *   *

While I had already on various occasions in my life experienced fits of profound gloom, none of them, not even that which overwhelmed me on my first afternoon at Pageites while awaiting the return of my future playmates, could compare with what engulfed me at eight o'clock on a January morning when I stepped out of my sleeper on to the platform at Sion. At the best of times the upper Rhône valley can hardly be described as *un paysage riant*; on that particular morning with all the mountain-tops masked by a low grey ceiling of cloud and an Arctic wind blowing puffs of grit along roads of which the bleakness was not yet, despite the temperature, mercifully disguised by snow, it was dreary beyond all telling. As the funicular to Montana crawled slowly up into the blanket of cloud my heart sank to hitherto unplumbed depths.

Gradually, however, my spirits responded to an observable lightening of the surrounding fog and when finally we were clear of the last dirty grey wisps I experienced an extraordinary sensation of liberation which caused me temporarily to forget the depressing reason for my journey. I had never before been in the high mountains in winter and snow had hitherto been no more for me than an occasional welcome phenomenon which if sufficiently thick led to the cancellation of football matches, so that I was totally unprepared for the beauty and grandeur of the scene revealed on our emergence above the cloud-level. The sky was of an intense dazzling blue and although no more snow was at the moment being added to the fresh fall which covered all the distant peaks and adjacent slopes, the air appeared to be full of minute specks of glittering mica mysteriously suspended. When to this visual surprise was joined the novel sensation of a sleigh-ride I managed to arrive at my destination in a far more balanced state of mind than an hour before I should have thought conceivable. In the circumstances this was just as well, for my welcome was of the defiantly cheerful kind only achieved by the medical profession which is guaranteed to make the stoutest heart quail. Moreover the excessive cleanliness of everything, coupled with the pervasive smell of some medicated floor-polish, made it abundantly clear that this was not, as all the staff nobly did their best to pretend, just another luxury hotel.

In the days which followed I gradually accommodated myself to the strict routine of temperature-taking and sputum tests; breakfast in bed, then, after the doctor's mid-morning visit, a short walk before lunch, a long rest in the afternoon and in the evening a little bridge with bed sharp at nine. My room, bright and functional with a large balcony, became slightly less impersonal when I had arranged the large supply of books I had brought with me that no longer included, I was surprised to discover, *The Magic Mountain*, thoughtfully presented to me by Graham Shephard on the eve of my departure, which I appeared, thanks perhaps to some subconscious failure of nerve, to have left on the train. The food, owing to the fact that Doctor Roche, the principal, was married to a daughter of the chairman of the Savoy, who regularly sent out the more delicate of their kitchen staff for a health-giving holiday, was excellent; drink was in theory strictly confined to a single nourishing glass of stout with meals. My fellow sufferers were a widely representative collection of all ages; there was a glamorous and recently married deb of the previous year, a North Country manufacturer's son, tea-planters, a retired colonel, vicars' daughters and business men, all united by a frenzied interest in each other's progress, in which it was not long before I myself became completely absorbed. Very soon the outside world grew shadowy and remote, the fall of governments and the movements of Wall Street paled into insignificance alongside questions of such burning interest as whether or not Mrs. Padstow-Trench was going to have a pneumothorax or how far the authorities were aware of Colonel Golightly's regular morning visits to that chic little bar in the village. Curiously enough this intense preoccupation was just as strong among those, like me, whose sojourn was largely preventive or restorative, as with the older inhabitants who were likely to have to remain at this altitude for an indefinite period. And as all my blood-counts and tests remained resolutely negative I felt increasingly compelled frequently to refer to my haemorrhage which, whatever its cause, had in this company definite value as a status symbol.

In due course the time I was made to stay in bed was reduced, I was allowed to skate and permitted myself an occasional visit, in the company of some of the more dashing inmates, to Colonel Golightly's little bar which on most mornings was enlivened by the presence of that exotic figure of my Oxford days, Cara Pilkington, now surprisingly married to a very dull and apparently tubercular hearty from my old college. This, however, remained the limit of my dissipation, for the moral tone of Doctor Roche's establishment (which was wholly English), unlike that of some of its local rivals, was unshakeably high, and sex never in my experience raised its head much above ground level. Later, I was subsequently informed by Sir Malcolm Sargent, who arrived for treatment shortly after my own departure, the situation changed.

With surprising speed the months slipped by and the snow had already vanished from the lower slopes, and round the sanatorium was pitted with those little dents through which would shortly appear the tell-tale necks of the bottles lightly cast from upper windows during winter storms, when, having put on the required weight, all tests triumphantly passed, I was judged fit to resume normal life. Curiously enough my departure proved almost as painful a wrench as had my arrival. After months of cherishing and regimentation, during which I had had to take for myself no decision more vital than that posed by the question of whether to call four no trumps over my partner's four hearts, once outside, my feelings were akin to those of some unfortunate inmate of an enclosed order at the time of the Dissolution of the Monasteries. Taking tickets, booking in at hotels, changing trains, all now presented problems with which I felt totally incapable of coping, and the Rhône valley, deep in slush, seemed no more welcoming than it had in January. I had decided, rather unwisely as it turned out, to go straight to Milan, and thence to join friends in Venice for Easter. The Principe di Savoia, at which I put up for the night, was packed with black-bearded little Fascist bosses in tasselled caps, and the barman and waiters seemed, after the familiar and friendly staff at Montana, markedly off-hand. My room looked out over the railway-yards and sleep I soon realised was likely to prove impossible. As the night wore on I became increasingly a prey to irrational fears, suffered *crises d'étouffement* and was finally seized with a panic depression from which dawn rescued me just in time. No one, of course, had thought fit to warn me of the disastrous, though mercifully temporary, effects of descending straight to sea-level after a long period spent at an altitude of about five thousand feet.

When, after a highly enjoyable week in Venice, I finally returned home I was at pains to stress that my health, although now restored, had still to be cherished; above all the avoidance of stuffy, ill-ventilated working conditions was, so I had been assured, essential to my continued well-being. And what could well be dustier and less bracing than a barrister's chambers? Whether because she had by now lost faith in astrology, or because she had always in her heart of hearts favoured the arts, my mother accepted these specious arguments and readily agreed that I should abandon the unhygienic surroundings of the Temple for the health-giving atmosphere of Gower Street.

When I arrived there the great days of the Slade were, alas, already over; the formidable Tonks had recently been succeeded by Randolph Schwabe, a charming but far from dynamic personality, and there were few among the students who seemed likely to rival the achievements of the immediately preceding generation, that of William Coldstream and Rex Whistler. The teaching was still dominated by an exclusive preoccupation with drawing and tone-values to which the basic techniques, the equivalent in oil-painting of Purple Johnson's flat wash, were rigorously subordinated. The direct touch was everything, and I doubt if there was a single student who understood the subtleties of under-painting or who was capable of putting on a glaze. Nevertheless I slogged happily away in the approved manner, and from time to time produced some sombre still-life or discreet understatement of landscape which duly appeared in the annual exhibition of the New English Art Club. But my happiest hours by far were those spent in the department of stage-design, at that time presided over by Vladimir Polunin.

It is a curious thing that all the Russians who have crossed my path have without exception conformed, in their own individual ways, as closely as possible to the traditional conception. Vladimir Polunin, although a quite dissimilar character, was as markedly and defiantly Slav as Komisarjevsky; with his wispy beard and high, flat cheek-bones one had the impression, on encountering him for the first time, that one had previously met in Madame Ranevsky's garden or hovering round Madame Arkadina's samovar. Hopelessly vague in all practical matters—he was continuously mislaying his keys or ordering the wrong canvas—and subject to alternating moods of hilarious merriment and

deepest gloom, his survival in the harsh world of exile had been largely due, I fancy, to his extremely capable English wife. As an original artist his achievement was limited—the sets after Constantin Guys for a de Basil ballet and the drop-curtain at Stratford*—but as an interpreter of other men's designs he was without rival.

During his long spell as the principal scene-painter for Diaghilev he had been involved in the production of innumerable master-pieces, and his account of working with Picasso on *The Three-cornered Hat*, which he subsequently published in his book on scene-painting, was in the highest degree enlightening. But for the ambitious British student his tuition was attended by one grave disadvantage; sincerely, and I think correctly, convinced that the continental method of painting on the floor was manifestly superior, he would have no truck with vertical paint-frames. Unfortunately there did not then exist, nor does today, any theatre or paintshop in England equipped with the necessary floor space to work in a manner in which, there is no doubt, one can achieve a far greater degree of fidelity to the original design than is possible on a paint-frame, so that one emerged from the course with a masterly technique for which, so long as one remained this side of the Channel, there was absolutely no demand. Nevertheless the time I spent in Vladimir Polunin's studio was by no means wasted, for the familiarity with handling distemper and mixing size which I there acquired stood me in good stead many years later when I found myself quite capable, should the need arise, which on more than one occasion it did, of painting a sky-border or finishing off a backcloth single-handed. A further and far greater debt of gratitude which I owe to that lovable man arises from the fact that he it was who first introduced me to the

* To these should properly be added *Three Generations*, an account of his childhood in Moscow during the last century. Written in Russian and admirably translated by his son, it was published shortly before his death about a dozen years ago. An unjustly neglected masterpiece of its kind, it presents a fascinating picture of a stratum of pre-revolutionary society, that of the well-to-do Moscow merchant families, of which few other descriptions are readily available.

fellow-student whom, after a long and frustrating courtship, I married some two years later.

In the following summer I embarked on the last, and in many ways the most enjoyable, of my bachelor outings. In my final year at Oxford I had formed a firm friendship with a Balliol undergraduate a year my junior whom I then regarded, and still do, as one of the most remarkable of all my contemporaries. Christopher Hobhouse had had a more difficult childhood than most, from the effects of which he was, when I first knew him, recovering at what seemed at times an alarming speed. When his father, an archdeacon of manic austerity, had mortified himself into a mental home, Christopher, whose mother was long since dead, was rescued by his guardian from the board school in which for reasons of conscience his father had maintained him and sent straight to Eton at a far more advanced age than is customary. When during my third year he arrived at Oxford on a scholarship, he had so far adjusted himself to his changed fortunes as to present a somewhat aloof Etonian front to the world while still maintaining a high and rather touching seriousness of purpose, fortunately modified by an irrepressible sense of the ridiculous that spared neither himself nor others. An intellectual, if ever there was one, he was constantly assigning to himself rôles which after much careful thought and rational justification he considered at the time to be correct and into which he flung himself with a thoroughness and enthusiasm that occasionally verged on the embarrassing.

When I first met him he was still playing Hobhouse the Quiet Scholar-with-a-taste-for-architecture, and his evenings were spent in his ground-floor rooms in the big quad of Balliol, which had for him the high distinction of having been the scene of Benjamin Jowett's proposal to Florence Nightingale, puffing away at a massive pipe and studying the latest publications of the Wren Society. After a term or two, however, this merged into that of Hobhouse the Epicurean; the rather subfusc suitings he had hitherto affected were exchanged for elegant tweeds, the pipe more often than not was replaced by a cigar, and his luncheon parties became so frequent and so prolonged as to attract the unfavourable attention of the Master, a dour Scots socialist and a dedicated foe of any form of self-indulgence. Through all his metamorphoses, however, he always retained a keen interest in politics which, during the year after I went down, was much strengthened by his friendship with Harold Nicolson and the company of Bob Boothby and Brendan Bracken, and was only temporarily dimmed by his unfortunate experience in 1931 when he stood as the New Party candidate for Ashton-under-Lyme. Despite an eloquent election pamphlet bearing on its cover a very dashing photograph above the legend 'Hobhouse the Children's Friend', which was much admired when handed out along with the Order of Service at the Pakenham wedding in St. Margaret's but which had, perhaps, a rather diminished impact when distributed at Ashton-under-Lyme, he, along with most of his party's candidates, forfeited his deposit.

For a less resilient character such a setback might well have proved, at least temporarily, disheartening, but for Christopher it was merely the signal for a further change of rôle. Having recently come into his small patrimony at a moment when there was some faint, delusive upward movement on the stock-market, a few moderately successful coups were sufficient to confirm him in the part of Hobhouse the Financial Wizard, one which he was playing for rather more than it was worth when we decided to go together to the South of France. The principal new prop which the current rôle demanded was an enormous touring Vauxhall which, as Christopher never tired of pointing out, had been the largest car obtainable on the second-hand market; undoubtedly impressive, it had for me, whose ego was not then in need of just that form of support, certain disadvantages. Not only did it consume petrol at an astronomical rate but it cost twice as much as any normal car to put on the ferry; moreover its performance hardly matched its appearance and our progress was from time to time punctuated by a series of shattering explosions.

One of the more curious side-effects of the extraordinary excess of self-confidence which accompanied this new rôle was Christopher's firm conviction that maps were quite unnecessary;

the roads of France, so he maintained, were so well-marked, and his own bump of locality so highly developed, that in a car such as this we could find our way blindfold. Unfortunately his bump of locality had failed entirely to register the existence of the Massif Central in one of the more forbidding clefts of which we found ourselves marooned as night fell on the second day of our pilgrimage. Finally we landed up in a dilapidated and quite empty caravanserai, half youth-hostel, half hotel, where neither the décor nor the cuisine in any way conformed to the Financial Wizard's idea of suitable accommodation and where he retired for the night very low-spirited and chastened.

Next day, however, all was more than well; the sun shone, the mountains fell away and as we dropped down into Provence the heat increased with every kilometre and our spirits rose with the mercury. At this stage in his career Christopher was firmly of the opinion that all talk of good little inns and plain bourgeois cooking was simply an expression of inverted snobbery and that the glossiest and most expensive restaurants were invariably the best. Fortunately the newly-opened Jules César at Nîmes served to confirm this view and the mere sight of its shaded terraces and white-coated waiters induced in him a very exalted mood, and it was with the keenest expectations of pleasure that, after a nourishing martini, he settled down to study the enormous menu. But what we did not realise, and only learnt from next day's papers, was that all Europe was in the grip of a heat-wave of which the highest midday temperature was recorded at Nîmes. It was, therefore, with alarmed surprise that I noticed Christopher's face, already fiercely sunburnt, turn slowly from puce to indigo after he had consumed no more than half a glass of rosé and a single helping of hors d'œuvre; acting for once with rare presence of mind I led him swiftly to a cool corner, stretched him out on a sofa, undid his collar and, being myself unaffected by the heat, returned to my luncheon. By the time I had finished the rosé he had so far recovered that we were able, after a brief interval, to resume our journey, albeit with me, highly apprehensive, at the wheel of the juggernaut. Mercifully towards evening he was so far himself again as to be able once more to take over the controls.

It was one of Christopher's most engaging characteristics that, however hard he might strive after sophistication, he was never able wholly to suppress the immediate and spontaneous expression of approval or enjoyment which with him took the rather surprising form of high, whinnying laughter, and from the moment we hit the coast this immoderate hooting was uncontrollable and almost continuous. At that time the South of France in summer was a comparatively recent phenomenon and still retained a prestigious atmosphere of chic and high-living which has long since been overwhelmed by coach-tours and development, and the glittering Hispanos and Cadillacs sweeping from beach to beach, the trousered blondes leaning on palm-shaded bamboo bars, the high-powered speed-boats cutting white swathes through the azure sea, all served to build up a picture of the gay life which exactly fulfilled his highest hopes. The climax came at sunset when once more the celebrated bump of locality let us down; we were searching for his cousin Geoffrey Moss's villa, tucked away somewhere behind St. Tropez, where Christopher was to stay and whence I was going on to Cannes the next day, and were now hopelessly lost in the maquis. Suddenly we heard the sound of excited voices coming from a ruined tower at the end of a track to the left which, as we drew nearer, turned out to be unmistakably those of two English lesbians enjoying an emotional scene. Christopher's cup of happiness was now full; leaning back in the driving seat with his hands still on the wheel he laughed and laughed until the tears rolled down his cheeks.

A day or two after I had arrived at Cannes Christopher turned up at the flat I was sharing with a friend of sanatorium days, John Puttock. Geoffrey's villa, a simple Provençal farm-house, standing remote among the olive trees on a secluded bay with the clearest water I had ever seen, which had appeared to me idyllic, had soon proved rather too rustic for Christopher in his present mood, and the lure of the flesh-pots had drawn him irresistibly eastward for a brief respite that in fact prolonged itself into a stay of weeks. Given his requirements he could hardly have made a better choice. Cannes in the early 'thirties, unlike Monte Carlo, possessed no period charm whatever; it was as contemporary as George Gershwin or the Blue Train and even the statue of Lord Brougham failed to evoke the faintest whiff of nostalgia. All the new buildings, such as the summer Casino, were in what was then known as 'Art-deco', a style deriving from the Exposition des Arts Decoratifs in 1926, characterised by an abundance of peach-coloured glass sand-blasted with vaguely cubist designs, gold-backed murals in the manner of José Maria Sert and a frequency of tapestry panels usually a long way after Lurçat. Against this background there paraded an extraordinary collection of peers, pimps, playboys, tycoons, film stars, celebrated mannequins (the term 'model' was not yet current), American princesses and Australian Ranees, dilapidated Barons and far from dilapidated Baronets.

The Financial Wizard felt immediately at home and at cocktail time sat for hours on the terrace of the Carlton in a state of blissful trance; but the spot which aroused his highest enthusiasm was the Eden Roc. This celebrated menagerie (the term is justified by its striking resemblance to the polar-bear pool on the Mappin Terraces) was then at the height of its fame and every day a wide selection of the celebrated and the notorious carefully disposed themselves on its bluffs and ledges and even occasionally went so far as to roll languidly into the sea. Here one could admire the chilly beauty of Miss Doris Duke, the tobacco heiress, albeit from a careful distance, as she was always attended by two hired muscle-men who went into action at the first sign of any undue familiarity; could respect, without fully understanding, the tender regard with which the Ranee of Pudokota watched her teenage son with gilded toe-nails and made up to the nines, feeding asparagus tips to a pet tortoise with a diamond-encrusted shell; appreciate the tenacity of the elderly Van Dongen plying his laborious breast-stroke in optimistic pursuit of some well-developed blonde. Prone on striped mattresses, members of the Greek syndicate, reposing after the labours of the previous night, filled in the time with a little half-serious backgammon, while in a strategic cleft on the water's edge Miss Elsa Maxwell lurked like Grendel's mother in her mere, ready to pounce out on the first worthwhile celebrity to swim past. From time to time an elegant cabin-cruiser swept round the point on its way to Antibes and a few moments later a succession of small waves would slap the isolated rocks on which my Lords Castlerosse and Portarlington were basking like a couple of exhausted sea-elephants, and caress the ankles of the *femmes-du-monde* dangling their legs over the side while engaged in pleasurable speculation as to who exactly had been responsible for the clearly visible tooth-marks on the shapely thigh of the Florentine marchesa with the honey-coloured hair.

Lacking both Christopher's stamina and his financial wizardry I took my departure after a week or so for the less glamorous, if socially more selective, season at Bembridge, I.O.W., to pay a visit of approval to my future parents-in-law, leaving him to drain the cup of pleasure to the dregs. The next time I saw him was in London a month or so later when he was waiting to go into a nursing home. After I had left him at Cannes he had, so he told me, formed a warm friendship with a young lady who subsequently became known to all his acquaintance as Boop-a-doop, and embarked on the comparatively new rôle of Hobhouse the Demon Lover. His performance had, however, unfortunately been a little marred by some trifling physical disability which, so he had been assured (I am happy to say, correctly) by a leading Harley Street authority whom, on Harold Nicolson's advice, he had consulted, could easily be remedied by circumcision. Having always heard that for those of riper years this simple operation is quite exceptionally painful, it was with some trepidation that in due course, and carrying the traditional grapes, I went to visit him. I need not have worried; his native resolution had seen him through and he was sitting up in bed alongside a bottle of champagne and smoking a large cigar in a fine state of righteous indignation. The pain he dismissed as trivial, but the indignity he found intolerable. In particular he was deeply shocked by what he described as the gross irreverence of the nurses. "Would you believe it," he asked in a voice of genuine outrage, "but they handle it just as though it were a *banana*!?" I displayed, I hope, a suitable incredulity.

Meanwhile my probationary visit to the Isle of Wight had passed off tolerably well, much helped by the presence of John Betjeman who was currently pursuing Karen's cousin, Camilla Russell, the Pasha's daughter, but as I was only twenty-two and Karen barely seventeen, it was made clear that a considerable period would have to elapse before there could be any question of announcing our engagement, and I did not go abroad again until this had duly taken place nearly a year later when, properly chaperoned, we went for a short skiing holiday at Garmisch. Unfortunately there was little or no snow and we were reduced to taking long walks in the mountains and inspecting the local Baroque. One day, having exhausted the architectural pleasures of the immediate neighbourhood we went down to Innsbruck, returning after dark by the local *bummelzug*. On arriving at the German frontier station at Mittenwald we noticed, without at once appreciating, a certain atmosphere of tension and suppressed excitement which remained for some time unexplained. Then, looking over the massive shoulder of the man in the next seat in the little wooden carriage, I read, by the dim light of the single bulb an enormous banner headline printed in blood-red, '*Hitler wird Kanzler sein!*'

That night we watched from our balcony the glow of the marching torches and heard the booming of the village band punctuated by throaty '*Sieg Heils*'. In the morning we asked the waiter what had happened downtown the previous evening; he assured us that it had been all very gay but quite orderly. There had, he admitted, been one or two slight scuffles but nothing serious and this morning everything was quite as usual, except, he added with a smile of rather sinister satisfaction, that one or two notorious local undesirables had completely vanished.

5. *"One of these days"*

IT WOULD, I fancied, as I arrived correctly dressed in white
tie and tails in the company of Nancy Rodd, turn out to be a
rather more interesting evening than that afforded by most
deb-dances of which, during the period preceding my wedding,
I had had my fill. The setting, Whistler's old house on Chelsea
Embankment, was a welcome change from those indistinguishable
residences in Pont Street or Hyde Park Gardens which nightly
resounded to the strains of Mr. Jack Harris's band; our hostess's
close connection with Oxford and the Bright Young People
would ensure, I thought, the presence of some of the more picturesque survivors of the previous decade not usually to be found at
such functions; and, by the same token, it seemed likely that the
girls from the shires and the beefy young ensigns from the Brigade
would for once be in a minority. Nevertheless I was in no way
prepared for the first departure from the customary routine. On
catching sight of the usual small crowd of sightseers gathered on
the pavement outside the gate, I braced myself to conceal the
embarrassment invariably induced by the appreciative cooing
which the appearance of the female guests normally provoked. I
need not have bothered. The smiles were sardonic rather than
welcoming and instead of 'Coo, ain't she lovely!' we received
solicitous but ironic enquiries after the health of Mrs. Barney and
pious expressions of hope that the lady had not forgotten her gun.
The Barney Case, in which the verdict just announced had
clearly not given any manifest satisfaction to the proletariat, had
already produced a widespread revulsion of feeling that involved,

I now realised, circles far distant from those in which that trigger-happy and rather sordid poor little rich girl normally moved. The 'Twenties, it was generally decided, had gone on quite long enough and the Bright Young People, of whom Mrs. Barney had never in fact been one, were to be swept smartly under the carpet. Hem-lines came tumbling down, chaperones were returning with a rush, and formality was, quite clearly, on the way back.

Once inside, however, it was not apparent that the critical barrage to which they had been subject on arrival had had any very lasting effect on the spirits of the guests. As I had hoped, the slightly older generation represented by Harold Acton and Mrs. Armstrong-Jones were present in force, and of the current crop of debs only the most glamorous appeared to have received invitations, and it would have taken more than a few snide comments to ruffle the mask-like composure of such reigning beauties as Miss Margaret Whigham or Lady Bridget Poulet even, which seemed unlikely, had they been fully comprehended. From the garden came the strains of 'Peanut Vendor' played by one of the newly fashionable rumba bands, and half-way up the stairs our hostess, glorious as some Nordic corn-goddess wearing a magnificent diamond tiara slightly on one side and presumably quite unaware of the views being expressed by the man in the street, radiated beauty and enjoyment as she received her guests. Nevertheless, I could not wholly rid myself, as I mounted the stairs, of a presentiment of coming, and probably unwelcome, change, which was almost immediately, and quite unexpectedly reinforced. Suddenly the queue came to an abrupt halt and drew to one side to make way for two descending footmen carrying between them the inanimate form of Augustus John who, it appeared, had been overcome by the heat rather early in the proceedings; and as I watched that defiantly noble, if temporarily horizontal, figure, beard pointing heavenwards, but still with an expression of quiet pride stamped on the unconscious features, being carried out into the night, I felt more strongly than ever that one epoch was ending and another, markedly less care-free, beginning. Mercifully lacking my mother's gift of precognition,

I was spared any full realisation of the exact nature of the doom which lay ahead, and it was only in retrospect that the fact that the ball was given by the future Lady Mosley for her sister, Unity Mitford, took on a symbolic significance.

Markedly different, and usually rather more rewarding than the evenings spent on the dance-floor, were those which at this period I passed once a week in the Café Royal. I had been so fortunate the previous summer as to have made the acquaintance, while on holiday in Austria, of Vernon Bartlett, who had on our return to London extended his friendship so far as to introduce me to a small group of his friends including, among others, Gerald Barry, Philip Jordan, Alan Thomas and Frank Owen, then the youngest member in the House, that on Thursday evenings had a regular *stammtisch* at the Café Royal, then enjoying a revival of popularity which was to last until the outbreak of war. The mirrors and the golden caryatids, amidst which greatly daring I had once sat as a schoolboy, only survived in the grill-room and had elsewhere been replaced by modernistic decorations in the worst possible contemporary taste, but the food was good and cheap, the house burgundy at five bob a bottle excellent, and, best of all, one could in the café end of the big room sit as long as one liked over a single glass of lager. In addition one enjoyed on certain evenings the pleasure of listening to Miss Haidée de Rance, who had in her youth sung 'Yip-i-addy-i-ay-i-ay' with George Grossmith himself, and her ladies' orchestra playing gems from Lehar at no extra charge. The clientèle was rewardingly mixed and on almost any night one could be certain of finding friends or acquaintances from Oxford, the Slade or Fleet Street, and in addition certain more established figures who were coming to play an increasingly important rôle in my life. For with the prospect of marriage it had become abundantly clear to me that the income I enjoyed from a small legacy from my grandfather, plus what I could hope to make as a painter, would have to be considerably augmented and so, greatly encouraged by the appearance of my first published cartoon (as I remember, a not very funny drawing in what I hoped was the

style of Peter Arno) in the old *Saturday Review*, then edited by Gerald Barry, I had launched out on a freelance career. At that time such a decision was not quite so reckless as today it might seem for there then flourished a number of enlightened patrons who were unfailing in their support and practical encouragement of the young, several of whom were regular habitués of the Café Royal. Principal among them were Jack Beddington of Shell and Christian Barman of the London Passenger Transport Board to whom I, and a high proportion of my contemporaries, remain eternally indebted; the former commissioned and paid for, whether or not they were used, a variety of illustrated pamphlets and brochures, and for the latter I did a whole series of small posters which in those days used regularly to draw the attention of Underground travellers to the more colourful spectacles they could witness during the coming week.

Nevertheless even in this agreeable, and to me highly stimulating, company one became increasingly conscious of a change in the climate. Naturally this awareness found a very different expression from what it did in the clubs and ballrooms further west; apprehension, which there led to a battening-down of the social hatches, was here replaced by a slowly rising indignation with things as they were, most forcefully and regularly voiced by Philip Jordan, culminating a year or two later in the great outburst of emotion immediately provoked by the Spanish Civil War.

*   *   *   *   *

Safely married at last, on a shatteringly hot day in June, by none other than Canon Carlyle whose personality triumphantly survived the imposition of a cope on which the High Anglican vicar of St. Peter's, Eaton Square, had insisted, and after a traditional honeymoon spent in Venice, we installed ourselves in a vast, unheated flat with a studio, on top of a late Victorian block in West Kensington, where I settled down to reviewing whatever books were sent me, designing anything from Christmas cards for laundries to posters for church bazaars and painting the occasional still-life for the New English. In the course of time, to these rather sporadic activities was added a regular connection with *The Architectural Review* which I owed partly to my mother's longstanding friendship with the mother of the editor, that remarkable and happily still-flourishing genius, Hubert de Cronin Hastings, whom I had known since childhood, and partly to the presence on the staff of John Betjeman. This took the form of writing a monthly column of architectural chit-chat which from time to time I embellished with drawings, endless caption-writing and the occasional contribution of a full-length feature article.

The Architectural Review was then, as I am happy to say it still is, far more than just a specialist monthly and many daring devices of lay-out and new typographical techniques, which have today become commonplace, were first pioneered in its adventur-ous pages. In those fine eighteenth-century rooms in Queen Anne's Gate, less gorgeously bizarre than they are today, there prevailed a stirring, almost hot-gospelling, determination to spread the doctrine of fitness for purpose and to proclaim from the functional roof-tops that there was no style but the inter-national style and Le Corbusier was its prophet. Fortunately, perhaps, the magazine possessed a built-in counterweight to too much modernismus in the shape of Betjeman who inhabited a small room on the top floor in which the Morris wallpaper had been ingeniously enlivened by the addition of coloured transfers of butterflies and insects, where he devoted himself to the re-habilitation of C. F. Voysey, recently discovered, much to every-one's surprise, to be still alive—a bald, period figure always in a hand-dyed blue shirt with his tie drawn through a ring—and a tireless advocacy of the merits of Norman Shaw.

Even more powerfully evocative of late Victorian aestheticism than his office was the poet's home in the country. Having married at the same time as we had, he and Penelope were now installed in a charming cottage, stone-walled and Morris-papered, in the Vale of the White Horse. At that time Uffington was one of the least spoiled villages in Berkshire which on an autumn evening, when the blue smoke was rising gently above the orchards and the thatch and the willow leaves were drifting slowly down, conformed with uncanny exactness to the vision of Eleanor Fortescue Brickdale and might well have been specially commissioned by Messrs. Black. This appearance of tranquillity was, however, deceptive, as life for the inhabitants was now no longer the undeviating round of rustic chores to which for generations they had been accustomed; for Penelope combined a missionary zeal for widening the cultural horizons of her rural neighbours with an energy and force of character inherited from her mother, the formidable Marschallin, and under her direction the Uffington Women's Institute became a transforming influence and its ceaseless activities demanded the full co-operation of all her friends. Its members were tirelessly lectured on Nepalese architecture and Indian religions, instructed in the preparation of mayonnaise (which, as none of them ever ate salad, they were rather puzzled to know what to do with) and firmly encouraged to keep and milk goats—animals they quite rightly detested and which regularly chewed up all their chrysanthemums. For their industry and perseverance they were from time to time rewarded by musical evenings in which all her guests, even if tone-deaf, were expected to take part. On the most memorable of these, which coincided with the annual prize-giving for the best home-made wine, the principal item on the programme was a performance of 'Sumer is icumen in' sung by Adrian Bishop, Maurice Bowra, my wife and the poet himself, accompanied on the piano by Lord Berners, and by Penelope on a strange instrument resembling a zither. My own contribution to the ensemble took the form of a flute *obbligato*. So powerful was the effect that all present remained rooted to their seats even when, as happened from time to time, a home-made wine bottle exploded, showering those unfortunates in the immediate vicinity with broken glass and elderberry juice. But the enjoyment of the audience was as nothing to that of the performers and I cannot now recall in all the years that have since elapsed, ever having spent an evening of such continuous and unalloyed pleasure.

The London in which Betjeman and I went about our cultural

business was still one of the most agreeable of capitals in which to live. We complained, of course, about the traffic, deplored the destruction of historic buildings, and resented every rise in the rates, but upon grounds which seem today inexcusably trivial. As night fell, young men in white ties still drifted down Piccadilly in the direction of the Café de Paris or whatever restaurant it was in which the incomparable Douglas Byng was appearing, and at midday old gentlemen in the Turf Club still sat down to luncheon in their bowlers. Dowagers in astonishing hats, of which the most spectacular was invariably Lady Alexander's, paraded annually at Burlington House and surrealist demonstrations frequently held up the traffic outside the Burlington Galleries. Levées were still regularly held at St. James's Palace, one of which, the first of the new reign, on my father-in-law's insistence, I attended. Quite why he was so keen on this anachronistic initiation ceremony, which even then lacked all practical significance, I was never quite sure but was none the less grateful for the chance it afforded of seeing inside the palace and gratifying my taste for uniforms. Not only was it a splendid spectacle but it also provided a convincing demonstration of the truth that whereas women dress up to impress men, so do men. Uninhibited by the presence of the opposite sex, everyone there was clearly deriving the keenest satisfaction from his personal appearance and doing his utmost to outshine his neighbour. Bishops puffed out their lawn and Hussar captains gave their moustaches an extra twist; judges ceaselessly readjusted their wigs and ambassadors their monocles, while those merchant bankers and prominent industrialists, who had felt that a Scots grandmother fully justified their dressing up as Bonnie Prince Charlie, shot their ruffles and played ostentatiously with their dirks; even those of us in little Lord Fauntleroy costume, from time to time smoothed out our silk stockings and patted our sword-hilts. On emerging rather self-consciously but none the less proudly into the everyday world, only the miners' dirge from street to street suggested that just possibly someone somewhere might be getting busy on old England's winding-sheet.

In the St. James's Club, which I had recently joined, the mournful Welsh cadences launched by the sad little groups shuffling past its geranium-fringed windows went almost unnoticed. The membership at that period was divided into the card-room set, dominated by such eye-catching personalities as Lord Castlerosse and 'Crinks' Johnson; the diplomats, British and foreign, active and retired—including such fascinating figures

as an immensely aged Russian prince in a skull-cap whose continental method of throat-clearing was clearly audible at Hyde Park Corner, and Mr. Zirkis, formerly first secretary at the Imperial Ottoman Embassy, so appreciated a bridge player that he had been prevailed upon to remain a member, uninterned and unmolested, throughout the First War; and a rather younger group several of whom had been my contemporaries at Oxford. Of those members who could not be exactly fitted into any of these categories the one in whose personality the club took perhaps the greatest pride was Lord Tenterden. With a purple face surmounting a wing-collar several sizes too small, a waxed moustache and a strong resemblance to a popular music-hall artist of the period called Billy Bennet ('Almost a gentleman'), this hereditary legislator was regularly turned out of the house by his strong-minded wife immediately after breakfast, given five shillings and told not to come home before lunch. Round about midday the five shillings was exhausted and all those entering the bar received a mournful and thirsty look from his lordship to which most responded. Nevertheless he could on occasion display remarkable resource and he once deflected a friend of mine from the tea-tent at a Buckingham Palace Garden Party on the grounds that what they both needed was a real drink and that most fortunately he had a couple of bottles of Bass, which he had brought with him in his top-hat, cooling in the lake—a claim which proved to be perfectly correct. On another occasion he was introduced by Patrick Balfour to Evelyn Waugh who, Patrick explained, was a well-known novelist. The interview proved agreeable to both and his lordship closely questioned Evelyn on his writing habits, technique and sales, and, when finally the latter took his leave, turned to Patrick and said in tones that betokened a lifelong ambition finally gratified, "So *that* was Mrs. Humphry Ward!"

Culturally the club's greatest asset was Dr. Tancred Borenius the great Finnish art-expert who presided over the meetings of a small weekly luncheon club of which I was a junior member. In the intervals of forming such notable collections of Old Masters as that which he assembled for the late Lord Harewood, the learned doctor devoted himself to propaganda for the White Rose League and the support and encouragement of Royal Pretenders, the dimmer the better, and was everlastingly excusing himself on the grounds that he had to go to Victoria to meet a long-forgotten Bourbon claimant or to Brown's Hotel to write his name in the book of some infinitely obscure Braganza princess. These little attentions did not go wholly unrewarded and no man in London could claim a finer collection of the insignia of orders generally believed to be extinct. Just how extensive this was I only realised when I was privileged to help him dress for the Coronation of King George VI at which Queen Mary, a friend of long standing, had obtained for him a prominent position as personal representative of the Carlist Pretender. Across the bottle-green uniform, heavily embroidered with gold, of a Knight

of the Order of Pope Gregory XIV there stretched the grand
cordon of the Order of Carlos IV of Spain; round his neck the
White Lion of Finland was entangled with the badge of the Order
of the Emperor Pedro I of Brazil and the Grand Cross of Saint
Vladimir; while the region of his liver was more than adequately
protected by the glittering stars of half-a-dozen dynasties which

Garter himself would have been hard
put to it to identify. As he was a large,
massively built man he could accommodate a great number of these sing-
ular distinctions and this, he had
decided, was the one occasion when he
could wear the lot, and it was in vain
that I appealed to his fine artistic
sense, suggesting that he was, perhaps,
in danger of ruining the overall effect
by slightly over-egging the pudding. It
was only when I hinted that he ran
some risk of being mistaken for an
assertive but rather unimportant rajah
that he agreed, albeit with tears in
his eyes, to divest himself of some of the gaudier indications of a
testified chivalry.

I had first met Tancred Borenius with my wife's parents who
entertained constantly rather than extensively in a large house in
Catherine Street, Westminster. My mother-in-law was a woman
of enormous charm and strong personality of which the visitor
was first likely to become aware as he turned the corner from
Buckingham Street to be welcomed by the strains of the *Liebestod*
filling the whole neighbourhood. As he was shown into the
drawing-room, in which all the ornaments and chandeliers were
quaking and shivering in the vast volume of sound, he would find
his hostess tranquilly asleep on a chaise-longue with her ear
pressed as close as she could get it to an enormous electric gramophone known, I think, as a Panatrope. The moment this was
turned off by the butler she would awaken with an expression of

considerable annoyance that would at once be replaced by a ravishing smile on catching sight of the visitor to whom she would explain, as though it was the most logical thing in the world, that owing to her deafness she could only sleep if there was a continuous noise. When I first knew her she was a woman of quite remarkable, although totally unfashionable, beauty, who at first glance gave the impression of having slipped into something loose on coming back from George V's Coronation and had remained in it ever since. The only child of one of those formidable Edwardian beauties who had enjoyed the close friendship of their genial sovereign when he was still Prince of Wales, her coiffure, her clothes, her conversation, indeed her whole style, were unshakeably pre-war, and she retained in full measure that generation's enthusiasm for practical jokes, fancy-dress and the music of Reynaldo Hahn. Anyone more dissimilar in temperament, background and education from my own dear mother it would be impossible to imagine, but fortunately they shared a common interest in all forms of psychic phenomena, and on this at first sight rather insubstantial basis an agreeable relationship was established, although they approached their subject from slightly different angles; my mother-in-law was an enthusiast for mediums, ouija-boards and table-turning and a keen member of the Society for Psychical Research, who lacked all interest in those problems of spiritual growth which from time to time so absorbed my mother. On the other hand my mother-in-law's preoccupation with physical well-being and all the ills (including many which might normally be considered remote) that might possibly endanger it, was, perhaps, excessive.

Her acquaintance among medical men was extensive and in her drawing-room Harley Street reputations were constantly coming up for reassessment; her devotion to *The Lancet* was fully equal to my mother's for *The National Message and Banner* involving her in flights of diagnosis which her immediate family found, on occasions, embarrassing. Her ceaseless preoccupation with 'les petits soins de la personne' and hygiene in general verged on the pathological; her bathroom and lavatory were kept permanently locked lest by some unhappy chance someone uninstructed in the rules of the house might stray into them in error, and she was constantly tortured by grave suspicions that her maid might have been using her hairbrushes. When travelling abroad she not only took her own sheets but also her own bidet, a Victorian model tastefully decorated with hand-painted violets and lilies-of-the-valley, which I had once to carry the whole length of the Blue Train after it had been mislaid on Calais quayside—an incident which led my wife to explain by way of easing my embarrassment, "You must realise, darling, that my poor, dear mother suffers from a bidet-fixe."

A very different character was my father-in-law although he too was, in his own way, if rather less wittingly, sufficiently remarkable. He was one of a brilliant quartet of brothers of whom the eldest, Leverton Harris, having been a not very successful member of Mr. Asquith's war-time government, finally abandoned politics for the arts; the second, Walter, was the celebrated *Times* correspondent in Tangier; while the youngest, Clement, a brilliant musician, a pupil of Wagner and a protégé of the Empress Frederick, had been killed at an early age while fighting with the Greek forces in the disastrous Greco-Turkish war of 1897. Although possibly less picturesque, Austin's career had been perhaps the most successful; his judgement, decisiveness and general know-how had earned for him a very enviable position in the banking world and he was the key-figure on innumerable boards. The unfortunate events of 1929 had shaken him badly; easily moved to tears he had, according to my wife, blubbed almost continuously throughout that disastrous winter, but when I first knew him the worst was over, although he was still liable to collapse into hopeless sobbing at the mere sight of the household books and, as a desperate measure of economy, used regularly to circulate the house after nightfall turning off all the lights quite regardless of whether the rooms were occupied or not. However, he derived a considerable, if gloomy, satisfaction from the knowledge that it had been in his dining-room, where he was entertaining Sir John Simon and Sir Montague Norman, that the decision to abandon the Gold Standard had finally been taken, an event which only the united protests of his family deterred him from commemorating by the setting-up of a bronze plaque.

Tall, handsome and dignified, despite an intimidatingly aloof manner which those who did not know him well attributed to shyness, he was in my experience outstandingly kind. Blessed with an unshakeable self-confidence, no matter what subject was under discussion, he was always sustained by a perfectly sincere conviction that he had forgotten more about it than anyone else had ever known; a conviction which led him from time to time to compromise with the strict truth. Thus when taking visitors round his magnificent gardens he would point to a tree and loftily proclaim that that was the tallest eucalyptus ever grown in England, despite the fact that his embarrassed family were well aware that there were a dozen others at least twenty feet taller within a radius of a quarter of a mile. Or he would draw his guests' attention to a plant, which had been regularly on display at Chelsea for years, proudly claiming that this was the only white agapanthus that had ever been successfully naturalized in England. He was, however, completely guiltless of any deliberate intention to deceive, and when he made such statements he was invariably completely convinced of their unassailable accuracy. As he grew older there were virtually no limits to his fantasy and on one occasion even my mother-in-law, who was seldom at a loss for words, was reduced to speechlessness on being told, after the gentlemen had been left to their port, by the guest who had sat next to her husband during dinner and whom he had held spellbound throughout, that she had always previously assumed that Bleriot had crossed the Channel alone and had had no idea that he had in fact been accompanied on his perilous trip by Sir Austin.

Occasionally embarrassing as was my father-in-law's extraordinary ability to transcend reality, it became fraught with peril whenever he took to the road. One of the earliest motorists, he did not finally relinquish the wheel, and then only under strong medical pressure, until well on in his eighties and throughout this long period was sustained by the irrational belief that all other traffic would know who he was and make due allowance;

a belief which, curiously enough, seemed only too frequently to be justified except, of course, in the case of trams with which he had one or two unfortunate brushes. For his passengers, who did not always share his god-like invulnerability, the experience was doubly alarming as he always regarded driving as a combined operation with himself in charge and expected prompt action from whoever was next him when, in a voice hoarse with excitement, he cried out, "My God! The handbrake!" Later in life he became subject to dizzy spells, almost invariably when travelling at over sixty miles an hour, when he would suddenly lean back clutching his head in his hands with the full weight of his foot pressed hard down on the accelerator, requesting in hollow tones that his companion should take over the wheel.

The fascinating but contrasted temperaments of my parents-in-law were accurately reflected in the lay-out of their establishment in the Isle of Wight where we annually spent July and August. 'Smoglands', as it was called for reasons understood by none save my mother-in-law, was a settlement rather than a house. Some years previously she had, while staying on the island, lighted on, and in a moment of caprice bought, a small and utterly undistinguished villa, pebble-dashed and intermittently half-timbered, on the outskirts of Bembridge, despite the strong discouragement of her entire family who had at once pointed out its manifest inadequacies and general inconvenience as a summer residence for one of her expansive nature. She was fully confident, however, that one or two minimal alterations would set all to rights and, from that moment on, every year saw new modifications and additions; half-timbering vanished, bow-windows burst forth, extra bathrooms blossomed, guest-wings projected. A large free-standing garage for several cars with servants' rooms above arose on the site of the shrubbery, the field which separated the original suburban garden from the cliff-edge was acquired and planted, and a number of gypsy caravans were parked at strategic points to accommodate an overflow of weekend guests. Not to be outdone my father-in-law, in the years immediately preceding the slump, purchased the whole of the available adjoining land on which he proceeded to erect not only a suitable holiday home for himself but also gazebos, ornamental pools and a walled garden, the whole in the then fashionable pseudo-Spanish style, all green tiles and wrought-iron grills, popularized by Mr. Oliver Hill, carefully separated from his wife's pleasaunce by a fuchsia hedge. These contrasted methods of home-building were nicely indicative of the temperamental differences between them. Any enterprise on which my mother-in-law embarked, no matter how small its beginnings, was destined to snowball into an avalanche of frenzied activity; thus within a year of acquiring a small ciné-camera she had mobilized the whole place into an amateur Pinewood, with flood lamps and light meters and transformers, for the production of full-length pictures of the most ambitious kind which involved the whole-time co-operation of family, friends and usually reluctant neighbours, while a casual visit to an exhibition of peasant pottery might easily lead to the transformation of entire rooms into replicas of a Portuguese fisherman's cottage or a Jugo-Slav farmstead. My father-in-law on the other hand always started with a grandiose conception in which, having carried it out to the letter, he quickly abandoned interest. Thus, soon after it was completed, his enthusiasm for the White City, as his Spanish fantasy came to be known in the family, evaporated and he seldom spent more than a couple of weeks there in the summer, whereupon it was promptly annexed by my mother-in-law as a useful addition to her own *cottage orné*.

The summers we spent at Smoglands are coloured in retrospect by an extraordinary quality of fantasy and insulation. The Isle of Wight was at that time still rich in the last enchantments of the Victorian age; once one had stepped off the paddle-steamer at Ryde Pier one entered a steel-engraved world of which the magic was proof against even the occasional aeroplane, which here at once reverted to the status of flying-machine, and where the giant Cunarders passing down the Solent seemed symbols of the nineteenth century's romantic conception of the future rather than contemporary realities. The barge-boarded villas of Ventnor and Shanklin, with their conservatories and ornamental palms, shrouded in a mist of fuchsias and passion-flowers, would have delighted the great Loudon himself; the downland farms, with the sunset breaking through the rook-haunted, embowering elms reflected in their duck-ponds, seemed patiently to await the coming of Birkett Foster; while at Seaview the chain-pier at once invested the children and donkeys on the sands below with all the period animation of a drawing by Leech. It was as though the whole island was striving to approximate to the locked and inviolate condition of that sanctified room at Osborne where more than thirty years previously the eponymous heroine of the age had breathed her last.

Bembridge was an island within an island. Protected physically by its silted harbour and single toll-road and socially by a rampart of ferocious snobbery, the inhabitants kept themselves to themselves with a tenacity of purpose worthy of Mrs. Vanderbilt's Newport. Within this charmed circle Smoglands was an alien and self-contained enclave maintaining only strictly diplomatic relations with the local society. My father-in-law, it is true, was a member of the Sailing Club, an institution which took much pride in the fact that it had from time to time blackballed members of the Squadron and had once closed its doors to the King of Spain, and used every so often rather half-heartedly to chide his wife on her neglect of her social obligations. Now and again neighbours called, but as their unheralded arrival invariably took place at a moment when my mother-in-law, dressed as a female explorer, was firing blank cartridges down the drive at the climax of a particularly lurid film-sequence or, seated at her easel, was drawing the more glamorous of the female house-guests erotically disposed in total nudity around the lily-pond, they more often than not beat a hasty retreat. Even when not in fancy-dress her appearance was sufficiently unusual to excite comment, for in a world of flowing imprimes, white flannels and yachting caps she was normally clad in a very old mackintosh of vaguely military cut, that might easily have seen service in the Easter Rising, and a conical straw-hat surrounded by a ribbon stamped 's.s. *Stella Polaris*' in letters of gold, and was never without an open parasol, for she retained quite unmodified an earlier generation's mistrust of the sun and even when bathing always wore a wide-brimmed picture hat decorated with faded Malmaison roses familiarly known as 'Trelawney of the Wells'. Too often the rare occasions when she did make a social effort and extended a conventional hospitality to her neighbours were, through no fault of hers, doomed to disaster. Once she braced herself to invite to tea a certain Colonel and Mrs. Savill, the most exalted and strait-laced of all the representatives of local society, and did her very best to create an unmistakeable atmosphere of gracious living. Exquisite in coffee-coloured lace she presided over tea on the lawn, the butler and parlour-maid hovered around with petits-fours and cucumber sandwiches, while all the house-party, for once properly attired, made polite conversation. Everything was going swimmingly and Mrs. Savill was just launched on a long account of last night's ball at the Garland Club when there came a voice from Heaven, "Fuck-off, you silly bitch!", and a gigantic orange and blue macaw planed gracefully down from the top of the Wellingtonia.

Almost the only Bembridge worthy, and one who was herself regarded rather askance by the Sailing Club set, with whom close and amiable relations were maintained, was Olive Opal Custance, the poetess, who dwelt in a small cottage near the church bearing on its gate the legend 'Safe Haven after a Stormy Passage'. A large, jolly woman, hung about with much amber and afflicted with a nervous and uncontrollable laugh, the safety of her haven was from time to time menaced by the arrival of her dilapidated husband, Lord Alfred Douglas, to whom, although they had long been parted, she gave summer shelter out of sheer kindness of heart. Bottle-nosed and rheumy-eyed, this deplorable old wreck, on whom his recent re-discovery by Betjeman had acted like a shot of adrenalin, used occasionally to accompany Olive Opal to Smoglands where his presence was responsible for a certain embarrassment that induced in his wife appalling gales of manic laughter. For one of the most regular of our summer visitors was the irrepressible and wholly delightful Dolly Wilde who on these occasions was torn between a feeling of loyalty to the memory of Uncle Oscar (whose favourite niece she always claimed to have been despite the difficulty of reconciling that rôle with her equally firmly held conviction that she was far too young to remember anything which took place before 1914) prompting immediate withdrawal, and her unconquerable reluctance ever to miss anything which might be going on. Needless to say she invariably stayed, contenting herself with the maintenance, for at least five minutes, of an attitude of strict reserve. During one of these visits I took the opportunity of having 'Bosie' pat my children's heads, thus forging for them an interesting link with the past which I trusted would in days to come prove as useful an anecdotal investment as Swinburne's kiss had been to me. Unfortunately, shortly afterwards, a kind friend hopelessly confused their infant minds by securing for them a similar accolade from Norman Douglas with the result that they remain to this day convinced that the author of *South Wind* was really responsible for Oscar's downfall.

* * * * *

In the insulated and self-absorbed world of Bembridge wars and rumours of wars passed unheeded and it was only in the winter months in London that I was uneasily aware that the righteous indignation so presciently expressed by Philip Jordan in the Café Royal was rapidly becoming general. Every other weekend, Hyde Park Corner or Trafalgar Square saw a monster rally with banners reading 'Abolish the Means Test' or 'Hands off Abyssinia' or simply 'Anti-Fascists Unite', supported by not only the Communists and the 'stage army of the good', stalwart veterans of the militant Suffragettes and knickerbockered opponents of the Boer War, but also by a high proportion of the students of both universities and the entire staff of the London School of Economics. Needless to say for all the effect such demonstrations had on Messrs. Baldwin and Chamberlain they might have been demanding the repeal of the Corn Laws or protesting against Catholic Emancipation; it was only with the outbreak of the Spanish Civil War that the justified unease of so large a proportion of the population reached dimensions which forced the Government to pay them the tribute of prevarication.

The emotional impact of that conflict was, and remains, in my experience, unique; neither the Abdication which for a very short time generated more heat than is generally remembered today, nor even Munich, aroused feelings of such intensity. It divided families, broke up love-affairs and provoked furious resignations from clubs; leading poets denounced Fascist excesses with all the fervour, if not invariably with quite the felicity, of Milton condemning the late massacres in Piedmont and some, not content with denunciation, followed the example of Tennyson and the Apostles and set off for Spain in person where their presence proved in most cases equally ineffectual. On the other side, outraged Papists circulated horrifying photographs of decapitated priests and violated nuns and amateurs of the bull-ring abandoned the bar at Whites to fight for Franco. Among my own friends and acquaintances attitudes varied; the Café Royal was solidly pro-Republican as was most of Oxford; Betjeman, for whom at that period Europe south of Tulse Hill did not exist, remained, I think, unaware of the conflict; Tancred Borenius regarded it as a heaven-sent opportunity to promote a Carlist restoration; Colonel Kolkhorst, although temperamentally one hundred per-cent reactionary, was still at that time hoping for academic preferment and took his cue from the head of the Spanish school, Professor Madariaga; while Angus Malcolm, always regarded as a died-in-the-wool Tory, who was then *en poste* in Spain was the only member of the Embassy staff bold enough to express any sympathy with the Government. Unfortunately Christopher Hobhouse was not at first able to give the struggle his full attention as he was once more busy changing rôles; one or two unlucky experiences on the stock market had recently encouraged him to abandon that of the Financial Wizard in favour of Hobhouse the Man of Letters, and he had accordingly realised what remained to him in the way of capital and purchased a dilapidated water-mill in Norfolk which he was fully occupied in restoring to a condition suitable for the serious pursuit of literature. I myself remained obstinately uninvolved. I had only once been in Spain for a few days when a child and was quite untouched by that mystique of espagnolism which powerfully affected so many of my contemporaries; neither Lorca nor flamenco meant a thing to me and from what I had read of Spanish history in the nineteenth century the fight in progress seemed to me to be a recurrent rather than an isolated phenomenon. Only the ridiculous and humiliating farce of non-intervention induced a feeling of shame and indignation.

When confronted with contemporary events in Germany, however, I could achieve no such lofty, pragmatic detachment and my attitude was at first ambivalent. Like many of those who grew up in the aftermath of the First War my reactions were conditioned by guilt. At Charterhouse we had regularly been addressed by earnest Quakers making moving appeals on behalf of innocent German children permanently under-nourished as a result of the maintenance of our inhuman blockade and later, like most readers of the *New Statesman*, I came to regard the Treaty of Versailles as a Punic settlement from which the victors derived neither credit nor advantage; a conviction which in my case had been much strengthened, when on holiday in Mainz, by the sight of respectable *hausfrauen* being pushed off the pavement by the Senegalese sentries of the occupying power. Moreover in the course of my summer wanderings I had developed a romantic fondness for an imaginary Germany which, if it had ever existed, had vanished for ever in 1870; and my view of the contemporary scene was bathed in the rosy light of a painting by Spitzweg and softened by the gentle melancholy of the Schöne Müllerin.

However, I was not so wholly absorbed in the *Biedermeierzeit* as not to be aware of certain more recent developments, but unfortunately I drew the wrong conclusions. The vitality and astringency displayed by such radical movements as those represented by Kurt Weil and Georg Grosz in Berlin and the *Simplicissimus* group in Munich encouraged the belief that there was a reliable, built-in opposition to the night-mare ascendency of lower middle-class nationalism. Unfortunately such guileless optimism was ill-founded; when the crunch came the Berliners were forced to retreat into exile, although still firing all the way*, while the Bavarians at once capitulated hook line and sinker. So sanguine was I that even the interest aroused by that startling headline seen on a January train had been untinged by over-much apprehension, and it was not until the following summer, when we crossed the Rhine for what was to be the last time, that I formed the painful impression that *gemütlichkeit* was being steadily eroded by mania.

The first disquieting revelation came in Munich, where we had gone to visit the household in which my wife had spent a year learning German, that of two elderly sisters both travelled and intelligent, one the widow of a South American grandee. In the days before his attainment of power Hitler had been for them, as for so many of the German upper-classes, that common little agitator whose name could not be mentioned in decent company, and my wife was, therefore, more than astounded when, after a long and lyrical account of the Führer's recent visit to his old stamping ground they both chanted in chorus, "*Schauen Sie, er war ganz wie Jesus Christi!*" Even for me, who had never met them before, this demonstration of that schizophrenic ability, possessed by ninety-nine out of a hundred Germans and of which I had always been dimly aware, suddenly to identify themselves with causes to which their temperament and background would normally render them unalterably opposed, came as a slight shock. It was therefore with a distinct sense of relief that a day or two later we went on to Vienna, which was still mercifully displaying all its old inefficiency and charm; superficial as the latter might be we remained grateful for the contrast it afforded, and on re-crossing the frontier on our way home the '*Heil Hitlers*', the slogans, the beefy young thugs of the *Hitlerjugend* rattling

* Gulbransson and Thöny, the two principal contributors to *Simplicissimus*, who had been as undeviating in their opposition to National Socialism before it came to power as they had been to Prussian militarism before 1914, in '33 not only immediately went into reverse but denounced their old editor and colleague, Th. Th. Heine, to the security police.

collecting boxes for the *Winterhilfe*, all seemed doubly distasteful.

The second, and less easily definable, moment of truth came in Hanover. After a nostalgic morning spent at Herrenhausen, which ever since reading *The Four Georges* had had for me a high aura of romance, we were relaxing in the town's principal beer-garden when there entered a plump middle-aged man in the tight brown uniform of a *Sturmbannfuehrer* or *Gauleiter* with wet red lips and a great deal of face-powder. The combination of homosexuality and arbitrary power has for me always been productive of an irrational disquiet—Tiberius, James I, Frederick the Great are none of them figures with whom I would greatly care to have been closely associated—and the spectacle of this arrogant queer, disdainfully acknowledging the sycophantic greetings of the other customers while playfully flicking the ears of the better-looking of his attendant storm-troopers with his shiny leather gloves, seemed quite suddenly indescribably sinister.

Curiously enough, returning to Bembridge a few days later, we found installed for the weekend a certain Baron von Bültzing-slöwen and his strapping daughter whose acquaintance my father-in-law had recently made at Baden-Baden. This insufferable Junker, whose presence was driving my mother-in-law mad with boredom, while admitting with a wholly unconvincing display of broadmindedness that there were, perhaps, certain aspects of National Socialism which those of gentle birth might find distaste-ful, nevertheless maintained that the movement had done much to restore a sense of high moral purpose to the youth of Germany and that Herr Hitler, whose manifest shortcomings were almost all attributable to his humble origins, was in many ways a figure comparable to Baden-Powell. It was, therefore, with considerable satisfaction that on Sunday morning I passed across the breakfast table a copy of the *Sunday Express* with its front page entirely devoted to a lurid, but not inaccurate, account of the Night of the Long Knives which not only reduced the Baron for once to silence but provided, I considered, ample justification for my emotional reaction in the beer-garden at Hanover.

Most of the time during the next few years I was too happily

engaged in writing books, begetting children and drawing architecture to entertain any very prolonged anxiety, but just occasionally I received a salutary and unexpected jolt. Walking one day along The Mall I was suddenly stopped in my tracks by the sight of a swastika-draped coffin escorted by a squadron of Life Guards and followed by a posse of high-ranking officers in the full-dress uniform of the *Wehrmacht*. After a moment's reflection I remembered that Herr von Hoesch had died a day or two before, and realized that protocol demanded a Sovereign's escort for the corpse of any ambassador dying *en poste*. Nevertheless the spectacle of the Household Cavalry jogging along in the wake of the swastika left a vivid and slightly unnerving impression which was by no means erased by subsequent knowledge of the circumstances leading up to it. For it was more than suspected that the unfortunate ambassador, an amiable and cultivated anglophil, had not in fact died of wholly natural causes and that his end had been hastened by a member of his own staff whom I had frequently met and cordially disliked in the St. James's Club; an incident which served powerfully to reinforce my reluctant acceptance of the possibility that the permitted period during which the Great Beast of Revelation was to exercise dominion was, as my mother had foretold, getting very close now.

My mother herself remained cheerfully convinced that Armageddon was inevitable and almost on us, and was not remotely surprised by the atrocity stories about life in the Third Reich which were beginning increasingly to circulate; for such goings-on she was quite prepared not so much by her prophetic gifts as by the shrewd estimate she had formed of the German character at a time when as a girl she had nearly become engaged to an officer in the Prussian Guard. In her experience sentimentality and cruelty invariably went hand in hand, therefore concentration camps and pogroms were no more than one would expect from a people who swooned in ecstasy in front of Böcklin's *Toteninsel* and were liable to burst into uncontrollable sobs on hearing some repellent six-year-old recite *Du bist wie eine Blume*. My mother-in-law on the other hand, despite a natural distaste for Germans that had been much strengthened by the Bültzingslöwen's visit, had as yet received no warnings from the Other Side. The Spirit Guides with whom her preferred medium was most frequently in touch seemed always to display a disinterest in current affairs almost equal to her own, and she was further protected from apprehension by a quite staggering ability to shut her eyes to all unpleasantness—an ability which had also, incidentally, prevented her, despite childhood friendships with such figures as Wilfred Scawen Blunt and Cunninghame Graham, from ever achieving the smallest idea of what socialism was all about.

The summer of 1938 witnessed no change in the established routine at Smoglands. Of the regular visitors few displayed any very lively political awareness and none was remotely interested in Czechoslovakia; only Victor Cunard who had been the *Morning Post* correspondent in Rome, whence he had been expelled on account of the consistently critical tone of his dispatches, occasionally betrayed a basic uneasiness by sudden bursts of furious indignation. My father-in-law, it is true, took to groaning loudly every time he picked up a newspaper but, as his normal reaction to the state of affairs prevailing at any time during the previous ten years had been a gloomy resignation to the worst, this caused neither surprise nor alarm. Every now and then, however, he would in a rare moment of optimism praise God for Sir John Simon, a vote of thanks which not even the most sanguine of his hearers could quite bring themselves to second, and it was left to a comparative newcomer to the circle, Christopher Hobhouse, for whom my mother-in-law had taken a great liking, to sound a mild note of alarm.

Originally Christopher had been inclined rather to underestimate the seriousness of the Nazi threat; he had at the time of the New Party paid a visit to Munich in the company of Bob Boothby and Tom Mosley and had met the Führer whom he had considered a very second-rate little man. "Would you believe it? He had the effrontery to start telling me about Cromwell, of whom he clearly knew nothing, and seemed quite put out when I was forced to point out one or two of his more glaring errors."

But the recent assumption of yet another new rôle had had the incidental effect of radically modifying this slightly contemptuous attitude. His recent period of literary activity had proved extremely fruitful and he had produced two works of unquestioned merit; a study of the Great Exhibition of 1851, which still remains by far the best account of that extraordinary enterprise, and a life of Fox which for me ranks with *Portrait of Zelide* by Geoffrey Scott as one of the two best eighteenth-century biographies produced between the wars. Nevertheless, great as had been his *succes d'estime* and comparatively satisfactory as were the sales, he was quite shrewd enough to see that literature alone was unlikely for many years to come to support him in the style to which he was determined to become accustomed. Decisive as well as clear-sighted, he lost no time in acting on this realization, sold the mill, moved to London and started to read for the Bar. The more conveniently to pursue his studies, he installed himself with Harold Nicolson in King's Bench Walk where the scales were very soon removed from his eyes, for no man in London was more firmly convinced than Harold of the ruthless and undeflectable nature of Hitler's ambition; a conviction of which he was to give dramatic proof a month or so later, when he was the only member of an hysterical House with the moral courage to remain firmly seated when Mr. Chamberlain blandly announced peace with honour.

Of the prolonged and pointless agony of Munich I retain no very coherent memory; only certain significant moments remain vivid. On September the seventh I went up to London on one of my regular visits to the offices of *Night and Day*, that admirable but short-lived magazine on which I served as art critic, and, having forgotten my book, acquired a copy of *The Times* on Portsmouth station. In my detached and carefree youth I was no great student of the daily Press and seldom, I am ashamed to say, opened *The Times* and then only to read the dramatic notices and the Court Page; but on this particular morning, having exhausted all else long before the sight of the distant pinnacles of Charterhouse had produced their accustomed *frisson* as we shot past Godalming, was driven by boredom for once to read the leader column. 'It might be worth while', hazarded Mr. Barrington-Ward, 'for the Czecho-Slovak government to consider whether they should exclude altogether the project, which has found favour in some quarters, of making Czecho-Slovakia a more homogeneous state by the cession of that fringe of alien population which are contiguous to the nation with which they are united by race'. Little attention as I had paid to the activities of the Runciman mission and non-existent as was my experience of international negotiations, such an expression of opinion in Printing House Square at this particular moment suggested even to me a willingness to capitulate unmatched since the days of Ethelred the Unready. It was of course true that very similar sentiments had been expressed a week before in the *New Statesman* but, being even then aware of the vagaries to which Mr. Kingsley Martin's political judgement was occasionally subject, I had neither taken them seriously myself nor expected others to do so. Shocked and baffled, I was re-reading these suave but ominous phrases for the third time, when the train pulled into Guildford Station where, to my great satisfaction, Vernon Bartlett got in, to whom I at once pointed them out. If I was shaken, he was appalled and at once confirmed my worst fears of a possible sell-out which he attributed entirely to the malign influence of Sir John Simon. Moreover he revealed that so alarming had he already considered the situation that he had that morning cabled his son who was on holiday in Germany to return home at once. I was still, however, hoping against hope that the leader did not in fact bear the meaning which I attached to it and was still pathetically eager for reassurance when I went to the club for luncheon. Little reassurance was forthcoming, for the St. James's, which was the home-from-home of Lord Vansittart whose views were shared by the majority of the Foreign Office members and endorsed by many others who had from time to time been affronted by the behaviour and conversation of their fellow-clubman—Herr von Ribbentrop—was to become during the next few weeks one of the principal strongholds of the opponents of appeasement. (Exceptions, alas, there unfortunately were and it was in this coffee-room that I heard, when all was over, a former British Ambassador to Prague loudly justify, within earshot of the Czech military attaché, the abandonment of our solemn obligations on the grounds that the Czechs possessed no officer class.)

During the following weeks two encounters stamped themselves on my memory by reason of their immediate impact and the revelation of character which they afforded. One evening we went by way of distraction to see De Basil's Russian Ballet at Covent Garden; the atmosphere in the auditorium was tense, for the day had been one during which it seemed that the limits of appeasement had finally been reached and that war was inevitable. It was just at the moment when fashion decreed that women should wear their hair piled on the tops of their heads, and their resultant transformation into Second Empire tarts drawn by Constantin Guys combined with the Offenbach music of the first ballet to induce an eerie sensation of revelling on the eve of Sedan. During the first interval I met Monty Shearman, come straight from the Foreign Office, who revealed to me with pardonable excitement the Prime Minister's intention of flying out to Godesberg, news which soon spread to produce a general if unworthy sense of relief which in my case was almost immediately and painfully dispelled. Going into the Crush Bar for a much-needed drink I saw a hushed and embarrassed group surrounding a familiar figure clutching a tankard of champagne who was giving the world in general his views on Hitler, Chamberlain and Sir Horace Wilson, expressed with a venomous intensity and uninhibited directness that I have never heard equalled. For the past year or more, abandoning all his hard-fought campaigns for the preservation of Georgian architecture, Robert Byron had devoted himself exclusively to dispelling any wishful thinking about the Third Reich by travel, fact-finding and tireless propaganda, both written and spoken. ("Do you mind telling me exactly how much the Germans are paying you?" he had recently electrified the luncheon table at the Beefsteak by asking a particularly pompous ex-ambassador who had been extolling the merits of the Führer and his régime.) Always pale, confronted with the ruin of all his hopes and efforts his face was now the colour of bleached Bromo, and beneath those heavy lids his red-rimmed eyes blazed with the cold fury he had once directed at the invading hearties along with a fusillade of well-aimed champagne bottles. Alas, his targets tonight were well out of range and he was left to pour out his scorn and fury on a gaggle of balletomanes who could not have been more pleasurably shocked had he physically exposed himself, a terrible scene which still returns to me whenever I hear the expression *saeva indignatio*.

My second encounter, although less dramatic, was equally effective. Walking across St. James's Park one afternoon on my way to *The Architectural Review*, I was crossing that elegant little suspension bridge (soon to be ruthlessly destroyed not by enemy action but by a civil servant's whim) when I was hailed by Ronnie Cartland, Lock-bowlered and clove-carnationed, whom I had hardly seen since Charterhouse days. He had come straight from the House where, I subsequently learnt, for he himself made no mention of it, he had just made a speech in which he had not only attacked his party's policy, but also foretold his own death. Regarded by all the *bien-pensants* as being in the worst possible taste, Harold Nicolson afterwards recalled it as the most moving he ever heard during all his years as member. Less violently but no less intensely, he now proceeded to deliver exactly the same message as had Robert Byron, emphasizing in particular the inevitable curtailment of civil liberties, in particular the right of free expression of unpopular views, which would ensue if the policy of appeasement were to be pursued to the bitter end. I never saw him again, but the memory of that slightly *exalté* but debonair figure prophesying woe, poised against the most romantic of all London vistas, remains undimmed.

During the next few days I, like everyone else, made a series of futile but unavailing efforts to overcome a feeling of all-engulfing frustration and helplessness; I enrolled myself in something called the Officers Emergency Reserve, from whom I was never subsequently to hear a word, supported Ed Stanley's enthusiastic but unconsummated attempt to recruit a party to dig slit-trenches in Hyde Park from among the regulars at the St. James's bar, and finally signed on at my local A.R.P. centre where I was promptly sat down to fit gas-masks. This rather macabre but necessary exercise was carried out in the Cardinal Vaughan Schools in the Addison Road, and here it was that I heard the news of our threadbare deliverance. I had just finished adjusting a mask to the bald and shining pate of Mr. Robertson Hare when a plump and excited priest rushed in, flung wide his arms in the gesture of one confidently expecting the Stigmata, and announced in a voice thick with near-hysteria, "Sure an' it's peace, praise be to the Blessed Virgin, Mr. Chamberlain and Signor Mussolini!"

Every month which elapsed between Munich and the outbreak of war witnessed a strengthening of my uneasy conviction that after all mother knew best. In the ordinary way the published portents of inevitable disaster would as likely as not have escaped my attention, busy as I was on a new book, but I had recently entered a world where awareness was not only an occupational requirement but was to become my principal stock-in-trade.

Like so many other developments in my life my appearance in Fleet Street was in the first instance due to John Betjeman. Having embarked on a powerful series of articles for the *Daily Express* tracing the rise of civilisation from the earliest times, optimistically entitled 'Man into Superman', he had found himself unable to cope with the earliest numbers, and knowing that I had always had a weakness for archaeology had suggested to the Features Editor, John Rayner, that I was the man for the job. Apprehensive but elated I set to work with a will and my enthusiasm was sufficient even to overcome the unexpected hazard, which for a more conscientious historian was likely to have proved insuperable, presented by the fact that at that period Lord Beaverbrook was still a staunch upholder of the Westminster Confession so that none of his newspapers could carry any statement likely to conflict with Archbishop Usher's careful calculation of the exact date of the Creation.

Whatever modest success the series may have enjoyed was for me of far less importance than the friendship with John Rayner which sprang from it. This distinguished bibliophil and pillar of the Foreign Office was then the youngest, and by far the best, Features Editor in Fleet Street; an erudite typographer, he had recently transformed the whole appearance of the *Express* by his energy and that of most of the other dailies by his example. One evening after dinner I mentioned to him how much I admired the little column-width cartoons which regularly appeared in the French papers and wondered why the English press had never adopted them. "Go ahead, give us some" was his unexpected but gratifying reaction and on the first day of 1939 I embarked on a career which, thanks to the mercy of God and the tolerance of editors, has continued ever since.

The *Daily Express*, when first I went there, was rather different from what it is today. The gleaming black glass façade struck a bold note of what we then considered uncompromising, up-to-the-minute functionalism; in the entrance hall the gilding on the complicated bas-reliefs, packed with the symbols and heraldry of an Empire upon which it was anathema to suppose the sun would ever set, was still dazzlingly bright; even the lifts worked. The editorial floor, the only one in London to be laid out on the American pattern, supported half the population it does today producing twice as much copy; the Hickey column, which is now maintained by a staff of at least half-a-dozen, was then produced single-handed by Tom Driberg, and the Women's Editor, Lucy Milner, made do with one part-time assistant. Moreover there still flourished serious rivals whose scoops and circulation had at all costs to be surpassed and every ear was always attuned to any slight change of note in the constant humming of the invisible dynamo in Stornoway House. Above all it had Arthur Christiansen.

Few subjects give rise to more unprofitable speculation than what makes a great editor. In Chris's case the undramatic answer was, I think, given by his possession of a quality rare in all walks of life and almost unknown in Fleet Street, a very exact knowledge of his own limitations. Unrivalled as a news-man, he was well aware that his political judgement was hopelessly unreliable, but he also knew that, however good it might have been, his proprietor would have been unlikely to have seen any necessity for his exercising it unaided. Not himself an outstanding judge of 'features', he made certain that his subordinates were, and on their urging was always quite willing to launch out on experiments which he privately thought fantastic, on the chance that the readers might approve; if they did then the series continued even though he himself remained unconvinced; if not they were promptly abandoned with no recriminations. He was entirely free from the prejudice, understandable enough, which at that time was still entertained by many of the old, born-and-bred Fleet Street professionals, against the bright young men from the Universities who were entering the field of popular journalism in ever-increasing numbers, and for nearly a quarter of a century I received from him nothing but kindness, encouragement and salutary criticism. From time to time he would turn down some drawing flat on grounds which I usually, but not quite always, afterwards came to accept as justified, but once a drawing was passed he upheld his decision against all comers so that one could leave the office with a reasonable confidence that, so long as he was on the bridge, what one had drawn or written would appear unaltered the next morning. In appearance he was comfortable-looking, almost chubby, with an encouraging smile of which the sincerity was in no way qualified by the gleaming falsity of the teeth it revealed. Usually soberly dressed, he developed later in life a regrettable weakness for those hand-painted American ties so popular in the Truman era.

Of the other influential characters then flourishing on the second floor, the one with whom I was most closely associated was Tom Driberg in whose column my drawings originally came out. His appearance was subtly changed from the dadaist days at Oxford, the silhouette was now more majestic and the manner more authoritative, while the centrally-parted hair had undeniably ebbed, leaving a couple of curls stranded on the forehead like a

151

misplaced moustache. His personality, however, happily remained as complex and fascinating as ever; at once staunchly Marxist and devoutly Anglo-Catholic, it was not always easy for those who knew him but slightly accurately to estimate whether he was at any particular moment fulfilling the demands of the class struggle or responding to the promptings of the confessional—an uncertainty from which he undoubtedly derived considerable pleasure. Although a product of it, he was not, naturally given his political views, an upholder of the public-school system: this made it all the more curious that all his dealings with his colleagues and subordinates were strongly coloured by the public-school ethos. Messenger boys were treated as fags, and assistants put on their honour to do well and praised for owning-up if they did not; all criticism and reprimands, so he always claimed, hurt him far more than they did the victims; and on one occasion I was sternly rebuked for not standing up when the headmaster, Mr. Christiansen, came into the room. This strict maintenance of alien standards did not exactly endear him to his fellows but none could withhold their respect from the creator of what was unquestionably the best gossip-column in Fleet Street, a literary form which he had not only completely transformed but to which he had given a new dimension.

My daily task, in fulfilling which I slowly, but very slowly, acquired a certain degree of confidence was not during this particular period rendered any easier by the unhealthy optimism which still remained the corner-stone of editorial policy. While it was being stoutly maintained day after day that there would be no war in Europe this year, anything which might possibly imperil the fulfilment of this comforting prophecy, including unkind and possibly aggravating jokes about the Führer and his minions, was rigorously taboo, and it was not until after the occupation of Prague that the reins were loosened. The news of this sombre confirmation of all our worst fears reached me not in Fleet Street but in Switzerland where I had gone for a fortnight's skiing. Arriving one morning at the top of the Parsenn I encountered Michael Spender who gloomily repeated to me the exultant German announcement he had just heard over the radio in the ski-hut. A day or two previously I had been in the cosy little bar on the roof of the old *Paris Soir* building in Paris which was then the chief rendezvous for newspapermen from all over Europe, where, rather to my surprise—for I was as yet not fully aware of that intense preoccupation with the immediate past to which all foreign correspondents are subject—central Europe was conspicuously not on the agenda and all interest was concentrated on the fate of the wretched remnants of the Republican forces in Spain. The impact of the present tidings had for me, therefore, the unbuffered force of the momentarily unexpected and all the distant, gleaming ranges stretching away below us were suddenly darkened as though by a storm long forecast but of which the advent nevertheless came as a surprise.

On my return to London I found a marked change in the atmosphere; in the office encouraging noises were still regularly being made but now carried no conviction, least of all with those charged with making them, and I found myself at last at liberty to do my worst with the rulers of the thousand-year Reich. While the feeling that the eleventh hour had long since struck was general, once accepted it was deliberately ignored, and on the surface life went on much as usual. Lucy Milner went off to Paris to cover the dress-shows with her customary but unconvincing air of long-suffering; on Wednesdays James Agate passed shiftily through the office with his weekly copy looking, in his flat-brimmed bowler and horsey overcoat, more than ever like an absconding bookie with intellectual pretensions; the great voice of Johnny Morton could still be heard from one end of Fleet Street to the other intransigently booming. Only in 'Poppins', where between six and seven most of the Features staff were regularly to be found, did one occasionally receive sotto-voce enquiries as to what 'arrangements' one was making for the not-so-distant future, to which I, fatalistically convinced that all arrangements had undoubtedly long since been made for one, firmly replied "None".

That summer we passed in a hired house at Beaulieu, my father-in-law having with notable prescience recently sold Smoglands. Early in August I grew apprehensive lest September, when Karen and I had planned to go to Italy, would not in fact prove to be an ideal holiday month and one night after dinner we drove into Southampton and jumped on the night-boat to Le Havre. My youthful passion for the Baroque had long since given way to a neo-classical enthusiasm which had in its turn been superseded by an all-absorbing interest in the Romanesque which now led us, just in time, to spend a week covering the area between Caen and Fécamps. It is not, I think, entirely hind-sight which invests the memory of this French excursion, so successful aesthetically, with a faint malaise; the fierce political excitement so evident in the days of the Popular Front had, it appeared, quite faded away and our fellow passengers in the local bus and the bourgeois families gingerly indulging in *bains-de-mer* on the perilous shingle at Etretat seemed sunk in a self-centred apathy which even Monsieur Daladier's *decrèts-lois* were powerless to disturb. On our return to Beaulieu a week later, laden with pâtés and camemberts and calvados, the fruit of a final inspired raid on Felix Potin at Le Havre, we were greeted on opening the morning paper by a carefully-posed photograph of Messrs. Molotov and Ribbentrop signing the Russo-German pact.

Back in London each day saw further signs that this time the storm was inescapably on us and the point of no return had finally been passed. On going into White's, which that month was giving hospitality to the St. James's, I was startled to notice among the bowlers and homburgs on the rack two scarlet-banded military caps and a gold-wreathed kepi; some of one's acquaintances disappeared altogether, others emerged wearing the unlikeliest uniforms and quite a number adopted a maddeningly discreet smile, with which during the next few years one was to become only too familiar, intended to indicate that their employment was of so secret a nature that no reference to it could possibly be made. Hobhouse, who was convinced that there would be no formal declaration of war and that death and destruction would rain down suddenly from the sky, never went out without his ear-plugs, having been informed by someone who had been in Barcelona that in an air-raid it was the ear-drums which went first. My father-in-law returning suddenly from a fishing trip in Iceland summoned me to dine with him at Pruniers where I found him unexpectedly braced by the prospect before us, but rather worried by the extraordinary efficiency of the German Intelligence. "Do you know," he said, "we were followed the whole way back from Reykjavik by a German U-boat. Now how on earth had they found out that I was on board?"

One golden evening the sky was dotted with barrage balloons, radiant and flashing in the sunset, and the next morning one noticed that the windows of many shops were criss-crossed with sticky paper. And then came the night when, having stayed even longer than usual in Poppins, where editors and executives were drooping over the bar in a state of total exhaustion induced by a week of working twenty-four hours a day marshalling news, accrediting war-correspondents, coping with the newly installed censorship, arranging emergency communications, I emerged with Lucy Milner and a waif-like girl-reporter in a pixie hat, who was to end the war as Mrs. Ernest Hemingway IV, and saw for the first time the fretwork Gothic of St. Dunstan's-in-the-West silhouetted against a still faintly glowing sky dominating a blacked-out Fleet Street.

At midnight, after a long session charged with a rather eerie gaiety at the Café Royal to which, in addition to the usual clientèle, half London appeared to have been drawn, I went to my A.R.P. post and was told to report for duty the next day at one o'clock. All that night I kept waking up in my empty house expecting to hear the roar of vast aerial armadas heading straight for West Kensington and in the morning I fell upon the newspapers the moment they arrived, although already fully aware of what they were likely to contain. So compulsive was this passion for news, by which during the last few weeks we had all been gripped, and which had lost none of its power even though now we all knew the Rubicon to have been crossed, that, noticing on my way to keep my watch the next morning that the post-office clock still wanted a minute to one, I decided to risk arriving late and turned smartly into the public bar of the Holland Arms.

"Just a song at twilight"

I CANNOT honestly say that my attitude to flying-bombs was ever one of gay insouciance. Nevertheless as they grew more frequent I developed a paper-thin tolerance which I had never achieved during the earlier, more orthodox, bombardment. For one thing there was not, after the first few days, any anti-aircraft fire, which brought two advantages; first an unaccustomed quiet, and second, and more important, a welcome freedom of movement. During the 'blitz' so long as I remained indoors I was ceaselessly assailed by what psychiatrists so unfeelingly describe as 'irrational fears', but on escape into the wide open spaces these were promptly transformed by the patter of shrapnel into anxieties to which my reason accorded every justification. But during the short summer nights of 1944 it was possible to cut short the long hours of bedroom terrors by escaping into streets unmenaced by our own defences. And so it came about that on such evenings as I was not on duty I developed the habit of taking long walks through the misty Kensington evening and exploring districts which had for so long aroused my curiosity as to have acquired an almost fabulous quality but which in ordinary times I had never had the opportunity, or had lacked the energy, to penetrate.

The Holland Road which leads northward from my house is not in itself a romantic thoroughfare but the back-drop framed by the wings of its long stucco perspectives had always had for me a certain sinister fascination. A circular building in the style that the mid-Victorians were pleased to call Palladian marks the entrance to a narrow street of cheap shops running into the main road at an acute angle, crowded in peace-time with stalls and costers' barrows, which had always from earliest childhood strangely affected my imagination. In part this was due to an occasion when my father had, as a great treat, taken me to the White City Exhibition and we had halted here on our return to enjoy the spectacle of the seething Saturday night crowds, the women all in tight sealskin jackets and vast plumed hats, the men in pearl-buttoned waistcoats and flared trousers, jostling round the street-market in the theatrical light of the gas-jets; in part to the mystery and surprise which always colours any sudden revelation of a crowded slum-life existing behind a pompous and familiar façade and which is as powerfully induced by suddenly coming on one of the tenement streets which emerge between the neo-Renaissance palazzi of Fifth Avenue as by the half-glimpse of the Venetian ghetto seen beneath the arch of the Merceria. Here, moreover, the romance had been much heightened by the fear and distaste for the neighbourhood beyond, to which the more nervous of my elders were accustomed from time to time to give whispered expression. For in my youth Notting Dale was held, not, I fancy, altogether unreasonably, as one of the most dangerous districts of London and it was confidently stated that it was impossible for a well-dressed man to walk the length of the Portobello Road and emerge intact.

So powerfully had the prevailing attitude reacted on my sub-conscious that, although I had never in fact had occasion to do so, I had never gone out of my way to investigate this Alsatia of North Kensington. Now, when it seemed probable that the more enter-prising thugs would be exercising their calling, thanks to the favourable conditions provided by the blackout, in the profitable districts of W.1, and the more nervous would be deep in the Tube shelters, was surely the ideal time for this long postponed exploration.

The deeper I penetrated into the stucco wilderness, deserted save for an occasional pathetic figure weighed down by bedding hurrying through the drizzle to the Shepherd's Bush Tube Station, the more insistent did the past become. A certain plenitude of frosted glass and bold Victorian display-types, still characteristic of Dublin and the lower East Side of New York, but elsewhere in London long since submerged beneath a flood of chromium plate and modernistic sans-serif, was doubtless chiefly responsible, but in addition long buried memories of streets half-seen in the distance from my pram, as nurse cautiously skirted the fringe of this City

of the Plain on our way to Wormwood Scrubs in the hope of seeing Mr. Graham White go up in his new flying machine, played their part. As I drifted on in a vaguely north-eastern direction, ears cocked for overhead chugging, the sense of familiarity deepened and finally achieved its maximum intensity at the end of a curving street of dilapidated semi-detacheds, all peeling paint and crumbling volutes.

As I paused to take in this panorama of decay my attention was irresistibly, but apparently illogically, drawn to a house immediately opposite across the street. Separated from the pavement by a few square feet of trampled grass and sooty laurels, the brickwork of the low wall still bearing scars that marked the recent out-wrenching of railings for the armaments drive, it in no way differed from any of its neighbours; the pillared portico and debased but still classical mouldings marked it as having been originally intended for some solid family of the Victorian *bourgeoisie*; the marked disparity of the window-curtains on the various floors, all subtly different in their general cheapness and vulgarity, indicated that it now sheltered three or perhaps foru separate establishments. My glance travelling disdainfully across this depressing façade, marking the broken balustrade above the cornice, the hacked and blackened lime-trees, the half erased 79 on the dirty umber of the door-pillars that had once been cream, came finally and shockingly to rest on the street name attached to the garden wall—Elgin Crescent. This, I suddenly realised, was my birthplace.

In my subconscious eagerness to prolong my evening stroll, I must have walked right through the haunted district I had set out to explore and emerged into the once familiar playground of my childhood on the slopes of Notting Hill. The fact that I had done so all unawares, that I had passed the formerly so firmly established boundary line without for a moment realising it, spoke far more clearly of what had happened here in the last thirty years than could many volumes of social history. As I walked on up the hill, regardless for once of a flying-bomb now following the course of Ladbroke Grove seemingly only just above the chimney-pots,

I noticed with a certain proprietary satisfaction that the progress of decay had not been halted at Elgin Crescent; that the squares and terraces that had once formed the very Acropolis of Edwardian propriety grouped round the church had suffered a hardly less severe decline. Some of the most obvious signs of degradation were certainly the result of five years of war and common to all parts of London, but here this enforced neglect was clearly but a temporary acceleration of a continuous process. The vast stucco palaces of Kensington Park Road and the adjoining streets had long ago been converted into self-contained flats where an ever-increasing stream of refugees from every part of the once civilised world had found improvised homes, like the dark-age troglodytes who sheltered in the galleries and boxes of the Colosseum. Long, long before the outbreak of war these classical façades had already ceased to bear any relevance to the life that was lived behind them; the eminent K.C.s and the Masters of City Companies had already given place to Viennese professors and Indian students and bed-sitter business girls years before the first siren sounded. And yet I who was only on the threshold of middle-age could clearly remember the days when they flourished in all their intended glory. At that house on the corner I used to go to dancing classes; outside that imposing front-door I had watched the carriages setting down for a reception; and in that now denuded garden I had once played hide and seek.

Many times since that wet wartime evening I have pondered on the implications of the dismal transformation then so suddenly brought home to me. This was not, it seemed to me, just a case of a once fashionable district declining slowly into slumdom but rather the outward and visible sign of the disappearance of a whole culture; a disappearance, moreover, which no one seems to have noticed and for which no tears had been shed. For it is a curious fact the term 'upper-middle-class' used as a social classification should only have achieved its maximum currency at a time when that class, or rather the cultural pattern which it established, had completely vanished; that while all the other labels which attached to the social stratifications of late Victorian life retain in varying degrees a certain relevance, this which is shiny from over-use by leader-writers and social analysts marks a completely empty drawer. The aristocracy and landed gentry, although Nationally Entrusted and sadly Thirkellised, are still, thank goodness, for all their constant complainings of extinction, visibly and abundantly there; the lower-middle-class is not only still with us but so enormously increased in numbers and influence as to impose its own colour and standards on our whole civilisation; the working-class although, anyhow in London, being rapidly reduced by the ever-increasing rate of its absorption into the lower-middle-class and steadily losing much of its peculiar character remains numerous and powerful. But the old upper-middles, in so far as they possessed a definite culture and set of values of their own, are as extinct as the speakers of Cornish.

It is customary to explain this disappearance either in terms of the Marxian dialectic or by reference to the immense burden of taxation which weighed on them more heavily than on any other section of the community. It can also be correctly maintained that the continuous process of social assimilation, based on a deep-rooted national instinct that bids us reject on the one hand the transatlantic vision of the equality of man and on the other all the continental foolishness of *Ebenburtigkeit* and sixty-four quarterings, has been immeasurably accelerated in the last fifty years. Whereas a couple of generations separated the mediaeval burgher from the Tudor squire and another couple intervened between the Tudor squire and the Stuart nobleman, in recent years the social barriers between class and class, which though always clearly marked were never happily insuperable, have often all been leapt in a single lifetime. But, although there has always been a two-way traffic, the probability is that only a very small proportion of the two and a half million direct descendants of John of Gaunt would not now be black balled for a suburban tennis club, and economic arguments remain as partial an explanation as dialectical materialism.

Far and away the most important single factor leading to the complete collapse of the upper-middle-class way of life was the invention of the internal combustion engine; for the coming of the motor-car made possible the 'week-end', and the week-end spelt doom. However formal may have been the religion of this section of the community, the whole pattern of their life, anyhow in London, yet centred round the church, and once the cohesive force exercised by 'Morning Prayer' became weakened by the disruptive influence of the golf-links and the week-end cottage the whole social organism collapsed into its individual units. Curiously enough one of the few who seems at the time to have been aware, doubtless purely intuitively, of what was afoot was His late Majesty King George V (always temperamentally far closer to the upper-middle-class than the aristocracy), for if we are to believe the memoirs of his eldest son, one of the chief of his many objections to the younger generation was based on their fondness for leaving London at week-ends.

The vacuum involuntarily created by Lord Nuffield and his peers was filled in two ways, of which only one was connected with the process of dissolution. The lure of the country, besides ruining the home-counties, created a new class whose way of life, although originally based in intent on the emulation of that of the landed gentry, was in fact far closer to that of the middle-class immediately below them. By the 'thirties the differences dividing the £10,000 a year stockbroker from his £800 a year clerk were all quantitative not qualitative. One lived in a gabled mansion standing in its own grounds at Sunningdale, the other in a semi-detached villa at Mitcham, but both residences were bogus Elizabethan and both householders caught the 8.28 every morning. The stockbroker had a six-cylindered Rolls and a Lagonda, the clerk a second-hand Morris, but both were as likely as not to spend Sunday on the golf-links. They saw the same films, listened to the same radio-programmes, read the same newspapers, and neither of them went near a church except to get married. The way of life of both was equally far removed from that of the stockbroker's father living in Egerton Gardens or Orme Square.

The second, and perhaps more extraordinary, of the twentieth-century inventions which remoulded English social life was that of the intelligentsia. Hitherto, this amenity so long established on the continent had here been lacking. In Victorian times writers and artists, save for one or two of the most exalted, living remote and inaccessible on private Sinais in the Isle of Wight or Cheyne Row, had conformed to the pattern of the upper-middle-class to which most of them belonged. Matthew Arnold, Browning, Millais were all indistinguishable in appearance and behaviour from the great army of Victorian clubmen, and took very good care that this should be so. The *haute Bohème* did not exist and the Athenaeum rather than the Closerie des Lilas shaped the social life of the literary world. Only at the very end of the century amidst the gilded mirrors of the Café Royal did there emerge a society which bore some faint resemblance to those which had long been flourishing in the life of Paris, Vienna and Berlin; and even this, by the equal importance that sporting peers and racing journalists—the 'Pink'un' world in fact—enjoyed along with the artists and writers to whom they were linked by such liaison figures as Phil May and a common devotion to the Music Hall, bore a peculiar British stamp.

By the time the 'twenties were half-way through the whole picture had completely changed. The immense increase in size and circulation of newspapers and magazines, the rapid development of the cinema industry, the coming of the B.B.C., the colossal expansion of advertising, and later, the establishment of such organisations as the British Council, had transformed the pocket *Vie de Bohème*, which flourished in the late 'nineties into a vast army of salaried culture-hounds, an army which recruited its main strength from the younger generation of the upper-middle-class.

Unlike all the earlier class divisions the intelligentsia forms a vertical rather than a horizontal section of the community. Connecting at the top with the world of artistic dukes and musical minor royalty it trails away at the bottom into the lower depths of communist advertising men and *avant-garde* film directors. But however different the social and financial standing of the various grades within the group may be, the pattern of their existence remains strangely consistent and utterly at variance with that of the old middle-class from which so many of the members sprang. Where the parents, even those in some way connected with the arts, lived in substantial houses in which they ate regular meals the children live in flats and eat at snack-bars and restaurants; while the fathers not infrequently tended to look rather over-dressed in the country the sons invariably appear underdressed in the town. A society which was predominantly Anglican with a handful of high-minded agnostics has been transformed into one which is predominantly agnostic with a handful of not so high-minded Roman Catholics. For the transformation is widespread and complete. So successfully was the New Bohemia glamourised by female novelists during the 'twenties and 'thirties that its way of life has gladly been adopted by thousands of the old upper-middles whose connection with the arts is non-existent. Thus even so late as twenty years ago one was fairly safe in assuming that any bearded figure in corduroys reading the *New Statesman* was at very least a photographer or a museum official, whereas now he is just as likely to be a chartered accountant or a dry-salter. In a world where only Guards officers and bookmakers still maintain a sartorial standard, the social ideals of Murger are everywhere triumphant and even ordained ministers of the Established Church do not hesitate to advertise their broad-mindedness with soft collars and grey flannel 'bags'.

Although the effects of the change did not become generally apparent until after the first German War it was, in fact, well under way by 1914; but due largely to the patriarchal organisation of my family I was the fortunate victim of a time-lag and in the halls of my youth there still flourished a way of life which in more sophisticated circles was already in visible dissolution. From the death of the old Queen until the outbreak of war this small society upheld the standards of Victorianism with the same unruffled tenacity with which the Sephardic community at Salonika per-sisted in speaking fifteenth-century Spanish; fully aware of Bernard Shaw, Diaghilev and Alexander's Ragtime Band their outlook remained as resolutely unmodified by these phenomena as that of the Adobe Indians by the airplane and the radio.

The present volume is not, therefore, primarily autobiographical in intent but rather, by using thematic material drawn from a few commonplace incidents of childhood, an attempt to raise not a monument but a small memorial plaque to a vanished world. Many of the principal characters may well appear to readers below the age of forty ridiculous, maladjusted and anachronistic, wilfully blind to the great changes going on about them and rashly presumptuous in their firm convictions. Such a view is easily justifiable and, indeed, is one which I myself frequently expressed in my heedless youth. But, sheltering from the chugging menace overhead in the shabby ruins of their citadel scrawled with slogans demanding a Second Front and scarred by blast yet still retaining in the evening light an almost Venetian grandeur of decay, self-confidence waned. Whether their disappearance is an irreparable loss or a welcome deliverance I am too close to them to say: I can only record that I have become increasingly conscious of the debt, which, for good or ill, I owe them.

1. *"Take me back to dear old Shepherd's Bush"*

I WAS BORN in the eighth year of the reign of King Edward the Seventh in the parish of St. John's, Notting Hill. At that time Elgin Crescent, the actual scene of this event, was situated on the Marches of respectability. Up the hill to the south, tree-shaded and freshly stuccoed, stretched the squares and terraces of the last great stronghold of Victorian propriety: below to the north lay the courts and alleys of Notting Dale, through which, so my nurse terrifyingly assured me, policemen could only proceed in pairs.

The Crescent, like all border districts, was distinguished by a certain colourful mixture in its inhabitants, lacking in the more securely sheltered central area, grouped in this case round the church. While residence there was socially approved and no traces of 'slumminess' were as yet apparent, there did cling to it a slight whiff of Bohemianism from which Kensington Park Road, for instance, was quite free. Of the residents several were connected with the Stage, and some were foreign, but neither group carried these eccentricities to excessive lengths. Among the former were numbered a Mr. Maskelyne (or was it a Mr. Devant?) who lived on the corner, and, right next door to us, the talented authoress of *Where the Rainbow Ends*, whose daughter, a dashing hobble-skirted croquet-player, remains a vivid memory. The foreigners

167

included some Japanese diplomats and a German family connected with the Embassy, whose son, a fair, chinless youth, was always at great pains to model his appearance on that of the Crown Prince Wilhelm, much to the delight of my father whom a long residence in Berlin had rendered expert in detecting the subtlest nuances of this elaborate masquerade. Fortunately my parents' arrival at Number 79 had done much to erase the principal blot on the fair name of the street, as our house had previously been the home of no less equivocal a figure than Madame Blavatsky.

Number 79 was a semi-detached stucco residence on three floors and a basement with a pillared porch, not differing stylistically in any way from the prevailing classicism of the neighbourhood. At the back was a small private garden opening into the large garden common to all the occupants of the south side of Elgin Crescent and the north side of Lansdowne Road. Such communal gardens, which are among the most attractive features of Victorian town-planning, are not uncommon in the residential districts of West London, but are carried to the highest point of their development in the Ladbroke estate. This area, which was laid out after the closure of the race-course that for a brief period encircled the summit of the hill, represents the last rational, unselfconscious piece of urban development in London. It was unfortunately dogged by misfortune, and the socially ambitious intention of Allom, the architect, and the promoters was largely defeated by the proximity of an existing pottery slum in Notting Dale, which received, just at the time the scheme was being launched, an enormous and deplorable influx of Irish labourers working on the Great Western Railway.

How different it all was in the years before 1914! Then the stucco, creamy and bright, gleamed softly beneath what seems in reminiscence to have been a perpetually cloudless sky. Geraniums in urns flanked each brass-enriched front door, while over the area railings moustachioed policemen made love to buxom cooks. And in every street there hung, all summer long, the heavy scent of limes.

The angel who drove the original inhabitants out of this gilt-edged Eden, not with a flaming sword but by a simple vanishing trick, was the domestic servant. The houses, even the small ones like ours, were planned on generous lines and labour-saving was still not only an unrealised but un-thought-of ideal. Fortunately my parents, whose joint income at the time of my birth amounted to all of £600 a year, were able to maintain a cook, a housemaid, a nurse and a boot-boy; my mother, moreover, had been through the hard school of a Victorian grandmother's household, and herself undertook such specialised, and now obsolete, labours as cleaning the chandeliers, washing the rubber-plant and superintending the linen.

The ideal of the servantless civilisation, already fully realised in the United States, is doubtless a noble one, and those who so bravely, and possibly sincerely, maintain that they feel degraded by being waited on by their fellow human beings compel our admiration, although personally they invariably provoke me to confess that I can tolerate without discomfort being waited on hand and foot. But it is an ideal attended by one grave disadvantage—whom is there left for the children to talk to? A mother's love is all very well, but it is only a poor substitute for good relations with the cook.

In my own case, the centre of the below-stairs world was Kate the housemaid. This remarkable woman, gaunt, near-sighted and invariably prepared for the worst, not only endeared herself to me by acts of kindness to which I could always be certain no strings were attached, but also provided my only contact with the real world which lay beyond the confines of my isolated nursery. Quick-witted and an omnivorous reader of the popular press, it was her habit to converse largely in political slogans and popular catch-phrases. Thus when I was detected sliding unobtrusively into the larder she would call out "Hands off the people's food", and if when driven out she suspected that I still retained some loot she would advance with simulated menace, jabbing the upturned palm of her left hand with the index finger of her right, in a gesture which a dozen cartoons of the then Chancellor of the Exchequer,

Mr. Lloyd George, had rendered universally familiar, exclaiming "Put it there!" And always when I asked what was for dinner she would remind me of Mr. Asquith and bid me "Wait and see". But by no means all of her sources of verbal inspiration were political; better even than the Harmsworth Press she loved the music-hall, and her evenings off were regularly spent at one or other of the many suburban houses then still happily flourishing on the sites of future Odeons. Her favourite performers were Wilkie Bard, George Mozart and Alfred Lester, and while engaged on her endless scrubbing and dusting she could usually be heard informing the household that she had got a motto, or wanted to sing in opera, or desired to be taken back to dear old Shepherd's Bush.

The popular music of the Edwardian era played an important rôle in the national life: these music-hall songs and ballads have today been so weakened and degraded by intensive plugging and self-conscious revival over the air that they are now as far removed from their former spontaneous popularity as are the careful prancings of latter-day Morris dancers from the village revels of the Elizabethans. In the strictly stratified social world of my childhood they seemed to me in my bourgeois pram to be the one thing enjoyed in common by the world represented by the whistling errand-boy and the ladies I occasionally observed, humming gaily, if a little off-key, as they emerged from the glittering paradise of *The Devonshire Arms* (in passing which my nurse always developed an additional turn of speed and on which she would never comment), and the world of which the pillars were Kate and my father. I specify my father rather than my parents as his taste was almost identical with Kate's (he perhaps rated Harry Lauder a little higher than she did), whereas my mother's was more accurately represented by *Traumerei* and *Songe d'automne*, beautiful works, doubtless, but hardly with so universal an appeal.

A few additional figures there were who stood in a rather closer relation to the small world of Number 79 than the anonymous ranks of passers-by I observed from my pram: they, while obviously debarred from the full club privileges of Kate, the cook, my parents and the boot-boy, yet enjoyed, as it were, the facilities of country membership. The Italian organ-grinder, a martyr to gastric troubles, who regularly appeared every Thursday afternoon; the crossing-sweeper in Ladbroke Grove whose function the internal combustion engine was even then rapidly rendering as decorative as that of the King's Champion; the muffin man, the lamplighter and the old gentleman who came out on winter

evenings to play the harp by the foggy radiance of the street lamp —Dickensian figures who have obviously no rôle to play in the Welfare State and have left no successors. Doubtless their disappearance should be welcomed, and yet they did not appear to be either downtrodden or exploited: indeed, the impression they gave was chiefly of a proper consciousness of the important rôle in the social fabric played by muffin men, lamplighters and organ-grinders. Certainly their spirits seemed higher and their manners were undoubtedly better than those of the majority of the present-day beneficiaries of enlightened social legislation. Even the crossing-sweeper, despite his ostentatious rags and traditional whine, displayed a certain individuality and professional pride which one seldom observes in the hygenically-uniformed Municipal Refuse Disposal Officer.

Apart from such figures, my relations and, later, fellow-pupils at my kindergarten, the most vivid and indirectly influential personality of my early childhood was our next-door neighbour to the west, old Mrs. Ullathorne. This imposing and always slightly mysterious *grande dame*, with whom I was bidden to tea at regular intervals, represented an era which, even at that date, seemed almost incredibly remote. She had enjoyed, so it was said, a considerable success at the court of Napoleon the Third, and there were prominently displayed amongst the palms and bibelots of her crowded drawing-room innumerable *carte-de-visite* size photographs of dashing cuirassiers in peg-top trousers sporting waxed moustaches and elegant lip-beards, and of crinolined beauties who had somewhat surprisingly elected to put on full ball-dress and all their diamonds for a good long read, of what appeared from the binding to be books of devotion, seated on rustic benches in a vaguely Alpine landscape. Certainly Mrs. Ullathorne herself gave a very definite impression of belonging to another, and far more sophisticated, world than that of Edwardian Notting Hill. Alone among all our female acquaintances she was heavily and unashamedly made-up (even the dashing daughter of our playwright neighbour, who was thought to be a suffragette and known to smoke, never, I fancy, went further than a discreet use of *papiers poudrés*). But the style in which her *maquillage* was conceived proclaimed her way behind, rather than daringly ahead, of the times. The whole surface of her face was delicately pale and matt, and only by imperceptible degrees did the pearly white take on a faint rosy flush above the cheekbones; the eyebrows, which although carefully shaped were not plucked thin, were a deep uncompromising auburn, contrasting very strikingly with the faded parma violet of the lids. Her toupet, a rich mahogany in colour, was dressed in tight curls and fringes in the manner of the reigning queen. The whole effect was one of extreme fragility which, one felt, the slightest contact or even a sneeze would irretrievably wreck, and was as far removed from that achieved by modern methods as is a Nattier from a Modigliani.

Whether due to Mrs. Ullathorne's long residence in foreign parts or to her extreme age, she displayed another peculiarity which set her still further apart from the rest of my world—she invariably insisted that in place of the customary handshake I should bow smartly from the waist and kiss her hand. This was for me always rather an alarming ordeal, and I can still see that long white hand delicately extended, criss-crossed with the purple hawsers of her veins standing out in as high relief as the yellowish diamonds in her many rings, and experience once more the ghastly apprehension that one day, overcome by unbearable curiosity, I should take a sharp nip at the most prominent of those vital pipelines.

The influence which the old lady exercised on my early development was not, however, direct, but the result of a gift. One day she presented me with a large quarto volume bound in dark green leather into which, with incredible neatness, she had in childhood pasted scraps.

Although I can still vividly remember the enchantment which was renewed every time I opened that magic volume, it is only quite fortuitously that its peculiar flavour, recognisable if faint, now and then returns to me. No effort of conscious memory will work the miracle, but just occasionally the sight of swans upon a castle lake, or some peculiar combination of Prussian blue and carmine, or the feel beneath the fingers of the embossed paper lace on an old-fashioned Christmas card, will play the part of Proust's Madeleine and fire the train. Many must have received such volumes in childhood, but not many I fancy so perfect an example of the genre as this; for the artists of no age have ever surpassed those of the romantic period in the production of keepsakes and *culs-de-lampes*, and this volume had been compiled at exactly the right moment. The shakoed, hand-coloured infantryman, who so gallantly assaulted that vaguely Oriental stronghold, were the soldiers of Louis Philippe subduing the fierce Goums of Ab-del-Kedir; this mysterious steel-engraved lake shadowed by twilit mountains was Lamartine; and the rather over-plumed knights, their armour gleaming with applied tinsel, were undoubtedly setting out for the Eglinton Tournament.

The charm and excitement of those vividly coloured vignettes must have made a powerful appeal to the imagination of any child but in my case it was reinforced by the contrast they provided to the illustrations in my other books. My mother suffered from that perpetual illusion common to all parents that the books which had meant the most to her in her own childhood (or possibly those which, later in life, she had persuaded herself had then been her favourites) would awaken a similar delighted response in her off-spring. My nursery library was therefore well stocked with the illustrated fairy-tales of the late 'seventies and early 'eighties. It cannot be denied that the skill of the great nineteenth-century school of English wood-engraving was then at its height and that many of these volumes were, in their way, masterpieces. Nevertheless, not only did I dislike them all with the solitary exception of Tenniel's *Alice*, but certain of them awoke in me feelings of fear and revulsion.

I do not think, looking back, that my reaction was purely personal nor wholly abnormal. Children are all firmly in favour of representational art up to a certain point (my lack of enthusiasm for Walter Crane, for instance, was caused by his tendency to subordinate accurate representation to decorative embroidery and was of a wholly different kind to my dislike of Linley Sambourne), but that point is reached when realism is carried over into the third dimension. They will welcome, and indeed demand, the maximum amount of realistic detail provided it is flat, but once an artist starts to give his illustrations depth and to visualise his figures in the round, his pre-adolescent public will begin to lose interest. Thanks to the incredibly responsive instrument which such figures as the Dalziels had made of the wood-engraver, the book illustrators of the 'eighties were able to exploit the third dimension, which still possessed in this medium the charm of comparative novelty, to their hearts' content, and they certainly made the most of the opportunity. The buxom flanks of the Water Babies sprang from the flat page with a startling illusion of rotundity; the more unpleasant creations of Hans Andersen's imagination displayed a devastating solidity; indeed, certain artists went rather too far in their three-dimensional enthusiasm and overstepping the bounds of realism achieved an effect which can only be described, in the strictest sense of the word, as surrealist. In our own day this irrational element in the wood-engraved illustrations of the late nineteenth century, against which I as a child had unconsciously reacted (in exactly the same way, incidentally, as did my own children some twenty-five years later), has been recognised and skilfully utilised for his own terrifying purposes by Max Ernst in such works as 'Le Lion de Belfort' and 'La Femme a cent têtes'.

Thus the world of Mrs. Ullathorne's scrap-book, with its brilliant green lawns and flat improbable trees peopled by kindly gendarmes in enormous tricornes and little girls in pork-pie hats and striped stockings practising archery in château parks, took on in addition to its own proper attraction the welcome character of a safe retreat from that other, boring yet terrifying, world of all too completely realised fantasy.

The work from which, next to the scrap-book, I derived the greatest enjoyment was also uncontemporary, being two bound volumes of the *Picture Magazine*, to which my father had regularly subscribed during his school days at the very end of the Victorian age. This admirable periodical nicely combined instruction with amusement, and among the regular features were a series of simple pseudo-scientific experiments (a cock mesmerised into following a chalked line with its beak and a daring criminal escaping from Vincennes by means of a home-made parachute), accounts of travel and exploration (whiskered tourists being hauled up to the monasteries of the Meteora in nets), and, best of all, strip cartoons by Caran d'Ache. In addition were included from time to time four-page supplements of photographs of the most distinguished figures in one particular walk of contemporary life—soldiers, scientists, painters . . . Of these my favourite was that devoted to the rulers of sovereign states who, thank Heaven, were at that date far more numerous than they are today.

Those long rows of royal torsos adorned with every variety of epaulette, plastron, and aiguillette, the necks compressed into collars of unbelievable height and tightness, the manly, if padded chests, hung with row upon row of improbable crosses and stars and criss-crossed by watered silk ribbons and tangles of gold cords, surmounted by so many extraordinary countenances adorned with immense moustaches, upstanding in the style of Potsdam or down-sweeping in the style of Vienna, some fish-eyed, some monocled, some vacant, some indignant but all self-conscious, had for me a fascination which never failed. And nor, when I had learnt to read, did the captions prove a disappointment; such names as Mecklenberg-Schwerin, Bourbon-Parme, Saxe-Coburg-Gotha held for me a flavour of high romance to which the very difficulty of pronouncing added rather than detracted. How drab by contrast did the still small handful of republican presidents appear, and how deep was my contempt for those pince-nezed, bourgeois figures to whom a gaudy silken diagonal across their stiff-shirted bosoms could not lend an air of even spurious distinction!

Incredible as it may seem, many of these paladins who now appear far more remote from our modern experience than Attila or Ivan the Terrible were actually still more or less firmly on their thrones at the time when I first grew familiar with their appearance. The whiskered porcine features of Franz Josef were still regularly revealed to his loyal Viennese as he drove every morning through the Hofburg; hardly a day passed without his German colleague, dressed as an Admiral, a Hussar, a Uhlan, a Cuirassier, or a Highland sportsman, making an appearance in the illustrated papers; and somewhere hidden away in the heart of the plaster mazes of Dolmabâghcheh, that last bastard offspring of a frenzied rococo which had reared itself so surprisingly on the shores of the Bosphorus, apprehensive, invisible but undoubtedly there, was Abdul the Damned.

Of all this I was at that time naturally unaware. All these characters were no more and no less real to me than Jack the Giant-Killer and the Infant Samuel of whom my mother was accustomed to read aloud, or Hackenschmidt and the Terrible Turk, in whose exploits the boot-boy took so keen an interest. Only Kaiser Wilhelm was for me in any way, and that very remotely, connected with real life; for I had once been sent a box of toy soldiers by an old friend of my mother, who was one of that monarch's A.D.C.s, and whose photograph in the full-dress uniform of the Prussian Guard stood on the piano.

Less colourful but more familiar were the pages devoted to the more prominent contemporary divines. No flourishing moustachios nor jewelled orders here, but every variety of whisker from the restrained mutton-chop to the full Newgate fringe, and billowing acres of episcopal lawn. At the time these portraits were taken the social prestige of the Establishment, and even, on a different level, of Nonconformity, was at its height, and although it had become a little dimmed in the intervening years it was still comparatively great. How complete has been the subsequent eclipse, a brief study of the representative novels of high life during the last half century will amply demonstrate; although the regiments of handsome curates, worldly Archdeacons and courtly Bishops who thronged the pages of late Victorian fiction thinned out a lot in Edwardian times, a sharp-tongued Mayfair incumbent or two, ex-curates doubtless of Canon Chasuble, still make a regular appearance in the tales of Saki: but in all the works of Michael Arlen I cannot recall a single dog-collar and the solitary cleric to appear in the novels of Mr. Waugh is Fr. Rothschild, S.J.

In real life, anyhow in the society in which my parents moved, the clergy still played a prominent and honoured rôle. Their merits as preachers were eagerly discussed and the exact degree of their 'Highness' or 'Lowness' keenly debated. Many of the originals of those portraits were, therefore, quite familiar to me by name as being preachers under whom members of my family had at one time or another sat, while on the knees of one of them, Prebendary Webb-Peploe, a celebrated Evangelical preacher from whose well-attended Watch Night sermons the more impressionable members of the congregation were regularly carried out on stretchers, I myself had once had the honour of being perched.

It may seem strange that my infant literature should have been so exclusively out-of-date, but at that time the modern renaissance of the children's book was in its infancy, and the prevailing standard of contemporary productions was unbelievably low. Exceptions there were, however, and I can vividly remember the pleasure I derived from the Nursery History of England, illustrated by that happily still flourishing artist, George Morrow, and, a little later, from the works of Edmund Dulac.

To the enjoyment of the pictures, appreciation of the text was soon added, as thanks to the brilliant educational methods of my mother I learned to read at a very tender age. Her system, simple as it was effective, was based on a chocolate alphabet. This was spread out twice a week on the dining-room table and such letters as I recognised I was allowed to eat; later, when my knowledge of the alphabet was faultless, I was entitled to such letters as I could form into a new word. Although never strong in arithmetic I soon grasped the simple fact that the longer the word the more the chocolate, and by the time I could spell 'suffragette' without an error this branch of my education was deemed complete and a tendency to biliousness had become increasingly apparent.

Once my ability was firmly established I read everything on which I could lay my hands, from *The Times* leaders to the preface to the Book of Common Prayer. This impressive zeal was not, I fancy, the result of any exceptional thirst for knowledge, but rather of boredom, and was far commoner among children at that time than it is today. Such cinemas as then existed were regarded by my parents as undesirably sensational and notoriously unhygienic, and there was no compulsion on grown-ups to make any pretence of enjoying the company of the young who were, quite rightly, expected to amuse themselves. The only addition which modern science had made to the sources of infant pleasure available to my parents, or even my grandparents, was the gramophone. On this archaic machine I was permitted, as a great treat, to listen to the exaggeratedly Scots voice of Harry Lauder, just audible through a barrage of scratching and whining, singing 'Stop your tickling, Jock', or to the waltzes of Archibald Joyce rendered, rather surprisingly, by the Earl of Lonsdale's private band and recorded on discs half an inch thick by Messrs. William Whiteley.

My appearances in the drawing-room, where the gramophone was kept, were determined in accordance with fixed rules, as indeed were those of almost all the children of my generation—on weekdays half an hour before going to bed and half an hour in the morning to practise my scales, the latter period being prolonged to an hour on Tuesdays when Miss Pearce, poor long-suffering woman, came to wrestle with my highly personal rendering of 'The Merry Peasant'. Apart from these daily occasions, the only times when the room knew me were when there were visitors.

The pattern of social life in archaic Bayswater, and all points west, differed almost as much from that prevailing today as it did from that of mediaeval times. Fixed rules prevailed governing the exact hours and days on which visits took place, the number and size of the cards left and when and how they should be 'cornered', the clothes to be worn, and the length of time which one was expected to stay; even such trivial gestures as those with which the ladies, once perched on the Edwardian Hepplewhite chairs, were accustomed to throw back their veils and roll down their gloves at the wrists, were formal and standardised. There was no casual dropping-in for drinks, as drinking between meals was confined exclusively to the restorative masculine whisky-and-soda (or among the older generation "a little b. and s.")—almost exclusively, for curiously enough I do recollect among certain of my older female relatives the ritual partaking of a glass of port wine and a slice of plum cake at eleven o'clock in the morning, although this was generally regarded as an old-fashioned survival only to be justified on grounds of old age or a delicate constitution. There was no ringing up and asking people round for a little cocktail party as we had no telephone and cocktails were still unknown, save perhaps to certain rather 'fast' Americans—the sort of people who patronised those 'tango teas' of which the papers spoke.

Where no casual appearance could possibly take place, and all was fixed and pre-ordained, I knew exactly when the summons to present myself below would come. My mother, like all the ladies of her acquaintance, had her Thursdays, when the silver teapot and the best china would be shiningly conspicuous and her friends and relations would dutifully appear to be entertained with cucumber sandwiches, *petit-fours*, slices of chocolate cake and, in winter, toasted buns. Those who could not come, either because the number of their friends who had also chosen Thursday as their 'At Home' day precluded a personal appearance at each or for some other valid reason, sent round their cards.

My own entry was always carefully timed by Nurse to coincide with the moment when the teacups, with which I was hardly to be trusted, were already distributed and the sandwiches and cakes were waiting to be handed round. My performance on these occasions was invariably masterly. Clad in a *soigné* little blue silk number, with Brussels lace collar and cut steel buckles on my shoes, in which I had recently made my first public appearance as a page at a wedding in All Saints, Margaret Street, I passed round the solids in a manner which combined efficiency with diffidence in exactly the right proportions. Moreover, although conspicuously well-behaved, I could always be relied on to go into the *enfant terrible* act at exactly the right moment, and produce embarrassing questions or comments of a laughable kind that yet just stopped short of being offensively personal or too outspokenly apt. The freely expressed admiration which my performance always produced was almost as gratifying to me as it was to my mother, particularly in such cases where I considered it was likely to pay a handsome dividend next Christmas. Only among my Lancaster relations was the rapture apt to be a little modified; my Aunt Hetty, for instance, was more than once heard to remark that if Mamie were not careful dear little Osbert would soon be developing a deplorable tendency to "play to the gallery".

The only other times (apart from the many-coursed dinner parties of the period, a fixed number of which my parents were accustomed to give during the year, which naturally affected my

life not at all) on which visitors appeared was when country relatives were in London and were of sufficient age or importance to be asked to tea or luncheon for themselves alone. The most memorable of these was my Great Aunt Martha, not only for her own personality and appearance which were remarkable enough, but also for the manner of her arrival. Having been born early in the reign of George IV she was relatively fixed in her ways, and when she came to stay with her younger brother, my grandfather, the victoria and the greys were put at her disposal: their use in London had otherwise come to be increasingly abandoned in favour of the Renault, and they were only still maintained, I fancy, out of respect for Mundy, the elderly coachman, and a deep-rooted enthusiasm for harness horses which was general in my father's family.

I can still recall the stately dignified clop-clop, quite different in rhythm from that of the brisk single-horsed baker's van or the heavy proletarian tattoo of the pantechnicon, which announced that Aunt Martha was rounding the corner, and which I had been eagerly awaiting at the nursery window for half an hour or more. Quickly snatching up some lumps of sugar from Nurse, I was down the stairs and at the horses' heads almost before the footman was off the box. Looking back, I confess myself lost in admiration at my youthful temerity, as nowadays my reluctance to go fumbling round the muzzles of relatively unfamiliar quadrupeds would hardly be so easily overcome.

Great Aunt Martha, although even older than Mrs. Ullathorne, gave no such impression of fragility; on the contrary she appeared, and indeed she was, exceedingly robust and just about as fragile as well-seasoned teak. Her eyebrows which were thick as doormats were jet-black and her hair, which she wore severely parted in the middle and swept smoothly down over each cheek, was only streaked with grey. She never appeared abroad save in the prescribed Victorian uniform for old ladies—black bonnet enriched with violets, a black jet-trimmed shoulder cape and very tight black kid gloves—which was becoming increasingly rare even at that date and now only survives among pantomime dames. Her features were strong and masculine and bore a close resemblance to those of Sir Robert Walpole as revealed in Van Loos' portrait, and she retained a marked Norfolk accent. Tolerant and composed, she radiated an air of genial and robust common sense, which none of the rest of the family displayed, anyhow in so marked a degree; and alone of all the Lancasters she professed a keen interest in food and was reputed to be the finest hand with a dumpling between King's Lynn and Norwich. In addition she was never at any pains to conceal an earthy relish for scandal which, linked to a prodigious memory, made her a far more entertaining, and quite possibly a more accurate, authority on the genealogies of most Norfolk families than Burke.

Despite her outward Victorianism, Great Aunt Martha nevertheless always gave a strong but indefinable impression of belonging to a still earlier era. This must, I think, have arisen largely from her gestures, for gestures remain the surest and least easily eradicable of all period hall-marks. Tricks and turns of speech are good guides but are generally indetectable when combined with a strong regional accent; clothes and hair styles may be deliberately and consciously adopted for their period value; but gestures are easy neither unconsciously to lose nor deliberately to acquire. One has only to compare the most accurate reconstruction of a 'twenties scene in a modern revue with a thirty-year-old film to appreciate this truth; no matter how skilfully the accents and fashions of the epoch may have been recaptured on the stage the film will always reveal a dozen little gestures—a peculiar fluttering of the hand or some trick of standing—which at the time were so natural as to be completely unnoticeable, and of which even the most knowledgeable spectator with an adult memory of the period and the keenest eye for detail will have remained completely unaware and may even, on seeing them again after a lapse of thirty years, fail to realise are the very hallmarks of that genuineness of which he is nevertheless completely convinced.

The particular gesture of Aunt Martha's which I found so revealing and which, had I not seen her so frequently employ it, I should have come to consider a stereotyped illustrator's convention, no more having an origin in nature than the Fascist salute or the sudden heart-clutching of an Italian tenor, was that with which she invariably registered surprise. This was an emotion constantly evoked in her by the unexpected brilliance (as she thought it) of her great-nephews and nieces or the extraordinary things of which the newspapers were nowadays so full. Maintaining her usual upright but placid attitude when seated, she would suddenly elevate her eyebrows to a remarkable height and in perfect unison raise her hands, which had been lying quietly in her lap, smartly at right angles to her wrists with palms outwards, at the same time, but more slowly, lifting her forearms until the tips of her outspread fingers were level with her shoulders, in a manner that was perfectly familiar to me from the illustrations of Cruickshank.

Such visits as those of Aunt Martha were, however, few and far between, and the rhythm of our daily life, monotonous as it would seem to a modern child, was but seldom interrupted by these intrusions from the outside world. Thus the drawing-room saw me chiefly in its familiar everyday dress, very different from the unnatural spruceness and formality it assumed on social occasions, and so it remains in my memory. Summoned down for my daily visit I would take my accustomed place beside my mother for the evening reading. My enjoyment at this performance depended in a very large measure on the choice of the book, which was governed partly by the day and partly by my mother's mood.

On Sundays and holy days, or on occasions when some recent display of temper or disobedience on my part was thought to have merited implied reproof, the volume chosen was a ghastly selection of pious fables, illustrated in that wood-engraved style I so much abominated. What particularly infuriated me about the author, and still infuriates me, was not so much his unctuous style, nor even the pious nature of the themes, but his abominable deceit. The hero, some gallant knight, would don his armour, leap on his trusty steed and go galloping off in pursuit of dragons in the most approved style, and then, just as my interest was getting aroused, it was revealed that the armour, on the exact style and manufacture of which I had been excitedly speculating, was the armour of Righteousness, the steed one learnt answered to the name of Perseverance, and the dragons against which the hero was off to do battle were called Self-Love, Indolence and Bad Temper. Thus one cold puff of piety instantly and irrevocably shattered the warm colourful world of romance and fantasy which had been building up in my imagination and my rage, though concealed, was boundless. But it was years before the sight of that thick little royal blue volume, so guileless and optimistic is the infant mind, warned me to expect the worst.

But in the course of time my so evident lack of response led to the gradual abandonment of this depressing volume, and the occasions on which I was firmly removed from the study of some illustrated volume of my own choice to listen to the far from hair-raising adventures of some smug paladin of evangelical piety became fewer and fewer. And in the picture which I chiefly retain of these early evenings of my childhood it plays no part.

The firelight is gleaming and flashing from the polished brass of the heavily defended hearth; on one side sits my father, freshly returned from the city, reading one of the pastel-coloured evening papers of the time; on the other my mother, studying with well-founded distrust the double-page spread of the interior of the newly-launched 'Titanic' in the *Illustrated London News*. The pleasantly depressing strains of 'The Count of Luxembourg', rendered of course by the Earl of Lonsdale's private band, faintly echo amidst the shiny chintz and gold-mounted watercolours, speaking of a far distant world of dashing Hussars and tight-waisted beauties in long white gloves with aigrettes in their golden hair, for ever dancing up and down some baroque staircase of exceptional length. While in the middle, flat on his stomach, lies a small boy of engaging appearance poring over an enormous green volume, the faintly dusty smell of the fur hearthrug heavy in his nostrils, perfectly happy counting the medals stretched across the manly chest of the Hereditary Prince of Hohenzollern Sigmaringen.

2. "Has anyone seen a German Band?"

FOR SHEER pleasure few methods of progression, one comes gradually to realise, can compare with the perambulator. The motion is agreeable, the range of vision extensive and one has always before one's eyes the rewarding spectacle of a grown-up maintaining prolonged physical exertion. Moreover, the sensation of pasha-like power which all this induces is not illusory for, by the simple device of repeatedly jettisoning a teddy-bear or a rattle, any display of independence on the part of the mahout can successfully be countered, and should she, maddened beyond endurance, be provoked to reprisals a piteous howling will soon attract the friendly interest of sympathetic passers-by and expose her to public, if unjustified, rebuke. The gondola alone, I think, can compare with the pram for pleasure, but only on those occasions when one is certain that someone else will charge themselves with the nerve-racking financial dispute which will inevitably mark the journey's end.

In the far-off days before the first German war, travelling by pram in London was even more enjoyable than it is today: for on the few occasions that I accompanied my own children on their outings (though never being so foolish as to provide the motive power) I was much struck by the decline of street-life in the very districts which in my own childhood had been so packed with colour and incident. First, there was then an infinitely greater variety of traffic: classical milk-chariots driven by straw-hatted Ben-hurs (so much more exciting than the dreary little waggonettes of the present-day dairy combines), the even more dashing butcher's vans with the striped-aproned driver perched way aloft, the little painted donkey-carts of the costers who still wore their earrings and their high-waisted pearl-decorated jackets without the slight air of embarrassment natural to those making a hospital collection, emphasised and threw into strong relief the novelty of the occasional motor-vans. Secondly, the number of the street-traders and itinerant musicians had not yet been reduced to identical ranks of nylon-selling spivs and an occasional ex-service-men's band. There were innumerable Italian organ-grinders, male and female complete with monkey, and in those days Italians looked like Italians, all flashing teeth and curled moustaches—figures from *Cavalleria Rusticana*—not the slick dummies of the Coca-Cola lads of modern Italy: the Punch and Judy show was still a robust and common entertainment, not just a carefully pre-served survival of British folk-drama, and that high, ghastly cry, which familiarity never wholly robbed of its menace, was liable suddenly to startle at any street-corner: while the musical per-formers ranged all the way from the immensely dignified old lady who sang 'Just a Song at Twilight' to a harp accompaniment to the virtuoso who played the 'Light Cavalry Overture' on the musical glasses. Any knot of people at the kerb-side held a promise of entertainment, and the exact feel of the old forgotten excite-ment, so intimately bound up with memories of Kensington, returned to me once more when, many years later, a small crowd in the market-place of Argos parted to reveal a spectacle which until that moment I had never consciously remembered having seen before—a performing bear.

Even today Notting Hill Gate retains something of its original village atmosphere. Tucked away behind the intruding shopfronts, which in Victorian times encroached further and further on to the old Oxford road, eighteenth-century façades occasionally betray their presence by a cornice or a moulding projecting unexpectedly above the level of the black glass and chromium plate, recalling the district as a self-contained village.

In my pram-travelling days the old importance of the junction of the main road out of London to the West and the lane by the sandpits leading to Kensington had been recently reinforced by the opening of the Central London Tube immediately opposite the old Inner Circle station, but the resulting bustle and *va-et-vient* had still a local, almost provincial flavour, quite different to the anonymous big-city congestion of today. A crowd of prams, many of whose occupants were known to me personally, would at this hour be making the crossing towards the Gardens; other children's mothers or cooks would be emerging from the green-grocers or the lending-library; and a number of kindly old Colonels or cooing maiden-ladies would stop to make the usual jocular remark or to praise my exceptional beauty in terms that were none the less gratifying for being familiar.

But to these routine encounters had recently been added the possibility of far more exceptional and dramatic excitements. The women of Britain were on the march, and a crowd round the Post Office was a sure sign that they had recently demonstrated their political competence by heaving a brick through the window or pouring acid into the pillar-box. It never, unfortunately, fell to my lot to see a Suffragette but I was vividly aware of their existence. A close study of the press cartoons had taught me exactly what to look for and I habitually scanned every stretch of public railings hoping desperately for the sight of some grim-visaged, spectacled, hammer-waving Andromeda self-enchained. My light-hearted attitude to this vital question rather distressed my mother, a keen Shavian who at one time had moved in the progressive-minded circles centred on the Cobden Sanderson house in Chiswick Mall, but received every encouragement from Kate whose views accurately reflected the prevailing music-hall opinion and for whom Mrs. Pankhurst was as inexhaustible a source of amusement as were, at other times, such diverse public figures as Pussyfoot Johnson and Sydney Stanley.

Although invariably doomed in the matter of Suffragette outrages to arrive after the action was over, I was more fortunate in respect to street accidents—in those days more varied and less lethal. For some reason these seemed always to be concentrated in that stretch of the Bayswater Road between Notting Hill Gate and Queen's Road, and here I was, at various times, privileged to witness the collapse of a carthorse (and to retain for years to come the memory of the astonishingly light pink colour of the blood frothing from its mouth and nostrils, and the surprising number of passers-by eager and willing to sit traditionally on the poor animal's head), a white 'Arrow' omnibus bursting into flames, and to hear a deafening report which announced the head-on collision of two fast De Dion Boutons outside the chemist's. But best of all I enjoyed the sight, which remains vivid to this day, of a fashionable lady in a very tight hobble skirt of vivid purple falling flat on her face while running for an omnibus, a mishap provoking peals of happy, childish laughter all the way to the Round Pond.

Once past the old lady selling balloons—so much more disagreeable untransformed by the whimsical imagination of Sir James Barrie—and actually inside the Gardens which were the goal of our outing, my exultation was customarily transposed into a minor key. I was not as a child much attracted by the beauties of nature and keenly regretted the shops and street accidents thus temporarily abandoned, for which the expected encounters with little friends (governed as they were by the number of nannies with whom my own was at any particular moment on speaking terms) provided inadequate compensation. True, there was the Dutch Garden where nature was kept under proper control and the pleached limes formed tunnels of delight, and the Round Pond with its complement of miniature shipping, but here I was constantly disappointed by the lack of variety and was only buoyed up by the hope, seldom realised, of seeing a junk or a galleon, or even a three-masted schooner, anything in fact other than the inevitable yachts which varied only in size. But chiefly was my rather jaundiced view of the Gardens coloured by the knowledge that sooner or later I should be forced to get out and walk, a development for which I could see no adequate justification, as even such an exceptional spectacle as workmen hanging fairy-lamps on the trees in celebration of the Coronation could be viewed just as well and in far greater comfort from the pram.

Our return route from the Gardens usually lay down the Queen's Road and Westbourne Grove, thoroughfares dominated and given character by the presence of Messrs. William Whiteley's emporium, an establishment which bulked very large in our family life. It is difficult nowadays to realise how very personal was then the relationship, even in London, between shop-keeper and customer and the enormous importance, comparable almost to that attained by rival churches, which late Victorian and Edwardian ladies attached to certain stores. All my female relatives had their own favourites, where some of them had been honoured customers for more than half a century and their arrival was greeted by frenzied bowing on the part of the frock-coated shopwalkers, and where certain of the older assistants stood to them almost in the relationship of confessors, receiving endless confidences on the state of their health, the behaviour of their pets and the general iniquity of the Liberal Government. Thus for my Great Aunt Bessie the Army and Navy Stores fulfilled all the functions of her husband's club and her undeviating loyalty was repaid by a respect and consideration which bore little or no relation to the size of her account. My mother's affections were chiefly centred on Harvey Nichols which her family had patronised for many years and which had been finally sanctified by her grandmother having met her death, at the age of ninety, at the wheels of a careless cyclist on leaving that establishment one summer morning in the last year of the old Queen's reign. However, although Harvey Nichols ever retained the first place in my mother's estimation, Knightsbridge was some way off and Queen's Road close at hand, so that Whiteley's had come to play the more important rôle. It was, moreover, already distinguished by being the favourite shop of her aged Cousin Jenny who lived hard by in Inverness Terrace.

*   *   *   *   *

In a period still very rich in vintage old ladies Cousin Jenny was remarkable not so much for any individual quality (although by no means lacking in character) as for her completeness, as of some antique pot which was not, perhaps, at the time of its manufacture an outstanding masterpiece but which has been raised by the correctness of its silhouette, the fine preservation of its glaze and the perfection of its patina to the status of the supreme example of its type, providing the standard by which all other finds are graded. The only daughter of an enterprising Scotsman Douglas Lepraik, who had made a large fortune by introducing steam navigation on the Yangtse-Kiang, she had been destined for an important marriage. Unfortunately while still a girl in a finishing school in Brussels she had contracted small-pox of which the ravages had been so severe as to outweigh in the eyes of hoped-for aristocratic suitors the attraction of a handsome dot. She had eventually married, late in life by the standards of the period, one of her father's sea-captains who had quite recently died after many years of blissfully happy union; since when she had adopted a way of life as rigidly limited, but within its narrow confines as intense, as that of Proust's Tante Eulalie.

The house in Inverness Terrace, which provided so perfect a setting for the endlessly repeated cycle of Cousin Jenny's daily life, had been presented to her completely furnished by her father as a present on her wedding in the late 'seventies or early 'eighties and not the smallest alteration nor addition had since been made. There in the big bow window of the drawing-room, which commanded a good, clear view of the street in both directions, discreetly veiled by Nottingham lace curtains, she passed most of her waking life, protected from all possibility of draught by thick velvet *portières* and from interruption or assault by an immensely fat and disagreeable fox-terrier. Her principal occupation was the careful study of the *Morning Post* and this took a far greater time,

even given the much larger newspapers of those days, than one would have imagined. Not only did she read every word, including the stock prices (for she had inherited something of her father's shrewd Scots business sense), in itself a formidable task, but was forced to do so with only half an eye or in short snatches in order that no important development in the life of Inverness Terrace, such as the visit of the doctor to Number 8 or the progress of the promising romance between the parlour-maid at Number 11 and the new baker's roundsman, should escape her notice. Thus she was seldom more than half-way through her task when it was time for her only excursion, her daily visit to Whiteley's.

No abbess ever identified herself so closely with the life of her convent, nor any archaeologist with his 'dig', as did Cousin Jenny with that of Whiteley's Universal Stores. She had watched it grow from a small oil and paint shop to Sir Aston Webb's Renaissance Palazzo covering several acres; and while she would stoutly maintain in conversation with Great Aunt Bessie its manifest superiority to the Army and Navy Stores she had nevertheless invariably deplored all innovation and expansion and had foreseen nothing but future disaster arising from each successive change, from the abandonment of oil-lamps in favour of gas to the introduction of the soda-fountain. No incident was too trivial to hold her attention and the appearance of a new cashier in the hardware or a change in the colour of the parcel tape were immediately noted and gave rise to fears for the firm's stability hardly less grave than those aroused by the assassination of its original founder at the hands of an illegitimate son in the sweet department, an incident of which it was alleged she had been an eyewitness.

Cousin Jenny's daily outing invariably took place in the morning, so that by tea-time when visits from her family usually occurred she had been able to put in another two hours with the *Morning Post* and was completely master of what was for her the most important section, the Court Page. She was thus fully equipped to take the lead in the conversation, which could be sustained almost indefinitely, that was certain to arise whenever two or three of the older generation of my female relations were gathered together, about the doings, personalities and relationships of the Royal Family.

Was it not strange that the Queen of Spain had not come over to Kensington Palace this year, and did not that perhaps indicate that there would soon be another little grandchild for dear Princess Beatrice? How curious that one heard so little of Prince Albert of Schleswig-Holstein these days! Perhaps it was true that Queen Alexandra couldn't bear the sight of him and that was why he never went to Sandringham. Of course, one had always heard that his father had drunk like a fish and that sort of thing so often runs in families! Well, they would soon have to be looking round for a bride for the Prince of Wales, in a year or two's time he would be quite grown up. Of course there were always those Swedish princesses and one had heard talk of one of the Queen of Greece's girls. Anyhow one did hope that it would not be another of those Germans, always so plain and far too many of them in the family already!

In this style of *causerie* my aged cousin was an acknowledged virtuoso, sharply correcting any slip in the calculation of exact degrees of consanguinity, such as confusing a first cousin once removed with a second cousin, and displaying an astounding memory for the correct dates of births, marriages and accessions. Indeed for her one of the gravest inconveniences caused by the War when it came, worse than the rationing or the Zeppelin raids, was the difficulty it imposed in keeping fully posted on the activities of all Queen Victoria's German descendants. Although she lived on for many years, dying at a very advanced age in the early 'twenties, nothing in her way of life was ever changed (fortunately she did not live to see the disappearance of the *Morning Post*), and her strong personality remained unmodified to the end—or maybe even beyond, for it was at her funeral that for the only time in my life I came within measurable distance of what could be possibly described as a psychic phenomenon.

One of the ways in which Cousin Jenny's staunch unyielding conservatism had most strikingly expressed itself during her lifetime was in her firm refusal ever to contemplate the shortest journey in a horseless carriage and her continued use of a hired brougham for the regular visits to her banker and solicitor, the sole occasions on which she moved more than a stone's throw from the Queen's Road. Most inconsiderately those in charge of the *pompes funèbres* had ignored this idiosyncrasy and arranged for her to make her last journey in a motor-hearse. However, on the way to Kensal Rise this machine, a glittering and apparently perfectly functioning Rolls-Royce, broke down no less than three times and on the final occasion so completely that a substitute had hastily to be summoned by telephone. No sooner had Cousin Jenny been transferred to the new vehicle than this, too, began to develop engine-trouble, coming at last to a complete halt in the very gates of the cemetery, so that after further fruitless tinkering, the mutes were forced to shoulder the coffin for the good quarter of a mile to the mortuary chapel. After the service was over the by this time nearly hysterical mourners emerged to find the hearse once more standing ready, for from the moment it was relieved of its burden, the engine had responded perfectly. There still remained, however, the final lap to the grave itself at the furthest end of the cemetery and, with what I judged to be an ill-conceived determination, the undertakers once more transferred Cousin Jenny's mortal remains to the horseless carriage. Once more we all climbed into the attendant cars, once more the chauffeur swung the starting handle, once more there was absolutely no response. At last, the protesting mutes admitted defeat, and triumphantly reactionary, even in death, my aged cousin was borne to her final resting-place by man-power alone.

*   *   *   *   *

Once past William Whiteley's the homeward way lost much of its interest, for Westbourne Grove, although curiously enough still at that date quite a fashionable shopping street, had little enough in it at all times of the year, save one, to hold my attention and in retrospect is only remarkable for being the place where I saw my last horse-bus. The reason which formed the exception was the week or so immediately preceding Christmas when both kerb-sides were thick with toy-vendors selling the most extraordinary variety of novelties and play-things now only to be seen in the London Museum. Miniature 'knuts', who by the manipulation of a string could be made to bow and raise their top-hats revealing a great shock of golliwog hair; squads of wooden guardsmen that formed fours or line in obedience to the pressure exerted on the green painted trellis on which they were marshalled; toy goldfish swimming in what were apparently flashing globes of water but were in

reality simple loops of tin set spinning on a swivel: and, perhaps most remarkable of all, tiny Bibles the size of one's thumb-nail. "Li'l 'Oly Boible! Li'l 'Oly Boible! 'Orl the Good Book for tuppence!"

Although on week-days our return journey from the park had, save at Christmas time, a certain melancholy and sense of flatness, on Sundays the excitement was maintained to the very end. Our progress was then so timed as to bring us opposite St. John's, Notting Hill, at the hour at which my parents, along with the rest of the congregation, would emerge. For the present generation it is almost impossible to imagine how impressive a spectacle was the weekly Church Parade outside any one of a dozen or more London churches at the close of Morning Prayer on any fine Sunday in the early years of the century. At the moment of our arrival the street would be deserted save for one or two victorias and broughams at the church gates (never very many for, although the congregation contained a high proportion of 'carriage-folk', St. John's was rather Low and it was not thought right for any except the frail and aged to work their coachmen on the Sabbath), and the soft strains of Dykes would come floating out among the plane trees of Ladbroke Hill as the verger opened the doors at the final verse of the closing hymn. Then a short pause, a rustling murmur as the congregation rose from its knees gathering up prayer books and feather-boas and adjusting veils and gloves, and the first worshippers would emerge blinking a little in the bright sun pursued by the rolling chords of the voluntary. Soon the whole churchyard and street was a mass of elaborate, pale-shaded millinery, great cart-wheels à la Lily Elsie decorated with monstrous roses and doves in flight, old-fashioned bonnets trimmed with parma-violets, among which the glittering top-hats, ceaselessly doffed and replaced, provided the sharper, more definite accents.

Owing to the fact of my father, who was a churchwarden, being usually a little delayed by financial transactions in the vestry, I had ample opportunity to study and recognise the principal notables of our little world before my parents finally appeared. There was Sir Aston Webb, not yet president of the Royal Academy, cross-eyed and severe, resting on the seventh day from the labours of creating a new Buckingham Palace in the current Potsdam style; there was old Dr. Waldo, side-whiskered and benign, whose daughters I played with but the exact nature of whose functions as Chief Coroner for London no one would ever explain to me, albeit that the importance of this position was held to reflect great credit on the local community; there was Professor Perry who with his long hair, glasses and thick walrus moustache was the very type of the stage scientist, whose researches in electro-physics were nevertheless to bear abundant fruit in the coming war; and, at long last, there came my father.

The family reunion did not, however, by any means mark the end of the proceedings. Friends had to be greeted, enquiries made as to the progress of Old Mrs. So-and-So's cold, and views exchanged about the sermon. This last duty was more than purely nominal for at St. John's sermons were taken seriously and the congregation included many *cognoscenti* of fine preaching. The Vicar in my earliest childhood was a certain Canon, of whom only a vision of an angry red face remains to me as the children's service was invariably left to the Curate. Originally a fine preacher he had come of recent years increasingly to deviate from the path of strict orthodoxy, which had caused considerable dissension among his flock, so that his departure, which took place in circumstances sufficiently remarkable, was neither wholly unforeseen nor altogether regretted. In the course of one of his most rousing sermons, fortunately at Evensong, he announced that it had recently been revealed to him in a dream that there were no women in Heaven, the female part of mankind having finally been judged incapable of salvation. While those of his hearers who were acquainted with the Canon's wife could quite appreciate the obvious satisfaction with which the Vicar promulgated this new dogma, few among a congregation that was largely female could be expected to share it, and complaints to the Bishop led to the Canon's sudden retirement for a long rest in the country from which, in fact, he never returned.

In due course his place was taken by Canon Dudden, whose great reputation as a preacher and magnificent presence (he was, I think, at this time one of the most strikingly handsome men I ever remember seeing) made the appointment a very popular one with the congregation of St. John's. Whether it was equally gratifying to the Canon may be doubted, though this was not to be guessed at the time, for many years later when he once more, albeit distantly, entered my life as Vice-Chancellor of Oxford he was reported to be in the habit, when looking back on his career, of referring somewhat bitterly to "years of penance in the draughty parish-halls of North Kensington".

On most Sundays, if my behaviour had been thought to warrant a treat, I now quitted my pram and accompanied my parents and the other churchwarden, old Colonel Hook, to the latter's house in the next street to ours for a pre-luncheon visit. Arrived, exhausted from the effort to keep up with the long strides of my companions, I would be plied with sweets and lemonade while they refreshed themselves with a whisky-and-soda. I would then be taken by the Colonel into his study where he would bring out for my benefit a series of military trophies culminating in his full-dress cocked hat which, if I were fortunate, I should be allowed to my immense satisfaction to try on.

Of all the extraordinary interiors of my childhood, of which the atmosphere has been rendered by subsequent events remote from all modern experience, the most difficult to convey to any reader under forty-five was Colonel Hook's study. The faded sepia ranks of brother-officers, moustachioed, whiskered, bearded, staring straight ahead from under the peaks of monstrously high topees or jaunty little pill-boxes, their gloved hands clasped on chased sword-hilts, the water-colour sketches of forgotten cantonments with long rows of bell-tents and skeletal pyramids of stacked rifles, the yellowing maps with little coloured oblongs marking the spot where the Company made their last stand and the route taken by the relieving column indicated by a straggling procession of beetle-like arrows, the knobkerries, the assegais, the Pathan knives—all spoke of a way of military life as far removed from that with which we are familiar as that of the Roman legions. For Colonel Hook belonged entirely to the world of Lady Butler and Sir Henry Newbolt, of thin red lines and broken squares, of stockades and fuzzy-wuzzies, and displayed all its very real virtues in the highest degree. Although a little bent by the years his figure, in the short-tailed old-fashioned cut-away he usually wore, remained unmistakably military; his Roman nose, thick brows and long walrus moustache combined with the high white collar to make him the very image of the fictional colonel. However, of the traditional failings of the type he was completely free, being extremely gentle in manner and the reverse of peppery so that it was quite as impossible to picture him ever losing his temper as it was to imagine that he could under any circumstances break his word. His whole life had centred round a single-minded devotion to his regiment and he could not conceive it possible that any man could ask for a more rewarding career than the army.

Even as he had lived it Colonel Hook's life, and that of all those whiskered captains, had been, one can now see, anachronistic. It was, at this date, some fifty years since General Sherman had ravaged Georgia (the full significance of which event seems at the time to have escaped the notice of almost everyone save Napoleon III), and yet here we all were, grown-ups just as vividly as little boys, on the very eve of disaster, still envisaging war in terms of bugle-calls and charging lancers. So ridiculous does this now seem to us that we tend in retrospect to dismiss all these little colonial wars as playing at soldiers and denigrate by implication the heroism and courage of Colonel Hook and his like. What they had been spared was the realisation which only came gradually even after 1914, of the immense gravity attaching to the outcome of the fight, the large-scale anxiety transcending the personal which must lie at the back of any modern mind, however much it may be deliberately or unconsciously suppressed in action. If the relieving column did not arrive, or the ammunition run out so much the worse for the regiment; it was unthinkable, so accustomed to victory was that generation, that the ultimate outcome of the campaign would be affected. And even if by some extraordinary and terrible turn of events, or an act of betrayal on the part of Liberal politicians, the war itself should be lost, no threat to the British way of life would result; a whole battalion might be wiped out, national prestige sadly dimmed, but not a penny more would go on the income-tax, the Derby would still be run, and silk hats and frock-coats would still be worn at church parade.

*　　*　　*　　*　　*

When the storm finally broke which blew Colonel Hook and all his paladins way down the corridor of history, I was at the seaside. Each summer at the beginning of August I was sent with my nurse to an admirable boarding-house kept by an old governess of my father's at Littlehampton, where in due course I would be joined by my parents. The unbutlined Littlehampton of those days represented the English seaside at its best. Separated from the sea by a wide expanse of green, rows of bow-fronted Regency villas looked across the channel; on the sands pierrots, nigger minstrels, and on Sundays Evangelical Missioners, provided simple entertainment for those who had temporarily exhausted the delights of digging, paddling and donkey rides; there was even a charming little harbour with shipyards on the Arun which ran into the sea alongside a severely-functional jetty raised by the presence of two slot-machines and some wooden benches to the dignity of a 'Pier' in the local esteem. So over-exciting did the atmosphere here normally prove—the heady smell of low-tide in the harbour, the salty taste on the back of one's hands, the feel of the firm sand under bare feet—that even had our arrival not preceded my birthday on the 4th by so short a space, I should have had little attention to spare for current events. It did, however, strike me as I waited at the station on the morning of the third for my mother, that the crowd meeting the London train was, perhaps, larger and more restless than usual; that the paper-sellers alongside large posters depicting figures wearing what appeared to be rather high bowlers decorated with cocks-plumes above the legend in purple type 'Gallant Little Belgium', were doing a brisker trade than usual. But as I had no idea as to who on earth the Belgians were I not unnaturally attributed the increased public excitement to a general awareness that tomorrow was my birthday. I did notice, however, that my mother when she arrived seemed more preoccupied than usual and answered my nurse's enquiries in that irritatingly swift low-pitched tone reserved by grown-ups for the discussion of matters declared to be 'above my head'. As a result I was instantly seized by a ghastly fear that my birthday present had been forgotten or mislaid.

Very early the next morning my fears proved groundless and the excitement produced by opening parcels, trying out a new pistol and aligning rows of topeed riflemen (the very spit and image of those commanded by Colonel Hook) in the correct formation for receiving the charge of an equal number of naked Zulus emerging from a grove of tastefully displayed tin palm-trees, lasted sufficiently long to prevent my remarking any untoward seriousness in the dining-room at breakfast. Moreover, my father had come down late the night before and the prospect of his company for a whole long morning on the sands was quite sufficient to engage my whole attention.

And yet the beach when we got there did seem subtly different. The number of long-legged little girls in floppy *broderie anglaise* sun-hats (the exact look of whom against the sea and sand has been so perfectly recorded for all time in the very early paintings of Wilson Steer) was not visibly reduced, most of my accustomed playmates and their nannies were there, and only the grown-ups and casual strollers seemed fewer than usual. In what then did this sense of the unusual lie? At last I discovered what was wrong; my favourite among all the beach entertainers—a small brass-band composed of rather plump elderly gentlemen with long hair and thick glasses clad rather improbably in tight-braided hussar uniforms, who would normally at this hour be giving a spirited rendering of a selection from *Tannhauser* two breakwaters away from our hut—were nowhere to be seen. After fruitless searching up and down the length of the beach, in which I accounted for the presence of the ice-cream seller, the pierrots, the donkey boy, I finally put the problem to my father who was lying flat on his back on the shingle with his panama tilted over his eyes. The only reply I got was the whistled refrain of a familiar popular tune—

"Has anyone seen a *Ger*man band,
"*Ger*man band,
"*Ger*man band,
"I've looked everywhere both *near* and far,
"*Near* and far,
"*Ja*, Ja, Ja,
"But I miss my Fritz
"What plays twiddley-bits
"On the big trombone."

3. "My little grey home in the West"

FROM THE TOP of the omnibus the cloudless sky over-arching the parallel uniformities of Redcliffe Gardens seemed both bluer and more immediate than from street-level. It was, indeed, one of the many advantages of the old open-deckers that on them one enjoyed a sense of spaciousness, an awareness of immensity, that has almost vanished from our modern urban life approximating ever more closely to the central-heated ideal of inter-communicating *machines-à-habiter*. As a child I was always, therefore, exceptionally conscious of the heavens above when riding on omnibuses, but on this particular Sunday afternoon my attention had been concentrated and rendered more intense by the fact that my fellow-passengers, as well as the passers-by on the flanking pavements, were one and all steadfastly scanning the brilliant strip of light South Kensington azure immediately above their heads. What I expected to see, I have no idea; a flight of wild swans, perhaps, or a belated competitor in the Gordon-Bennett balloon race. For what at length, my wondering gaze excitedly directed by my father, I saw, I could hardly have been more unprepared.

No one, who was so keen a reader of the *Illustrated London News* as I was, could possibly have remained ignorant of the existence of heavier-than-air craft, even if, unlike me, they had not been collectors of cigarette-cards, or been taken on so many fruitless expeditions to Wormwood Scrubs on the chance of seeing Mr. Graham White and his new flying-machine; nevertheless, the sudden spectacle of the fantastic, open-work reality elegantly suspended no great distance above the romantic towers of Mr. Waterhouse's museum, the sun gleaming through the oiled silk of the wings, a pair of bicycle wheels clearly visible beneath, afforded me one of the most powerful visual sensations of my whole childhood. That the passage immediately above our heads of a daring aeronaut should have thrown me, at the age I was in 1913, into a state of almost uncontrollable excitement was hardly surprising: that my father, who had frequently seen such sights before, should have been almost equally affected, and to a far greater degree than any other of our fellow-passengers, was less to be expected. The reason, which was revealed by the information he almost immediately imparted, was not at the time apparent to me. The aeroplane, he explained, was a 'Taube', which meant in German 'a dove', and was so called from the peculiar shape of the wings. My father, whose knowledge of Germany was first-hand and extensive, must in fact have been asking himself the question which was to vex so many leader-writers in the next few days. What was a German military flying-machine doing over London at so remarkably low a level on a brilliant Sunday afternoon in the summer of 1913?

Even when not rendered memorable by the incidence of the first swallow of the Luftwaffe, my regular expeditions to visit my grand-father on Putney Hill were always enjoyable, anyhow in part. For one thing I was frequently accompanied by my father, of whom I saw little during the week, and in whose company I delighted; for another, they always involved a ride on a bus. This latter circumstance was less welcome to my father than to me, for he had inherited to the full the Lancaster passion for healthy exercise, which unaccountably did not, in my case, survive a further generation, and he was usually accustomed on these occasions to walk the whole distance from Kensington to Putney and back. This was manifestly impossible when I was of the party, and so the greater part of the distance was then covered by omnibus. For only when some member of the family was recovering from illness, or the weather quite exceptionally inclement, did my grandfather consent to send either a carriage or the motor-car. This omission, which in no way sprang from any meanness of character, was in part due to the fact that our visits usually took place on a Sunday, and in my grandfather's house the Biblical injunctions on the Sabbath employment of men-servants and maid-servants still retained much of their force, and due even more, I fancy, to a fear which never left a true Lancaster lest any such trouble-saving gesture would encourage a 'softening' process against which he must always be on guard, both in himself and others. Indeed, the omnibus itself was considered an indulgence but partly justified by my short legs and tender years, and was only tolerated on the understanding that I was to get out at Putney station and walk up the hill.

This to me intolerably long ascent was seldom, when accom-panied by Lancaster relations other than my father, accomplished without frequent bickering and occasional tears, for my constant complaints of exhaustion were not only invariably disregarded but often provoked speculations which seemed to me uncalled for and irrelevant. What, I was asked, would I do were I in the army? Or how should I get on in the company of Captain Scott? In vain did I pant out that I had no intention of going into the army (in those halcyon days such assurance on the part of small boys was not seemingly unduly optimistic), still less of taking part in any expeditions to the Antarctic: all such protests were brushed aside as purely superficial and in no way affecting the principle at stake. Today, however, my father was with me and all was well, for not only did his conversation successfully dispel the boredom which this particular thoroughfare normally produced, but even had I felt tired I should in his company have made every effort to conceal the fact.

At that date my chief complaint against Putney Hill was the total absence of shops, for the fascinating vagaries of Victorian domestic architecture did not have for me the charm and interest which later they came to exercise, and its immense residential dullness was only occasionally relieved by a steam omnibus bursting into flames on approaching the summit, or the spectacle of my Uncle Jack with a coach-top full of my cousins driving his four-in-hand back to Wimbledon. Even the possibility of being kissed by Mr. Swinburne on his daily round from No. 2 The Pines to *The Green Man* on the heath had recently been removed by the great poet's death.

(Nevertheless I have always claimed, and shall continue to do so, that this honour was vouchsafed me at an age so tender as to be beyond the reach of memory, on the perfectly reasonable grounds that it is *just* chronologically possible, and, seeing that he kissed almost every small child he passed, including all my cousins who were noticeably less attractive than I was, it is highly unlikely that I should have been missed out when so frequently in the neighbourhood.)

Normally by the time we had reached the top all the petty diversions—such as counting the number of houses with names as opposed to those with numbers, or deliberately treading on dog's-mess in order to provoke my nurse or my aunt, or scuffling my new white shoes in the dead leaves in the gutter—had long since been exhausted, and the vision of my grandfather's house was greeted by me with an enthusiasm considerably greater than either its intrinsic beauty or the social delights there awaiting me would seem to have justified.

'South Lynn', as it was called, was a large four-square Victorian mansion in yellow brick set well back from the road behind a semi-circular drive encompassing a circle of superlatively well-kept lawn adorned with a flag-pole. To the right as one approached was a stable-yard with a glazed roof which was rendered chiefly remarkable for me by the branch of a tree which Mundy, the

coachman, there preserved, nailed alongside the garage door, from the appearance of which he was able to forecast the weather with remarkable accuracy. In the centre of the façade was an imposing front door approached by a flight of white marble steps of so lethal a slipperiness that they were each separately furnished with a little rubber mat, and flanked by a pair of stained glass damsels clutching sunflowers and dressed in the Burne-Jones taste, through which, having swung expectantly on the wrought-iron bell-pull, I was accustomed to peer in order to catch the first fuzzy glimpse of the approaching parlourmaid's white cap and apron.

On entering the hall the thing of which I was always immediately conscious, as in any house other than our own, was the smell. Is smell the first of the senses to atrophy, or have the rich individual smells of forty years ago fallen victim, along with so much else, to the hygienic standardisation of the age? Certainly the houses and places of my childhood seem in retrospect to have been far more richly endowed in this respect than they are today. Even the mingled flavour of 'caporals', garlic and cheap Belgian coal, which was formerly far more evocative of Paris than the sight of the Arc-de-Triomphe or even the sound of taxi horns in the night, seemed on my last visit far fainter than formerly, while no nostrils under thirty-five could now possibly recognise, in the unlikely event of their ever encountering it, that extraordinary mixture of hot tar, horse-dung and lime trees which to me in my childhood spelt London in the early summer.

The peculiar smell of South Lynn, now unrecallable but instantly to be detected—a subtle mingling of Havana cigars and Knight's Castile soap—although general in all the houses of my Lancaster relatives, was as different as possible from that prevailing in my other grandfather's house, and instantly set in motion a whole related train of ideas and reactions, so that had it ever happened by some supernatural fluke that the smells of the one house should have greeted me on entering the other, I should have been as hopelessly at sea as one of Professor Pavlov's dogs for whom the wrong bell has tolled.

Quite apart from its smell, the hall was remarkable enough and in the highest degree characteristic of my grandfather and his way of life. Immediately facing one on entering, a broad flight of stairs rose to the darkness of a half-landing; balustered in polished oak they ended in a newel post surmounted by a carved figure in vaguely mediaeval costume holding aloft an electric *flambeau* with the red rose of Lancaster blazoned in colour on his surcoat. The walls between massively architectural oak doors leading to other rooms were adorned by a series of portraits of ladies and gentlemen in the wigs and stomachers of Queen Anne's day, reputedly ancestral, in whose features the more credulous of my relations, such as my mother, were constantly detecting striking resemblances to existing aunts and uncles, but whose connection with the family the more sceptical were occasionally heard to describe, when sagely out of earshot of my grandfather, as tenuous. Even I, as romantic and uncritical a child as ever thumbed through Burke, was never able to work out quite to my satisfaction exactly how a seventeenth-century worthy, wearing what appeared to be the robes of an Elector of the Holy Roman Empire, was to be fitted in to our not over-glamorous family tree. Further to emphasise, although perhaps a little confusedly, the prevailing atmosphere of antiquity, the space immediately above the drawing-room door had been tastefully adorned with a suit of Arab chain-mail, a mediaeval helmet and a couple of scimitars, the whole achievement being underlined, as it were, by a Zulu knobkerrie brought back from Africa by an uncle who had served in the Boer war.

The drawing-room, into which on these occasions we were immediately shown, always seemed enormous. Even allowing for the notorious enlargement effected by the eye of memory, it must, I think, have been an extensive apartment in order to have accommodated the quite extraordinarily large quantity of furniture without ever appearing over-crowded. In addition to the usual complement of chintz-covered sofas and armchairs and a concert grand, there were enough occasional tables, china cabinets, escritoires, bureaux, pouffes, side-tables, ottomans and footstools to have furnished a Cunarder. These pieces—mainly in rosewood or satinwood—it was obvious did not exist for themselves alone but rather for the functional purpose of providing a resting-ground for an enormous population of china, ivory and bronze figures which my grandfather had brought back, chained to his chariot-wheels, from his regular triumphant tours of foreign parts. The mantel-piece, draped in green velvet, harboured a quantity of eighteenth-century gods and goddesses, whose amorous abandon and equi-vocal attitudes could only be justified by their being Dresden of the best period. In the china cabinet were further witnesses to the affection which that city always inspired in the Lancaster family, not so valuable perhaps, but less embarrassing; dainty rogues in porcelain whose clothes, meticulously rendered with every lace frill standing out in neurasthenic detail, were indeed of eighteenth-century cut but whose simpering expressions and arch posturing proclaimed them natives of that Victorian version of the Georgian age—all candlelight, sedan-chairs and "Fie, Lady Betty", the world in fact of Lewis Waller in *Monsieur Beaucaire*—which found its fullest expression in the works of Marcus Stone and Dendy Sadler, and which has today been happily perpetuated by the producers of Hollywood.

Hardly less numerous than the porcelain beaux and belles, and even more astounding in their realistic rendering of detail, were the ivories. Japanese peasants carrying bundles of wood in which every branch and twig was separately and convincingly carved: pot-bellied sages the size of one's thumbnail: geishas whose elaborately pleated and embroidered robes were in striking contrast to the expressionless formality of their faces. My favourite in this collection, however, was not oriental, but a bust of Mary Queen of Scots whose bosom opened to reveal the whole scene of her execution complete with clergyman, headsman and weeping attendants, contained in the space of her lungs. The bronze population was of less interest, for the intractable nature of the material did not allow of such detailed modelling, and for me, as for all normal children, it was detail that counted. Indeed, I can only recall, out of all that dusky host, a Moroccan runner carrying the good news from Fez to Rabat and a melancholy Zouave resting on a rocky promontory.

But these studies from life were not by any means the sole witnesses to my family's familiarity with foreign culture. In addition there were several reproductions carried out in low relief in marble and gilding of the arcading of the Alhambra, framed and backed with red velvet; an alabaster model of the Tower of Pisa, and several large plates bearing hand-painted views of the Royal Palace at Stockholm; and a really very fine bronze model of the equestrian statue of Marcus Aurelius on the Campodoglio.

Curiously enough, the innumerable water-colours on the surrounding walls, though less exotic in subject-matter than the marshalled rows of *Reise-andenken*, came far closer to being works of art. A river-scene by David Cox, a view of Antwerp by Prout, several interiors of Italian Palaces, an anonymous drawing of the Boston Stump and a number of Birkett-Fosters reflected a taste that even then was old-fashioned and has not yet come back again into favour, but which was nevertheless genuine.

In appearance my grandfather, for whom this whole crowded scene existed to provide a background, was at this time, and indeed remained until his death at an advanced age many years later, one of the most completely realised personalities on whom I have ever set eyes. A tall, big man, he did not give the impression of great height owing largely to the size of his head, which was enormous, square and completely, shinily bald; but for the austerity conditions prevailing above the line of the ears he had been richly, perhaps over-compensated on a lower-level. Beneath immensely thick brows, jutting out like cornices, were just visible a pair of extremely bright hazel eyes, a determined nose, roman-esque rather than Roman, and two round and polished cheeks, thrusting up like twin tumuli from a hawthorn thicket. And that was all. From immediately below the nostrils right down to the navel there cascaded a snow-white beard of that particular strength and thickness only achieved by those who have never in their life employed a razor. The general effect was one of extreme benevo-lence, but nevertheless one was conscious that Father Christmas could, if necessary, double the part of Jove. This awareness of latent strength, which certainly justified the nervous awe which tempered the affectionate regard in which his whole family held him, was partly due, I think, to the slightly enigmatic expression—so marked in Moslem women—of those whose mouths are always hidden. For contrary to popular belief the mouth is a far more revealing feature than the eyes, and in my grandfather's case I constantly found myself speculating as to its exact size and shape, and whether it supported or contradicted the impression of warm-hearted joviality which the visible part of his countenance established. Was it perpetually wreathed in laughing curves, as one would at first sight assume, or was it set in a firm determined line as his reputation and career might have suggested? No one could tell me for by this time no man living had ever seen it; but, curiously enough, the only available evidence, a childhood portrait, indicated that it was, or once had been, delicately curved and rather feminine.

The greeting which I received never varied; after prolonged chuckling, as though my appearance recalled some side-splitting joke temporarily forgotten, my grandfather always made the same announcement which dated, I fancy, from my first visit in some early sailor-suit, " 'Pon my word, ain't he a howlin' swell!"

Having smirked embarrassedly at this familiar sally, I dived into the undergrowth and planted a kiss in what I hoped was the general direction of his cheek, after which I respectfully saluted whatever aunts happened to be present in the same manner. These formalities over, there came, if it were summer, the expected, and by me not over-enthusiastically received, feminine proposal, "Well, I think we've just time for a little run in the garden before tea."

Although never as a child a friend to violent exercise, I would not have it thought that I was so incurably soft as not to be able to face a gentle turn round an ordinary suburban garden; but this was not an ordinary suburban garden, and the phrase 'a little run' in the Lancastrian usage had sinister implications. First we passed through a conservatory attached at right angles to the drawing-room, which was in itself a source of frustration for I would gladly have lingered for longer than I was ever given a chance to do in an apartment which for me was always steeped in a curious, jungle romance. Around a tiled pool, in which two depressed golden carp of immense size circulated among improbable conch-shells, there flourished palms and giant ferns and banks of potted lobelias and calceolarias beneath a glazed sky barely visible through a tangle of maiden-hair.

All my life I have retained a deep affection for conservatories. To have gathered and selected all the more strikingly unfamiliar plant-forms, many of them sounding overtones of the highest

romance—of oases, of desert islands, of the Promenade des Anglais —behind glass walls through which the reality of Nature with all its untidiness, insects and dirt is clearly visible, and further, as here, to have reinforced this Douanier Rousseau-like treatment of the jungle with the addition of water and fish which are themselves a living testimony to the transforming power of art, has always seemed among our most civilised achievements. Unfortunately, although my enthusiasm was in no way shared by my aunts, they must, I fancy, have guessed at it, and classed it as unhealthy—part and parcel in fact of little Osbert's tendency to 'softness'—against which they waged so incessant and disinterested a warfare; and we always descended the iron stairs to the garden with a noticeable briskness.

As it was a Sunday, and anyhow I was still considered too young, the risk of being involved in a game of tennis was not yet serious, and the only danger I had to fear in this upper part of the garden was that of inadvertently treading on the grass edges of the lawn. The reaction which this mishap always produced in my grandfather was immediate and terrifying; indeed, his outbursts if the risk of any damage to his lawns (which invariably met the surface of the gravel in a right-angled turn as sharp and clean-cut as any architectural moulding) was imminent, were the only signs of rage I ever saw him exhibit, and so lent colour to the view which I had frequently heard expressed, but should otherwise have found difficult to credit, that "your grandfather can be very terrible when roused".

From the upper garden we descended by a flight of Italianate balustraded steps flanked with geraniums in urns to a region of flower and vegetable beds. The time spent here depended very largely on whether there were any little tasks at which it was thought I could usefully assist. If there were no sweet-peas to be cut, or green-fly to be sprayed, or, worst of all, some patch which the gardener's boy had neglected properly to weed, the whole party passed admiringly but swiftly to the greenhouses, my grandfather's especial pride. Here in the dry, clean heat hung row upon row of slowly ripening, still translucent, grapes which would later be cut down and distributed round the various Lancaster house-holds. But never, alas, in quite the quantity which their present abundance would seem to warrant, for despite this encouraging display the patriarchal vines never completely fulfilled their early promise. The fact was, of course, that my grandfather, like so many men who have justly acquired a great reputation as shrewd judges of character, impossible to hoodwink, was always taken in by his gardener who habitually reserved a sizeable proportion of the crop for private sale to the greengrocer down the road.

Beyond the greenhouses lay a coach-house and a yard in which a sheepdog of demonstrative friendliness but appalling smell was kennelled, and here, were it not for 'The Field', the garden would have ended.

'The Field', which was separated from the main garden by a still surprisingly rural lane, was, curiously enough, all that the same implied. Roughly oval in shape and bordered by elms, through the branches of which the roofs of the villas in Putney Vale were only just visible, it sloped down to a pond and a rustic summerhouse diagonally across from the gate in the lane. Despite the summer-house and the villas it fulfilled many of the functions of a proper country field, bearing an annual crop of hay and from time to time witnessing church fêtes and school sports, and its apparent size cannot have been wholly illusory as it is today covered by a hous-ing estate. Nevertheless, apart from a snobbish satisfaction that my grandfather's demesne was thereby rendered so much more exten-sive than his neighbours', the feelings which the existence of this unexpected *pleasaunce* aroused in me were mixed: it was, except in the immediate vicinity of the pond, quite unromantic and its bleak open spaces afforded far too many opportunities for violent exercise. Indeed, my worst fears were usually confirmed imme-diately on entering by the spectacle of a band of cousins already engaged in a heavily organised game of rounders, tiny gesticulat-ing figures, all black stockings and *broderie anglaise*, silhouetted against the yellowish green of the grass, away in the middle distance.

My childish reluctance to involve myself in violent sport, which

I have but partially overcome in later life, did not spring, as my aunts thought, so much from congenital laziness as from causes which, from the moral point of view, were hardly less censurable—a vanity which robbed of pleasure almost all occupations at which I was unable to shine, and a sad lack of the 'team spirit'. Added to these was a natural garrulity which, for reasons that I have never fully understood, was always firmly checked in the interests of 'playing the game'. Of this, years have not brought understanding, and I remain of the opinion that there is no game from bridge to cricket that is not improved by a little light conversation; a view which, I discovered in my pilgrimage from prep school to University, is shared only by a small and unjustly despised minority.

In the Lancaster family, games were not considered as suitable opportunities for individual self-expression and were invariably strictly supervised, and while failure to shine was never allowed to pass without jocular comment, success, in view of the danger of 'getting a swollen head', was always passed over in silence, or greeted in such a way that the victor was left in no doubt that his triumph was either undeserved or could easily have been surpassed had he but exerted himself a little more. The appearance of a housemaid at the gate of the field announcing tea was ready was, therefore, always a welcome sight despite the fact the grown-up in charge had invariably, with an infinite cunning, so arranged matters that the whole party were by this time at the extreme low bottom of the field and the ensuing race back to the house, from which there was no escape and in which I would inevitably come in an inglorious last easily outdistanced both by those who were younger and by those of gentler sex, was thereby stretched to its uphill maximum.

Of all the rooms in my grandfather's house, the dining-room where we finally ended up, panting and vaguely ashamed, has left the deepest impression. This was in no way the result of any superlative excellence of the meals there consumed, for the Lancasters had no understanding, and but very limited appreciation, of food (their ideal of a gastronomic paradise was one where cold roast mutton appeared at every meal and the cook, a vile-tempered

Devonshire woman, would have earned unfavourable comment in a British Railways hotel). It was rather the decoration, and prevailing atmosphere of immeasurable solidity, which made it memorable. On the walls pictures were ranged so thick it was impossible to get any clear idea of the exact pattern of the tooled and stamped wallpaper in the fractional spaces left between the heavy gold frames; pictures chiefly of storms at sea, blasted heaths and gloomy woods to many of which had been attached, rather optimistically as it was later to turn out, such names as Van der Velde and Old Crome. The only bright spots among the menacing storm-clouds and angry seas were provided by two portraits, one of my grandfather in mayoral robes, the other of an uncle in full regimentals.

The room, which ran almost the whole depth of the house, divided itself into sections on either side of the door. That to the left, already rendered menacing by the presence of a concentration of all the stormier works of art, was made still more sombre by the fact that its only source of illumination was a window which, as it looked out on to the stable-yard, was enriched by stained glass in the style of Walter Crane: that to the right was more cheerful not only thanks to the presence of the military uncle but also to a large bow-window in which stood a bronze tripod copied from the one in the Naples Museum (with, in so far as the more virile aspect of the supporting satyrs was concerned, rather less than a painstaking fidelity) and which was always gay with hothouse plants. On an extraordinary chest, carved in high relief by a well-known A.R.A. with frenzied mediaeval joustings, was kept the greatest of the room's treasures. In an elaborately chased gold casket decorated in a style which nicely combined a proper awareness of civic antiquity with an up-to-date acquaintance with the vagaries of art-nouveau in its more readily accepted academic form, enriched with enamel plaques bearing views of the town of which the painstaking realism would, in another setting, have taken on some of the quality of coloured post-cards, lay the Freedom of King's Lynn, presented to my grandfather at an impressive ceremony some years earlier.

Of all the numberless teas, luncheons, and dinners which I consumed in that gloomy apartment only a vague generalised memory remains. The food never varied, the well-named rock-cakes, the 'shapes' presumably so called because they had no other attribute, a peculiarly nauseating cocoa-flavoured rice-pudding, along with the inevitable cold mutton and excellent Stilton made their regular appearance year after year. Just as familiar were the faces of those around the table for, save for occasional dinner-parties to city friends which had practically come to an end for lack of contemporaries by the time I was of an age to attend them, my grandfather was unaccustomed to extend his hospitality much beyond the family circle. Even then the range was more limited than it need have been, for at any given moment my unmarried aunts were certain not to be on speaking terms with at least two of their sisters-in-law. It was only under the pressure of a European war that any noticeable extension was affected.

I have frequently thought that the coming of the Belgian refugees in 1914, and the resultant clash of cultures, provides one of the most psychologically rewarding, and strangely neglected, themes for which any dramatist or novelist could ask. For at that time not only were the English middle classes, who received the major proportion, far more insular than they are today—in the average household no member, save perhaps a daughter who had 'finished' in Paris, was likely ever to have exchanged a word with a foreigner, apart from the porters, customs-officials and guides encountered on conducted tours—but the whole conception of the refugee, now of so melancholy a familiarity, was utterly new and startling. How many fantastic encounters, inevitable readjustments and strange awakenings, one wonders, resulted from this brief incursion?

In my grandfather's case two circumstances combined to render the situation more than normally fantastic. His family had not indeed been isolated from continental experience so rigidly as most, but as their foreign contacts had been exclusively German, in which country most of them had finished their education, this was naturally most productive of awkward pauses and hasty rephrasings. And, as I now recognise, they had been subject to a peculiar time-lag which rendered their way of life strangely old-fashioned and caused them staunchly to uphold values which even in their native land had been called in question at least a quarter of a century before.

Of the two bewildered Belgian families who found an asylum at South Lynn the first was the more colourful, the second the more interesting, and in my case, as things turned out, rewarding. Commandant Kroll and his wife impressed themselves on my memory partly by his uniform (how strange in the eyes of childhood is the first sight of a uniform, normally associated with guardsmen, policemen and other hieratic and unreal figures of the outside world, when worn indoors!), but even more by the strange nature of the mortifications which wounded patriotism caused them to inflict on themselves. Mme Kroll's refusal, frequently announced, to wear her wedding-ring so long as a single German remained on Belgian soil was, to my mind, illogical rather than spectacular, but her husband's resolution to refrain from dying his purple-black moustaches for a similar period produced a result, anyhow in the early days, gratifyingly piebald and bizarre. However, apart from the Commandant's persistent efforts, vaguely resented, to cut up my meat for me at table, my relations with this monolingual pair remained distant. And anyhow they soon vanished after a dramatic scene, involving enraged stepsons, waved revolvers and passionate behaviour all round, that confirmed my family in their worst suspicions about Continental home-life.

Very different were the Van den Eckhoudts who succeeded the Krolls. Although, as I only came to realise many years later, their way of life was possibly even further removed, albeit in a totally different direction, from that of their hosts, there soon developed a mutual regard warming to affection which far outlasted the period of exile. Monsieur 'Van den', as he came to be called, was burdened by the grave disadvantage, in the eyes of his hosts, of being a painter; and, moreover, not one who had been driven into that employment by force of circumstance but who had deliberately

chosen it in preference to what would doubtless have been a highly profitable, and from the Lancastrian viewpoint eminently praise-worthy, business career open to him as the son of a wealthy Brussels banker. To make matters still worse it soon became apparent that his work, upon which he immediately engaged, bore little or no resemblance to that of dear old Mr. Roe, the brother of the Rector of St. Nicholas at Lynn, whose colourful presentation of such scenes as 'Nelson on the bridge of the Victory' or 'The Old Chelsea Pensioner' had recently gained for him an A.R.A. and many of whose masterpieces, including the Mayoral portrait and the mediaeval chest, were scattered round the house. M. Van den was, in fact, a modern painter; and unfortunately the scandal of the First Post-Impressionist Exhibition had been so heavily publicised that even a household as utterly cut off from all contact with contemporary art as was South Lynn had by now been made fully aware of its appalling implications.

The slight nervousness which the nature of M. Van den's occupation induced in my aunts—reinforced as it was by the unfortunate incident of the Krolls—while it could not possibly, in face of his extreme gentleness of manner (his appearance with his large features and rich mane of hair suggested the attempt of some archaic sculptor only acquainted with sheep to achieve a lion by hearsay) and the charm and evident good nature of his remarkably handsome wife, amount to anything as strong as antagonism, did at first make for a certain restraint which, curiously enough, worked ultimately to my great advantage. For my mother, alone of the whole Lancaster clan, had had personal experience of the artist's life, and her sympathy with modern painting was con-siderably greater than the fact that she was a pupil of the late G. F. Watts might have suggested. She had, moreover, been educated in Brussels and worked for a time in the studio of a master under whom M. Van den had himself studied, and she it was who provided him with the tools of his trade, lost with all the rest of his luggage on the flight, and constituted herself the champion of his work in all family discussions. In this she was undoubtedly actuated by a genuine admiration, for it was obvious to all who were not blinded by the unaccustomed lightness of his palette and a very restrained simplification of form, that M. Van den was an artist of the greatest sensibility and accomplishment, but almost certainly her defence derived an additional zest from the opportunity it afforded of, for once, putting her sisters-in-law in the wrong.

It was natural, therefore, that our household should have seen rather more of the Van dens than did the other branches of the family: with the fortunate sequel, some fifteen years later, that it was to their home, by then removed to Roquebrune, that I was sent to learn French. It was only at this later period that I was able fully to realise how extraordinary a transposition their sojourn on Putney Hill must in fact have been, and to gain, from their reminiscences, a completely detached and unengaged picture of my grandfather and his way of life.

The Van dens' household in the South of France when first I visited it in the late 'twenties, a callow but absorbent undergraduate, proved the gateway to a world of which, until that time, I had been ignorant of the very existence. The villa itself, 'La Couala', very white and simple, seemed by contrast with home bare and under-furnished. Even the books which stretched from floor to ceiling on plain unvarnished shelves looked in their yellow or white paper naked and temporary, while the austere peasant-made chairs and tables seemed but the frames of furniture still awaiting their padding and chintz. Only the grand piano had a vaguely familiar look which did not, however, extend to the music-rest, for the works there lying open were signed not by Amy Woodforde-Findon or Sir Arthur Sullivan, but such unknown personalities as Poulenc and Satie.

Still stranger by contrast to Lancastrian relations and protégées, who, together with a few school friends, had hitherto made up my social world, was the Roquebrune circle in which the Van dens moved, for almost all were concerned with the arts, and business and politics were never mentioned. Even when, as occasionally happened, a Belgian friend arrived on a visit, whom one learnt was in fact 'un grand industriel' or 'le premier chirurgien de Bruxelles', he was as likely as not immediately to seat himself at the piano and play half a dozen Bach fugues at a stretch. Among the close friends and neighbours were Simon Bussy, Gabriel Hano-teaux, and Paul Valéry. Names such as Matisse and Stravinsky, which had hitherto sounded in my ears as remote as Ingres or Beethoven, occurred constantly in the conversation as those of friends and acquaintances, while the post regularly brought long letters and sheaves of magnificent photographs from M. Gide at that time voyaging in the Congo. Nor could the width of the gulf separating this circle from that of my family be wholly attributed to differences of nationality for at least two English figures, Roger Fry and Dorothy Bussy, were regular members. But Gordon Square and Putney Hill, I soon realised, were far, far more than a sixpenny bus-ride apart.

Most adolescents are, I suppose, at some time or other, filled with a snobbish shame at the supposed inadequacy, social, intel-lectual or political, of their families. The reaction this induces changes according to the climate of the period; in my own case it led to an uncritical rejection of all the artistic values which my parents still upheld, and a ridiculous exaltation of contemporary masters at the expense of those they revered, which found expres-sion in the illogical view that because Proust was a great novelist, Dickens could not be; five years later it would have taken the form of joining the Communist party and maintaining that no essential difference divided Fascists and Tories.

Having quickly adapted myself to what I imagined to be the intellectual outlook of 'La Couala' I was tortured with anxiety as to how unspeakably bourgeois and philistine must the Van dens have found the Lancasters during their sojourn in England.

What could they have thought, I asked myself, of the bogus Dutch landscapes, the Academy portraits, the heraldic furniture of South Lynn? How bored and horrified must they have been in a household where a total unawareness of the world of ideas not only existed but was regarded as a matter for congratulation, and where all the arts, save one, were judged to be but enjoyable pastimes, more praiseworthy than bridge but less ennobling than riding. In particular the Lancastrian attitude to the only art which they did consider perhaps more easily justified (largely on moral grounds) than the rest—music—must, I felt, have been peculiarly unsympathetic.

In this last supposition, it must be admitted, I had some justification, for the theory that music was 'a good thing' produced in practice some very strange results. My grandfather's failure completely to master the violin late in life, a failure which the more critical of his long-suffering relations considered he was an unconscionable time in accepting, had determined him that none of his family should have to go through life similarly ill-equipped. Thus my Aunt Mary, who almost alone of the family had some genuine musical feeling, was an extremely competent clarinettist; my Uncle Harry's rich and confident baritone had easily gained him a place in the Bach choir and combined with a handsome presence earned him many a request to 'bring his music' when dining out; and my Aunt Hetty, although never a carefree, was nevertheless an infinitely painstaking performer of Beethoven's easier piano pieces. As the third generation advanced in years various gaps in the ensemble were steadily filled. My cousin Barbara, who had inherited something of her mother's skill, was allotted the 'cello; my Cousin Peggy took over her grandfather's violin, a choice which only he, rendered indulgent perhaps by his personal experience of the difficulties of the instrument and protected, moreover, by almost total deafness, regarded as anything but unfortunate; her sister Ruth had come to be considered as having a very pretty contralto, although few went so far as to maintain an equally satisfactory ear; and to me fell that beautiful, but temperamental instrument, the flute.

On ceremonial occasions, such as my grandfather's birthday or Christmas, we all arrived carrying our instruments and each equipped with some little concert piece laboriously practised for many months beforehand. The great object of the whole exercise, that all my grandfather's descendants should combine in some single paean of praise or thanksgiving, was never, alas, achieved, partly due to the fact that few composers seem to have worked for just this exact combination of instruments and voices, and partly to the rather varied degrees of accomplishment to which the performers had attained. This was doubly unfortunate for not only did it prolong the agony but also gave rise to internecine feuds and rivalries. While all had to admit little Barbara's remarkable

mastery of the 'cello, some thought it was rather an ungainly instrument for a girl, and although few, except her own parents, pretended to have much pleasure from little Ruth's rendering of 'Tit-willow', more, perhaps, might have made the effort. My own show-piece 'La Paloma' was usually greeted with a due appreciation of its difficulty, but some there were who appeared by their reception of it to assume a non-existent comic intent on the part of the composer.

Painful as these occasions had been at the time, they had become doubly so in recollection. It was, therefore, with considerable satisfaction that I reflected, while listening to Miss Van den giving a masterly rendering of Poulenc's 'La Bestiaire', that to such musical evenings as her parents may have had to endure at South Lynn I had been debarred by my age from contributing personally.

As the picture which the Van dens retained of life at South Lynn was gradually unfolded in conversation and reminiscence it provided, in its patent unlikeness to the sombre and embarrassing conception which my nervous imagination had built up, a chastening and much-needed lesson. It was true that they had not been much impressed by either the musical understanding nor the executive ability revealed in the family concerts, but the grandpaternal enthusiasm which had prompted them they considered wholly praiseworthy. My grandfather himself they regarded as the beau ideal of 'le grand seigneur anglais' and in the highest degree aristocratic. Here, I think they were misled by that rather too exclusively chivalric conception of the honour of knighthood still current abroad, for while my grandfather could rightly be described as patriarchal, possibly even patrician, aristocratic was, strictly speaking, an overstatement. Far more astonishing, however, was the tribute they paid to his intellect. His complete lack of sympathy with the sort of art they practised and admired in no way surprised them but his tolerance and freedom from all affectation in such matters they thought unusual and wholly admirable. His literary judgements which were confined to English and the classics, they were prepared to accept unquestioningly, and they had been deeply impressed by his privately printed volume of verse, of the very existence of which I was now made for the first time somewhat apprehensively aware. For his way of life, for the whole complicated machine of South Lynn existence, with its unalterable mealtimes, its Sabbath calm, its starched maidservants, its gleaming carriages, they expressed the most genuine admiration. And if this admiration had something in common with the fascinated delight of the anthropologist over some perfectly preserved example of a culture hitherto thought to be extinct, it was based on a full appreciation of the moral values that lay beneath.

Only once had the Van dens' understanding failed them, and this on the only occasion on which my grandfather had displayed that Jove-like side to his character of which his family were always so nervously aware. In some discussion of English literature M. Van den had chanced to speak appreciatively of Oscar Wilde and the reaction had proved the more alarming for being wholly unexpected. His host's expression had immediately become thunderous and in a tone of awful gravity ('c'etait une voix terrible, vous savez') he had been informed that had he not been a foreigner he would have realised that that was a name which could never be mentioned in a gentleman's house. While this confusion of moral and aesthetic judgements had remained for ever inexplicable the incident itself had undoubtedly left a deep impression, for I noticed that while during my stay with the Van dens the works not only of Stendhal and Fromentin, but of such contemporary writers as Valéry and Claudel, were pressed on me, my fondness for Proust met with little encouragement and the only work of their friend M. Gide which I was led to study was *Isabelle*.

The doubts of the validity of my personal conception of my grandfather's character which the Van dens' recollections had sown were strengthened soon after my return to England. My grandfather who was by this time a very old man had recently taken to his bed for almost the first time in his life and there was a certain urgency about the summons to South Lynn which awaited me. On arrival I was taken straight up to his bedroom, an apartment I now penetrated for the first time, overlooking the tops of the elm-trees in The Field and the wooded heights of East Putney deceptively rural-looking in the late afternoon sun. He was sitting up in bed, rather thinner than I remembered him, his white beard flowing over woollen pyjamas and with his hands, palm down, lying flat on the coverlet. His eyes had a slightly glazed look and there was a heavy charnel house smell in the room, but his voice was as firm as ever. As we talked, in a studiously matter-of-fact way, it suddenly occurred to me for the first time, that despite the impression created by his unshakable joviality, my grandfather was not, and had not been for a long time, a happy man: and that as he now looked back on his life he did not feel quite the satisfaction which he might justifiably have expected.

On the face of it, it was hard to see what had gone wrong, for if ever a man had fully accomplished what he set out to do that man was my grandfather. An only son of a widowed mother, largely dependent on the charity of friends for his education, he had, in his 'teens, set forth on the stage coach from Lynn to Cambridge which was as far as the railway at that time reached, determined to make his way in London and restore his family to their former affluence. In this he had completely succeeded, making a fortune large enough for him to discharge all his obligations many times over. Anyone claiming the remotest connection with the family, or whose parents or grandparents had had any hand in his education, was liberally rewarded. He had completely rebuilt and re-equipped the grammar school which had given him an education for which he had always been deeply grateful; he had founded prizes and scholarships and endowed hospital beds and charities without number; he had restored churches (not always, admittedly, with the happiest results) and erected innumerable memorials. His marriage had been singularly happy, and his pride in his children was manifest if uncritical. Why, then, should I have gained so distinct an impression that as he surveyed his life from his death-bed he found something lacking: that while his career testified so strikingly to the truth of the assumption that if a man wants anything sufficiently strongly he will always get it, it yet quite failed to contradict the rider that this is only too likely to happen after he had ceased to want it?

His life, it was true, had not been wholly free from disappointments and sorrows; his electoral campaigns had never been crowned with success, and several of the beneficiaries of his educational enthusiasm had turned out unsatisfactorily, notably one highly promising lad who had won every conceivable scholarship and exhibition only to go, immediately on leaving the University, straight to Hollywood. These, however, were minor blows. Infinitely graver were the death of his wife, after a few years of blissfully happy marriage, and the fact that two of his sons, and those perhaps the best loved, had predeceased him. Nevertheless, the abiding sorrow which these losses had brought seemed in so resilient a character the effect rather than the cause of a deeper melancholy, and one, moreover, which could certainly not be attributed to universal causes, for his religious faith, though simple, was robust, and never, I think, for a moment was he visited by any doubts as to the justice of an economic system which he so perfectly understood and which had brought him such prosperity.

On looking back it seems to me that the trouble may have lain in the very perfection of his achievement; that while his success story had followed so undeviatingly the classic lines he himself was, fundamentally, a romantic, and a frustrated one at that. In support of this view I can only call up small scraps of unrelated evidence, by themselves of no great significance, perhaps, but which when combined provide, if not proof, at least an indication. That strangely feminine mouth which according to the boyhood portrait lurked beneath the beard; the desperate violin playing and the privately printed poems; even the slightly ridiculous passion for heraldry which certainly had in it nothing of the snobbish. And in addition a scrap of conversation which has stuck in my mind through the years.

One night after dinner he told me, apropos of some genealogical discussion, that at a time when he was in constant correspondence with the College of Heralds, he had received a letter from an old antiquary in Norwich upbraiding him for relinquishing the crest which the family had up till that time borne in favour of a new grant of arms, adding the information that the former dated from a time long past when the Lancasters had been the largest landowners in the county. "Complete nonsense, of course," said my grandfather, "and not worth the expense and trouble of following up." But the tone of voice in which this forthright piece of common sense was pronounced indicated quite clearly that in his heart of hearts he held the exactly contrary view.

In fact the head had here attained too complete a victory over the heart, a fact which my grandfather, I suspect, had himself come half to realise, though never to admit. For it was impossible to think of him ever undertaking any action, of making any gesture, without due consideration, and while naturally the most kind-hearted of men, he had long ago convinced himself, perfectly rightly, that even kindness, if it is to attain its maximum effect, must be directed and thought out.

Thus, while I have no doubt that the hints of the Norwich antiquary brought instantly before his inner eye an impossibly glamorous world peopled with mythical Lancasters in shining armour ablaze with heraldry, a glittering mediaeval never-never-land in the probably quite fruitless exploration of which he would have had infinite pleasure, I am equally certain that a still small voice had pointed out to him that while a certain degree of interest in one's forebears and their quarterings was perfectly appropriate to the hero of a Victorian success story, to pursue it too far would not only involve unjustifiable time and expense but lay one open to ridicule and sarcasm.

It may well be that these reflections were in fact quite baseless; that I was only driven thus to speculate by the feeling that this was, or should have been, a dramatic moment; and the very fact that there was no heightening of the tension led me to give an unwarranted significance to its absence. But whether or not the emotion was purely subjective, I was, at that moment, for the first time made suddenly and vividly aware of one of the central facts of human existence—the terrifying isolation of the individual and the resultant impossibility of ever really knowing another human being. For I felt that if ever I were to receive an answer to the riddle which had for so long puzzled me, of what exactly my grand-father was like beneath the protecting envelope of bearded *bon-homie*, it should have been now, and no answer was forthcoming.

Certainly nothing in this final interview lent any support to my thwarted romantic theory. Our conversation was factual in the extreme, ranging over my progress at Oxford, the desirability of my being called to the Bar, and what London Clubs it would be suitable for me to join, and was brought to an end by a firm hand-shake and a "Well, good-bye, my boy, I don't suppose I shall be seeing you again". Feeling more than usually inadequate I turned

232

to go and had already reached the door when I was called back. Handing me a sheet of paper and a stamped envelope my grandfather asked me if I would mind giving the former to my Aunt Kate and put the latter out for posting. Examining them on the way downstairs I noticed that on the paper was a list of numbers relating to Hymns A. and M. ending with the 'Dead March in Saul', and the envelope was addressed in a firm clear hand,

The Editor,
(Obituaries)
The Times,
Printing House Square.

4. *"There was I waiting at the church"*

THERE IS no silence in the world so overwhelming as that which prevails on a small country station when a train has just left. The fact that it is by no means complete, that the fading echoes of the engine are still clearly audible from beyond the signal-box behind which the guard's van is finally disappearing, that one now hears for the first time the cawing of the rooks, a distant dog's bark, the hum of the bees in the station-master's garden, in no way detracts from its quality. The rattling world of points and sleepers, of gossiping fellow-passengers and sepia views of Cromer beach has been whirled away leaving a void which, for some moments yet, the sounds and smells of the countryside will be powerless to fill.

At Eastwinch station, lost amidst the un-by-passed fields of my Edwardian childhood, this period of suspension was apt to be longer than elsewhere. The platform, though I suppose no higher than most, appeared in the flat East Anglian landscape to be a raised island, isolated way above the surrounding elm-broken cornlands. Nor did it ever, at first glance, exhibit any sign of life, as the solitary porter's immediate duty was to open the level-crossing gates regardless of the passengers, alone with their luggage amidst the shiny tinplates advertising Stephens' Blueblack Ink and Venos Lightning Cough Cure. And it was only just as we were beginning to wonder whether or not this was the right day, that an aunt would suddenly emerge from the waiting-room.

Her greeting never varied. After the usual brisk, no-nonsense kiss and the routine enquiries she would announce that Jones had brought the trap (the Renault was never sent to the station save for my grandfather himself or some guest of more than usual age or decrepitude) and would take Nurse and the luggage, but that she expected that Osbert would like a little walk after all that time in the stuffy train. This was always said with a richly sardonic smile, she knowing full well that there was nothing Osbert so much abominated as little walks, no matter how many hours had been spent in stuffy trains; he, however, had long since learnt the use-lessness of protest and would inevitably find himself a few minutes later trudging along the Station Road gazing regretfully at Nurse, comfortably ensconced in the trap, bowling briskly away in a cloud of dust.

Even today Eastwinch is a very small village; at that date it was smaller still. Small, that is, judged by the number of its inhabitants rather than by its extent. Strung out for a mile or more along the Lynn-Swaffham road it started at the Lynn end with the church, a decent enough fourteenth-century Norfolk structure without, but scraped and scrubbed into insignificance within by the late Sir Gilbert Scott, standing on an outlying ridge of the Breckland, that scruffy, sandy waste which runs like some horrid birthmark across the homely face of East Anglia. Alongside, dank and laurel-shaded, was the vicarage; beyond, down the hill, lay the straight village street, hardly differing in character from the rest of the highway, so widely separated were the cottages, the four public-houses (two of them no longer licensed since my grandfather had decided that the needs of the villagers were being, perhaps, too amply cared for), and the solitary village shop. Half a mile beyond the point where it was entered by the Station Road, an ordinary country lane crossing the branch line from Lynn some three-quarters of a mile away, the street ended in a sharp fork, in the apex of which, facing directly up the village to the church, stood the imposing, globe-topped entrance gates of Eastwinch Hall.

The gates, once entered, were generally felt to be an overstatement. On the right lay a croquet lawn screened from the converg-

ing roads by a plantation of copper beeches; less than a hundred yards ahead was the house itself. Built a century earlier by some modest nabob who had done well in the tea trade, tradition maintained that it had been deliberately designed on the model of a tea-caddy. Although at the time I never dreamed of doubting this theory, on looking back it seems to me to have been a perfectly ordinary, four-square late Georgian residence with a rather low-pitched roof. Such idiosyncrasies as it displayed were all, in fact, the work of my grandfather; they took the form of terra-cotta masks of Comedy and Tragedy with which he had seen fit to enliven the plain expanse of yellow brick between the first and second storeys, unexpected bow-windows bulging out on ground level, and a vast gabled porch masking the front door. The erection of this last had unfortunately coincided with the height of the old gentleman's genealogical enthusiasm, and the pediment was adorned with a highly baroque version of his coat of arms in terra-cotta. So unexpectedly heavy had this forthright statement of the Lancaster family's inclusion among the armigerous classes proved that the fretted and white-painted wooden supports were already visibly straining beneath their burden of heraldry.

Structurally unsound and decoratively over-emphatic, the front porch nevertheless provided the focal point round which, during the long summer days, the whole life of the house revolved. Here my grandfather would sit reading his day-old *Times*, and to it would come the gardener with his offering of flowers which my aunts would painstakingly 'arrange' in a series of unattractive vases lined up on the tiled floor. As a vantage point from which nurses and parents could keep an eye on the younger children, and sporting uncles could give unsolicited advice to tennis-playing nephews and nieces, it was in constant demand. And always, on arrival, one found there the whole house-party grouped in a welcoming tableau.

I here use the word house-party simply as a convenient noun of assembly, disregarding its overtones. For us, particularly when speaking of the years before the first German war, the term has taken on a certain glamour, suggesting almost exclusively assemblies of the smart and the beautiful pursuing worldly pleasures in a constantly changed variety of expensive clothes. Nothing could bear less resemblance to the gatherings at Eastwinch Hall; no baccarat scandals ever darkened the fair name of a house where the only permitted card games were strictly educational; the conversation was seldom of a brilliance to have fired the imagination of Mr. Henry James; and it can safely be said that never, never did these corridors echo to whispered speculations about the geography of the bedrooms.

The two over-riding interests of my grandfather's life were his family and philanthropy. The first made it difficult for him, although fundamentally a social character, to take any great pleasure in the company under his own roof of those who were not in some way connected with the clan; the second provided ample opportunities for the employment of his large fortune without having recourse to the pursuit of expensive social ambitions. However, as the only son of an only son, despite the fact that of his seven children all but two had married and produced families, his circle would have been more restricted than he liked had not his genealogical researches helped to extend it. Diligent combing of the further branches of the family tree had revealed the existence of extraordinary survivals from a long-vanished Norfolk of gloomy farmers and manic-depressive yeomen. Unfortunately these had turned out to be exclusively female, and while they afforded many opportunities for the exercise of philanthropy their social gifts were seldom of an order effectively to enrich life at the Hall. They had, therefore, been comfortably installed in small villas on the outskirts of Lynn and in cosy cottages dotted round the country where their maintenance had been made the responsibility of my father and uncles. Deeply and volubly appreciative of their good fortune they were known collectively as the Grateful Hearts but seldom asked to the house.

In course of time the place which they should have taken had been filled by a second outer circle of Grateful Hearts differing in certain important respects from the original collection. Although its members could boast no blood relationship with the family they had all, at some time or another, been connected with it, usually in a dependent capacity. For inclusion in this group from which house-guests were selected three things, beyond a modicum of gentility, were necessary—poverty, piety and physical affliction. Naturally the senior members had soon developed so highly skilled a technique for the display of these attributes that a certain rivalry had sprung up. In my day the two prized exhibits, between whose merits no distinction was possible, were Miss Childs and Miss Marple. The former was an elderly lady of extreme bad temper suffering from advanced cataract; the latter a kindly, timid creature with curvature of the spine. While Miss Childs could rightly claim cataract as the worse affliction, Miss Marple was undoubtedly the poorer, and as their piety was equal and unquestioned there could be no supremacy on points. The fact that Miss Marple in addition to her hump-back had also a heavy cavalry moustache did not count, as the Lancasters themselves were a hirsute lot (one of my great-aunts had several times been mistaken for Lord Kitchener), and among them such an adornment was considered rather a source of pride than of shame.

The runners-up in these depressing stakes were undoubtedly Mr. and Mrs. Phipps. The husband, a seedy clergyman who was still, at an advanced age, a curate in the West of England, was generally known among the younger generation as 'Filthy Phipps' from the fact that his neck and hands invariably matched the greasy black of his clerical boater. His wife, a faded and depressed woman only slightly cleaner than her husband, suffered from an obscure malady the exact nature of which remained undisclosed. To this and to Mr. Phipps' guaranteed professional piety they owed their position, but remained debarred from further advancement by a certain whining dissatisfaction with their lot. For it was *de rigueur* that all afflictions should be bravely and brightly borne.

Rather less secure was the position of Frau Schmiegelow. Originally my aunts' German governess, this stout Prussian was bidden from time to time to quit her native land and revisit her former pupils. Her piety, which was of the aggressively Lutheran kind, was undoubted, and thanks to an unfortunate marriage to the postmaster of a small town in Schleswig-Holstein, her poverty was assured. At her afflictions it was more difficult, at first sight, to guess; extremely well-covered and bursting with health and self-assurance it was far from easy to see how she qualified on this score. It was rumoured that the postmaster drank, but what was an alcoholic husband compared to cataract or curvature of the spine? Looking back I now realise that her affliction was held to lie in her foreign birth. Not to be English was for my family so terrible a handicap as almost to place the sufferer in the permanent invalid class: the only difference being that, while it was the height of uncharitableness to laugh at invalids, foreigners were always legitimate targets for a robust sense of fun.

In the case of Frau Schmiegelow this grave disadvantage was, of course, mitigated by the fact that she was a German, for if one had to be foreign it was far better to be German, preferably a Prussian. Not only did the Lancasters find in the Germans all those virtues which they most admired—discipline, industry, physical courage and simple, unaffected Evangelical piety—but several of them had completed their education in Germany and all spoke the language fluently. Indeed, had the Germans only possessed a sense of humour they might almost have qualified as honorary Englishmen. In Frau Schmiegelow's case this deficiency was principally apparent in her attitude to Wilhelm II, a personality whom her hosts regarded as richly comic; and while good manners prevented this source of quiet fun from being exploited too openly, the gluey, hypnotised reverence with which the devoted Frau pronounced the syllables "der liebe Kaiser" strained forbearance to the utmost.

However, although occasionally a trial, Frau Schmiegelow nevertheless served a useful social purpose in consolidating the opinion of the other Grateful Hearts and, by her provocative advocacy of her sovereign's merits, in restoring a unity which at times showed signs of strain. In Frau Schmiegelow's presence Miss Childs, who was very Low, would forget for a moment her annoyance at the ecclesiastical lace on which Miss Marple, who was very High, was for ever engaged. (Despite her affliction some sixth sense enabled Miss Childs to be instantly aware of the Paschal Lamb or Sacred Monogram taking shape beneath the clever fingers of her rival.) Similarly Miss Marple, confronted with the greater menace, would overlook the fact of the Reverend Phipps' notorious indifference to the Eastward Position; while the Phipps themselves ceased for a few moments to be consumed by the jealousy constantly provoked by the greater regard in which the two old spinsters were generally held.

So powerfully, indeed, did the other Grateful Hearts react to

Frau Schmiegelow that she was able to exercise her restorative spell even by remote control. In the summers immediately preceding 1914, when her visits had ceased, the mere sight of her thin Gothic writing on an envelope was sufficient to promote harmony, while her lyrical account of the All-Highest's latest speech at Kiel or Potsdam, which one of my aunts would always make a point of immediately translating, produced a gratifying unanimity lasting for several days.

Far more powerful than poor Frau Schmiegelow's was the personality, and infinitely more disruptive the influence, of Miss Redpath. Whereas the other Grateful Hearts live on in my memory distinct but flat, Miss Redpath remains a three-dimensional figure, fully realised and complete. Indeed she was the first person outside my immediate family of whose individuality I was fully aware, and even as a very small child I was always conscious that she was not to be ranged with the lay-figures on the porch, whom I could not conceive of as functioning away from their familiar base, but enjoyed an independent existence far beyond the confines of the Hall. Nor was this difference merely apparent; Miss Redpath in fact fulfilled none of the conditions attached to the status of a Grateful Heart. Although by no means rich she had a small income of her own; her good health, despite the fact that she was well over seventy, was aggressive; and so far from being pious, or even indifferent to religion, she was a convinced and militant agnostic.

Lacking all the necessary stigmata it was difficult at first to explain her inclusion among us. If, as it is charitable to suppose, her hostesses were prompted by a disinterested desire to help and give pleasure to the lonely and unfortunate, it was quite obvious that she rightly considered herself in no way distressed, nor did she conceal the fact that she had a host of friends and that Eastwinch was only one of several country houses that she would be visiting in the course of the summer. If, as was sometimes disloyally suggested by their in-laws, the Lancasters suffered from an ingrained distaste for the company of their equals and were only really happy when surrounded by those they were in a position to patronise, then one would have said it would have been impossible to find a more difficult subject for the exercise of this discreditable family weakness than Miss Redpath.

The real reason, I fancy, why every summer this forthright and unaccommodating figure appeared for a week or a fortnight was, largely, fear. She had been the extremely capable Principal of the excellent girls' school at which my mother and my aunts (and indeed even some of my great-aunts) had received their education, and the awe in which they still held her made it impossible for them, having once asked her, to discontinue their invitations. Moreover she was a firm favourite of my grandfather who sometimes, I think, was hard put to it to conceal the boredom which the company of his other guests induced, and who fully appreciated the masculine qualities of her extremely well-trained mind.

Miss Redpath's appearance was completely in keeping with her character. Although very small, the extreme rigidity of her bearing fully compensated for any lack of inches, and her square face, with its great width of jaw, was distinguished by two peculiarities of expression which greatly added to the awe which she inspired. Her eyes always kept a look of astonished ferocity due to the fact that the bright blue irises were surrounded by a complete circle of white, their circumference nowhere broken by the lids, a phenomenon I have only otherwise observed among professional hypnotists and in photographs of Mussolini. In speaking she was never known to move her jaw, so that behind her exaggeratedly mobile lips (she was always very particular about elocution and would never tolerate 'mumbling') one was always conscious of the rigidly clenched teeth. Her costume, which was well chosen to set off her personality, never varied. Her coat and skirt of rich purple broadcloth trimmed with black braid were cut to allow the maximum movement; her black boots were thick and sensible; and beneath the high lace collar supported on either side by little serpentine wires one could clearly distinguish the vigorous movement of the neck-muscles occasioned by her peculiar manner of speech.

Whereas my cousins and the majority of their parents regarded the coming of Miss Redpath with marked apprehension I looked forward to it with the keenest pleasure. Not only had I long since discounted her alarming appearance and abrupt manner (for I had frequently been taken by my mother to visit her in London) but I much appreciated her powers as a story-teller and the fact that in addressing children she did not consider it necessary to adopt a manner of speaking in any way different from that in which she conversed with their elders. Moreover she lived in what I firmly considered to be the most beautiful house in the world.

In my childhood the sight of the trim green lawns of Hampstead Garden Suburb shaded by the carefully preserved elms, the white-painted posts linked by chains, the leaded casements and tile-hung gables, above all the miniature scale on which everything was conceived, induced a feeling of inexpressible delight; a feeling that suffered no lessening when the green-painted front door of Miss R.'s residence, with its heartshaped, bottle-glazed wicket, was finally opened.

Miss Redpath was a cousin of one of the leading Pre-Raphaelites (I think Holman Hunt) and the interior of her house had already acquired a strong period flavour. Immediately on entering one was confronted with a large reproduction of 'May Morning on Magdalen Tower' with an affectionate message from the artist scrawled on the mount, and on all sides one was conscious of Burne-Jones maidens yearning at one in sanguine chalk above bosky thickets of honesty and cape-gooseberries tastefully arranged in polished copper pots. Elsewhere were many brass-rubbings of recumbent knights and innumerable Arundel prints, while the presence of several Della Robbia plaques, a set of faded, purplish photographs of the Gozzoli frescoes in the Medici Chapel and some small, painstaking water-colours of Assisi, indicated that their owner shared to the full the Italophil enthusiasm of the late Victorians. The two small ground-floor rooms in which, against Morris wallpapers, all these treasures were displayed were connected by an open arch so that it was possible on the moment of entry to see right through the house to the little orchard beyond.

This, besides filling the interior with a green, filtered light, invariably suggested to me the scene that would be revealed were one to walk through the range of buildings in the background of Millais' *Autumn Leaves*.

Whether or not my childish whimseys were far-fetched, it was certain that no apartments could be further removed in atmosphere from the interior of Eastwinch Hall, but so powerful was the impression they created that Miss Redpath, who was not in herself a romantic figure, when seen against the familiar background of pitch-pine panelling, foxed sporting prints, and stuffed birds allegedly shot by an uncle in the Fayyum, still trailed clouds of Italo-Arthurian glory.

Nevertheless, there was nothing of the 'greenery-yallery' about her; a daughter of the manse she had learnt Latin and Greek at her father's knee, had been among the very first women to graduate at Bedford College, and was a distinguished Anglo-Saxon scholar, the friend and pupil of Professor Skeat. In addition she was a foundation member of the Fabian Society and a convinced, if not militant, Suffragette. Her standards of judgement were, therefore, high, and while her admiration for the achievements of the Pre-Raphaelites and their contemporaries was sincere it by no means invariably extended to their personalities.

It will readily be understood that the annual appearance of Miss Redpath, then at the height of her powers, in the close and docile circle of the Hall, was attended by a certain heightening of tension. Both sides, it is true, made allowances; my aunts for their part, although never finally abandoning hope of their old mistress's ultimate conversion, forewent the pleasure of open proselytising, while she made a genuine, if sometimes rather too obvious, effort to suffer fools gladly and to achieve the soft answer which turneth away wrath. Nevertheless, all present were conscious of the strain which steadily increased as her visit drew to its appointed close and it was obvious that sooner or later someone would go too far. I count it among the great privileges of my childhood that when the inevitable happened I was an eye-witness.

The day of Miss Redpath's downfall was a Sunday; a fact which, besides providing the very circumstances of the disaster, immeasurably heightened the drama. For at Eastwinch Hall even so late as the early years of George V the Victorian Sabbath retained all its rigours unmodified. Whatever books we had been reading during the week were put away and their places taken by bound volumes of *The Quiver*, dating from the period of my father's childhood. For me personally this was no great hardship as it merely involved handing in the G. A. Henty which had been my ostensible reading for the week while retaining concealed the W. W. Jacobs which I had been devouring under cover. Besides I rather enjoyed *The Quiver*; I was developing a keen period sense and derived much simple pleasure from the wood-engravings of whiskered curates and bonneted social workers. But my poor cousins, whose home-life was more emancipated than mine, were less resigned; already condemned, owing to our remoteness from any centre of modern civilisation, to miss at least three vital sequences of the *Perils of Pauline*, they regarded the weekly confiscation of *Comic Cuts* and *Buffalo Bill* as the most unjustifiable and high-handed curtailment of personal liberty. And their lot was rendered all the harder by the strict rules governing Sunday games, which I for my part rather welcomed. For after a week of humiliating and unrelieved defeat on the tennis court the enforced substitution of croquet, at which I early manifested a careless mastery, caused me no pain. But even the right to play croquet had been a hardly won concession granted only on appeal to my grandfather. He had ruled, very sensibly, that whereas the tennis-court was visible from the road and the vicar feared that the spectacle of the gentry at play might lead the villagers into sin, the croquet-lawn was concealed by a dense shrubbery so that only our own salvation was imperilled, and this was a risk which he thought, on the whole, we were justified in taking. Clock-golf, however, remained a bone of contention, my cousins maintaining that it was only a form of croquet and equally well-concealed, my aunts sticking firmly to the belief that it was in some way a 'worldlier' sport and therefore unsuited to the Lord's Day.

This particular Sunday dawned bright and fair with a brisk

245

wind sending small white clouds scudding across the vast East Anglian sky. As it was not the first Sunday in the month only Miss Marple had gone to Early Service, and the house party, with the exception of Miss Redpath, assembled for the first time at family prayers. When these were at long last concluded and the domestic staff in their unfamiliar morning prints had bustled back to their own quarters, all trooped in to breakfast where, as usual, the conversation turned exclusively on the events of the previous twelve hours.

One of the principal differences between our parents' generation and our own would seem to be that their nights were so much more tightly packed with incident. Not only were they constantly assailed by the pangs of hunger in the small hours, so that even in so austere a house as the Hall a tin of Marie biscuits stood at every visitor's bedside, but they never, apparently, enjoyed a single night of unbroken slumber. On this occasion Miss Childs had been aroused by the most extraordinary noise around midnight, while Miss Marple had been so convinced that there was a bat in her room that she had not dared to light her candle. And whatever door was it that had banged so persistently? My aunt said that she had been so certain that it was the upstairs bathroom that she had actually gone to close it only to find it firmly shut. And would somebody please remind her to speak to Scarlett about cutting back the Virginia creeper over the front porch as, really, last night the noise it made scraping against the landing window was too uncanny? As usual the conversation was only brought to an end by one of the ladies appealing to my father for confirmation of some particular nocturnal phenomenon and receiving the reply that he had heard nothing as, unlike some people, he went to bed to sleep.

Breakfast over I was summoned by my grandfather to take part in the elaborate Sunday morning ritual at which all the grand-children took it in turns to assist. First I went into the hall and fetched the freshly cut rose left by the gardener in a particular little vase on the hall-table, and returning to the breakfast-room slipped it neatly into my grandfather's button-hole. Then I waited, matches ready, while he carefully selected a handful of cigars for his case, reserving one for immediate smoking which he finally placed in his mouth very slowly, as if even he were not quite sure of the exact whereabouts of that feature, lost amidst the hawthorn hedgerows of his beard. After we were both satisfied that it was truly alight and drawing properly, I departed to the gun-room and removed with almost sacramental care from the locker, where it was kept neatly folded throughout the week, a Union Jack. Taking this carefully under my arm I rejoined my grandfather on the porch and we both then marched at a solemn pace across the tennis lawn to where, close by the road, there rose a flagpole.

Looking back I confess myself slightly puzzled by my family's passion for flagpoles; no member of it, except a half-legendary great-uncle, said to have served as a cabin-boy on the *Bellerophon*, had ever been in the Navy, nor had any of them lived in those far-flung outposts of Empire where showing the flag is an established ritual. Nevertheless, all of them in their country houses, and frequently in London as well if the garden was sufficiently large to allow of them doing so without inviting ridicule, had erected these impressive totems. However, in those pre-Freudian days the field of speculation was limited and I had long since come to accept a flagpole as being as normal an adjunct to a gentleman's residence as a greenhouse or a bathroom.

Once the bunting was safely aloft my mind was immediately occupied with a single overriding care—to avoid, in the short time that remained before Church, being sent to the lavatory. This anxiety had no physiological nor psychological foundation but arose quite naturally from the local plumbing arrangements. The single water-closet at the Hall was strictly reserved for the use of females; all the masculine members of the party, provided they were in good health, were expected to go to the earth closet which was housed in a tasteful neo-classic building discreetly surrounded by laurels, adjoining the stables. Unfortunately this structure was of wood and in the course of time a plank had worked loose at the back allowing the chickens, which were constantly straying into the stable-yard, free access at ground level. Originally this had intrigued rather than worried me, but ever since I had received a sharp nip on the tenderest, and at the time the most exposed, portion of my anatomy, my daily visits had been rendered hideous by fear and apprehension. With the usual false shame of childhood I had never revealed the cause of my reluctance, which was put down to obstinacy or constipation or both and treated accordingly. On week-days there was no possibility of escape, but just occasionally on Sundays my nurse and parents would be too busy getting ready for Divine Service to remember to make the usual enquiries.

Whether or not on this occasion I succeeded in avoiding my fate I cannot now recall, but I was certainly present, brushed and tidy, a quarter of an hour later, when the house party was assembled ready on the porch, the ladies all elaborately gloved and veiled and the gentlemen in dark suits and Homburg hats, for the frock coats and silk hats which were still *de rigueur* for urban worship had come by this date to be considered a little too ostentatious in the country. The only non-starter was Miss Redpath whose absence was perfectly well understood and resolutely ignored.

Ignored, that is, by the grown-ups but not by my Cousin John, a relentlessly inquisitive youth with an insatiable desire for information.

"Auntie, where's Miss Redpath?"

"That's nothing to do with you, dear."

"Auntie, isn't Miss Redpath coming to Church?"

Silence.

"Auntie, why isn't Miss Redpath coming to Church?"

Even then I well understood the nature of the dilemma with which my unfortunate relatives were thus confronted, for when it came to a strict regard for truth Matilda's aunt had nothing on mine. Their whole life was based on abhorrence of the Lie, and their definition of what constituted an untruth was wide indeed. All prevarication, euphemism and tactful understatement were for them impossible and resolutely to be discouraged in others. Often I myself, always an imaginative child, had been pulled up short in some harmless exaggeration by the soft question "Osbert dear, is that quite true?" In my younger days I found these exalted standards slightly ridiculous but now, when the politicians and the advertisers and the propagandists have succeeded in hiding the face of truth behind a thick veil of sophistry and illusion, the uncompromising attitude of my aunts (which I am happy to say they both maintain completely unabated at this present day) appears to me in a wholly admirable, if uncomfortably brilliant, light.

Truth, however, is notoriously a two-edged sword and on this occasion its revelation was attended with the gravest perils. To give the real reason for Miss Redpath's non-appearance would not only destroy our childish faith in the undeviating orthodoxy of all grown-up persons, and with it our respect, but it would reveal to us for the first time, and in the most unfortunate way, the existence of Doubt. For ordinary mortals it would have been possible to say that Miss Redpath had a headache—but not for my aunts; which was, perhaps, just as well because at that very moment the subject of the discussion was clearly visible marching off down the drive for one of her six-mile walks. Their normal reaction would then have been to have said that John must ask her himself, but they well knew that their nephew was a literal-minded and persistent lad who would undoubtedly act on this suggestion at the first opportunity, when Miss Redpath would unhesitatingly give her reasons accurately and at length. Finally after unavailing efforts to ignore the whole business they went so far as to say that Miss Redpath did not wish to come *this time*, hoping thus to give the impression that her absence was something quite uncustomary, and briskly started up a general conversation on other topics in which the Grateful Hearts loyally and loudly joined.

The interior of Eastwinch Church although of noble proportions was utterly without character. So well had Sir Gilbert done his work that, even for so romantic a mediaevalist as I then was, the scraped pillars and recut capitals had no message. All I can now remember is the extreme brightness and newness of the fittings. The crimson of the fleur-de-lys patterned felt which carpeted the chancel and covered the hassocks was hardly less startling than that of Elijah's robe in the East window; the brass oil-lamps rising above the stripped pine pews shone with a celestial brightness; and so dazzling was the lectern that it almost hurt to look at it.

The service itself, it must be confessed, displayed rather less sparkle, and was only enlivened for me by the recurrent astonishment I always experienced on hearing grown-ups sing. It was not so much the actual fact of their singing which amazed, but the feeling they put into it and the curious intonation, so utterly removed from their everyday manner of speech, which they appeared to consider it necessary to adopt the moment they opened Hymns A. and M. But long before we had come to the end of the *Te Deum* this source of pleasure had begun to lose its power, and it was with a very real sense of relief that at long last I saw Canon Pelly move across in the direction of the pulpit and knew that for the next twenty minutes at least I could devote myself fully to the particular costume drama that was then running in the private theatre of my mind, undisturbed by constantly having to rise and sing or kneel and pray.

Of a sermon which was in its way to prove historic I consciously remembered, when the usual mumbled "and now to God the Father . . ." had recalled me from the broad acres where I had been grinding the faces of the Saxon peasantry in my new rôle of a Norman baron of immense strength and ferocity, not one word. Nor, had it not been for the subsequent drama at the luncheon table, would I ever have given it another thought.

On leaving church the weather which had been fine enough earlier was seen to have changed. The wind had dropped and the small white clouds of early morning had swollen and coalesced. At the best of times the dining-room at the Hall was not a cheerful apartment; the sombre red walls were not noticeably relieved by the overframed battle scenes of Wouwerman which hung there (we knew they were by Wouwerman because each contained a white horse), and the closeness of the immense beech trees to the north-facing windows cast a sullen gloom even on the sunniest day. By the time we were all seated at table the sky had become heavily overcast and with it the natural brightness which was always encouraged at Sunday luncheon.

Normally the best one could hope for by way of entertainment at this weekly ceremony was a scene provoked by my Cousin John's refusal to eat his gristle, but today I had regretfully noticed he had drawn a helping at which even one of his notorious 'daintiness' could hardly protest, and I soon abandoned myself to speculation as to whether we should receive one sweet or two at the end of the meal.

Among the grown-ups the conversation, as usual, was steered by my aunts to a discussion of this morning's sermon. It was generally agreed by those who had been privileged to hear it, that seldom had Canon Pelly been so inspired, and how lucky they were to have so eloquent and powerful a preacher in a small place like Eastwinch! Amidst the chorus of agreement which these sentiments provoked among the Grateful Hearts, Miss Redpath, who had her own opinion of Canon Pelly, maintained a menacing silence. Although it was the last day of her visit, when her patience was invariably approaching exhaustion, all might yet have been well had not one of my aunts, ignoring the danger-signals and unable to leave well alone, gone on to describe this historic sermon as "a real intellectual treat".

"Really, my dear Harriet, and pray what makes you think so?"

The use of my aunt's full name instead of the customary diminutive was a sure sign that Miss Redpath was now fully roused.

"Well," explained my aunt, rashly but with determination, "it was so wonderfully *clear*. I don't think I have ever before properly understood the parable of the labourers in the vineyard. It always seemed rather *unfair* but this morning I was made to realise its true meaning for the first time."

Miss Redpath was plainly astonished that any ex-pupil of hers could be so mentally deficient as to have gone through life failing to understand the workings of a wage system so completely in accordance with the best Trade Union practice.

"And what, dear, did the Canon choose as the text for this enlightening sermon?"

"The first shall be last and the last first."

"One hardly needs to have gone to church, dear, to know exactly what the dear Canon would have to say on that rather trite theme."

At this point my grandfather, who had been listening with a quiet enjoyment which even the snowy smoke-screen of his beard could not wholly conceal, entered the discussion. "Well, Miss Redpath, as the only person not present tell us what you think the Canon would have said."

That my grandfather realised he was playing with fire, and did so deliberately, seems fairly certain; but I doubt that even he, shrewd as he was, anticipated exactly what he got.

Miss Redpath, hands folded on her lap, leant back and after one or two preliminary flexings of the corners of her mouth, through firmly clenched teeth, began.

For the next five minutes Canon Pelly was in the room with us: every unctuous intonation, every sniff, even the faint trace of transatlantic accent that had remained to him from his missionary days in the Canadian backwoods, was faithfully reproduced. As with his elocutionary effects, so with his mental processes, all were devastatingly recorded. No cliché, no hackneyed phrase, no false argument was missed. Even I, who had been lost in private fantasies during the sermon itself, was dumbfounded at the uncanny accuracy of the performance.

When at last Miss Redpath, with a final contemptuous but still all too convincing "dearly beloved", had finished, for the first time in the recorded history of the Hall a general exodus took place without a previous request to my grandfather to say Grace. Left in the dining-room were only Miss Redpath, her host and myself. Although deeply anxious to hear my grandfather's comments, my presence was in no way an attempt to eavesdrop; but, unlike my cousins who had been plainly appalled by the whole performance and fled in panic with their elders, I had kept my head and alone of those present remembered that in the excitement the Sunday distribution of sweets had been forgotten. I was not, therefore, deliberately hiding behind the screen which half concealed the sideboard, but was principally engaged in making good this oversight, and my rôle in the last act of the drama was involuntary.

At first silence reigned. My grandfather indeed, whose whole form was heaving rhythmically beneath his beard and down whose rosy cheeks the tears were helplessly pouring, seemed incapable of speech, and contented himself with jabbing his cigar in the general direction of Miss Redpath. She for her part was smiling like the happy warrior at the end of a hard day's dragon-slaying. At long last my grandfather after many splutterings and guffaws found his voice. "You listened!"

"Of course," replied Miss Redpath smugly. "I was sitting in the porch the whole time. Not that it was really necessary. Given that particular text it was perfectly obvious to anyone of the meanest intelligence what the invincibly commonplace mind of the Canon would make of it. Still, there were one or two finer points of stupidity which even I had not foreseen."

Of this conversation one fact and one fact only stuck in my mind—Miss Redpath had listened—and I lost no time in slipping from the room and publishing the news to the world.

In the drawing-room, where I found the rest of the party assembled, a certain uneasiness reigned. Some of those present, including my mother and all **my uncles,** had obviously reacted in the same way as my grandfather, and were making little attempt to conceal their enjoyment. My aunts, on the other hand, loyally supported by the Grateful Hearts, were maintaining a strained and disapproving silence. Only on the receipt of my startling news did their brows clear.

At the time I did not understand the significance of my aunts' reaction. Now I can see that as a result of my revelation the uncertainties to which they had been prey had been resolved, and the necessary justification for action provided. So long as Miss Redpath's performance was to be regarded as a feat of creative imagination, such was their integrity and regard for intellectual honesty, that deeply as they deplored the whole scene (particularly before the children too!), they did not feel entitled to act. Now that it was made clear that her triumph had been scored as the result of eavesdropping, she stood convicted of 'playing to the gallery'. And worse: truth itself had been tampered with, for by allowing her audience to assume that she was relying entirely on brilliant speculation and concealing her presence in the porch, she had been Acting a Lie! She had, in fact, finally gone too far.

In all the long summers which I subsequently passed at the Hall, never again, by some curious chance, was it found possible so to arrange the holiday timetable as to allow Miss Redpath's visit to be fitted in to the tight schedule of the Grateful Hearts.

5. "*The last rose of Summer*"

AN AWARENESS of social distinctions is among the earliest
senses to develop in the infant mind. All children, although
in varying degrees, are snobs and if their snobbishness is
based on differences and attributes incomprehensible to the adult
mind their perception is none the less acute: which always makes
for a certain self-consciousness in the sensitive grown-up knowing
himself to be under the scrutiny of a little rompered Proust who
is weighing him up in accordance with a scale of values which,
although it may bear little relation to those of the Lord Chamberlain's Office or the Faubourg St. Germain, is none the less rigid
for being arbitrary. Fortunately so few grown-ups do, in fact, in
this respect appear to be sensitive.

Thus as a child I was always convinced that my maternal

grandfather Alfred was in some subtle way 'grander' than my father's father. And this in the face of a considerable amount of superficial evidence supporting the contrary view. The latter, thanks to his beard, was the more imposing in appearance, and although both were rich he was the richer; moreover not only did he possess a town house *and* a country house but had also been knighted. Nevertheless, the former's house was approached by far the longer drive and was graced by a butler, and these two distinctions, particularly the latter, I considered decisive.

Naïve as may have been the premises on which my decision was based it was nevertheless accurately indicative of a subtle difference, not so much of social position as of character, existing between the two men. Alike in the circumstances of their origins and their careers they differed completely in everything else. Both were copy-book examples of the Victorian middle-class success story, but in their reactions to success no two men could have been less alike. While my Lancaster grandfather continued to work ceaselessly until almost his eightieth year, my mother's father, having made a large fortune by his early thirties, never did another hand's turn in his life. While Grandfather William gave enormous sums to charity he was always very tight-fisted when it came to tipping which made family outings to restaurants always a little embarrassing. Grandfather Alfred, on the other hand, while always adjusting his charitable benefactions strictly in accordance with what he considered the minimum obligations of a country gentleman, was noticeably lavish in the matter of casual largesse. And while both kept their offspring permanently short of cash, they did so for very different reasons: the former because he was sincerely convinced of the corrupting influence of affluence on the young, the latter because he was temperamentally opposed to anyone spending his money but himself. Moreover, while my Lancaster grandfather, despite his genealogical preoccupations, remained always the least snobbish of men scorning—indeed disapproving—all social pretensions, his opposite number had never, according to his sisters, hesitated to cut his own father when the latter was still in 'trade' on any occasion when recognition would have been an

imagined embarrassment. Alas, so desperately wicked is the heart of man and so blind to moral worth the eye of childhood, that while deeply respecting Grandfather William, my admiration for Grandfather Alfred knew no bounds.

My grandfather's great-grandfather had been a refugee who had preferred the more liberal climate of England to that prevailing in his native Marburg during the Revolutionary wars, and had settled in this country and married a lady known as 'the Rose of Shropshire' (whether or not she was so known outside the family circle I have been unable to discover). All his descendants had married in this country, and the only traces of their Teutonic origin that my mother's family still retained were exceedingly blonde colouring with very light Baltic eyes and the manuscript of a sermon allegedly preached by an ancestor, who had been Hof-Prädiger to the Elector of Hesse-Cassel, before Gustavus Adolphus on the eve of the Battle of Lützen. All that was known of their German relatives was due to a correspondence with an engaging Baron entered into by my great-grandmother which had produced a rather dull coat-of-arms with the forthright, if non-committal, motto *Ich Halte*, and a request for a loan. However, on the strength of this my great-grandfather had at one time considered adding the prefix *von* to his surname but fortunately had finally rejected the idea and thus saved his descendants considerable embarrassment in 1914.

In youth my grandfather's prospects had not been particularly rosy; his father, although in 'trade', was not very prosperously so, and all efforts to improve the family position by financial speculation had been markedly unsuccessful. A younger member of a large family he had in addition been considered delicate; but this in fact so far from being a disadvantage had proved a blessing. Thought to suffer from weak lungs it was arranged that the beardless youth should take a long sea voyage far from the fogs of South Kensington on a ship belonging to a maternal uncle who was establishing himself as a shipping magnate on the Yang-tse. Arrived in Hong-Kong he discovered that his elder brother, for whom a place had been secured in the uncle's business, was

heartily sick of the Far East and unconcealedly anxious to return. My grandfather, then barely seventeen but apparently now well set up by the sea voyage, willingly exchanged places and remained at Hong-Kong for the next fifteen years during which period he married a dashing widow, succeeded his uncle as head of the line, and made a comfortable fortune.

Of all the various subsidiary Victorian societies, firmly bound by culture and temperament to the great central organisation yet flourishing in conditions almost unimaginably different, that of the China merchants—the 'tai-pans'—must, one fancies, have been one of the most extraordinary. The picture that presents itself, founded admittedly on no detailed knowledge but rather on half-remembered gossip, on the fantastic furniture and ornaments which adorned my grandfather's house, and above all on the testimony of old photograph albums, is one that can only be compared to that of the Lusignan régime in Cyprus; a small dominant group settled on the fringe of a far older but decayed civilisation, rigidly conservative and nationalist in some things, unexpectedly assimilative in others. In the matter of clothes, for instance, no compromise appears to have been made; indeed, to judge from portraits of my grandfather at this period an almost propagandist assertiveness of Victorianism was *de rigueur*. Certainly the dundrearies would seem to be longer, the eyeglass more glistening, the neckwear heavier and more restrictive than they were even in St. James's Street. And nothing could well have made fewer concessions to local taste and conditions than Douglas Castle, the house built by the original Lepraik on the top of the Peak, a heavily machicolated granite mansion in the Scottish baronial style, in which my grandfather wed and my mother was born.

However, despite this architectural and sartorial rigidity, in other matters a far closer liaison would appear to have existed with the local culture than, say, in contemporary India. The British merchants met their Chinese colleagues on equal terms both socially and in business, and my grandfather had numerous Chinese friends, among them that Celestial Talleyrand Li-Hung-

Chang, and if cases of intermarriage were rare, less regular unions would appear to have been frequent. But the field in which the maximum co-operation would seem to have been achieved, and in which the results were most spectacular, was that of furniture design.

No generation in recorded history, with the possible exception of the Renaissance Rhinelanders, conceived beauty so exclusively in terms of ornament as did the Victorians; no race at any time has achieved so great and terrifying a mastery of intricate detail as the Chinese of the post-Ming Period; it was not therefore surprising that the resulting combination of Victorian taste and Chinese craftsmanship produced a series of objects of transcendental monstrosity of which a very large proportion appeared to have found their way into the houses of my mother's relations. The one thing which these masterpieces of tortured ingenuity had in common was a total disregard of comfort or convenience. Thus china cupboards were supplied with such a multiplicity of little shelves projecting at all levels that it was impossible to dust or remove a single object without sending six others crashing; and chairs, the lines of whose framework were, although partially blurred by an abundance of prickly carving, flowing and sinuous, would be furnished with marble seats inlaid with mother-of-pearl of the most unyielding and chilly rigidity. But of all these mixed masterpieces the most extraordinary were my grandfather's racing trophies gained at Kailoon. Here the traditional debased vase-shape common to all such objects had been retained, but in the decoration the Chinese silversmiths had been allowed the utmost licence, so that every inch of surface was covered with spirited steeplechasers conceived in the accepted Alken tradition, entangled with dragons, whips and horseshoes wreathed with tiger-lilies and horses' masks peering out from bamboo thickets amid clouds of butterflies, all carried out in the highest possible relief.

Our annual arrival at the maternal homestead to which the treasures of Cathay lent so individual an atmosphere was very different to our descent on Norfolk. G—, Dorset, is not among the more attractive of West Country towns: always pervaded by a smell of brewing, neither its beer nor its inhabitants enjoyed much regard in the surrounding countryside and its station, although larger, completely lacked the rustic charm of Eastwinch. Nevertheless, so keen was my anticipation of the pleasure to come, so powerful the recollected atmosphere, annually reinforced, of my grandfather's house, that the dreary yellow brick station yard had for me a quite indescribable magic. In part this was no doubt due to the presence there of the grand-paternal automobile—a dashing, crimson Talbot-Darracq that made the Lancastrian Renault appear very dowdy and dowager-like; and standing alongside it smiling, rug-laden and gleamingly gaitered, the Chauffeur Bates.

It is not uncommon for a rare degree of insight and perception to be attributed to the innocent age of childhood; instances are constantly quoted of practised deceivers who had successfully hoodwinked the shrewdest adults but whose pretences were immediately penetrated by an innocent child. If there is any truth in such assumptions I can only suppose myself to have been, in this respect at least, abnormal. For my affection for Bates, whose insolence, sycophancy and drunkenness made him detested by the whole family except my grandfather, was deep and boundless. Ruddy-complexioned, fair-moustached and, as I now realise, distressingly familiar, he continued to tyrannise over the whole household until one fatal day in 1914 when, heavily in liquor, he went too far in the presence of the son of the house returned from the Front who knocked him for six across the stable-yard. But fortunately his failings were as hidden from me as was his fate, when perched beside him on the driving seat I was borne at what seemed an unbelievable speed past the flying hedgerows up the dusty hill which led out of the town.

The gate-pillars of S—, my grandfather's residence, were also globe-topped, but this was the only thing which they had in common with those of Eastwinch Hall. Whereas the latter were, perhaps, over-prominent in view of the almost suburban drive on to which they gave, the former, half concealed by trees and shrubs, hardly suggested the long winding carriageway leading from the small Gothic lodge across the fields and finally disappearing over the hill behind a distant clump of trees. The house itself was not remarkable architecturally and exists in my memory solely as a medium-sized confusion of ivy, gables and white barge boards, but the gardens established for ever an ideal to which none subsequently encountered have ever attained. My grandfather was a skilled and enthusiastic gardener but in the style of Loudon rather than Miss Jekyll; here were none of those messy herbaceous borders and vulgar 'riots of colour' which make so many modern gardens look like the worst sort of Christmas Calendar, but terraced lawns and geometrical flower-beds symmetrically placed, their harvest of geraniums and lobelias protected by a ring of little wrought-iron hoops. Here was no crazy-paving overgrown with monstrous delphiniums stretching between sun-dial and bird-bath, but winding gravel paths arched by trellises leading to rustic summerhouses across wooden footbridges spanning contrived, fern-shaded water-falls. And the boundary was not marked by some crumbling brick wall untidy with rock-plants but by a ha-ha neatly stretched between balancing clumps of rare coniferous trees allowing a clear view across the fields to the home-farm.

The neatness and order so evident in the garden were not, curiously enough, reflected in the way of life prevailing indoors. On looking back, existence at S— has taken on rather a Tchekov flavour, but this may perhaps be due in part to art. It so happened that all my visits there in childhood seem to have been blessed with weather of exceptional heat and brightness which led, my grandfather being markedly photophobic, to the green venetian blinds being almost permanently down. This produced that filtered sub-aqueous light which, those who are old enough to remember the earliest Komisajevsky productions of Tchekov will recall, invariably flooded the country house interiors of theatrical Russia. Nevertheless, this coincidence seems to me to have reinforced rather than induced an impression which owed its origin to a certain inconsequence and lack of decision on the part of the family cast.

In strong contrast to life at Eastwinch, governed by Median

rules where no expedition or enterprise outside the normal routine was ever embarked on without the maximum planning rigidly adhered to, at S— plans were only made in order to be changed, and the whole rhythm of everyday existence was liable to be completely upset for the merest whim. Moreover while in Norfolk ill-health, anyhow in anyone under seventy, was regarded as a sign of weakness and rigorously discouraged, in Dorset no day passed without some member of the family being laid low with a migraine or a *crise de nerfs*. This was the least easily overlooked in the case of my grandfather himself for whom the stoic fortitude on which the Lancasters set so great a store made no appeal, and who saw little point in suffering if it were to be concealed and not to be shared with the largest number possible.

Thus on such days as he was attacked by one of his 'heads' the whole life of the household was completely overturned. The utmost quiet was insisted on and everyone went on tip-toe, which naturally reinforced the lugubrious effect created by the groans and bellows coming from behind his bedroom door. Within, no matter how hot the day, all the windows were tight closed, the blinds drawn and a roaring fire blazed in the grate, a condition of affairs which inevitably increased the casualty list as my grandfather could not be left alone and some member of the family had always to sit at his bedside. Even for those not so called, life was sufficiently disrupted; for, although the domestic staff was large, the constant supply of light meals on trays, most of which the invalid promptly sent back to the cook with a few acid comments and fresh instructions, the dispatch of numerous contradictory telegrams to Harley Street, all of which had to be taken by groom or chauffeur five miles to the nearest post-office, in addition to the condition of hopeless hysteria to which my grandfather sooner or later succeeded in reducing at least one of the housemaids, taxed its resources to the utmost. But while always remaining the principal sufferer, in comparison with whose agonies those of others were as nothing, my grandfather seldom remained the sole invalid for long. His second wife, although subservient to her lord in all things, was a martyr to ill health, in part genuinely so, and her children, my mother's step-sisters, had inherited from their parents the liability to take to their beds at the drop of a hat. Thus it frequently happened that I and my mother found ourselves alone for days on end, save perhaps for an uncle on vacation from Oxford or on leave from his regiment who was made of rather tougher stuff than the rest of the family.

Normally when good health was general the whole household assembled, as at Eastwinch, for the first time at family prayers, the only difference being that here absenteeism was more frequent, and less censured. The dining-room was a spacious apartment decorated in what I have always considered the appropriate style —crimson flock wallpaper, steel engravings after Gustave Doré and a massive side-board on which, together with the Chinoiserie racing-trophies, there rested at this hour a whole battery of silver dishes from which arose a gentle steam to mingle with the souls of the righteous who were being conveyed, immediately above, by a flock of angels from the moon-lit Colosseum where their earthly bodies were still being ruminatively chewed by lions. The length of the religious ceremony which preceded our own meal depended largely on whether my grandfather himself was conducting it and if so on the state of his appetite. If he had arisen brisk and early, eagerly appreciative of the whiff of fried bacon, our devotions would be carried out at breakneck speed; if, on the other hand, his night had been disturbed and he was convinced, as he frequently was, that his enfeebled health could hardly hold out much longer, the ceremony would be prolonged by the addition of a selected passage of Holy Writ read in a suitably lugubrious tone. When, as very frequently happened, the reading was taken from that passage in the Epistle to the Ephesians where the Apostle stresses the importance of submission to temporal authority the effect was immensely impressive. "Wives, submit yourselves unto your own husbands"—pause during which my grandfather's light blue eye would rest rather sorrowfully on my grandmother; " . . . children, obey your parents"—up would go the monocle and a stern glance would fall on my aunts and uncles; " . . . servants, be obedient to them that are your masters"—and it was transferred upon the ranged rows of the domestic staff. Curiously enough, I do not remember ever hearing on these occasions the verses in which the writer goes on to outline the obligations of the head of the household.

Thus spiritually purged we all sat down to an enormous and excellent breakfast which would usually pass pleasantly enough in the discussion of plans for the day which lost nothing in excitement from the knowledge that they would almost certainly not be carried out. The only interruption likely to occur was if the bacon did not attain the exact degree of crispness insisted on by my grandfather, in which case this mood of Christian resignation would vanish in a flash, and the butler would receive a brisk message for the cook, to whom, incidentally, he was married, couched in decidedly more forceful terms than those employed by Saint Paul.

For me the rest of the day passed in a series of delicious, un-organised pleasures. No one sent me on little errands; my presence was not demanded on the tennis-lawn; I was at full liberty to take what books I liked from my grandfather's library. I could spend the morning in the stable with Hodder, the groom, a splendid primeval rustic figure who had never been further than Shaftesbury in his life, or wander unshepherded along the stream in the wood, or reconstruct the battle of Tsushima with a wooden model of the Japanese fleet, belonging to an uncle still at Wellington, in the water-tank in the kitchen garden. No one bothered me until it was time for one of the large meals which punctuated the day, and here these too were sources of keen pleasure and eager anticipation; for, unlike the Lancasters, my maternal relatives were far from indifferent to what they ate and the simple country fare provided by the home-farm was reinforced by a regular supply of more exotic dainties sent down from Jacksons. All of which forces the conclusion that, on the whole, children are likely to have a far better time where the adults are reasonably self-centred.

While the enlightened self-interest, which was the guiding principle of my grandfather's life, operated happily enough in my own case, it must be confessed it showed him in rather less admirable light when dealing with other relatives. Unlike his opposite number he entertained no very exalted conception of family obligations and, apart from his own children, his affection for his relations was at its warmest when they were furthest removed, and this was particularly so in the case of his elder sister, my Great Aunt A. Left to himself, it seems likely that this remarkable old lady's visits to S— would have been even more spaced out than they were, but fortunately my mother, aided by her step-sister, was at hand to see that he did not shirk his obligations.

It must be admitted that his reluctance to entertain his sister, although undoubtedly blame-worthy, was not altogether incomprehensible. Great Aunt A was certainly, in some ways, a problem. Unmarried, her emotional life had been a series of disappointments, none the less bitter for the fact that they had been, when not wholly imaginary, largely her own fault. Her girlhood had coincided with that peculiarly sentimental period, the mid-'seventies, when clad in an art-silk bustle she had studied water-colour painting at South Kensington and lost her heart to innumerable curates. But as time went on she found a certain compensation in the extraordinary number of disagreeable encounters and impertinent suggestions to which her beauty, so she was convinced, subjected her, and she abandoned painting in favour of cultivating the more socially useful gift of a magnificent *coloratura* soprano. However, despite her blighted youth she looked forward to a dignified old age when, as she would frequently announce, she intended to put on a neat little mob-cap with lace tippets and a plain but rich watered silk dress. As at the time of her visits to S— she was invariably dressed in flowered muslins of the most youthful cut and girlish straw hats heavily over-laden with cabbage roses and was known to be close on seventy, it was not exactly clear as to when she expected the final stage of her earthly pilgrimage to begin.

My grandfather's attitude towards his sister, disgraceful as it was, was founded on a very clear-sighted appreciation of the exact nature of the caste system as it prevailed in the English country-side in the Edwardian period, and of his own position in the local hierarchy. Thanks to an engaging presence, thirty years' residence, and a stable full of hunters he was at long last established as being of 'the county' and sat on the local Bench and visited, and was visited by, all the neighbouring landowners. Nevertheless, he fully realised that there were still subtle distinctions within the closed circle into which he had been at such pains to enter, and whereas the local baronet, whose family had been resident in the neighbourhood for generations, could easily afford the presence beneath his roof of any number of the most wildly eccentric female relations, unfavourable comment was only too likely to be aroused by any too great prominence attaching to the mildly ridiculous elder sister of a retired China merchant. Eccentricity, to be socially acceptable, had still to have at least four or five generations of inbreeding behind it.

Thus, during the period of Great Aunt A's visit there was always a marked reduction in the number of little luncheon-parties for the local gentry and my grandfather's health would seldom permit his attendance at church on Sunday. In the latter instance his lack of moral fibre was, perhaps, forgivable, for even those with nerves of iron might well be shaken on finding themselves in the close proximity of Great Aunt A at Divine Service. For not only did that indomitable old lady always on these occasions take particular pains with her dress which led to the most fantastic superfluity of large pale blue bows, dangling ear-rings and enormous brooches strategically placed, but invariably made the most of the opportunity afforded for the fullest exercise of her remarkable voice. All was moderately well so long as she sang in unison; gradually almost complete silence would fall on the neighbouring pews as they realised the uselessness of competition, and one or two of the more impressionable choir-boys would collapse in hysterics, though a semblance of harmony was maintained; but once she started to sing seconds, as sooner or later she invariably did, all hope was lost and the organist could do nothing but immediately switch to ff and put on what speed he could, hoping for the best. Then it was that the more stalwart members of the family thought enviously of its head, comfortably tucked up in bed reading Meredith, and wondered whether or not their own displays of unflinching loyalty had really been worth it.

In addition to her vocal enthusiasm and bizarre taste in dress, Great Aunt A brought with her another cause of disruption. Like many maiden ladies living alone her affection for her domestic pets had long since passed way beyond the limits of normality, and all the passion which the curates had so unthinkingly rejected was now directed on her canary and her Pekinese. The former, whose vocal range was even more piercingly extended than Great Aunt A's own, was fortunately left behind, together with endless instructions and ample supplies of groundsel, with the landlady (to whom numerous admonitory post-cards on the subject of fresh water and cage-cleaning would regularly be dispatched) but the latter invariably accompanied his mistress on all her travels. Even by Pekinese standards, which in my experience are exalted, Mr. Wu rated as a menace of the highest order. Ostentatiously conscious of his aristocratic breeding, like so many of the bluest blood, he made no effort to conceal his arrogance and selfishness, and regarded it as completely absolving him from all effort to conform to the usages of decent canine society. House training was only for the middle-classes and he constantly dirtied carpets and chintz with all the insouciance of Louis XIV relieving himself in the open fireplace at Versailles. In addition he gloried in the possession of a delicate digestion and not only insisted on the most tender meals but threw up his dinner with an uninhibited frequency when and where he chose. His temper was as uncontrolled as his personal habits and despite the aristocratic flatness of his features he was perfectly capable of producing a nasty flesh wound at ankle level. In no house, therefore, was Mr. Wu a welcome guest, but at my grandfather's his presence always proved more than usually disruptive, as here, for probably the only times in his life, he encountered stiff opposition.

S—, like so many houses wherein all summer-long there reigns a thwarted restlessness due to the fact that for the majority of the inhabitants life only begins with the hunting season, was heavily over-dogged, as if a constant yapping and baying, faint echoes of the glorious music of the winter-months, was absolutely necessary to maintain vitality during a period insufficiently enlivened by tennis parties: and despite the constant protests of my grandfather, who was no friend to the lower orders of creation and for whom the hunting field had a purely social justification, vast hordes of his offsprings' pets constantly roamed the whole place. In the case of my Uncle Jack's spaniels, Budge and Toddy, as kindly and affectionate as their master, the rule barring entry to the house itself was fairly strictly observed; with the fox-terrier Jacky who had developed a mania for snapping off the heads of chickens (and with great speed and skill, for I well remember the surrealist

spectacle of several headless birds all running round the farm-yard at once) a certain feeling of relief was induced by his presence indoors; but over my youngest aunt's kennel no control had ever been effectively achieved. This last usually consisted of at least half a dozen Sealyhams, of unbounded energy and considerable ferocity, and a couple of Irish wolf-hounds, friendly and amiable enough, but one friendly wag of whose tails was capable of obliterating a whole regiment of netsukés and any quantity of Satsuma ware. Thus life was constantly being enlivened by a series of appalling scenes between parents and children and brothers and sisters arising from vain attempts to establish the exact responsibility for the latest canine misdemeanour. Sometimes, as when half-way through a smart little luncheon party at which my grandfather was entertaining an important local magnate all the cream for the strawberries was discovered to have been devoured by Jacky, these reached epic proportions and went rumbling on for years. On other occasions, such as when the new curate paying his first call had been brought down on the drawing-room carpet by the whole pack of Sealyhams in full cry and rescued only just in the nick of time, the incident passed off in peals of happy laughter and soon became a favourite subject for joyous reminiscence. With the arrival of Mr. Wu the incidence of such disasters not only immensely increased but, owing to Great Aunt A's almost insane affection for her repellent hound, left a trail of much intensified bitterness behind them. And it was to a disaster thus brought about that I owed my earliest acquaintance with one of the fundamental, and least agreeable, facts of life.

The garden at S— had been laid out on a slight incline, the ground falling away from the highest point outside the drawing-room windows to the ha-ha which marked the boundary of the level fields, and in order to accommodate both a croquet-lawn and a tennis court two fairly steep cuttings had been made so that the terrace was separated from the tennis and the tennis from the croquet by neatly turfed embankments of considerable height and steepness. One fine morning I was pleasantly engaged in rolling down the upper and steeper of these two ramps—an occupation to which I had devoted much practice and in which, while giving a gratifying illusion of distress to uninformed witnesses, I was able to indulge with no hurt or inconvenience to myself—in the indulgent charge of Great Aunt A who was reading *Home Chat* in a deck-chair on the terrace. Alongside her and slobbering over a disgusting rubber ball was Mr. Wu, who had only been allowed to expose himself to the perils of the outer world on the strict understanding that all the various gates and doors which gave access from this part of the garden to the stable-yard, to which the rest of the canine population had been banished, were securely locked.

Quite suddenly the desultory barking which formed an almost continuous ground-bass to the confused melody of our daily life became much louder and more purposeful and almost before I or

Great Aunt A had fully registered this fact, the whole pack of Sealyhams came skidding round the geraniums in full cry. The reason for their sudden appearance was not for a second in doubt to any of us, least of all Mr. Wu, whose fully justified fears of a *jacquerie* he at last saw terrifyingly realised. With one bound he was

on his mistress' lap only to be immediately snatched up by my terrified aunt and clasped tight to her shoulder as far out of the aggressors' range as possible. They, however, quite obviously meant business; their views of the mandarin-class coincided exactly with those of Sun-Yat-Sen and they were clearly in no doubt at all as to who was the cause of their enforced seclusion of the last few days. Realising, after a few abortive leaps, that their

272

predestined victim was out of reach, they changed their tactics and concentrated on getting his protectress down. I, meanwhile, seeing that the Sealyhams, of whom I entertained a healthy and not unjustified dread, were at the moment quite single-minded, gave myself up to a fascinated contemplation of Great Aunt A in the lead-rôle of 'Fireman save my child', from which her frenzied shrieks of "Osbert, don't just sit there! *Do* Something!" quite failed to rouse me. The end was inevitable and terrifying; my great aunt, her tartan skirt already loosened from its moorings, still clutching her darling whose aristocratic calm had for once, I was happy to observe, quite deserted him, backed steadily towards the edge of the terrace. One moment she was aloft and upright, assailed, frightened but still dominant—the next she was falling helpless through the air to land backwards on the croquet-lawn only a split second before the whole pack had galloped down the incline on top of her. At the exact moment that she lost her balance a shocking truth was suddenly made apparent to me; that grown-ups, whom I had always regarded as exempt from falling down and hurting themselves, were as liable to physical mishaps as children, and that being grown-up did not automatically give one complete and certain control over all events whatsoever. Then the fear so clearly discernible in the eyes of poor Aunt A aroused an echo in my own heart, chilly and far-reaching.

*　　*　　*　　*　　*

All too soon our visit would come to an end. One day a complicated timetable would be worked out in which my grandfather's visit to the dentist in Bath could conveniently be combined with our catching the fast train to London, readjusted to allow of my aunt's taking one of the Sealyhams to the vet in Wincanton, a picnic *en route* substituted for luncheon at the Grand Pump Room Hotel, and finally abandoned entirely amidst a storm of argument and counter-suggestions. In due course the car would come round to take us to G— station as usual and I would be led up to take leave of my grandfather, trying hard not to look expectant but always nevertheless relieved on hearing the faint crackle of a fiver as my hand was warmly shaken, provoking profuse thanks from me and distressed cries of "Really, Father, you shouldn't! It's far too much!" from my mother, and, I am deeply ashamed to say, in the depths of my heart scornful reflections on my grandfather Lancaster who on such occasions (which I did not pause to consider were in his case far more numerous) seldom rose to more than half a sovereign.

In the homeward train I was always a prey to the deepest gloom from which neither the latest *Rainbow* nor the arrival of the luncheon basket with the inevitable leg of L.S.W.R. chicken, strangely blue in colour, could rouse me. No more long afternoons reading Kenneth Grahame in the hammock, no more ponies, no more young and indulgent aunts and uncles, no more making myself sick on lemonade in the butler's pantry—even the prospect of once more seeing Kate could not compensate for all I was losing. At last I could bear it no longer and would angrily demand in a voice not far from tears why, when I was so happy, did we have to come away? Gentle but firm the answer was always the same, "Osbert dear, you are old enough now to realise that we are not put into this world just to be happy."